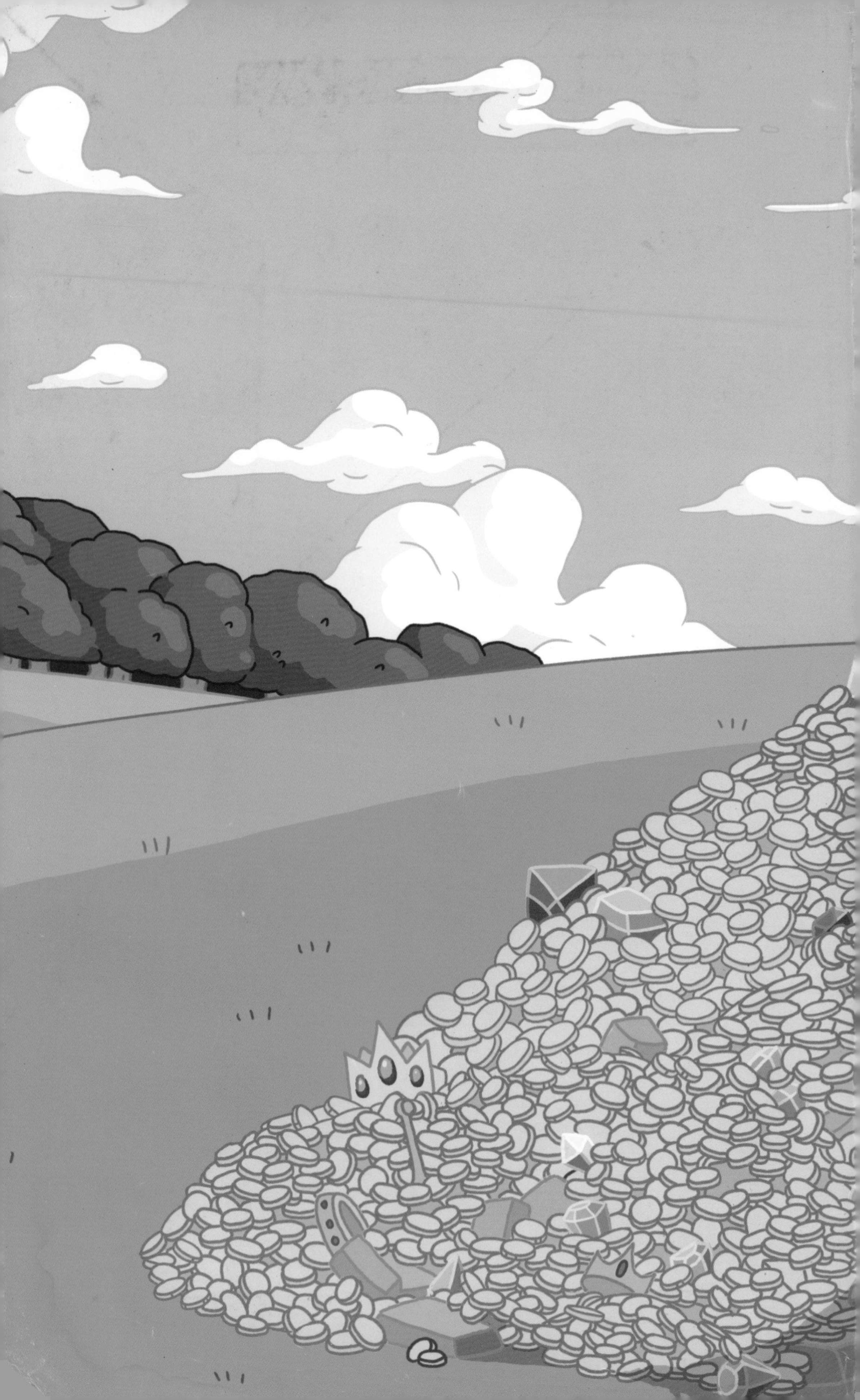

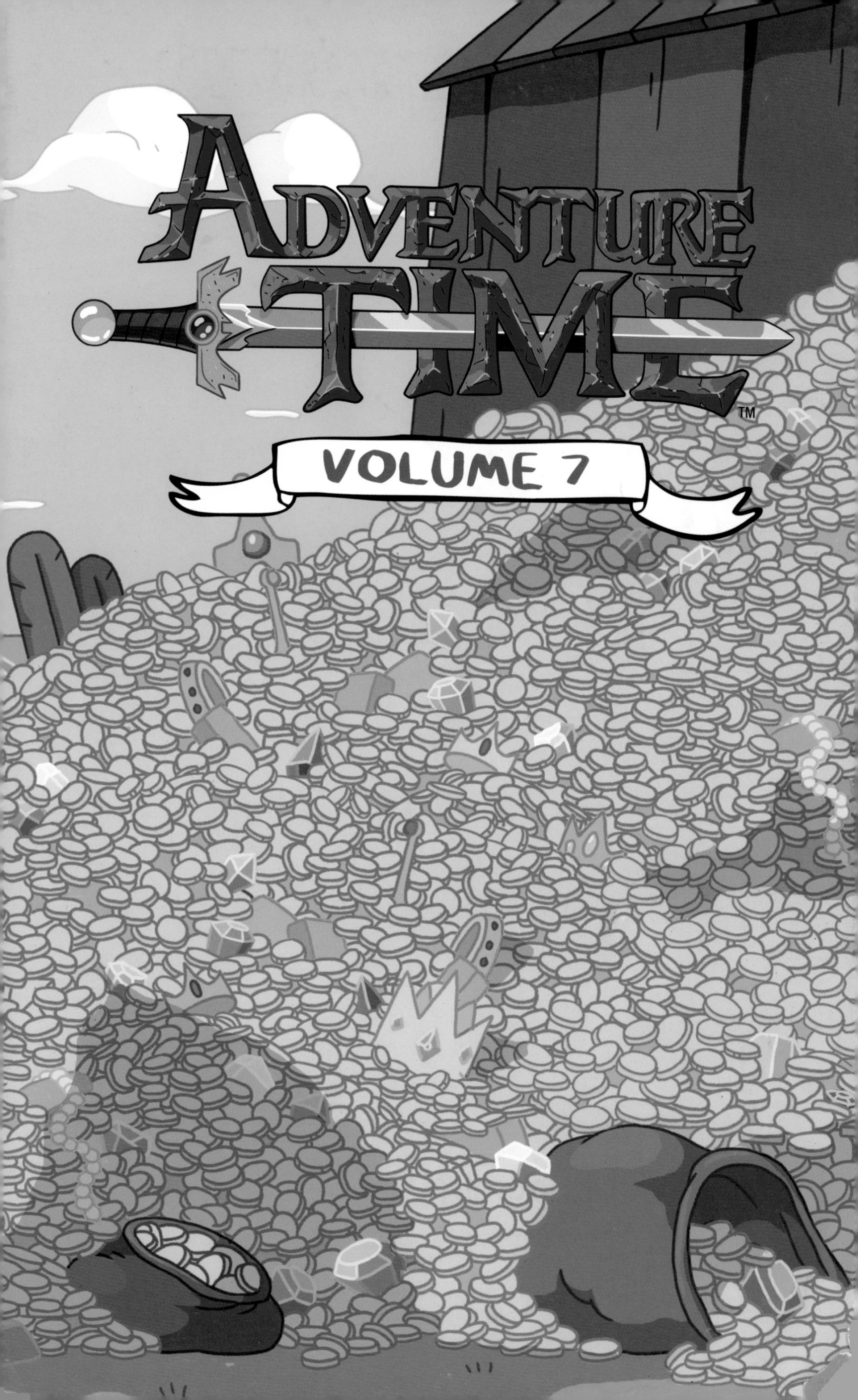
ADVENTURE TIME™
VOLUME 7

ROSS RICHIE CEO & Founder • MARK SMYLIE Founder of Archaia • MATT GAGNON Editor-in-Chief • FILIP SABLIK President of Publishing & Marketing • STEPHEN CHRISTY President of Development
LANCE KREITER VP of Licensing & Merchandising • PHIL BARBARO VP of Finance • BRYCE CARLSON Managing Editor • MEL CAYLO Marketing Manager • SCOTT NEWMAN Production Design Manager
IRENE BRADISH Operations Manager • CHRISTINE DINH Brand Communications Manager • DAFNA PLEBAN Editor • SHANNON WATTERS Editor • ERIC HARBURN Editor • IAN BRILL Editor • WHITNEY LEOPARD Associate Editor
JASMINE AMIRI Associate Editor • CHRIS ROSA Assistant Editor • ALEX GALER Assistant Editor • CAMERON CHITTOCK Assistant Editor • MARY GUMPORT Assistant Editor • KELSEY DIETERICH Production Designer
JILLIAN CRAB Production Designer • KARA LEOPARD Production Designer • MICHELLE ANKLEY Production Design Assistant • DEVIN FUNCHES E-Commerce & Inventory Coordinator • AARON FERRARA Operations Coordinator
JOSÉ MEZA Sales Assistant • ELIZABETH LOUGHRIDGE Accounting Assistant • STEPHANIE HOCUTT Marketing Assistant • HILLARY LEVI Executive Assistant • KATE ALBIN Administrative Assistant • JAMES ARRIOLA Mailroom Assistant

BOOM! Studios, 5670 Wilshire Boulevard, Suite 450, Los Angeles, CA 90036-5679. Printed in China. First Printing.
ISBN: 978-1-60886-746-2, eISBN: 978-1-61398-417-8

CREATED BY

Pendleton Ward

WRITTEN BY

Ryan North

MARCELZINE (Issue #30)
INTRO illustrated by Kat Philbin
COOL BEAR THE BEAR illustrated by Missy Pena
PEPPERMINT BARK RECIPE illustrated by Becca Tobin
HOURLY COMICS illustrated by Liz Prince
CHICKEN EXPERIMENT COMICS illustrated by Yumi Sakugawa
THE MANBABE'S LAMENT illustrated by Carey Pietsch
MY CA-RAZY DAY illustrated by Jesse Tise
FAVORITE KISSING SPOTS illustrated by Ian McGinty
colored and lettered by Fred Stresing
HOW TO LEAVE ME ALONE illustrated by T. Zysk
FINN THE SUPERHUMAN illustrated by David Cutler
colored by Gerardo Alba and lettered by Steve Wands
AFTERWORD illustrated by Shelli Paroline and Braden Lamb

ISSUES 31-34 ILLUSTRATED BY

Shelli Paroline & Braden Lamb

LETTERS BY

Steve Wands

COVER BY

Tait Howard

DESIGNER
Kara Leopard

ASSOCIATE EDITOR
Whitney Leopard

EDITOR
Shannon Watters

With special thanks to
Marisa Marionakis, Rick Blanco, Nicole Rivera, Conrad Montgomery, Meghan Bradley,
Curtis Lelash, Kelly Crews and the wonderful folks at Cartoon Network.

iii

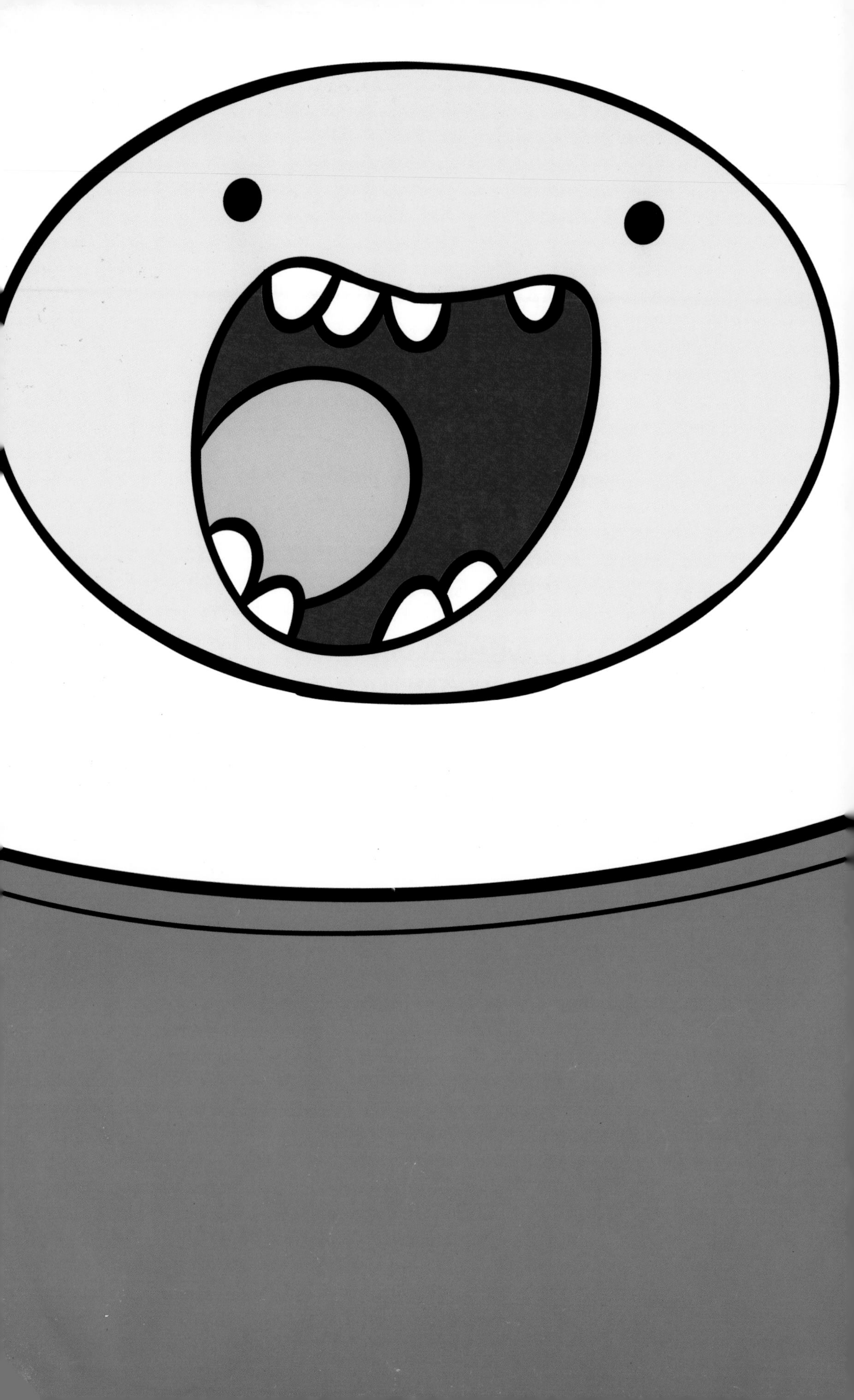

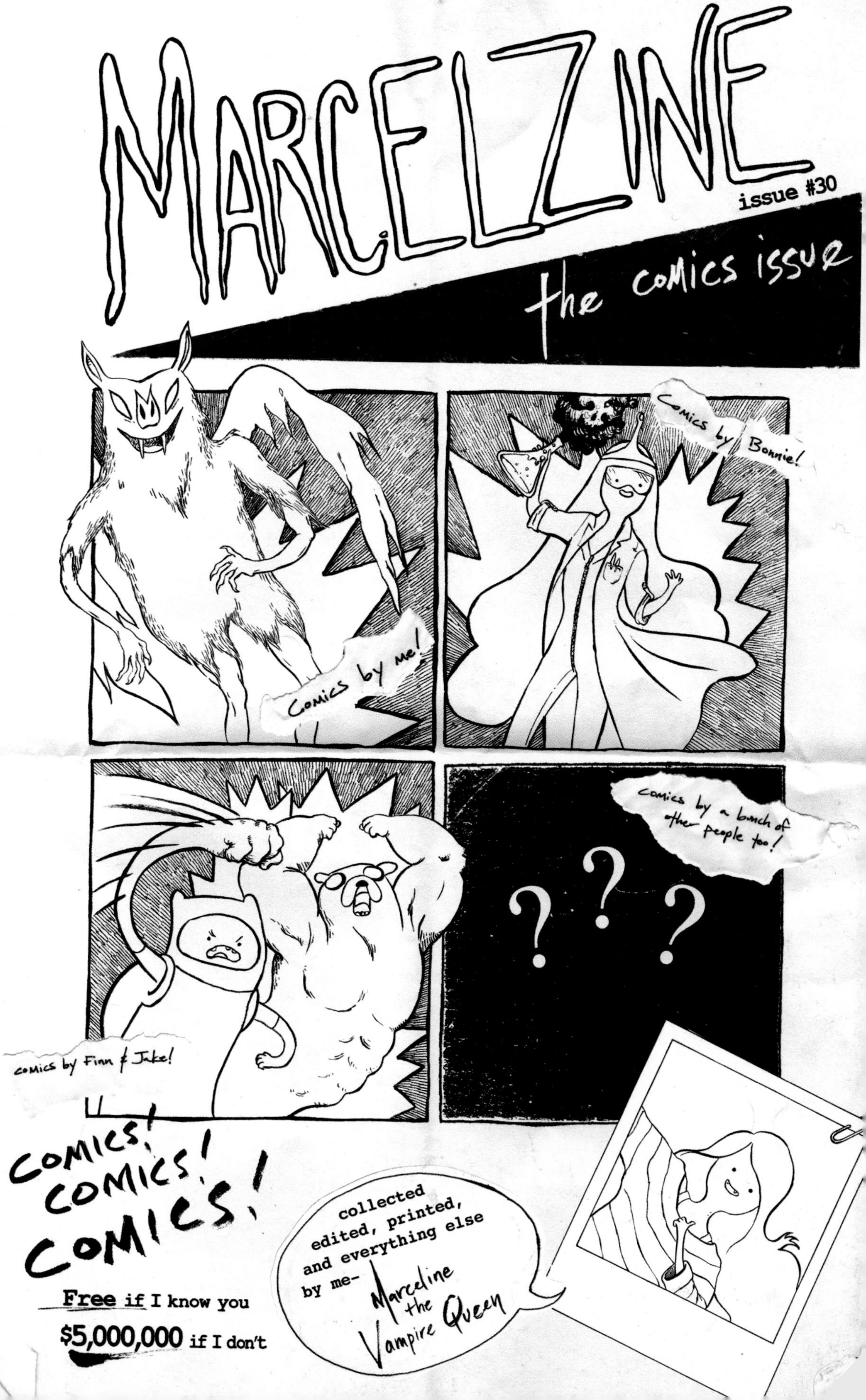
MARCELZINE
issue #30
the comics issue
Comics by me!
Comics by Bonnie!
comics by a bunch of other people too!
comics by Finn & Jake!
COMICS! COMICS! COMICS!
Free if I know you
$5,000,000 if I don't
collected edited, printed, and everything else by me-
Marceline the Vampire Queen

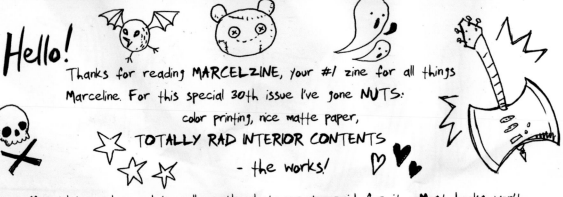

Hello!

Thanks for reading MARCELZINE, your #1 zine for all things Marceline. For this special 30th issue I've gone NUTS:

color printing, nice matte paper,

☆ TOTALLY RAD INTERIOR CONTENTS ☆☆

— the works! ♡ ♥ ♥

Marcelzine rules and is well worth whatever you paid for it. Most books won't tell you that they rule on the first page, but that's because they're afraid that it won't turn out to be true. But this book objectively rules, so I'm not afraid to give you a heads up on that:

this is awesome, you're lucky you get to read it, THE END.

I thought it'd be fun to have a theme for this issue, so I put up an open call for comics. Everyone loves comics, right? All the comics here either have my **OFFICIAL STAMP OF APPROVAL** or are here because honestly it was easier to print them than listen to people complain.

Lumpy Space Princess, I am looking in your direction. I know she's only going to flip through this once to make sure her comic is included, so she'll never read this. LSP, if you do actually read this, come up to me and say "syzygy" and I will give you a can of beans. A full can. Mmm-MMM, beans.

(SPOILER ALERT: SHE WILL NEVER SEE THOSE BEANS BECAUSE SHE WILL NEVER ASK. IN FACT I'M SO CERTAIN I'M EATING THE BEANS RIGHT NOW)

★ (UPDATE: THEY WERE ACTUALLY PRETTY GOOD) ★

Anyway, enjoy the comics! If you've got your own comics that you'd like to include in future issues, send 'em my way! Here is my address:

```
Vampire Queen, Marceline the
#1 Marceline's House Road
Land of Ooo
Earth, the Solar System
Local Interstellar Cloud, the Gould Belt
Orion Arm, the Milky Way Galaxy
Virgo Supercluster, the Observable Universe
The Entire Universe, Even The Parts We Can't See
```

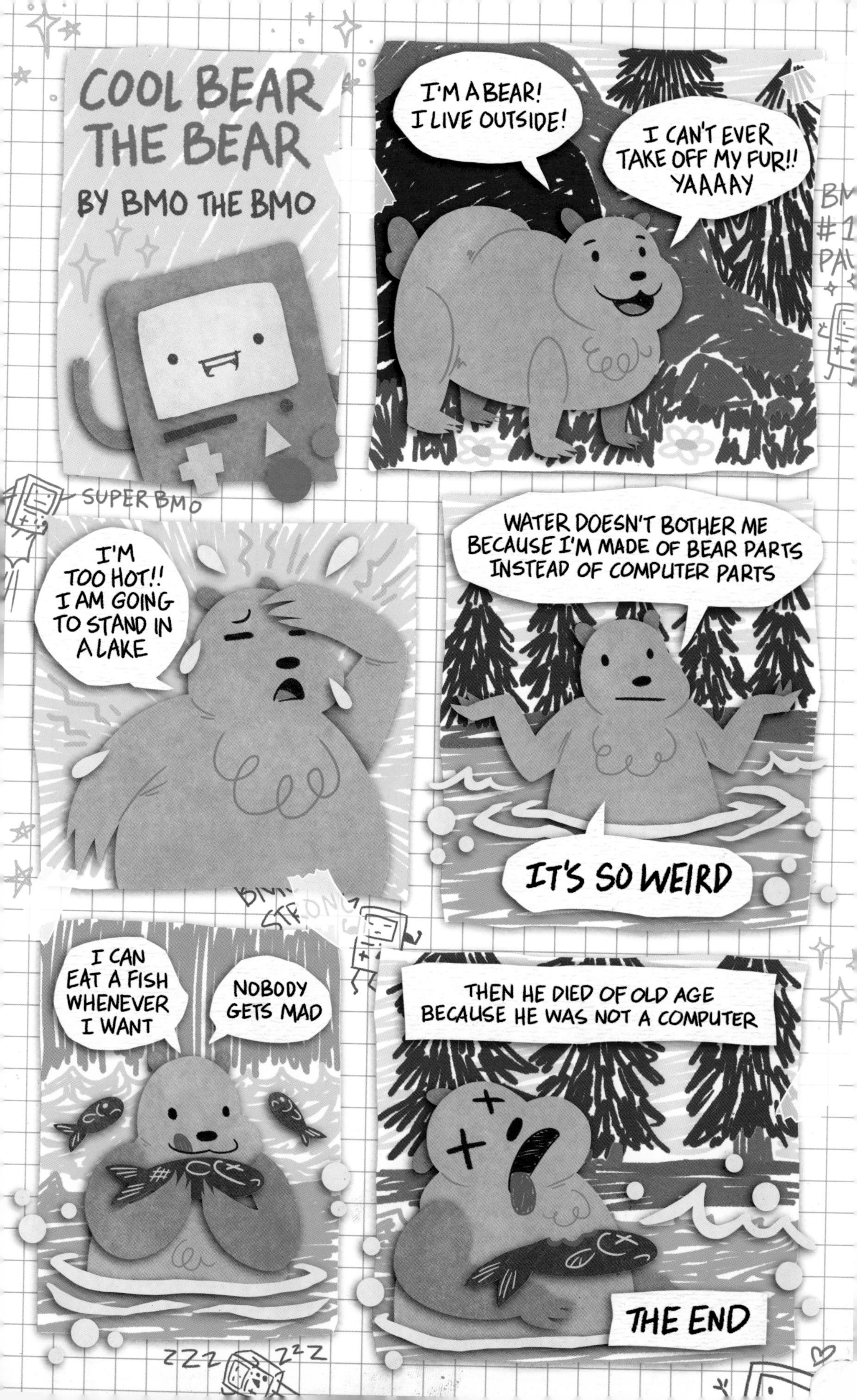
COOL BEAR THE BEAR
BY BMO THE BMO
I'M A BEAR! I LIVE OUTSIDE!
I CAN'T EVER TAKE OFF MY FUR!! YAAAAY
SUPER BMO
I'M TOO HOT!! I AM GOING TO STAND IN A LAKE
WATER DOESN'T BOTHER ME BECAUSE I'M MADE OF BEAR PARTS INSTEAD OF COMPUTER PARTS
IT'S SO WEIRD
I CAN EAT A FISH WHENEVER I WANT
NOBODY GETS MAD
THEN HE DIED OF OLD AGE BECAUSE HE WAS NOT A COMPUTER
THE END
ZZZ ZZZ

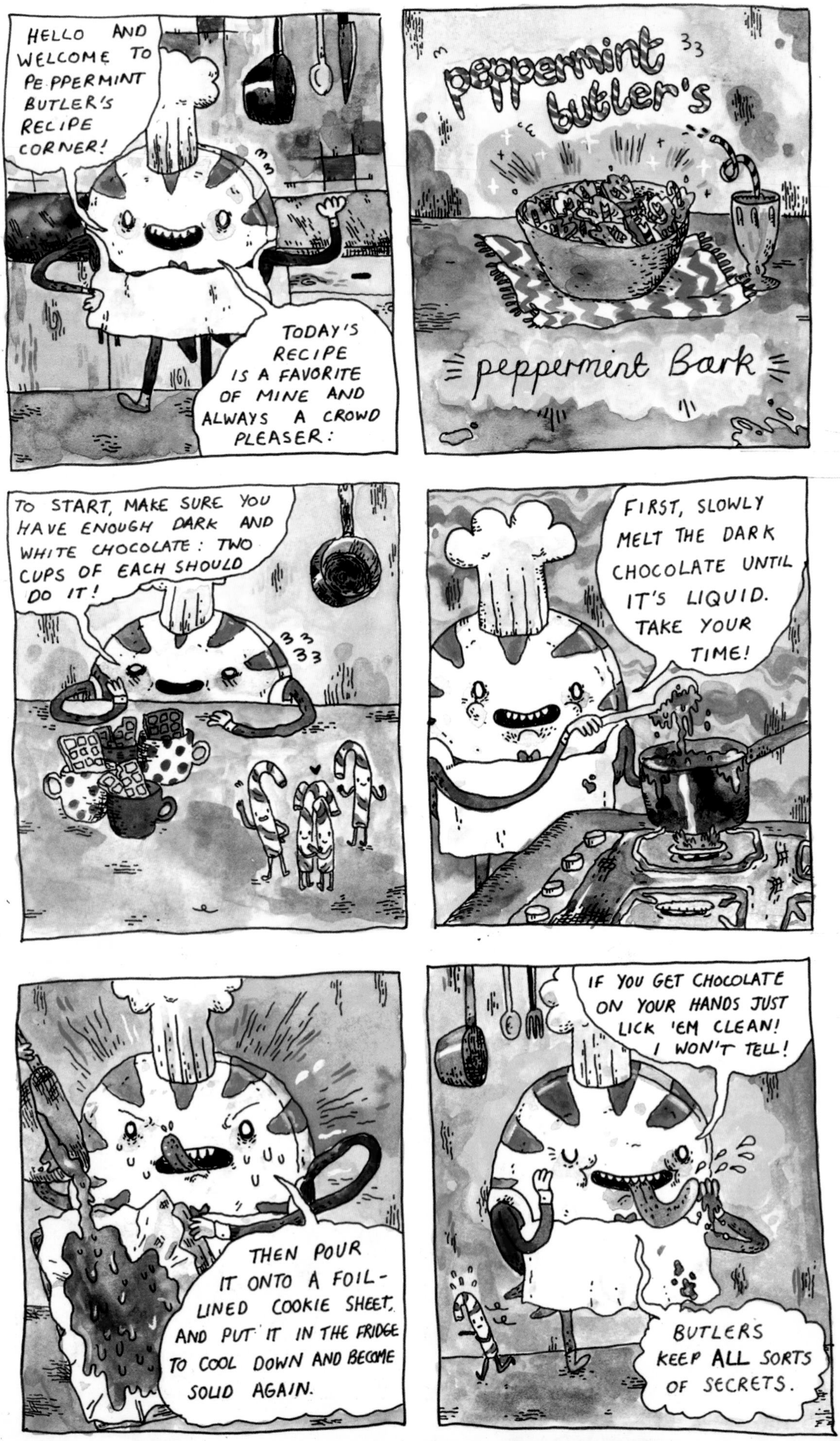
HELLO AND WELCOME TO PEPPERMINT BUTLER'S RECIPE CORNER!
TODAY'S RECIPE IS A FAVORITE OF MINE AND ALWAYS A CROWD PLEASER:
peppermint butler's
peppermint Bark
TO START, MAKE SURE YOU HAVE ENOUGH DARK AND WHITE CHOCOLATE: TWO CUPS OF EACH SHOULD DO IT!
FIRST, SLOWLY MELT THE DARK CHOCOLATE UNTIL IT'S LIQUID. TAKE YOUR TIME!
THEN POUR IT ONTO A FOIL-LINED COOKIE SHEET, AND PUT IT IN THE FRIDGE TO COOL DOWN AND BECOME SOLID AGAIN.
IF YOU GET CHOCOLATE ON YOUR HANDS JUST LICK 'EM CLEAN! I WON'T TELL!
BUTLERS KEEP ALL SORTS OF SECRETS.

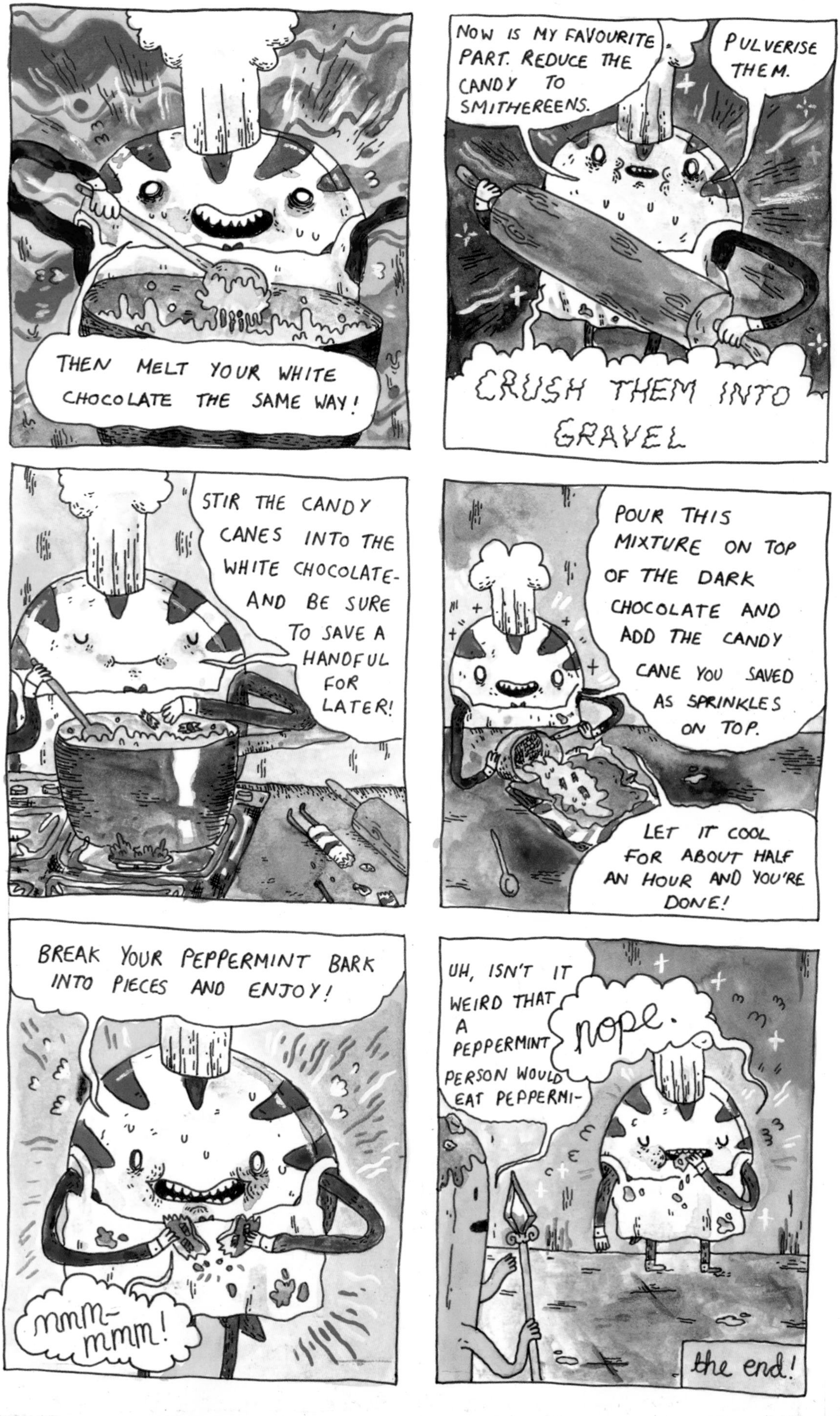
THEN MELT YOUR WHITE CHOCOLATE THE SAME WAY!
NOW IS MY FAVOURITE PART. REDUCE THE CANDY TO SMITHEREENS.
PULVERISE THEM.
CRUSH THEM INTO GRAVEL
STIR THE CANDY CANES INTO THE WHITE CHOCOLATE- AND BE SURE TO SAVE A HANDFUL FOR LATER!
POUR THIS MIXTURE ON TOP OF THE DARK CHOCOLATE AND ADD THE CANDY CANE YOU SAVED AS SPRINKLES ON TOP.
LET IT COOL FOR ABOUT HALF AN HOUR AND YOU'RE DONE!
BREAK YOUR PEPPERMINT BARK INTO PIECES AND ENJOY!
mmm-mmm!
UH, ISN'T IT WEIRD THAT A PEPPERMINT PERSON WOULD EAT PEPPERMI-
nope.
the end!

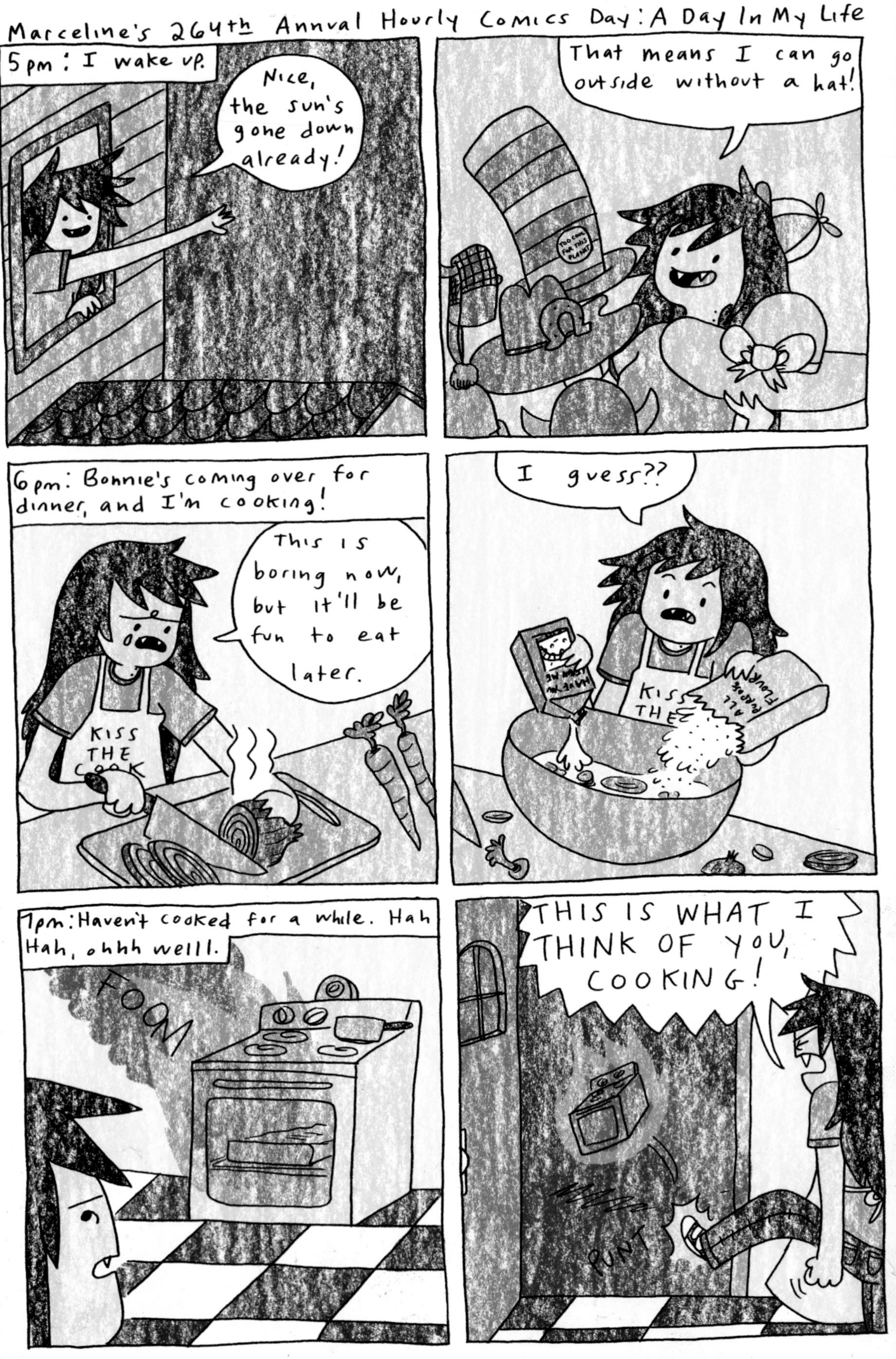

Marceline's 264th Annual Hourly Comics Day: A Day In My Life
5pm: I wake up.
Nice, the sun's gone down already!
That means I can go outside without a hat!
TOO COOL FOR THIS PLANET
6pm: Bonnie's coming over for dinner, and I'm cooking!
This is boring now, but it'll be fun to eat later.
KISS THE COOK
I guess??
KISS THE
7pm: Haven't cooked for a while. Hah Hah, ohhh welll.
FOOM
THIS IS WHAT I THINK OF YOU, COOKING!
PUNT

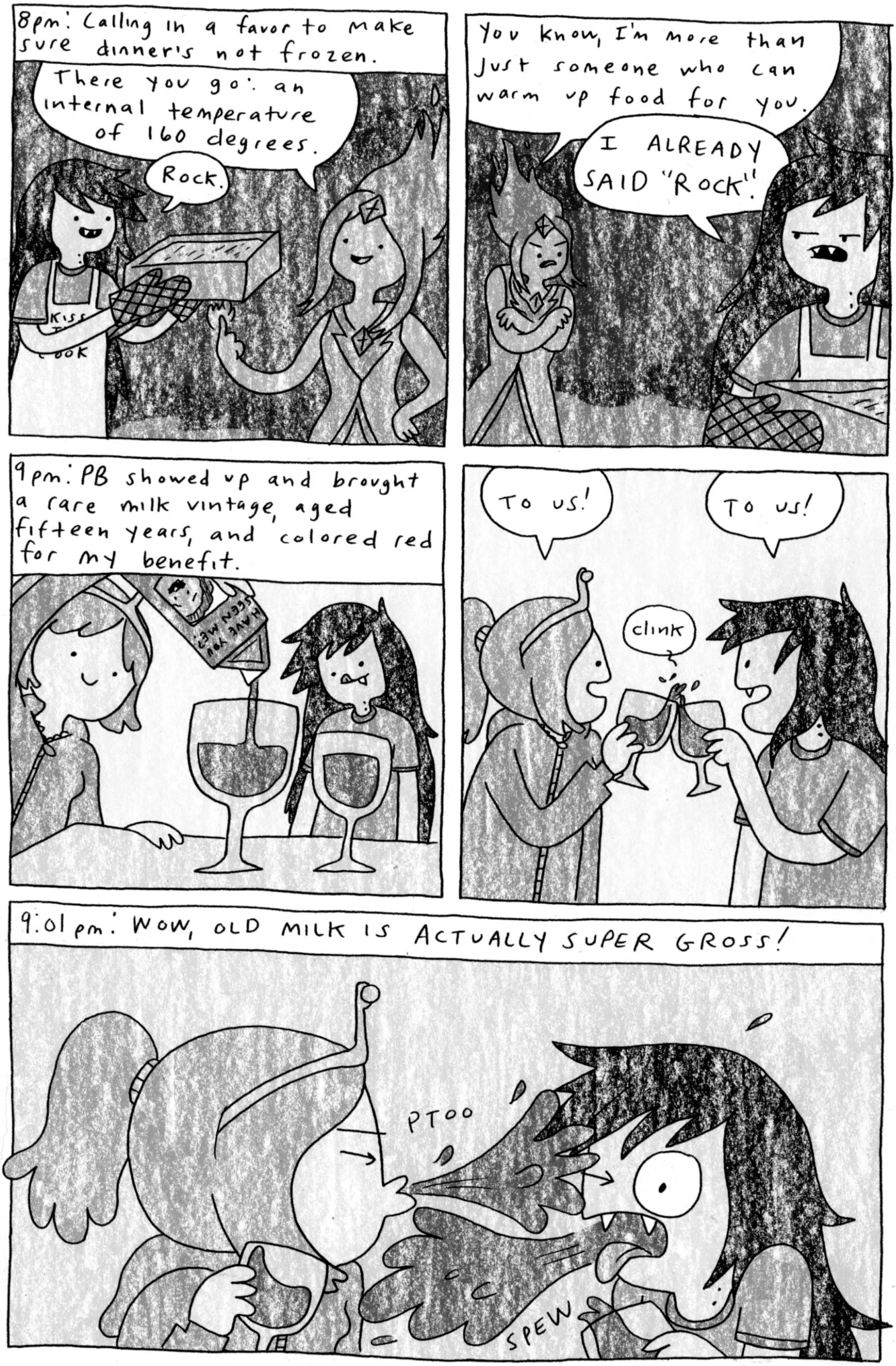
8pm: Calling in a favor to make sure dinner's not frozen.
There you go: an internal temperature of 160 degrees.
Rock.
KISS THE COOK
You know, I'm more than just someone who can warm up food for you.
I ALREADY SAID "ROCK".
9pm: PB showed up and brought a rare milk vintage, aged fifteen years, and colored red for my benefit.
HAVE YOU SEEN ME?
To us!
To us!
clink
9:01pm: WOW, OLD MILK IS ACTUALLY SUPER GROSS!
PTOO
SPEW

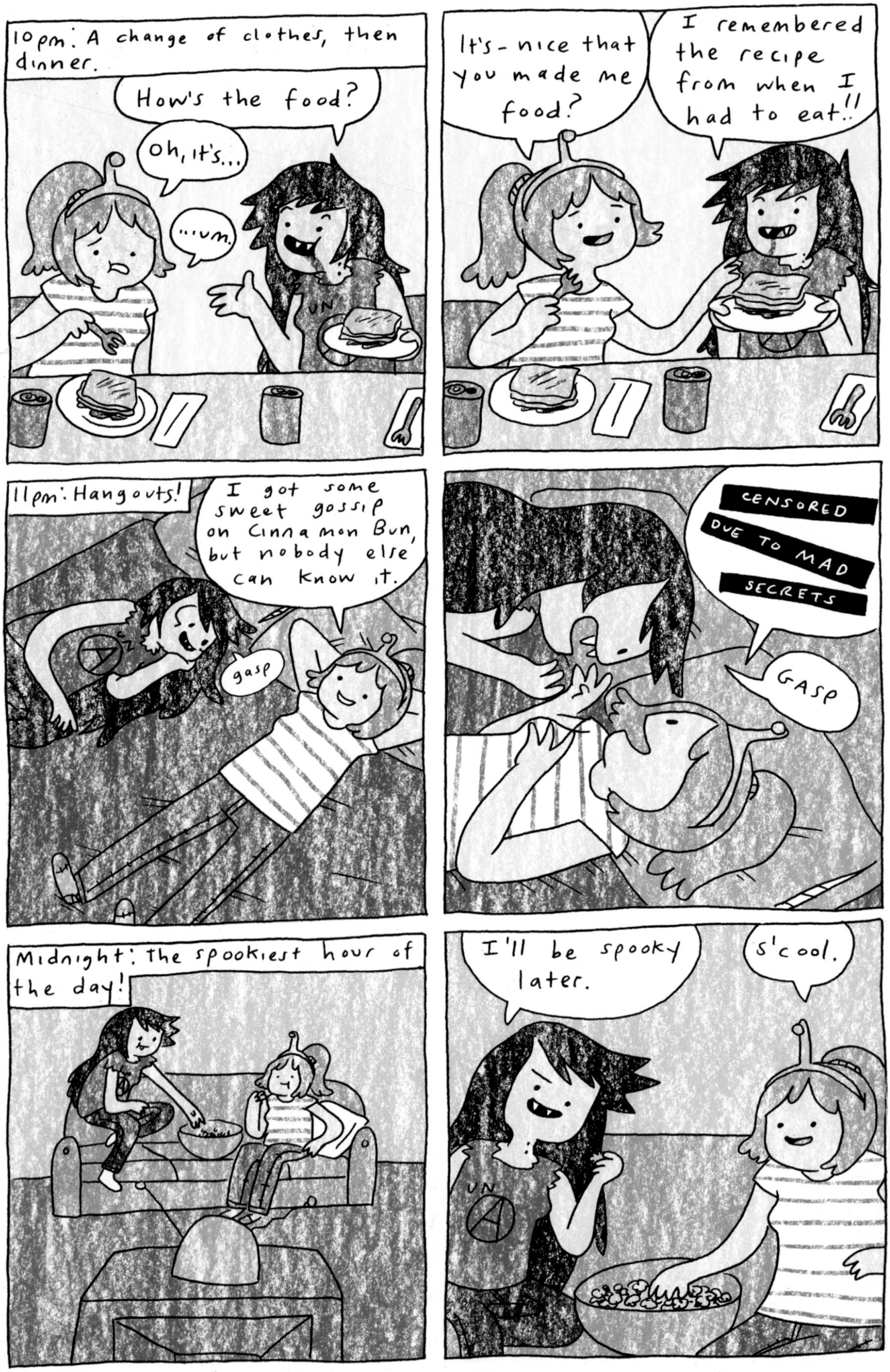

10pm: A change of clothes, then dinner.
How's the food?
Oh, it's...
...um.
It's- nice that you made me food?
I remembered the recipe from when I had to eat!!
11pm: Hangouts!
I got some sweet gossip on Cinnamon Bun, but nobody else can know it.
gasp
CENSORED DUE TO MAD SECRETS
GASP
Midnight: the spookiest hour of the day!
I'll be spooky later.
s'cool.

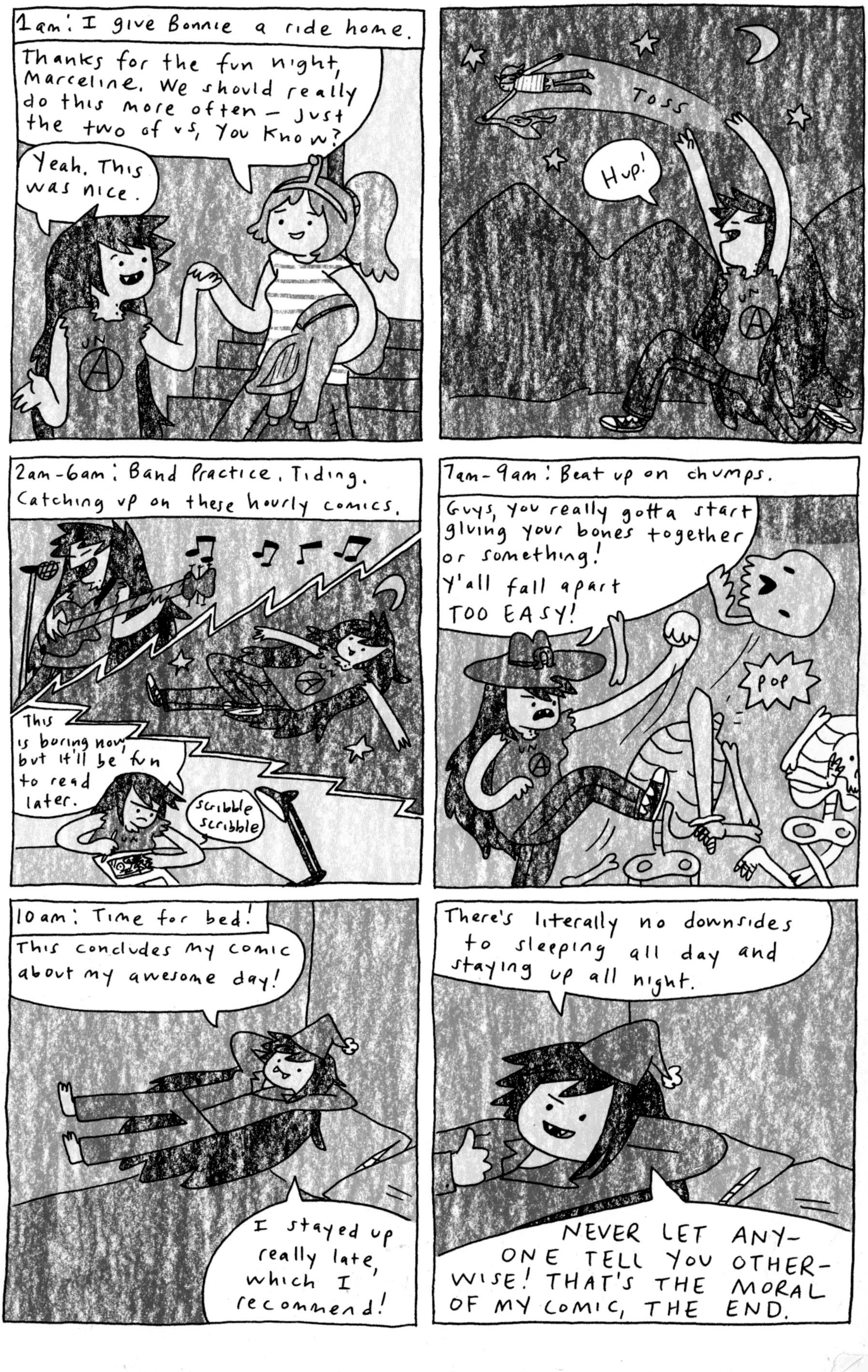
1am: I give Bonnie a ride home.
Thanks for the fun night, Marceline. We should really do this more often – just the two of us, you know?
Yeah. This was nice.
TOSS
Hup!
2am-6am: Band Practice. Tiding. Catching up on these hourly comics.
This is boring now, but it'll be fun to read later.
scribble scribble
7am-9am: Beat up on chumps.
Guys, you really gotta start gluing your bones together or something!
Y'all fall apart TOO EASY!
POP
10am: Time for bed!
This concludes my comic about my awesome day!
I stayed up really late, which I recommend!
There's literally no downsides to sleeping all day and staying up all night.
NEVER LET ANY-ONE TELL YOU OTHER-WISE! THAT'S THE MORAL OF MY COMIC, THE END.

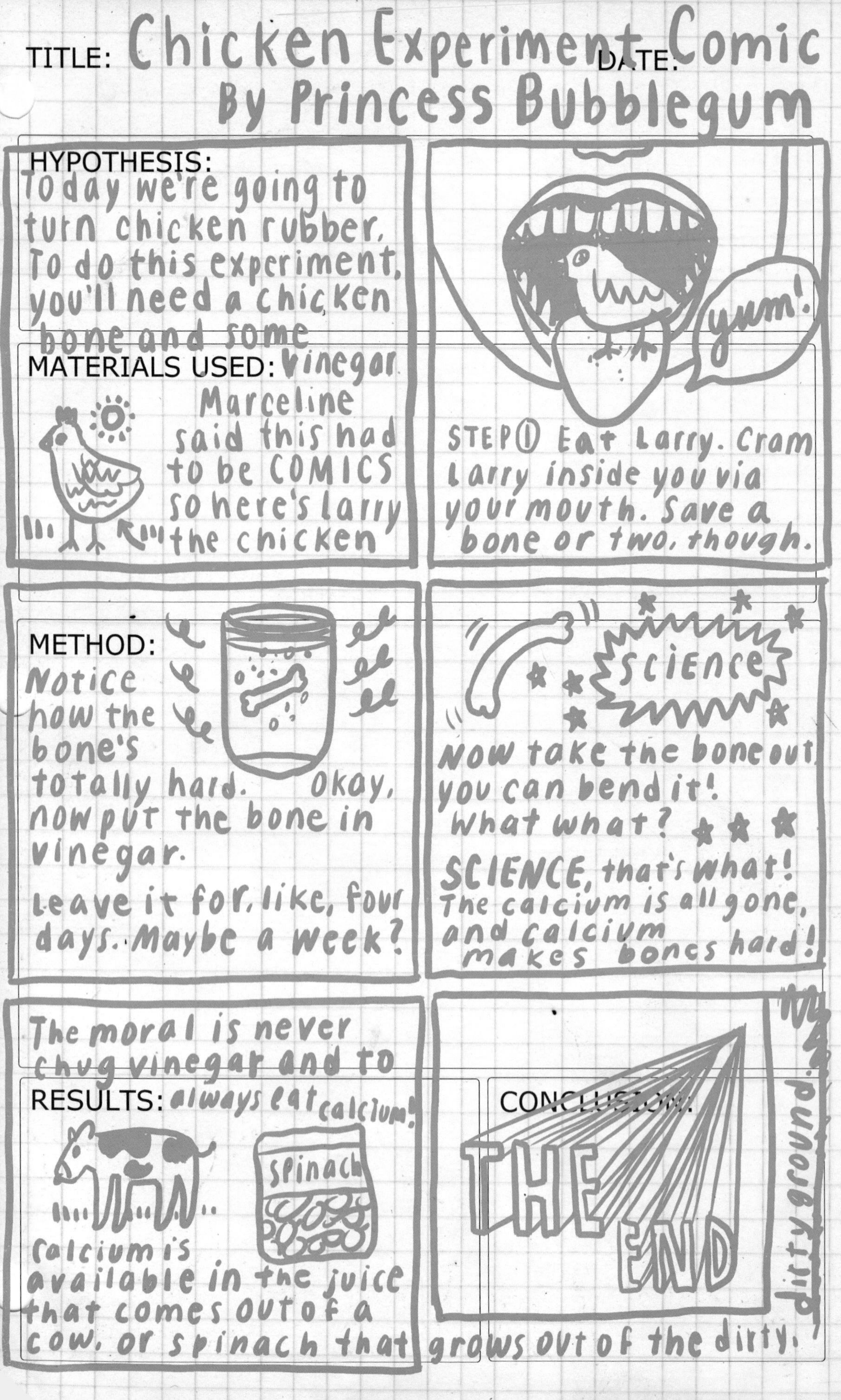
TITLE: Chicken Experiment Comic
DATE:
By Princess Bubblegum
HYPOTHESIS: Today we're going to turn chicken rubber. To do this experiment, you'll need a chicken bone and some
MATERIALS USED: vinegar
Marceline said this had to be COMICS so here's Larry the chicken
yum!
STEP① Eat Larry. Cram Larry inside you via your mouth. Save a bone or two, though.
METHOD: Notice how the bone's totally hard. Okay, now put the bone in vinegar.
Leave it for, like, four days. Maybe a week?
SCIENCE
Now take the bone out, you can bend it! What what?
SCIENCE, that's what! The calcium is all gone, and calcium makes bones hard!
The moral is never chug vinegar and to
RESULTS: always eat calcium!
Spinach
Calcium is available in the juice that comes out of a cow, or spinach that grows out of the dirty. dirty ground.
CONCLUSION:
THE END

THE MANBABE'S LAMENT:

A LUMPIN' ROMANCE COMIC

Y'ALL ARE GONNA **LOVE** THIS * BY LUMPY SPACE PRINCESS

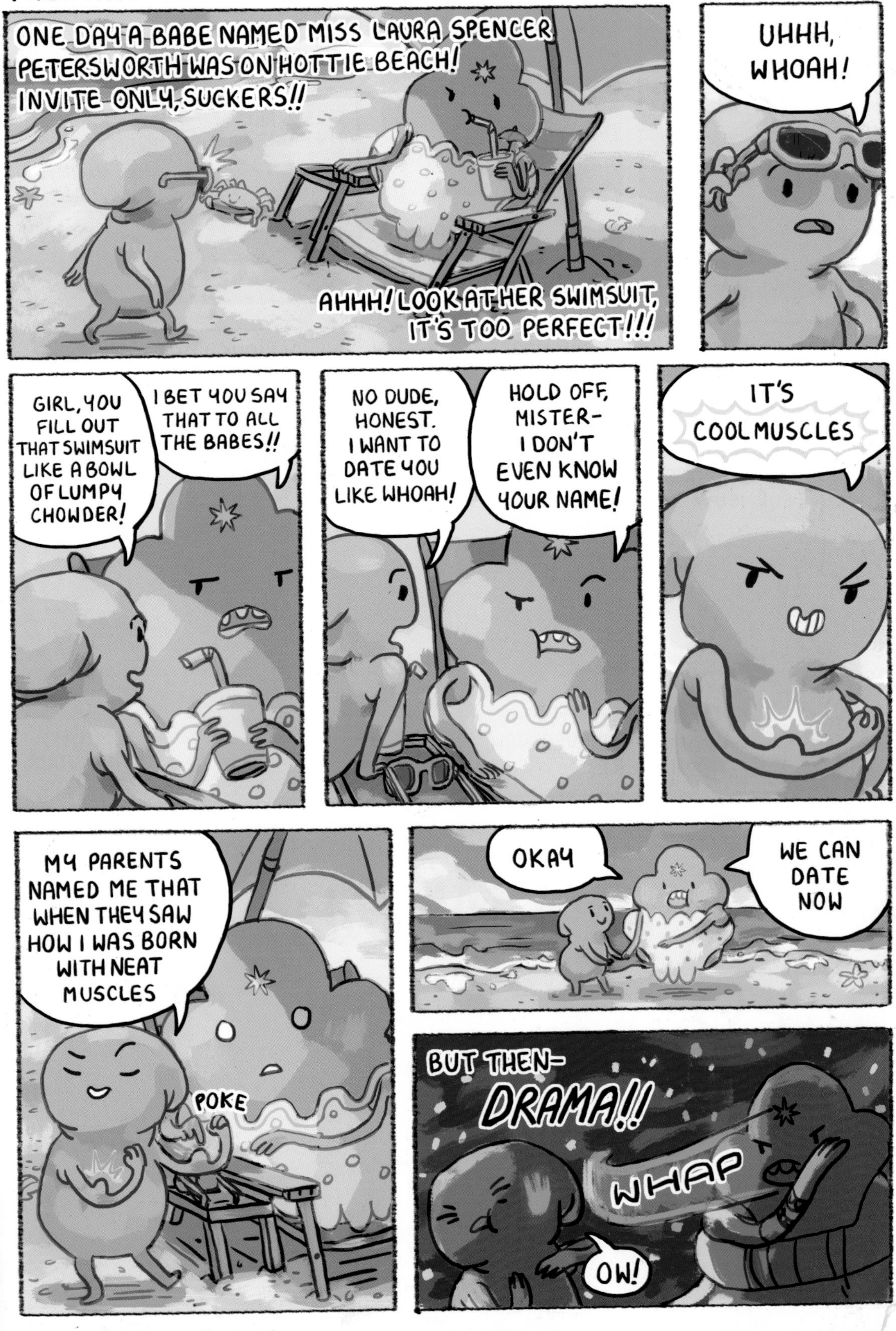

ONE DAY A BABE NAMED MISS LAURA SPENCER PETERSWORTH WAS ON HOTTIE BEACH! INVITE ONLY, SUCKERS!!
AHHH! LOOK AT HER SWIMSUIT, IT'S TOO PERFECT!!!
UHHH, WHOAH!
GIRL, YOU FILL OUT THAT SWIMSUIT LIKE A BOWL OF LUMPY CHOWDER!
I BET YOU SAY THAT TO ALL THE BABES!!
NO DUDE, HONEST. I WANT TO DATE YOU LIKE WHOAH!
HOLD OFF, MISTER- I DON'T EVEN KNOW YOUR NAME!
IT'S COOL MUSCLES
MY PARENTS NAMED ME THAT WHEN THEY SAW HOW I WAS BORN WITH NEAT MUSCLES
POKE
OKAY
WE CAN DATE NOW
BUT THEN-
DRAMA!!
WHAP
OW!

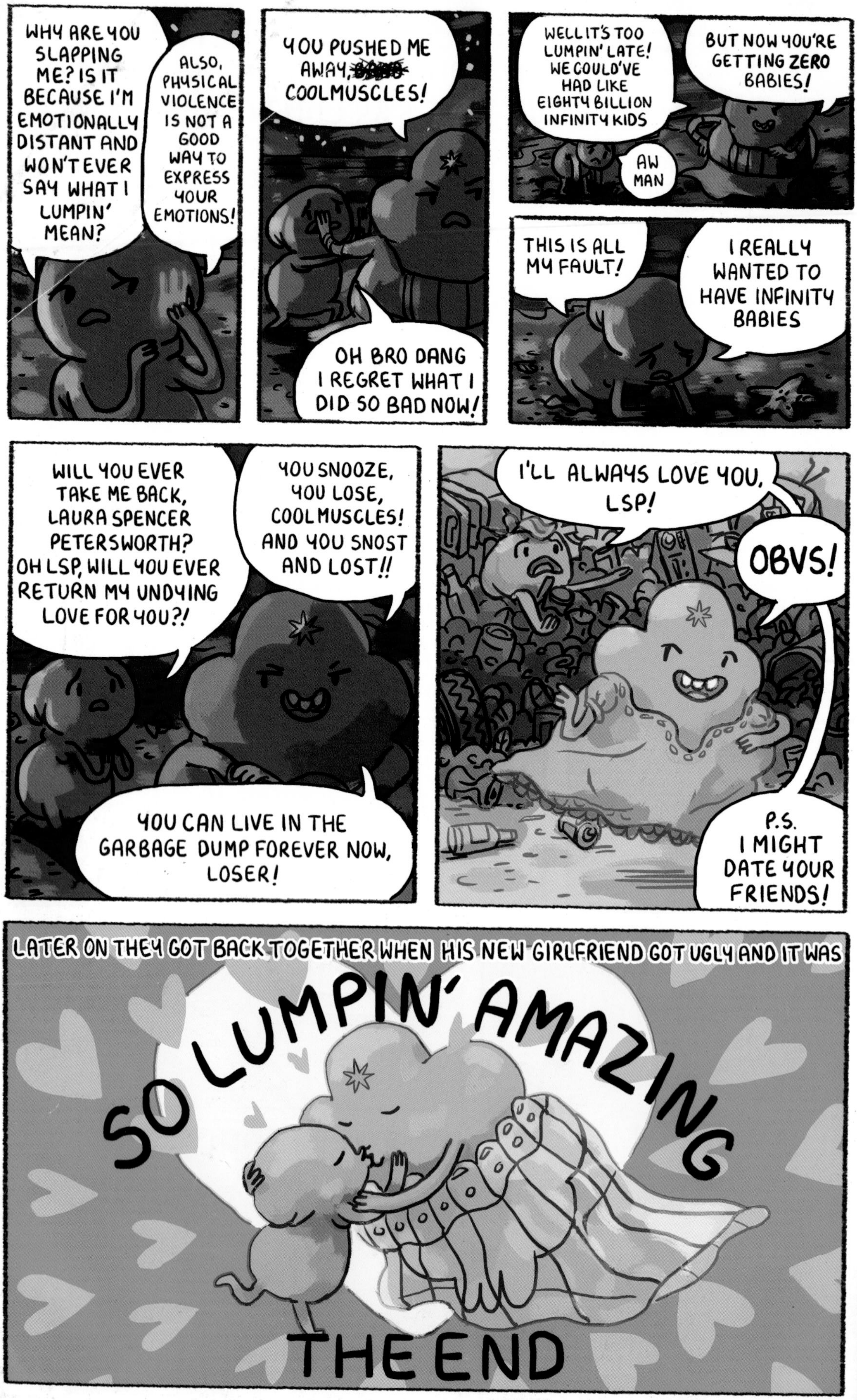
WHY ARE YOU SLAPPING ME? IS IT BECAUSE I'M EMOTIONALLY DISTANT AND WON'T EVER SAY WHAT I LUMPIN' MEAN?
ALSO, PHYSICAL VIOLENCE IS NOT A GOOD WAY TO EXPRESS YOUR EMOTIONS!
YOU PUSHED ME AWAY, [redacted] COOLMUSCLES!
OH BRO DANG I REGRET WHAT I DID SO BAD NOW!
WELL IT'S TOO LUMPIN' LATE! WE COULD'VE HAD LIKE EIGHTY BILLION INFINITY KIDS
BUT NOW YOU'RE GETTING ZERO BABIES!
AW MAN
THIS IS ALL MY FAULT!
I REALLY WANTED TO HAVE INFINITY BABIES
WILL YOU EVER TAKE ME BACK, LAURA SPENCER PETERSWORTH? OH LSP, WILL YOU EVER RETURN MY UNDYING LOVE FOR YOU?!
YOU SNOOZE, YOU LOSE, COOLMUSCLES! AND YOU SNOST AND LOST!!
YOU CAN LIVE IN THE GARBAGE DUMP FOREVER NOW, LOSER!
I'LL ALWAYS LOVE YOU, LSP!
OBVS!
P.S. I MIGHT DATE YOUR FRIENDS!
LATER ON THEY GOT BACK TOGETHER WHEN HIS NEW GIRLFRIEND GOT UGLY AND IT WAS
SO LUMPIN' AMAZING
THE END

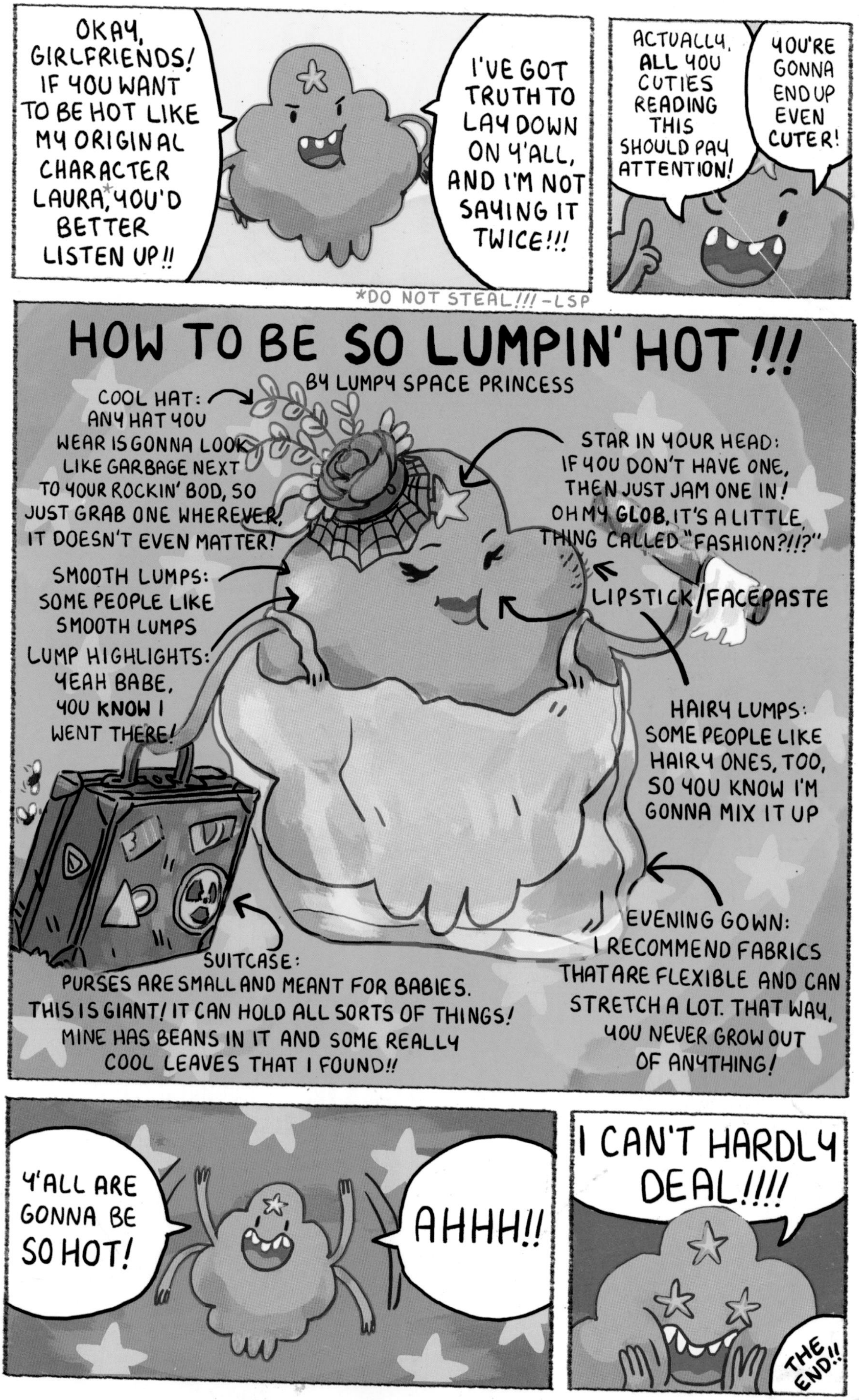

OKAY, GIRLFRIENDS! IF YOU WANT TO BE HOT LIKE MY ORIGINAL CHARACTER LAURA*, YOU'D BETTER LISTEN UP!!
I'VE GOT TRUTH TO LAY DOWN ON Y'ALL, AND I'M NOT SAYING IT TWICE!!!
ACTUALLY, ALL YOU CUTIES READING THIS SHOULD PAY ATTENTION!
YOU'RE GONNA END UP EVEN CUTER!
*DO NOT STEAL!!! -LSP
HOW TO BE SO LUMPIN' HOT!!!
BY LUMPY SPACE PRINCESS
COOL HAT: ANY HAT YOU WEAR IS GONNA LOOK LIKE GARBAGE NEXT TO YOUR ROCKIN' BOD, SO JUST GRAB ONE WHEREVER, IT DOESN'T EVEN MATTER!
STAR IN YOUR HEAD: IF YOU DON'T HAVE ONE, THEN JUST JAM ONE IN! OH MY GLOB, IT'S A LITTLE THING CALLED "FASHION?!!?"
SMOOTH LUMPS: SOME PEOPLE LIKE SMOOTH LUMPS
LIPSTICK/FACEPASTE
LUMP HIGHLIGHTS: YEAH BABE, YOU KNOW I WENT THERE!
HAIRY LUMPS: SOME PEOPLE LIKE HAIRY ONES, TOO, SO YOU KNOW I'M GONNA MIX IT UP
SUITCASE: PURSES ARE SMALL AND MEANT FOR BABIES. THIS IS GIANT! IT CAN HOLD ALL SORTS OF THINGS! MINE HAS BEANS IN IT AND SOME REALLY COOL LEAVES THAT I FOUND!!
EVENING GOWN: I RECOMMEND FABRICS THAT ARE FLEXIBLE AND CAN STRETCH A LOT. THAT WAY, YOU NEVER GROW OUT OF ANYTHING!
Y'ALL ARE GONNA BE SO HOT!
AHHH!!
I CAN'T HARDLY DEAL!!!!
THE END!!

My CA-RAZY Day

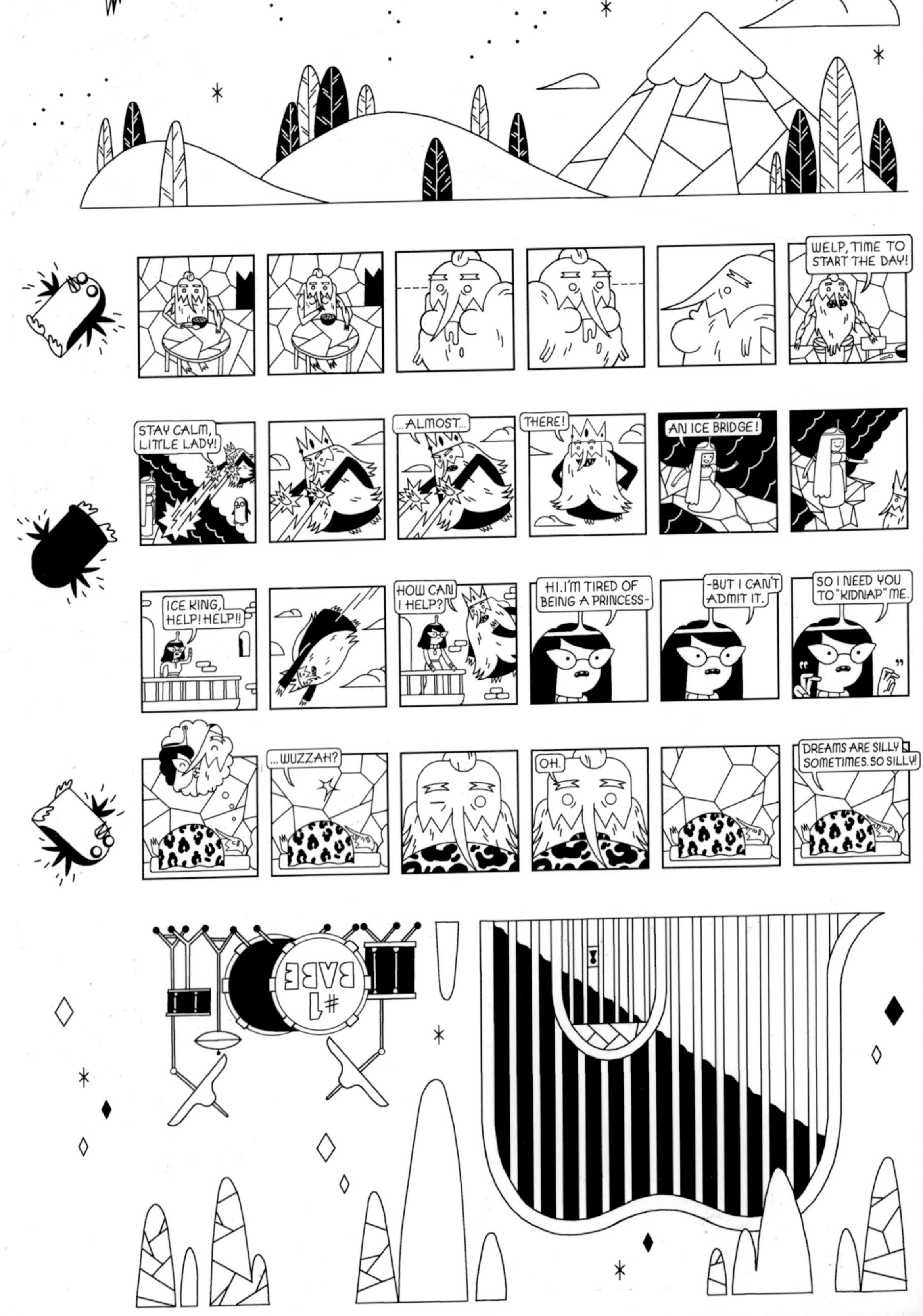

WELP, TIME TO START THE DAY!
STAY CALM, LITTLE LADY!
...ALMOST...
THERE!
AN ICE BRIDGE!
ICE KING, HELP! HELP!!
HOW CAN I HELP?
HI. I'M TIRED OF BEING A PRINCESS-
-BUT I CAN'T ADMIT IT.
SO I NEED YOU TO "KIDNAP" ME.
...WUZZAH?
OH.
DREAMS ARE SILLY SOMETIMES. SO SILLY!

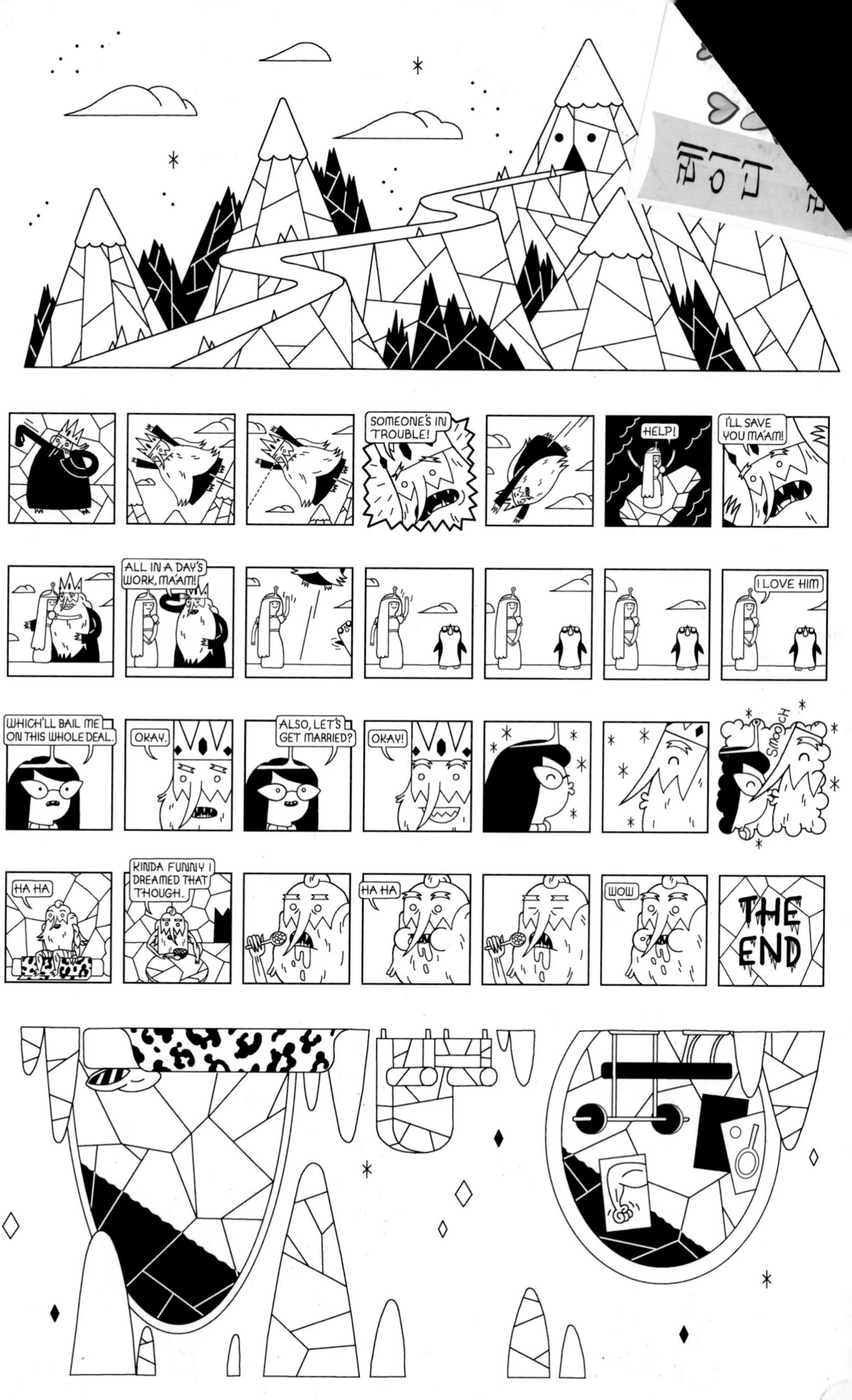
SOMEONE'S IN TROUBLE!
HELP!
I'LL SAVE YOU MA'AM!
ALL IN A DAY'S WORK, MA'AM!
I LOVE HIM
WHICH'LL BAIL ME ON THIS WHOLE DEAL.
OKAY.
ALSO, LET'S GET MARRIED?
OKAY!
SMOOCH
HA HA
KINDA FUNNY I DREAMED THAT THOUGH.
HA HA
WOW
THE END

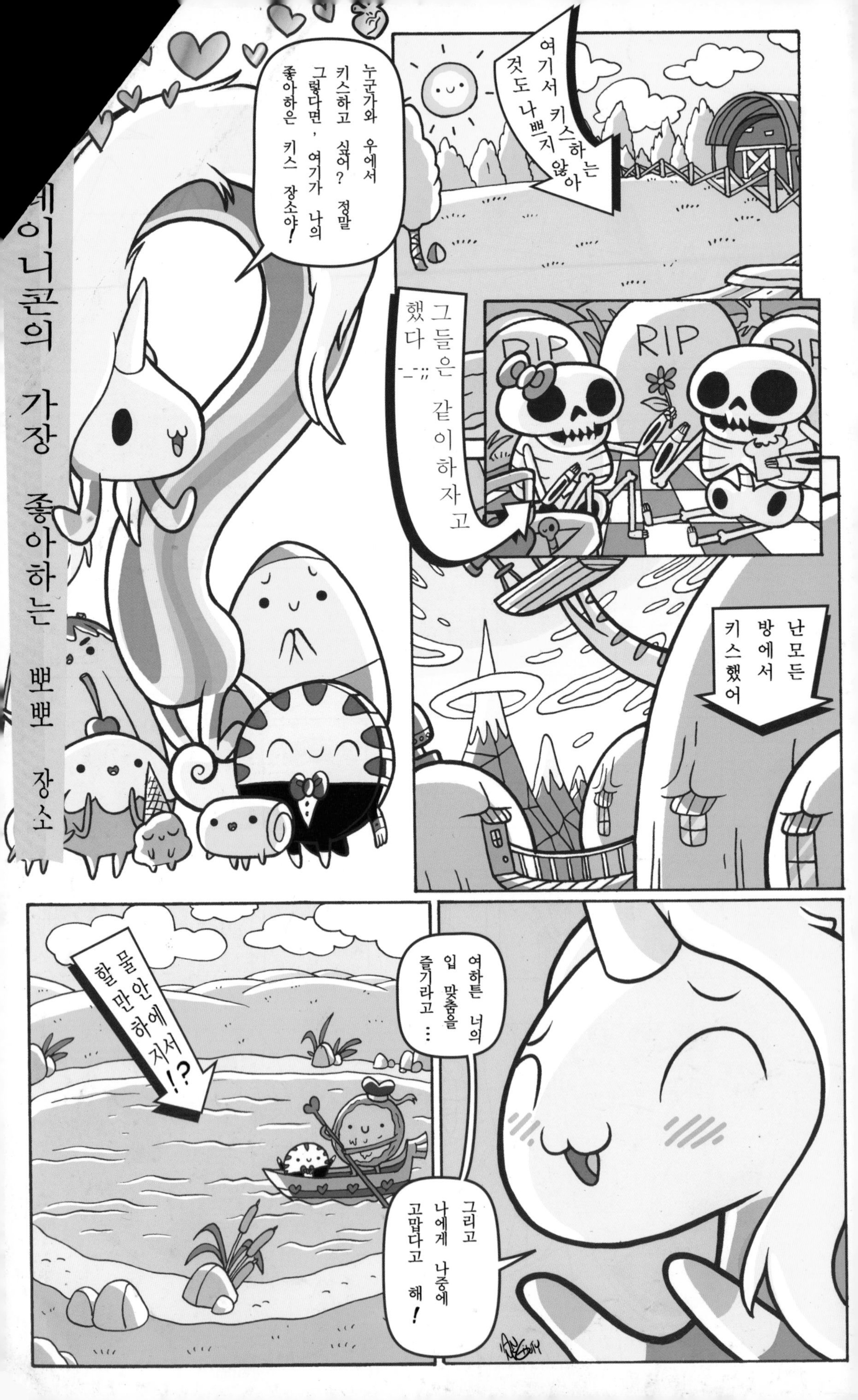
이니콘의 가장 좋아하는 뽀뽀 장소
누군가와 우에서 키스하고 싶어? 정말 그렇다면, 여기가 나의 좋아하은 키스 장소야!
여기서 키스하는 것도 나쁘지 않아
그들은 같이하자고 했다 -_-;;
난 모든 방에서 키스했어
물 안에서 할만하지!?
여하튼 너의 입 맞춤을 즐기라고…
그리고 나에게 나중에 고맙다고 해!

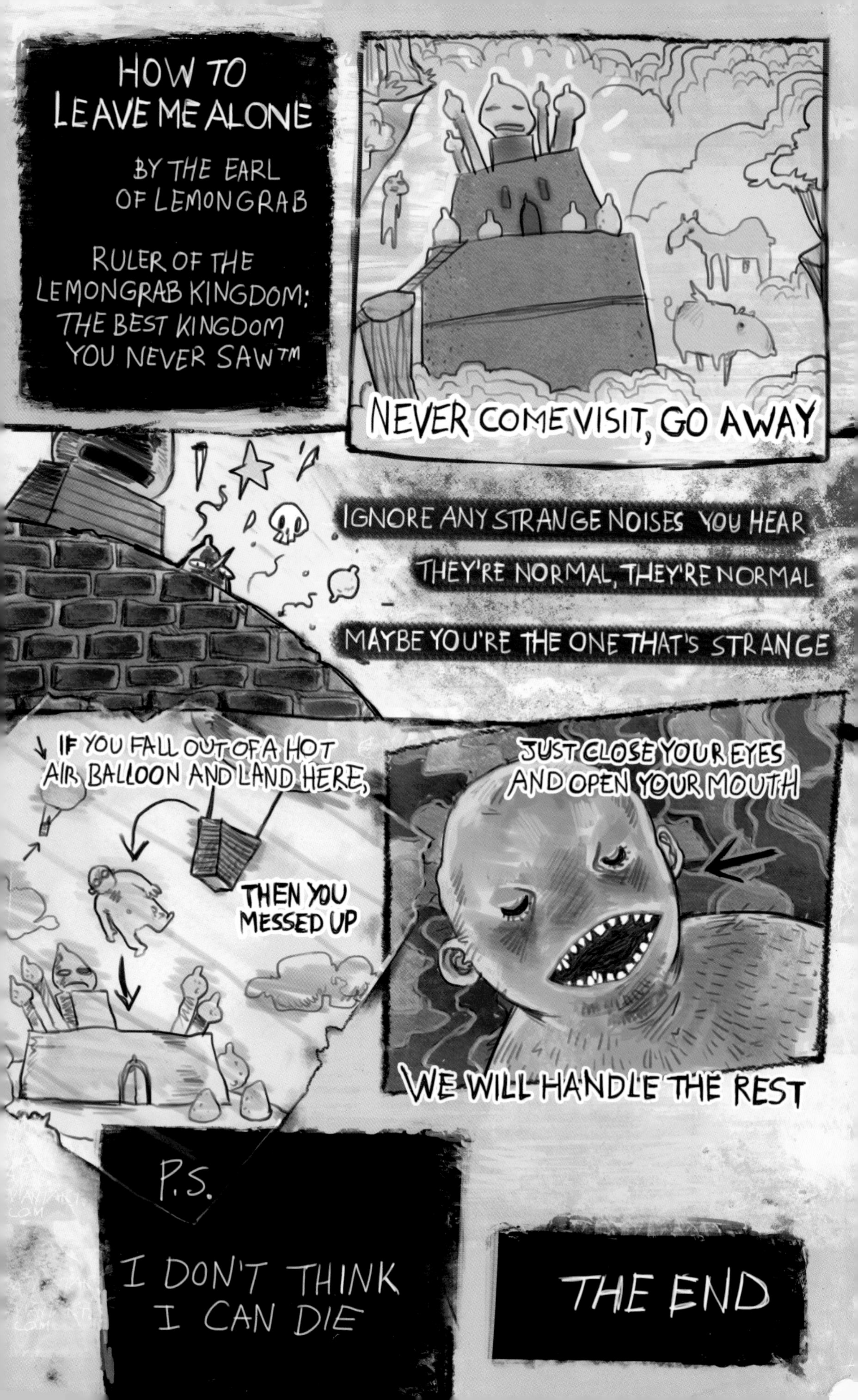
HOW TO
LEAVE ME ALONE
BY THE EARL
OF LEMONGRAB
RULER OF THE
LEMONGRAB KINGDOM:
THE BEST KINGDOM
YOU NEVER SAW™
NEVER COME VISIT, GO AWAY
IGNORE ANY STRANGE NOISES YOU HEAR
THEY'RE NORMAL, THEY'RE NORMAL
MAYBE YOU'RE THE ONE THAT'S STRANGE
IF YOU FALL OUT OF A HOT
AIR BALLOON AND LAND HERE,
THEN YOU
MESSED UP
JUST CLOSE YOUR EYES
AND OPEN YOUR MOUTH
WE WILL HANDLE THE REST
P.S.
I DON'T THINK
I CAN DIE
THE END

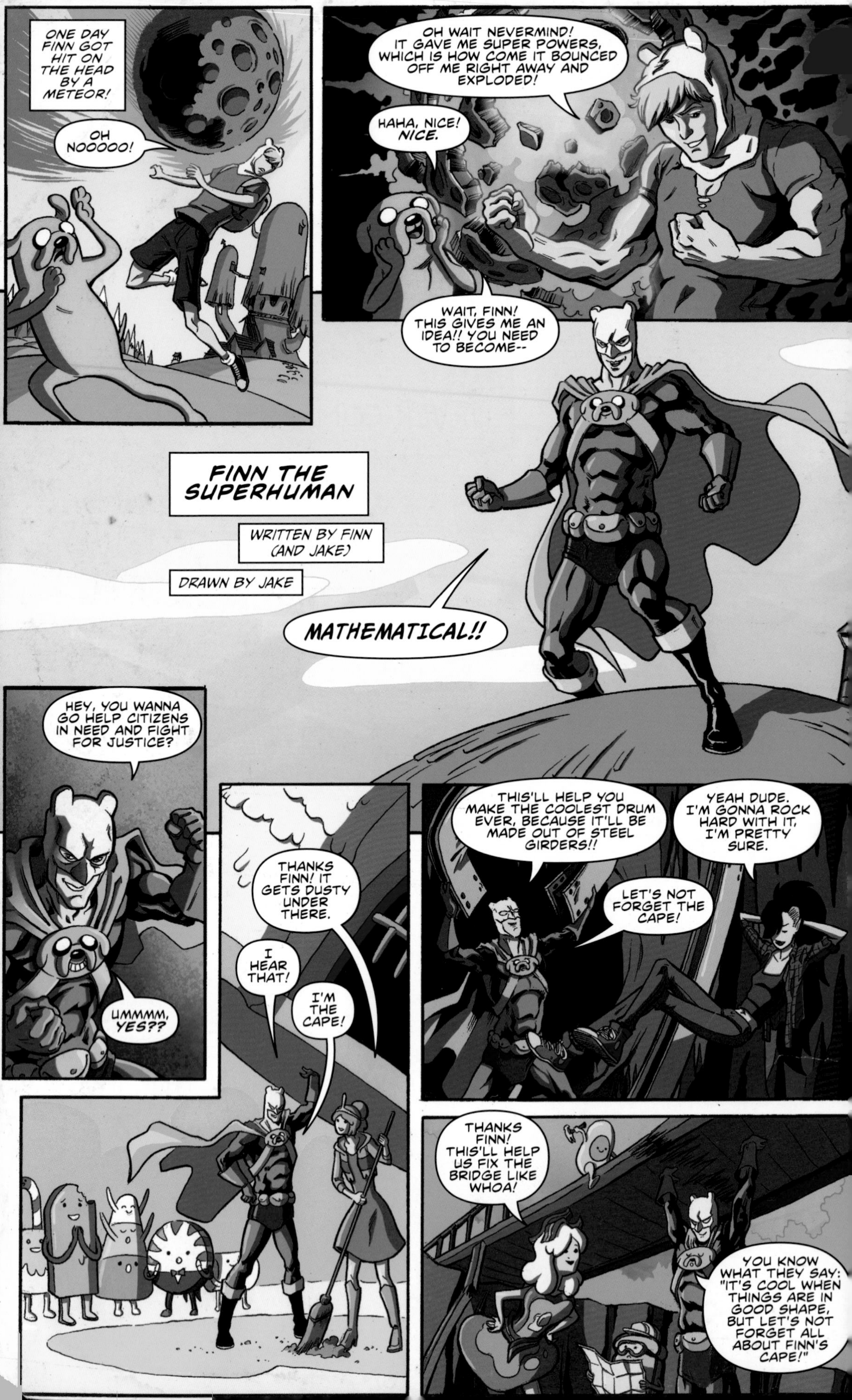
ONE DAY FINN GOT HIT ON THE HEAD BY A METEOR!
OH NOOOOO!
OH WAIT NEVERMIND! IT GAVE ME SUPER POWERS, WHICH IS HOW COME IT BOUNCED OFF ME RIGHT AWAY AND EXPLODED!
HAHA, NICE! NICE.
WAIT, FINN! THIS GIVES ME AN IDEA!! YOU NEED TO BECOME--
FINN THE SUPERHUMAN
WRITTEN BY FINN (AND JAKE)
DRAWN BY JAKE
MATHEMATICAL!!
HEY, YOU WANNA GO HELP CITIZENS IN NEED AND FIGHT FOR JUSTICE?
UMMMM, YES??
THANKS FINN! IT GETS DUSTY UNDER THERE.
I HEAR THAT!
I'M THE CAPE!
THIS'LL HELP YOU MAKE THE COOLEST DRUM EVER, BECAUSE IT'LL BE MADE OUT OF STEEL GIRDERS!!
YEAH DUDE. I'M GONNA ROCK HARD WITH IT, I'M PRETTY SURE.
LET'S NOT FORGET THE CAPE!
THANKS FINN! THIS'LL HELP US FIX THE BRIDGE LIKE WHOA!
YOU KNOW WHAT THEY SAY: "IT'S COOL WHEN THINGS ARE IN GOOD SHAPE, BUT LET'S NOT FORGET ALL ABOUT FINN'S CAPE!"

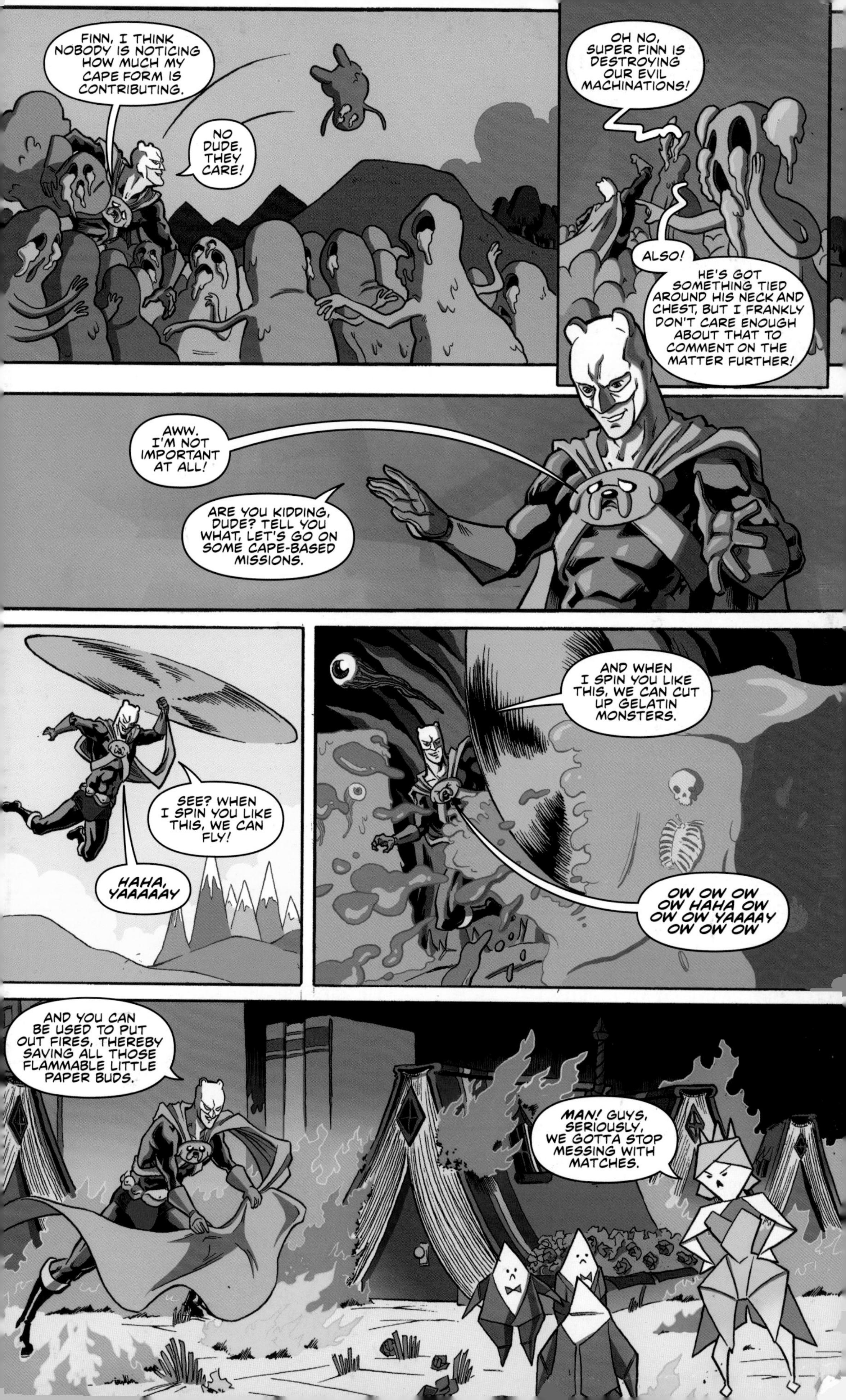
FINN, I THINK NOBODY IS NOTICING HOW MUCH MY CAPE FORM IS CONTRIBUTING.
NO DUDE, THEY CARE!
OH NO, SUPER FINN IS DESTROYING OUR EVIL MACHINATIONS!
ALSO!
HE'S GOT SOMETHING TIED AROUND HIS NECK AND CHEST, BUT I FRANKLY DON'T CARE ENOUGH ABOUT THAT TO COMMENT ON THE MATTER FURTHER!
AWW. I'M NOT IMPORTANT AT ALL!
ARE YOU KIDDING, DUDE? TELL YOU WHAT, LET'S GO ON SOME CAPE-BASED MISSIONS.
SEE? WHEN I SPIN YOU LIKE THIS, WE CAN FLY!
HAHA, YAAAAAY
AND WHEN I SPIN YOU LIKE THIS, WE CAN CUT UP GELATIN MONSTERS.
OW OW OW OW HAHA OW OW OW YAAAAY OW OW OW
AND YOU CAN BE USED TO PUT OUT FIRES, THEREBY SAVING ALL THOSE FLAMMABLE LITTLE PAPER BUDS.
MAN! GUYS, SERIOUSLY, WE GOTTA STOP MESSING WITH MATCHES.

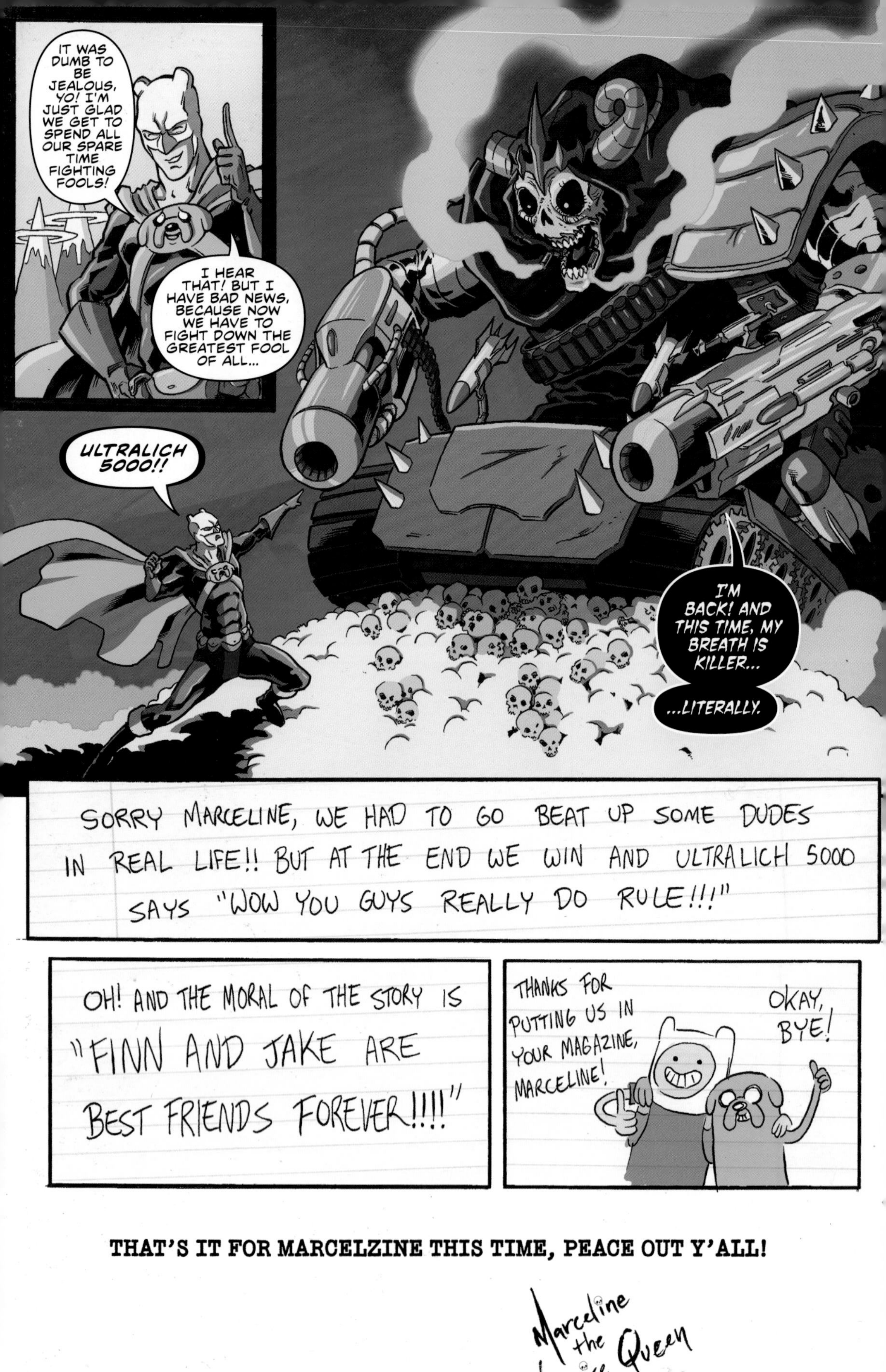

IT WAS DUMB TO BE JEALOUS, YO! I'M JUST GLAD WE GET TO SPEND ALL OUR SPARE TIME FIGHTING FOOLS!
I HEAR THAT! BUT I HAVE BAD NEWS, BECAUSE NOW WE HAVE TO FIGHT DOWN THE GREATEST FOOL OF ALL...
ULTRALICH 5000!!
I'M BACK! AND THIS TIME, MY BREATH IS KILLER...
...LITERALLY.
SORRY MARCELINE, WE HAD TO GO BEAT UP SOME DUDES IN REAL LIFE!! BUT AT THE END WE WIN AND ULTRALICH 5000 SAYS "WOW YOU GUYS REALLY DO RULE!!!"
OH! AND THE MORAL OF THE STORY IS "FINN AND JAKE ARE BEST FRIENDS FOREVER!!!!"
THANKS FOR PUTTING US IN YOUR MAGAZINE, MARCELINE!
OKAY, BYE!

THAT'S IT FOR MARCELZINE THIS TIME, PEACE OUT Y'ALL!

Marceline the Vampire Queen

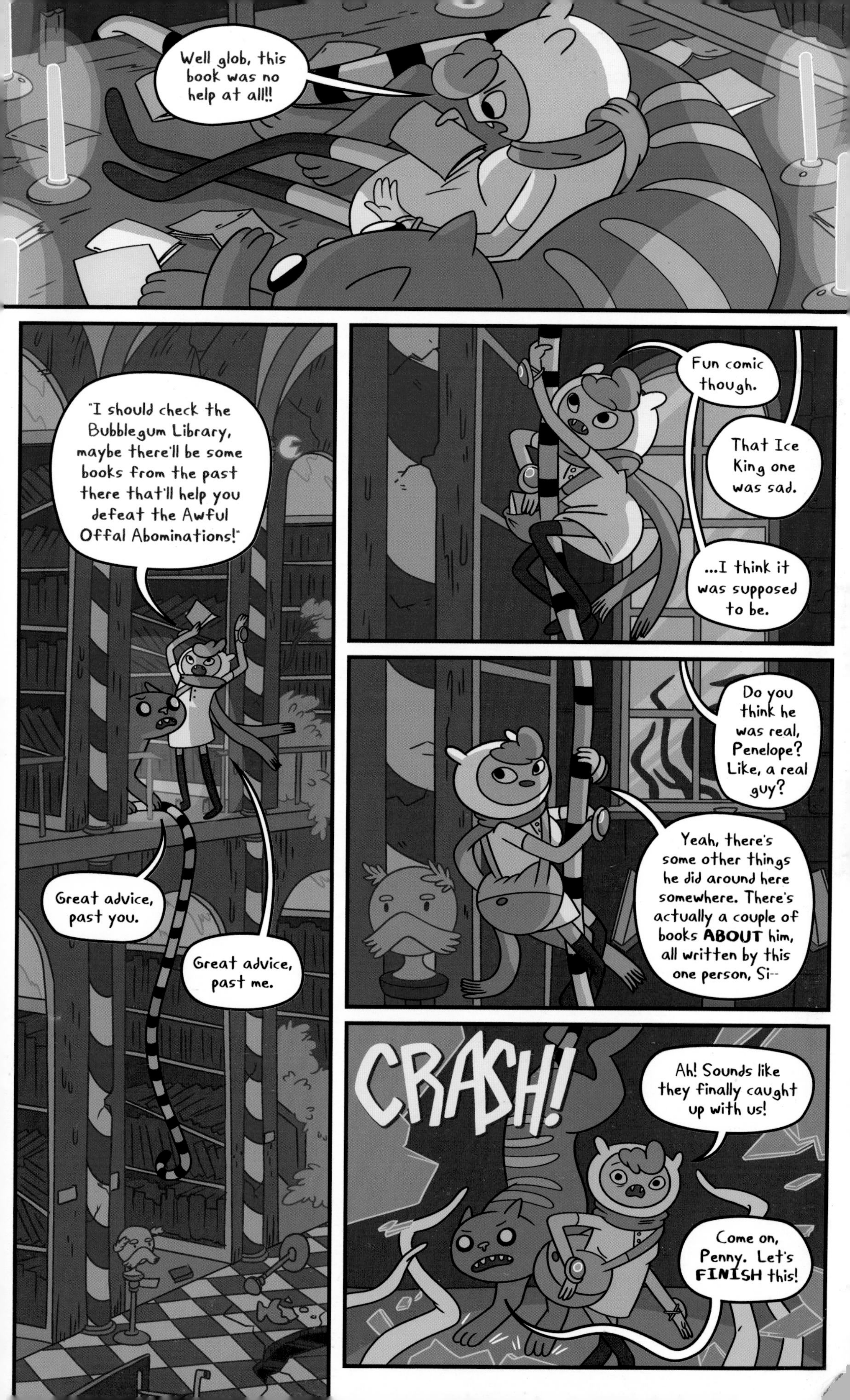
Well glob, this book was no help at all!!
"I should check the Bubblegum Library, maybe there'll be some books from the past there that'll help you defeat the Awful Offal Abominations!"
Great advice, past you.
Great advice, past me.
Fun comic though.
That Ice King one was sad.
...I think it was supposed to be.
Do you think he was real, Penelope? Like, a real guy?
Yeah, there's some other things he did around here somewhere. There's actually a couple of books ABOUT him, all written by this one person, Si--
CRASH!
Ah! Sounds like they finally caught up with us!
Come on, Penny. Let's FINISH this!

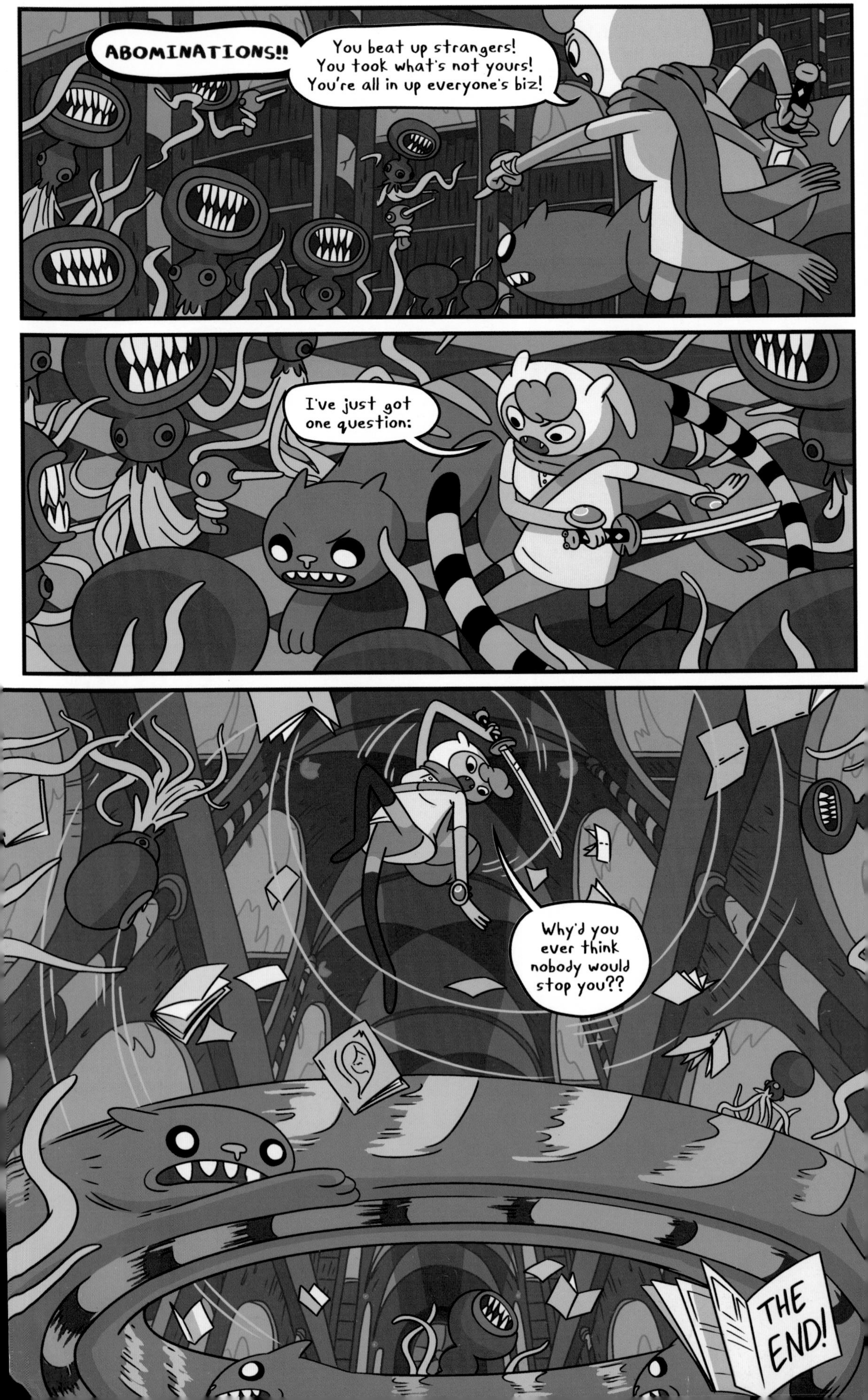
ABOMINATIONS!!
You beat up strangers! You took what's not yours! You're all in up everyone's biz!
I've just got one question:
Why'd you ever think nobody would stop you??
THE END!

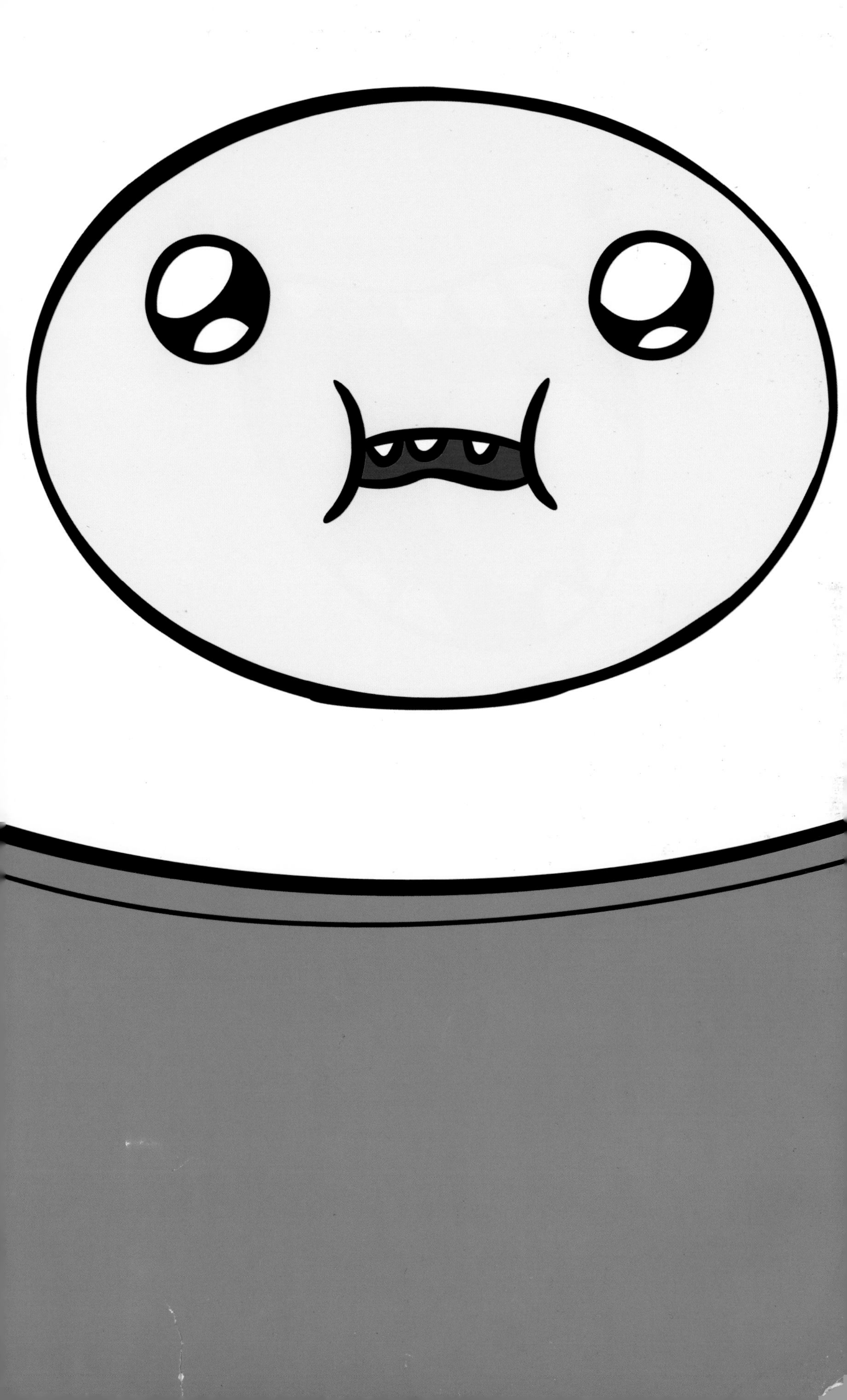

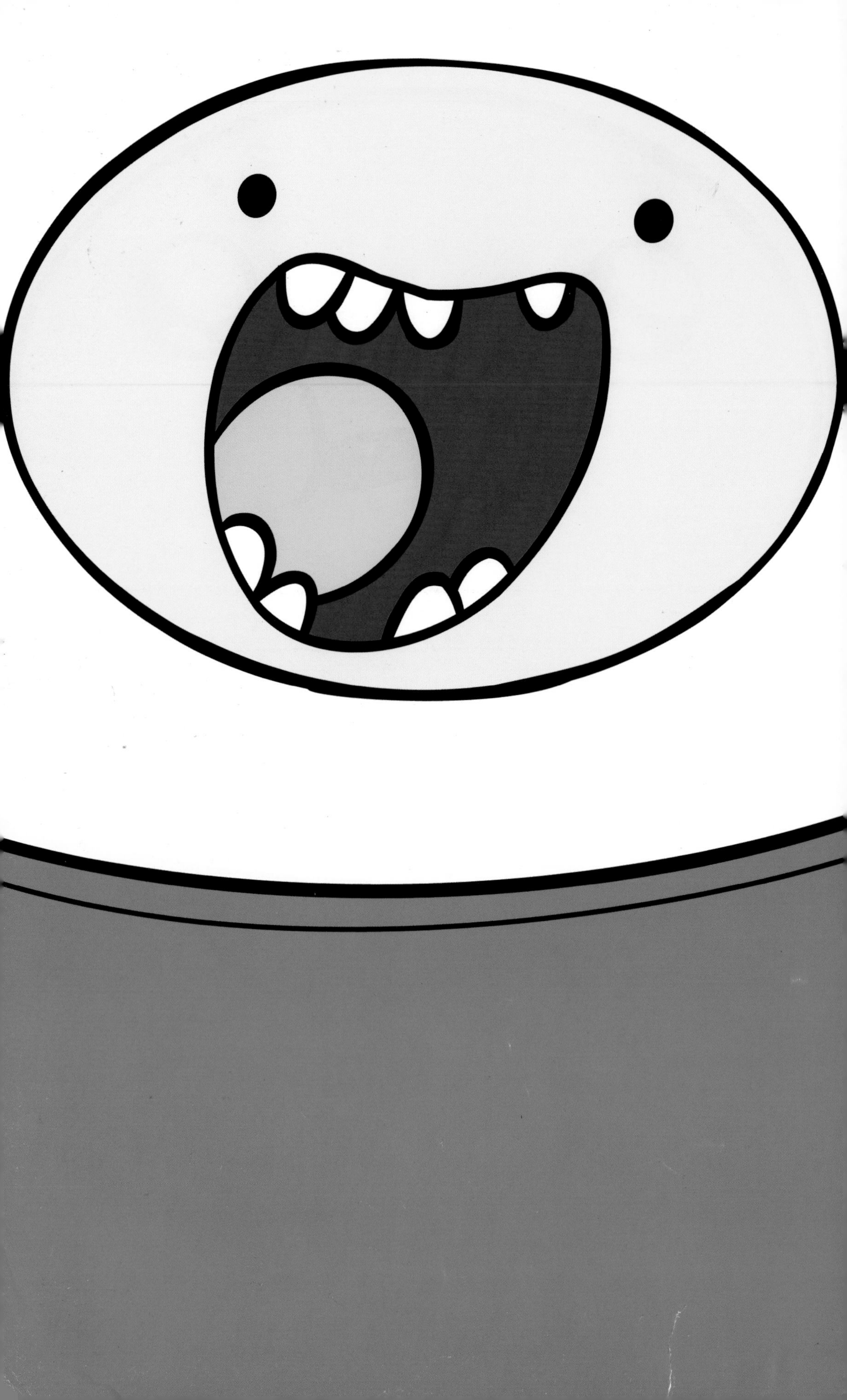

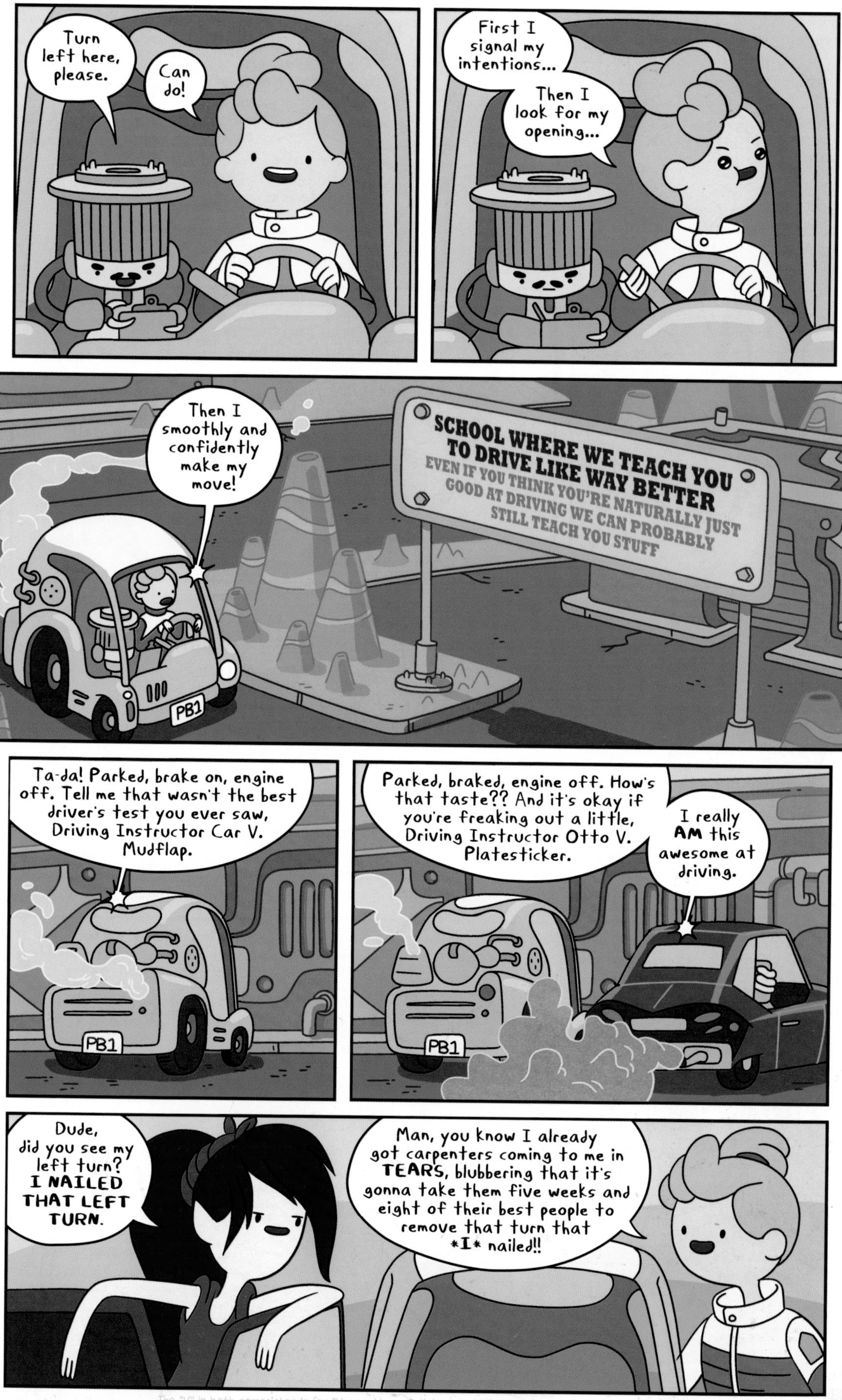
Turn left here, please.
Can do!
First I signal my intentions...
Then I look for my opening...
Then I smoothly and confidently make my move!
SCHOOL WHERE WE TEACH YOU TO DRIVE LIKE WAY BETTER
EVEN IF YOU THINK YOU'RE NATURALLY JUST GOOD AT DRIVING WE CAN PROBABLY STILL TEACH YOU STUFF
PB1
Ta-da! Parked, brake on, engine off. Tell me that wasn't the best driver's test you ever saw, Driving Instructor Car V. Mudflap.
PB1
Parked, braked, engine off. How's that taste?? And it's okay if you're freaking out a little, Driving Instructor Otto V. Platesticker.
I really AM this awesome at driving.
PB1
Dude, did you see my left turn? I NAILED THAT LEFT TURN.
Man, you know I already got carpenters coming to me in TEARS, blubbering that it's gonna take them five weeks and eight of their best people to remove that turn that *I* nailed!!

The "V" in both names stands for "Vroom Vroom". It is a very popular name amongst the car folk.

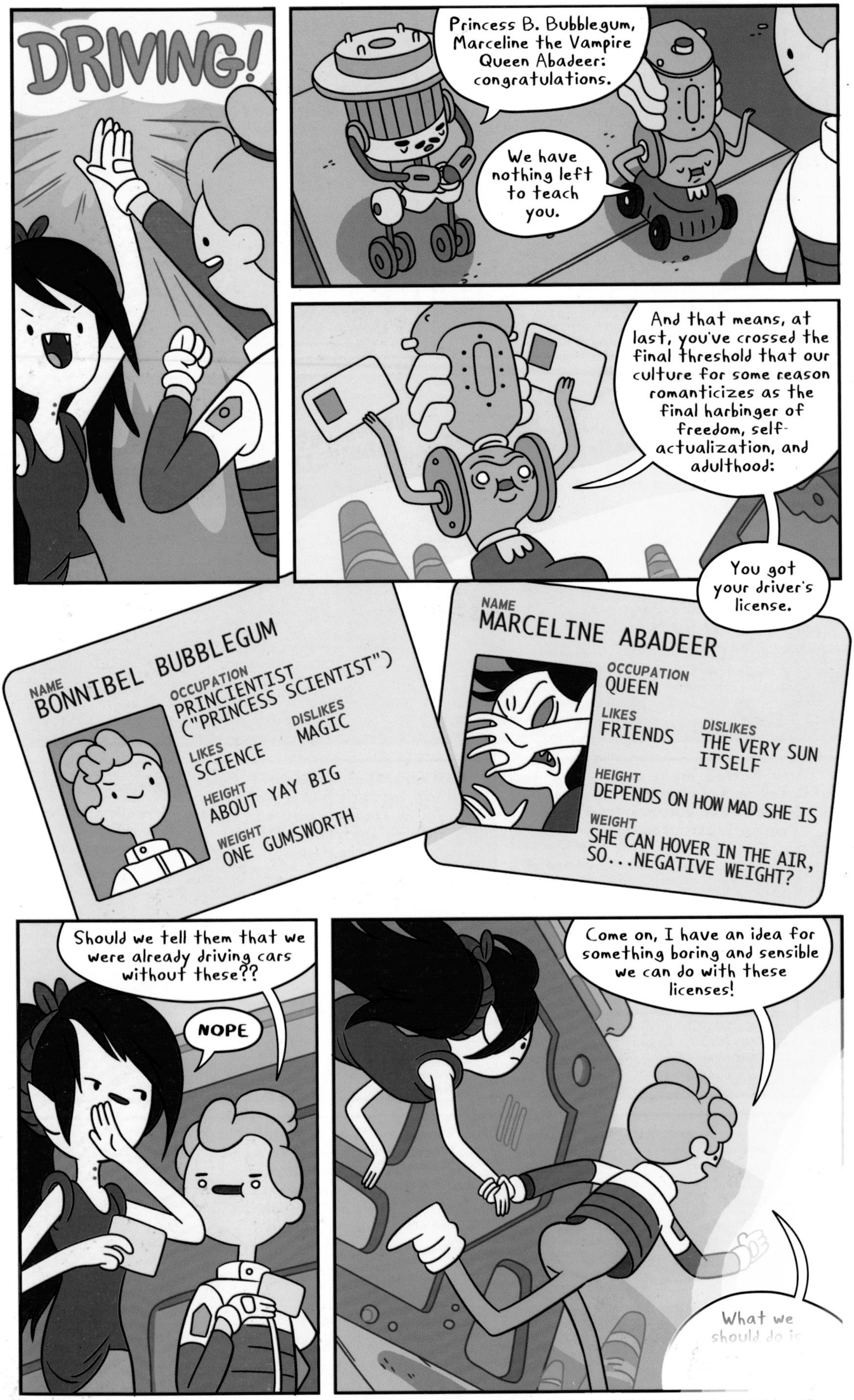
DRIVING!
Princess B. Bubblegum, Marceline the Vampire Queen Abadeer: congratulations.
We have nothing left to teach you.
And that means, at last, you've crossed the final threshold that our culture for some reason romanticizes as the final harbinger of freedom, self-actualization, and adulthood:
You got your driver's license.
NAME
BONNIBEL BUBBLEGUM
OCCUPATION
PRINCIENTIST ("PRINCESS SCIENTIST")
LIKES
SCIENCE
DISLIKES
MAGIC
HEIGHT
ABOUT YAY BIG
WEIGHT
ONE GUMSWORTH
NAME
MARCELINE ABADEER
OCCUPATION
QUEEN
LIKES
FRIENDS
DISLIKES
THE VERY SUN ITSELF
HEIGHT
DEPENDS ON HOW MAD SHE IS
WEIGHT
SHE CAN HOVER IN THE AIR, SO...NEGATIVE WEIGHT?
Should we tell them that we were already driving cars without these??
NOPE
Come on, I have an idea for something boring and sensible we can do with these licenses!
What we should do is

To be fair, I'm not a huge fan of the sun either. Responsible for all life on the planet, SURE, but sometimes it's TOO bright, you know what I mean?

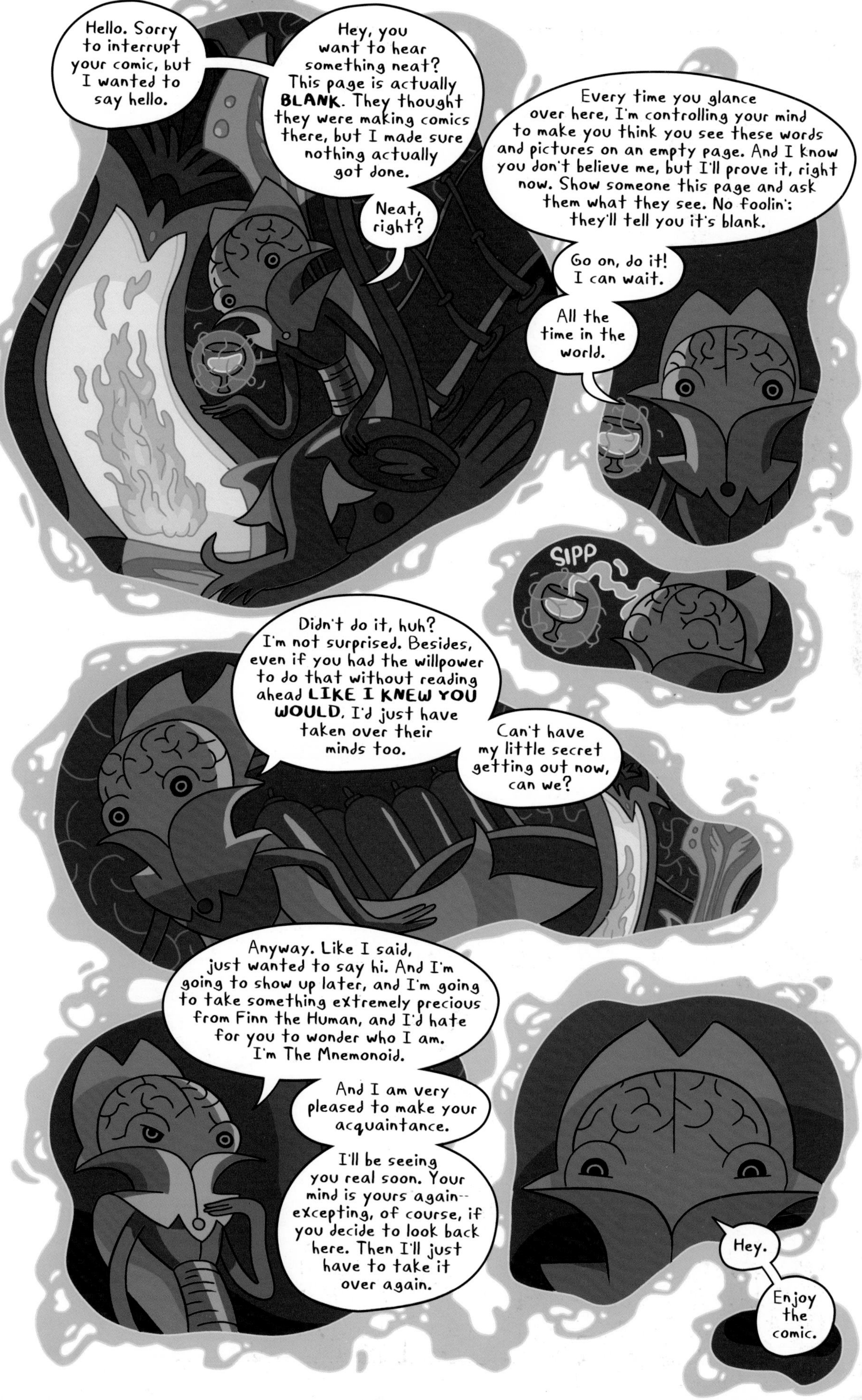
Hello. Sorry to interrupt your comic, but I wanted to say hello.
Hey, you want to hear something neat? This page is actually BLANK. They thought they were making comics there, but I made sure nothing actually got done.
Neat, right?
Every time you glance over here, I'm controlling your mind to make you think you see these words and pictures on an empty page. And I know you don't believe me, but I'll prove it, right now. Show someone this page and ask them what they see. No foolin': they'll tell you it's blank.
Go on, do it! I can wait.
All the time in the world.
SIPP
Didn't do it, huh? I'm not surprised. Besides, even if you had the willpower to do that without reading ahead LIKE I KNEW YOU WOULD, I'd just have taken over their minds too.
Can't have my little secret getting out now, can we?
Anyway. Like I said, just wanted to say hi. And I'm going to show up later, and I'm going to take something extremely precious from Finn the Human, and I'd hate for you to wonder who I am. I'm The Mnemonoid.
And I am very pleased to make your acquaintance.
I'll be seeing you real soon. Your mind is yours again--excepting, of course, if you decide to look back here. Then I'll just have to take it over again.
Hey.
Enjoy the comic.

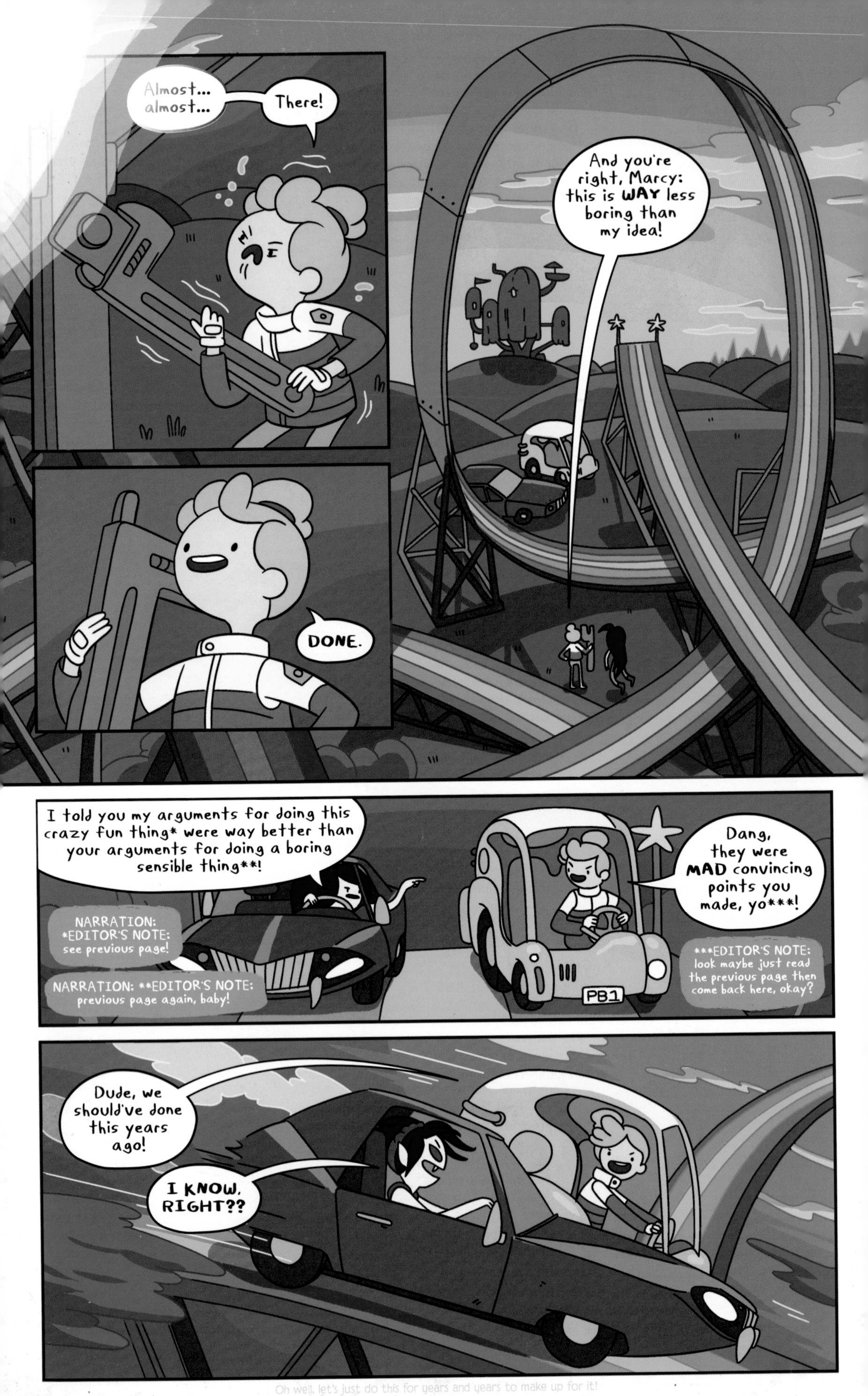
Almost... almost...
There!
And you're right, Marcy: this is WAY less boring than my idea!
DONE.
I told you my arguments for doing this crazy fun thing* were way better than your arguments for doing a boring sensible thing**!
NARRATION: *EDITOR'S NOTE: see previous page!
NARRATION: **EDITOR'S NOTE: previous page again, baby!
Dang, they were MAD convincing points you made, yo***!
***EDITOR'S NOTE: look maybe just read the previous page then come back here, okay?
PB1
Dude, we should've done this years ago!
I KNOW, RIGHT??

Oh well, let's just do this for years and years to make up for it!

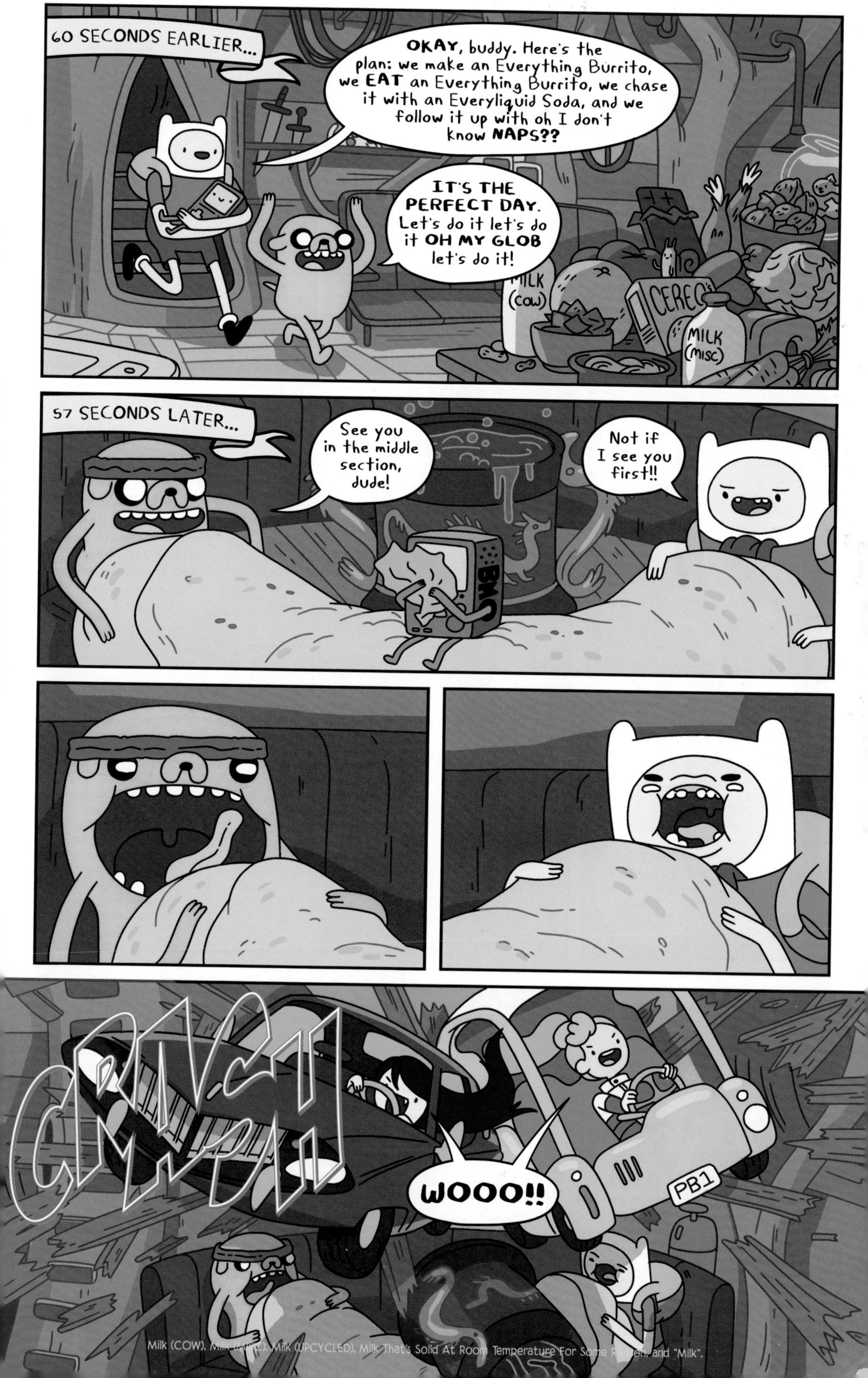
60 SECONDS EARLIER...
OKAY, buddy. Here's the plan: we make an Everything Burrito, we EAT an Everything Burrito, we chase it with an Everyliquid Soda, and we follow it up with oh I don't know NAPS??
IT'S THE PERFECT DAY. Let's do it let's do it OH MY GLOB let's do it!
MILK (COW)
CEREO
MILK (MISC)
57 SECONDS LATER...
See you in the middle section, dude!
Not if I see you first!!
BMO
CRUNCH
WOOO!!
PB1
Milk (COW), Milk (MISC), Milk (UPCYCLED), Milk That's Solid At Room Temperature For Some Reason, and "Milk".

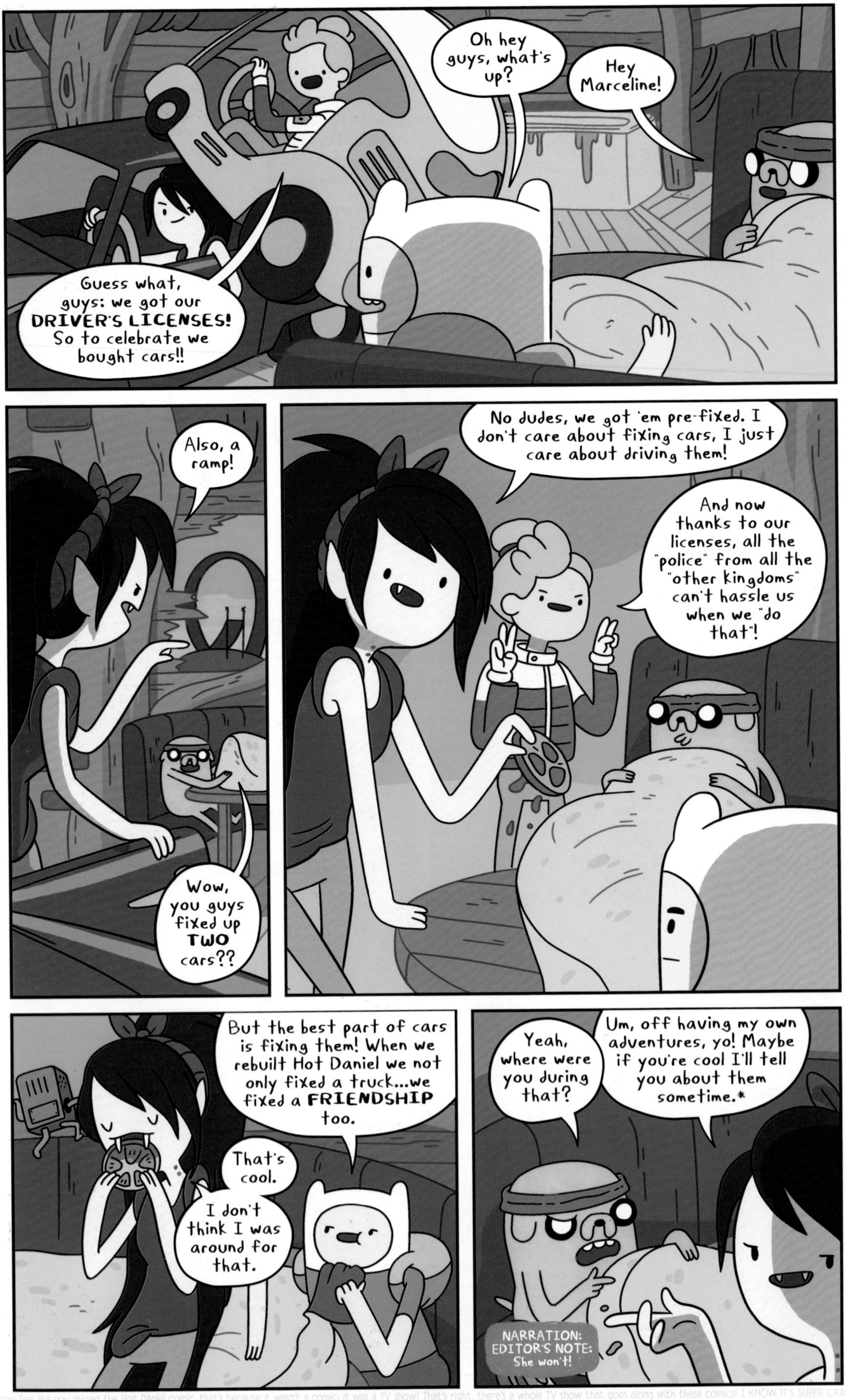
Oh hey guys, what's up?
Hey Marceline!
Guess what, guys: we got our **DRIVER'S LICENSES!** So to celebrate we bought cars!!
Also, a ramp!
Wow, you guys fixed up **TWO** cars??
No dudes, we got 'em pre-fixed. I don't care about fixing cars, I just care about driving them!
And now thanks to our licenses, all the "police" from all the "other kingdoms" can't hassle us when we "do that"!
But the best part of cars is fixing them! When we rebuilt Hot Daniel we not only fixed a truck...we fixed a **FRIENDSHIP** too.
That's cool.
I don't think I was around for that.
Yeah, where were you during that?
Um, off having my own adventures, yo! Maybe if you're cool I'll tell you about them sometime.*
NARRATION: EDITOR'S NOTE: She won't!

*If you feel like you missed the Hot Daniel comic, that's because it wasn't a comic: it was a TV show! That's right, there's a whole TV show that goes along with these comics! I KNOW, IT'S SUPER CRAZY!!

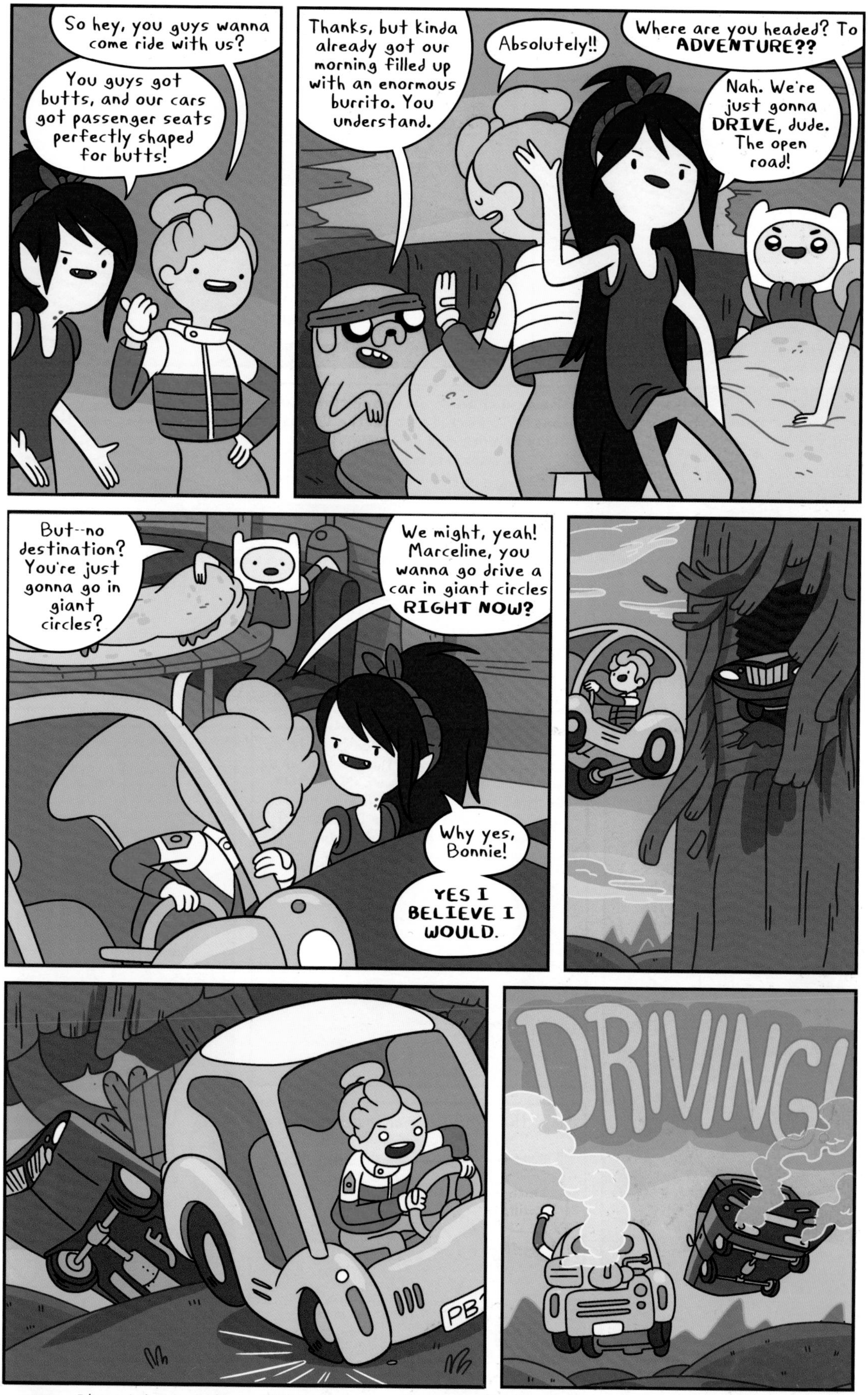
So hey, you guys wanna come ride with us?
You guys got butts, and our cars got passenger seats perfectly shaped for butts!
Thanks, but kinda already got our morning filled up with an enormous burrito. You understand.
Absolutely!!
Where are you headed? To **ADVENTURE??**
Nah. We're just gonna **DRIVE**, dude. The open road!
But--no destination? You're just gonna go in giant circles?
We might, yeah! Marceline, you wanna go drive a car in giant circles **RIGHT NOW?**
Why yes, Bonnie!
YES I BELIEVE I WOULD.
PB
DRIVING!

I know what you're thinking, and **NO**, the precious thing I'm taking from Finn is not "part of his rad wall because it's so rad". Come on. — It's at three out of a possible five stars wall **AT BEST**.

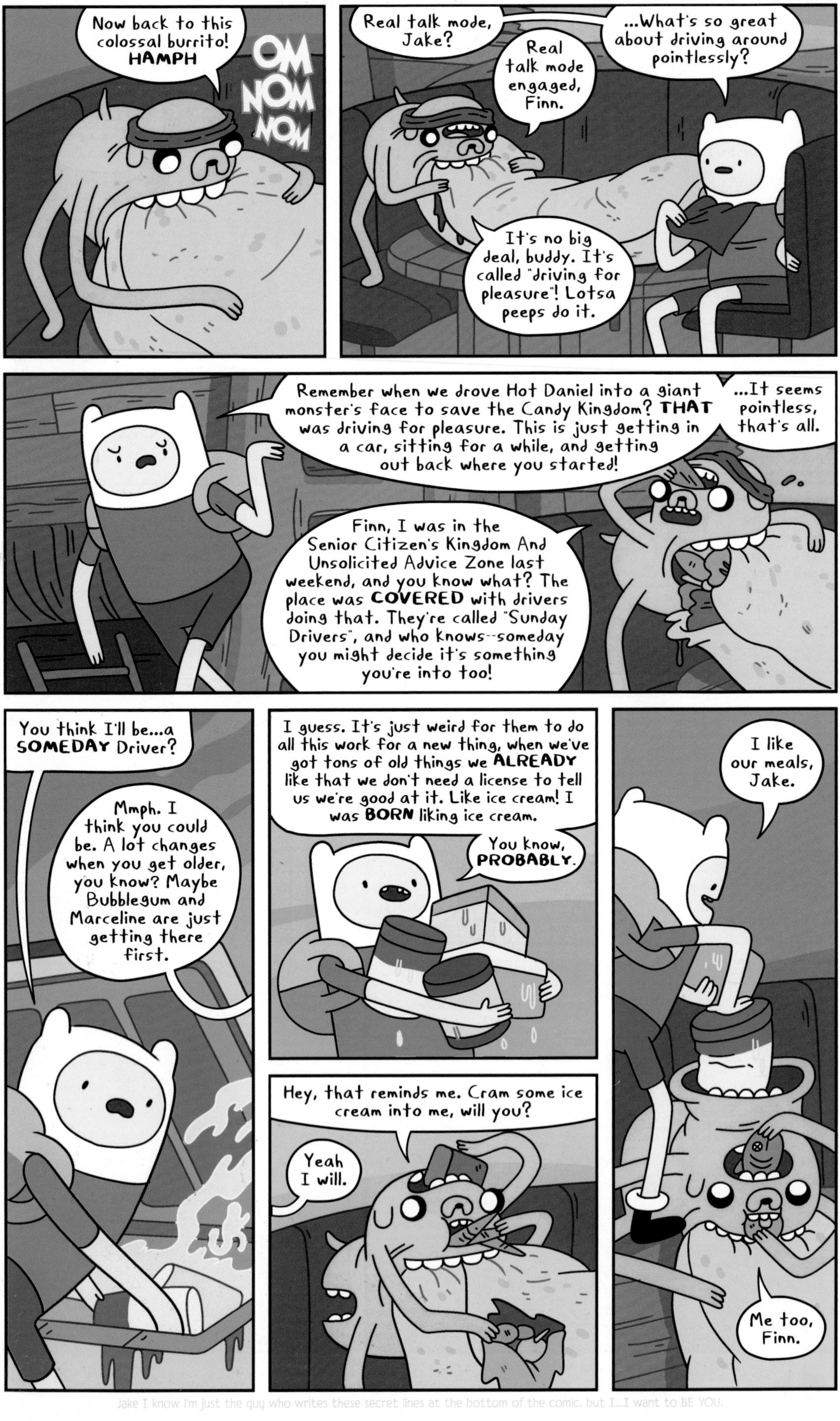
Now back to this colossal burrito! HAMPH
OM NOM NOM
Real talk mode, Jake?
Real talk mode engaged, Finn.
...What's so great about driving around pointlessly?
It's no big deal, buddy. It's called "driving for pleasure"! Lotsa peeps do it.
Remember when we drove Hot Daniel into a giant monster's face to save the Candy Kingdom? THAT was driving for pleasure. This is just getting in a car, sitting for a while, and getting out back where you started!
...It seems pointless, that's all.
Finn, I was in the Senior Citizen's Kingdom And Unsolicited Advice Zone last weekend, and you know what? The place was COVERED with drivers doing that. They're called "Sunday Drivers", and who knows--someday you might decide it's something you're into too!
You think I'll be...a SOMEDAY Driver?
Mmph. I think you could be. A lot changes when you get older, you know? Maybe Bubblegum and Marceline are just getting there first.
I guess. It's just weird for them to do all this work for a new thing, when we've got tons of old things we ALREADY like that we don't need a license to tell us we're good at it. Like ice cream! I was BORN liking ice cream.
You know, PROBABLY.
Hey, that reminds me. Cram some ice cream into me, will you?
Yeah I will.
I like our meals, Jake.
Me too, Finn.

Jake I know I'm just the guy who writes these secret lines at the bottom of the comic, but I...I want to BE YOU.

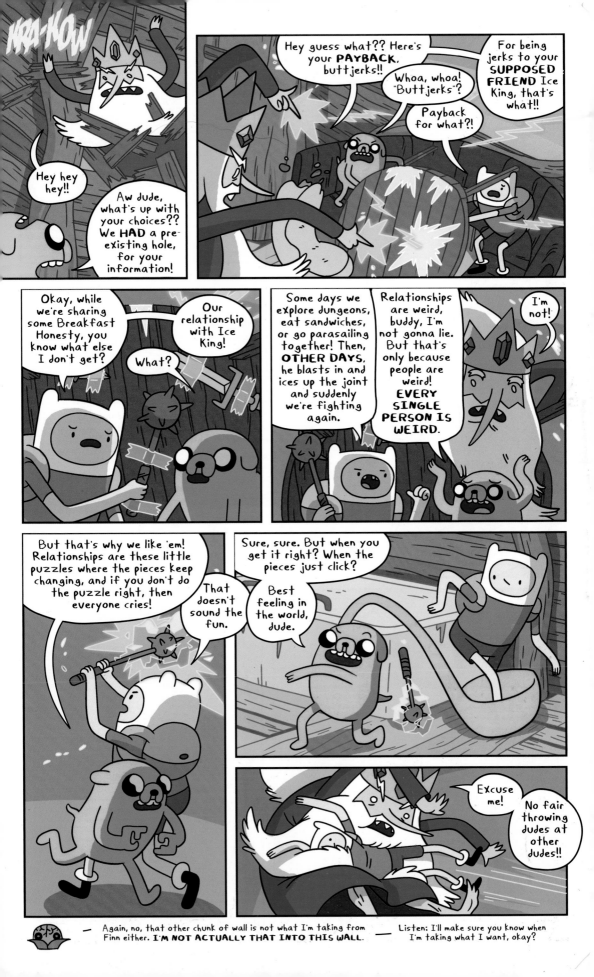

KRA-KOW

Hey hey hey!!

Aw dude, what's up with your choices?? We **HAD** a pre-existing hole, for your information!

Hey guess what?? Here's your **PAYBACK**, buttjerks!!

Whoa, whoa! "Buttjerks"?

Payback for what?!

For being jerks to your **SUPPOSED FRIEND** Ice King, that's what!!

Okay, while we're sharing some Breakfast Honesty, you know what else I don't get?

What?

Our relationship with Ice King!

Some days we explore dungeons, eat sandwiches, or go parasailing together! Then, **OTHER DAYS**, he blasts in and ices up the joint and suddenly we're fighting again.

Relationships are weird, buddy, I'm not gonna lie. But that's only because people are weird! **EVERY SINGLE PERSON IS WEIRD.**

I'm not!

But that's why we like 'em! Relationships are these little puzzles where the pieces keep changing, and if you don't do the puzzle right, then everyone cries!

That doesn't sound the fun.

Sure, sure. But when you get it right? When the pieces just click?

Best feeling in the world, dude.

Excuse me!

No fair throwing dudes at other dudes!!

— Again, no, that other chunk of wall is not what I'm taking from Finn either. **I'M NOT ACTUALLY THAT INTO THIS WALL.** — Listen: I'll make sure you know when I'm taking what I want, okay?

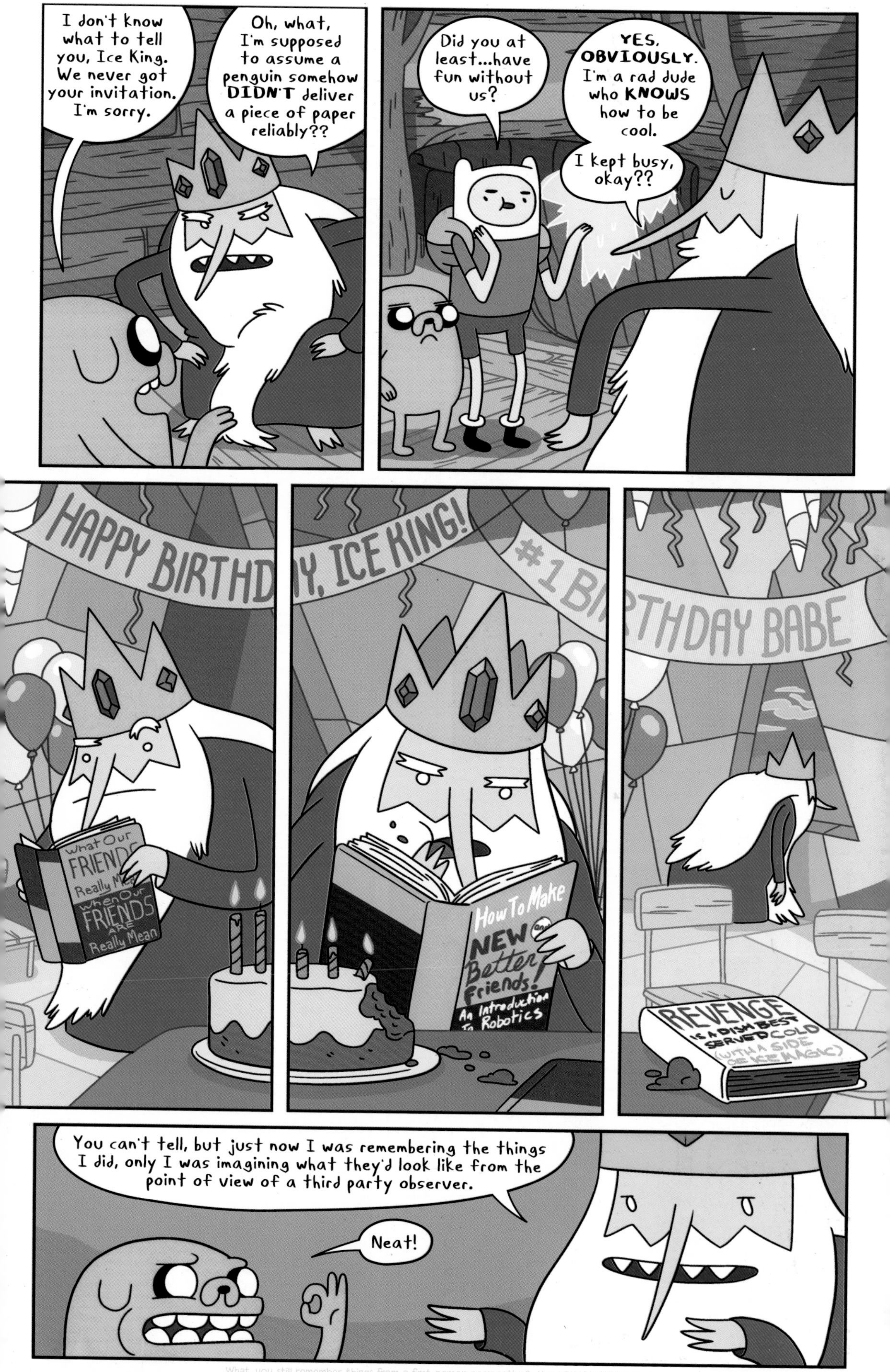
I don't know what to tell you, Ice King. We never got your invitation. I'm sorry.
Oh, what, I'm supposed to assume a penguin somehow DIDN'T deliver a piece of paper reliably??
Did you at least...have fun without us?
YES, OBVIOUSLY. I'm a rad dude who KNOWS how to be cool.
I kept busy, okay??
HAPPY BIRTHDAY, ICE KING!
#1 BIRTHDAY BABE
What Our FRIENDS Really Mean When Our FRIENDS ARE Really Mean
How To Make NEW and Better Friends! An Introduction To Robotics
REVENGE IS A DISH BEST SERVED COLD (WITH A SIDE OF ICE MAGIC)
You can't tell, but just now I was remembering the things I did, only I was imagining what they'd look like from the point of view of a third party observer.
Neat!

What, you still remember things from a first-person perspective? How CHARMINGLY retro.

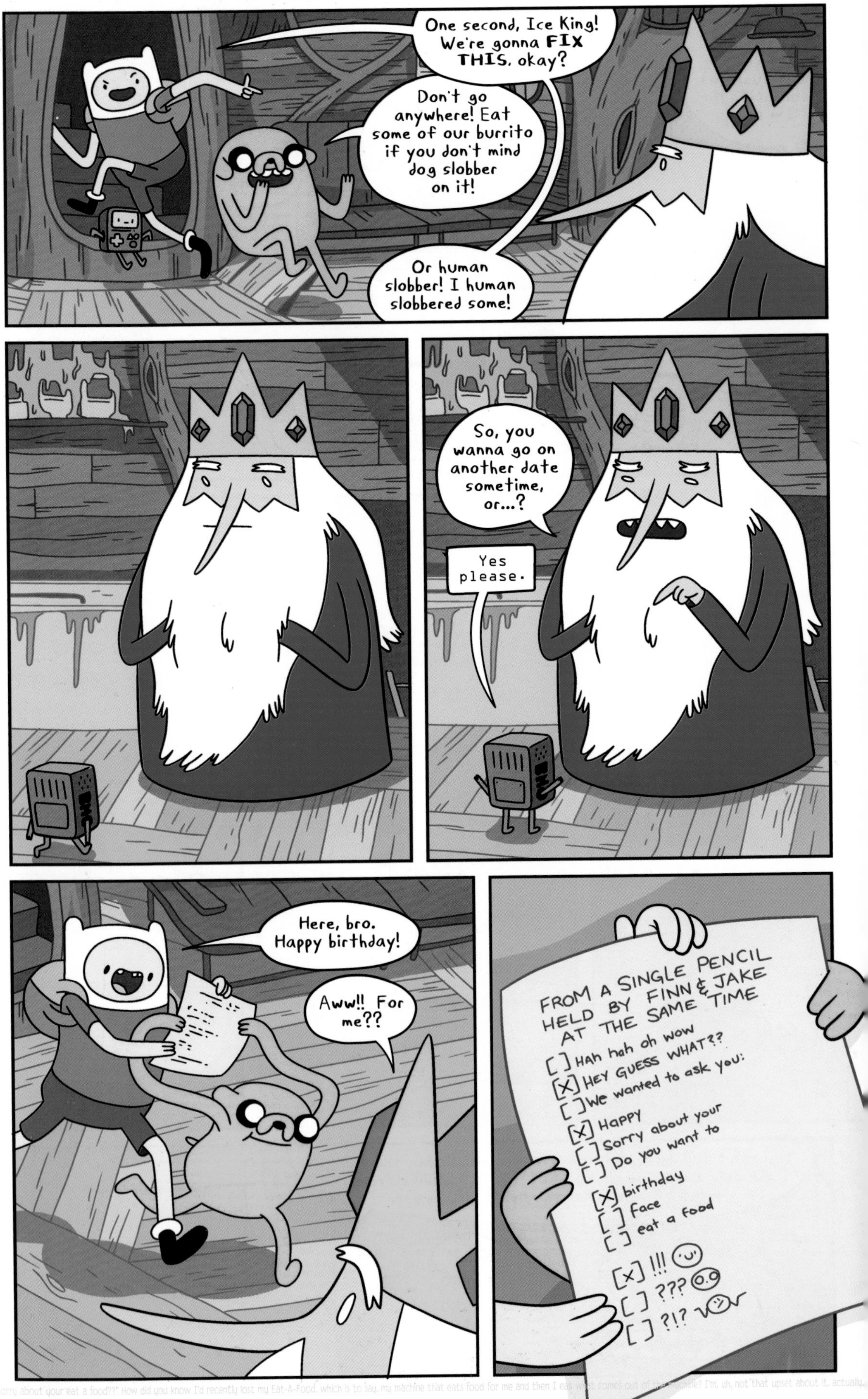
One second, Ice King! We're gonna **FIX THIS**, okay?
Don't go anywhere! Eat some of our burrito if you don't mind dog slobber on it!
Or human slobber! I human slobbered some!
So, you wanna go on another date sometime, or...?
Yes please.
Here, bro. Happy birthday!
Aww!! For me??
FROM A SINGLE PENCIL HELD BY FINN & JAKE AT THE SAME TIME
[ ] HAH hah oh wow
[X] HEY GUESS WHAT??
[ ] We wanted to ask you:
[X] Happy
[ ] Sorry about your
[ ] Do you want to
[X] birthday
[ ] Face
[ ] eat a food
[X] !!!
[ ] ???
[ ] ?!?

"Sorry about your 'eat a food??' How did you know I'd recently lost my Eat-A-Food, which is to say, my machine that eats food for me and then I eat what comes out of the machine? I'm, uh, not that upset about it, actually.

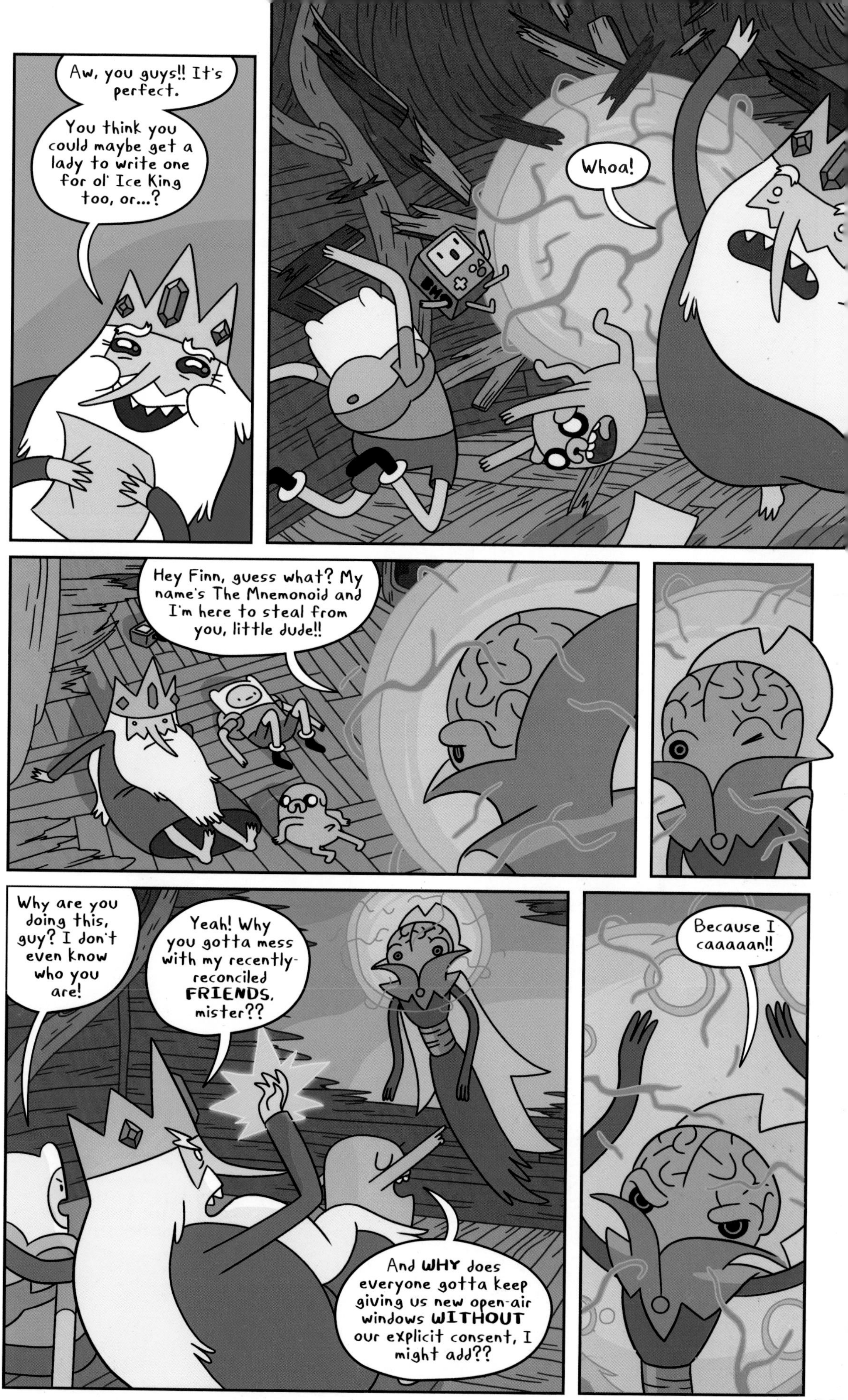
Aw, you guys!! It's perfect.
You think you could maybe get a lady to write one for ol' Ice King too, or...?
Whoa!
Hey Finn, guess what? My name's The Mnemonoid and I'm here to steal from you, little dude!!
Why are you doing this, guy? I don't even know who you are!
Yeah! Why you gotta mess with my recently-reconciled FRIENDS, mister??
And WHY does everyone gotta keep giving us new open-air windows WITHOUT our explicit consent, I might add??
Because I caaaaan!!

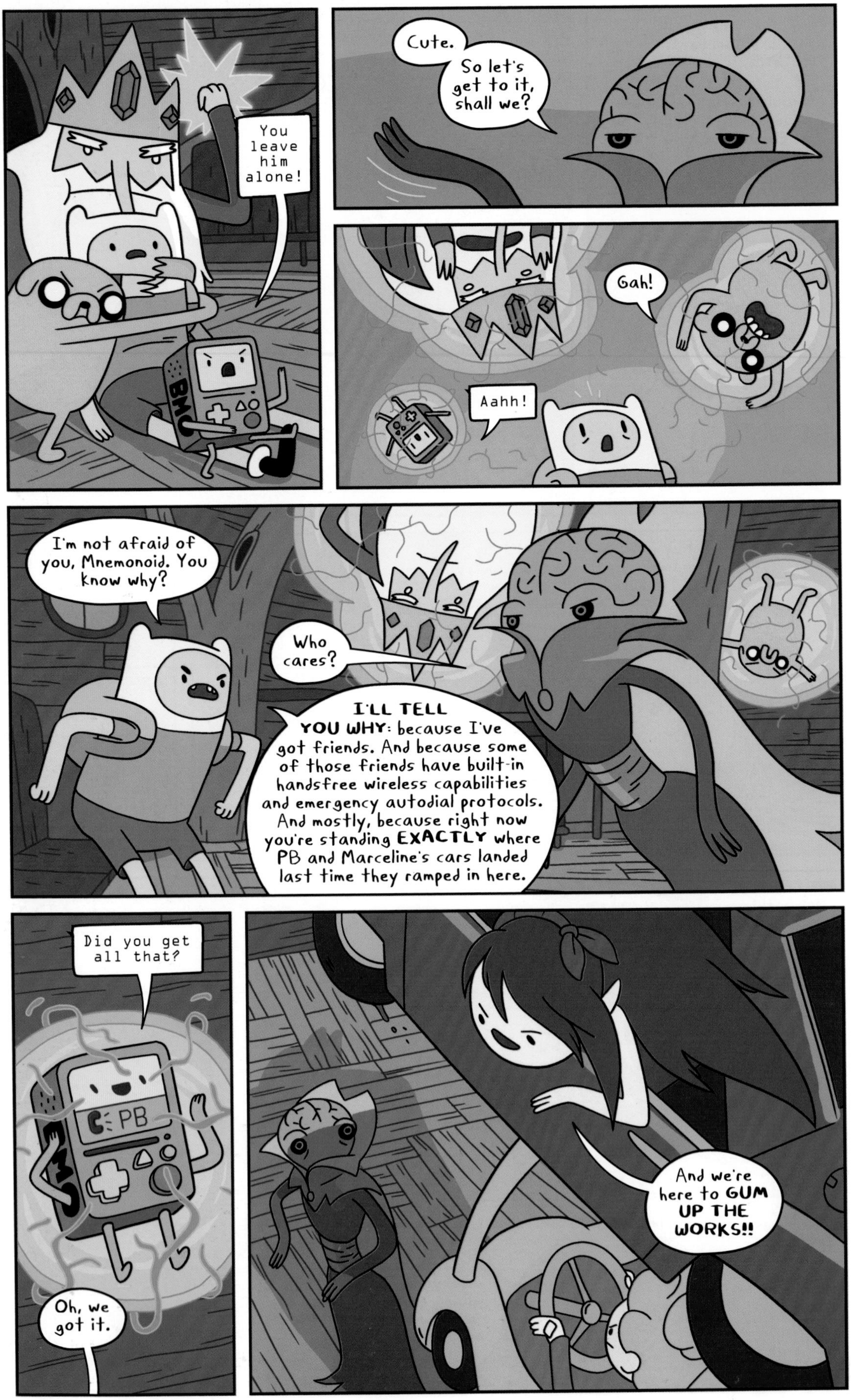
You leave him alone!
Cute.
So let's get to it, shall we?
Gah!
Aahh!
I'm not afraid of you, Mnemonoid. You know why?
Who cares?
I'LL TELL YOU WHY: because I've got friends. And because some of those friends have built-in handsfree wireless capabilities and emergency autodial protocols. And mostly, because right now you're standing EXACTLY where PB and Marceline's cars landed last time they ramped in here.
Did you get all that?
PB
Oh, we got it.
And we're here to GUM UP THE WORKS!!

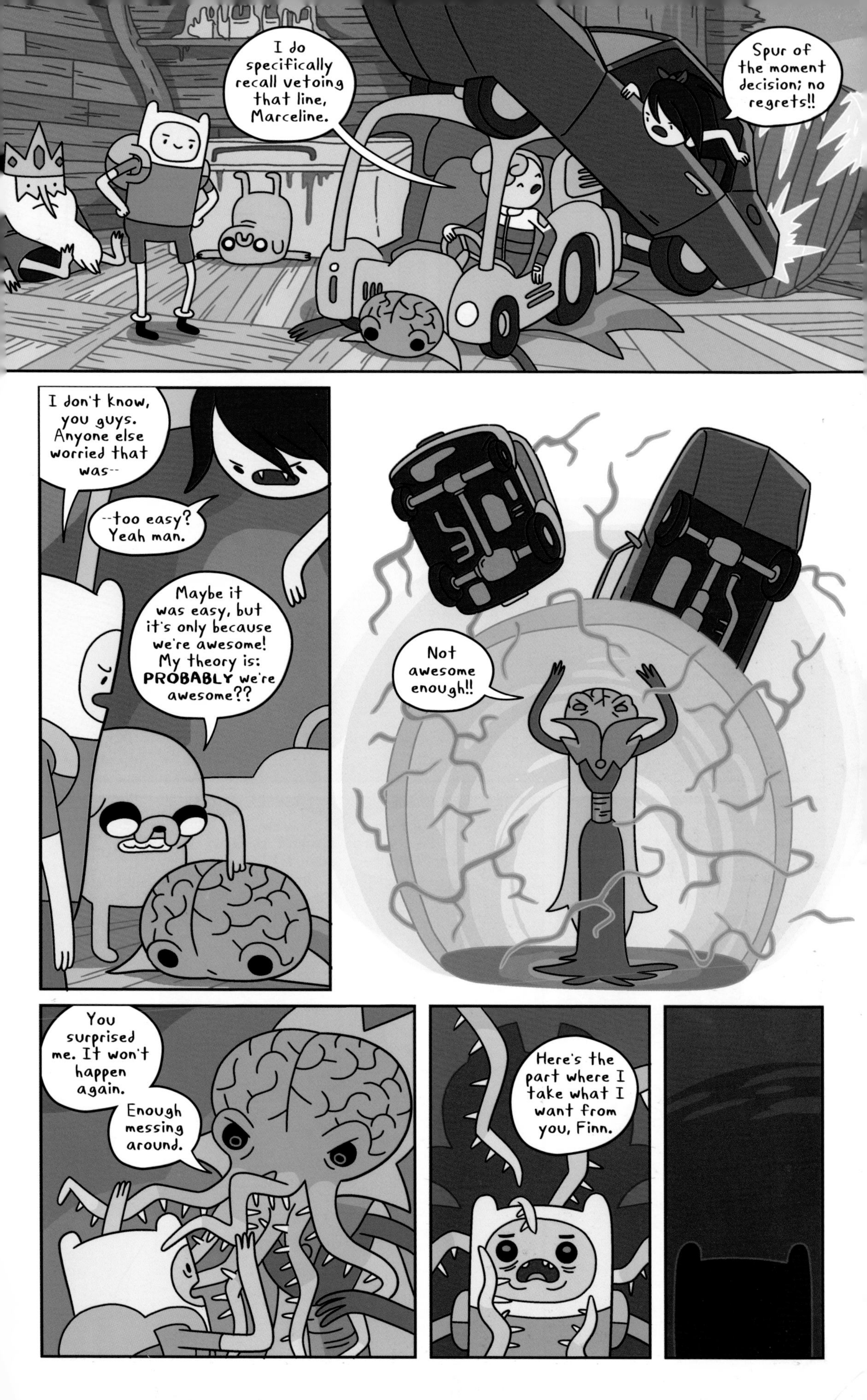
I do specifically recall vetoing that line, Marceline.
Spur of the moment decision; no regrets!!
I don't know, you guys. Anyone else worried that was--
--too easy? Yeah man.
Maybe it was easy, but it's only because we're awesome! My theory is: PROBABLY we're awesome??
Not awesome enough!!
You surprised me. It won't happen again.
Enough messing around.
Here's the part where I take what I want from you, Finn.

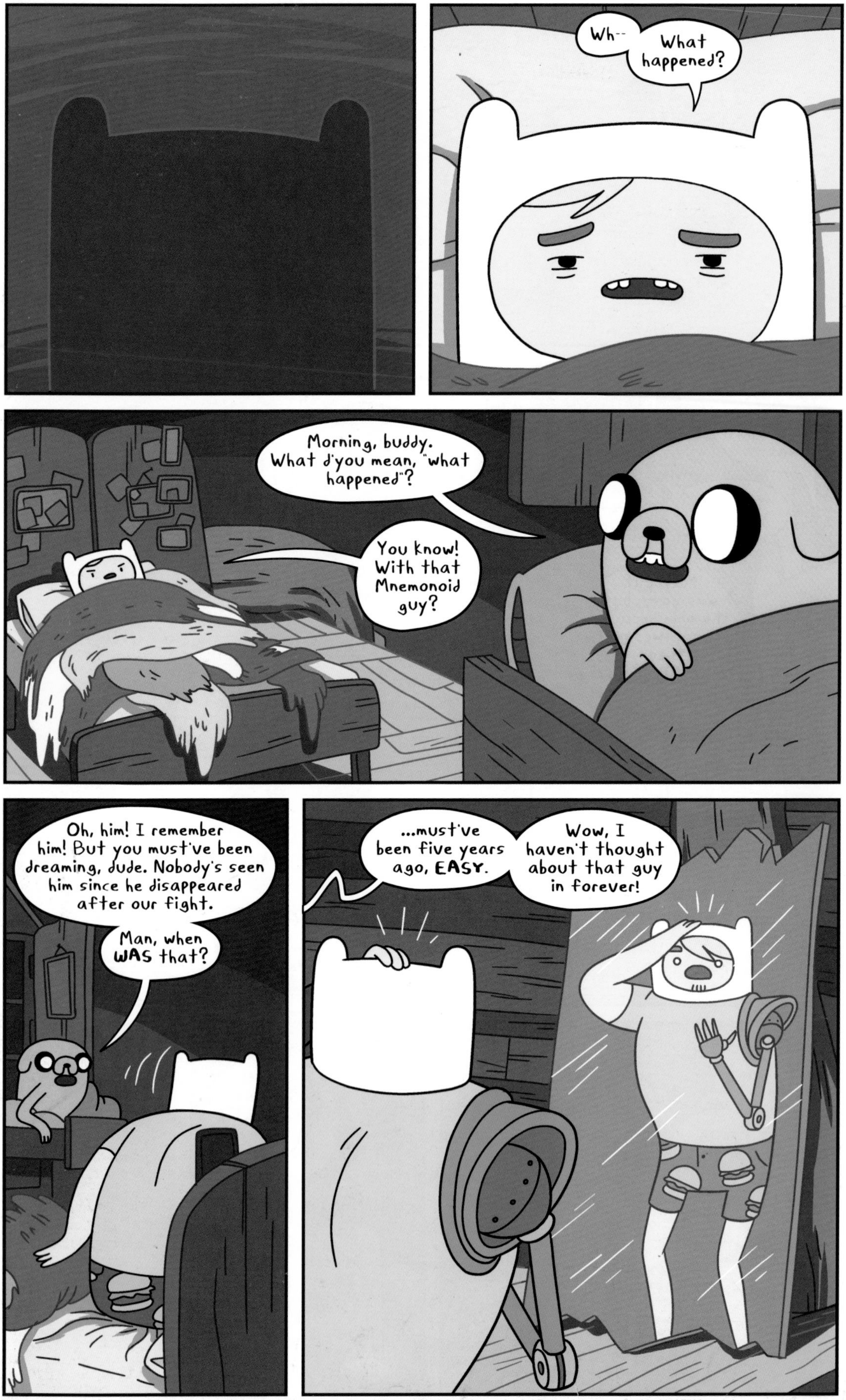
Wh--
What happened?
Morning, buddy. What d'you mean, "what happened"?
You know! With that Mnemonoid guy?
Oh, him! I remember him! But you must've been dreaming, dude. Nobody's seen him since he disappeared after our fight.
Man, when WAS that?
...must've been five years ago, EASY.
Wow, I haven't thought about that guy in forever!

If your name is "Hamburger Underwear", then good news: this comic just included a visual shout out to your frankly AMAZING name!

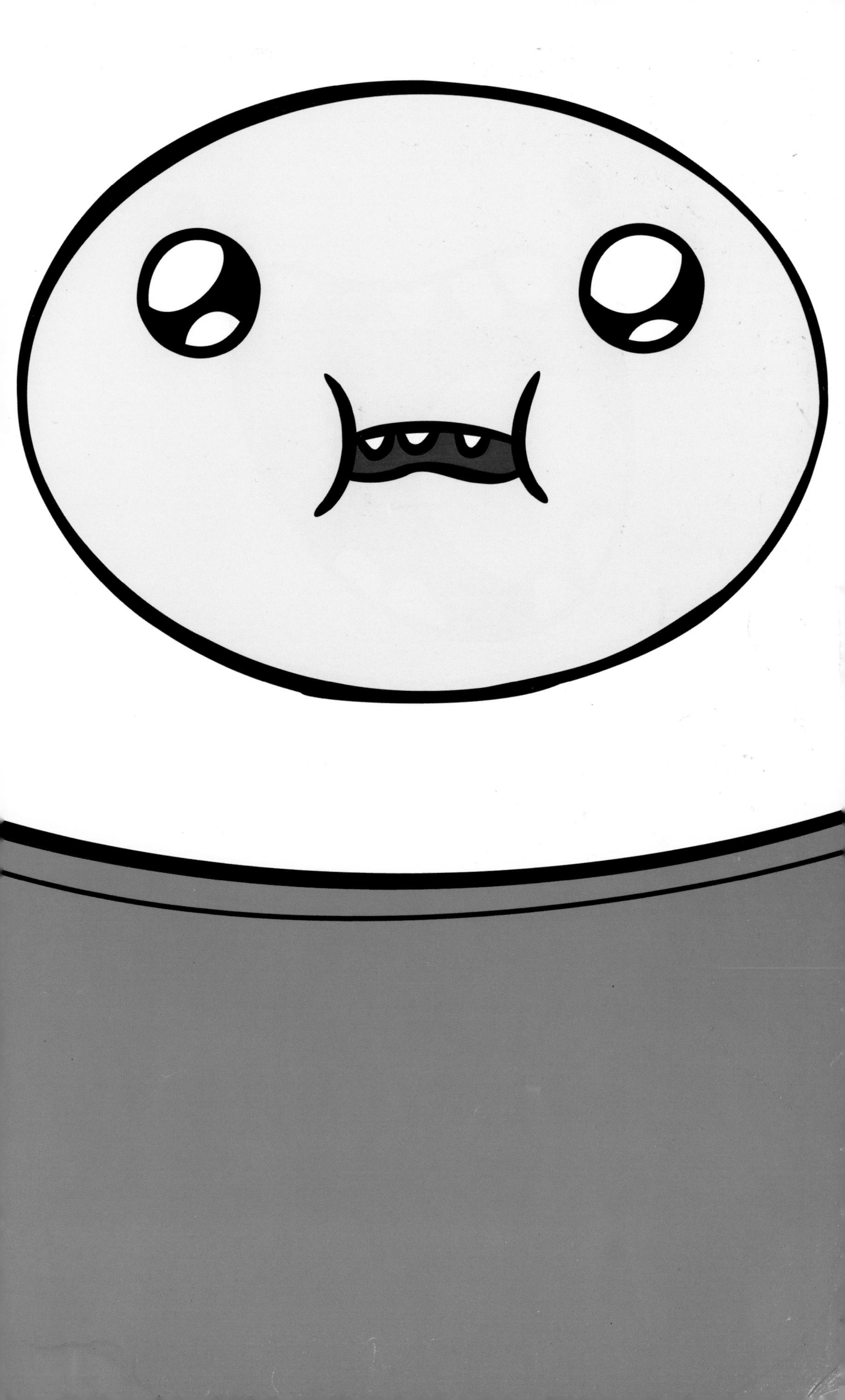

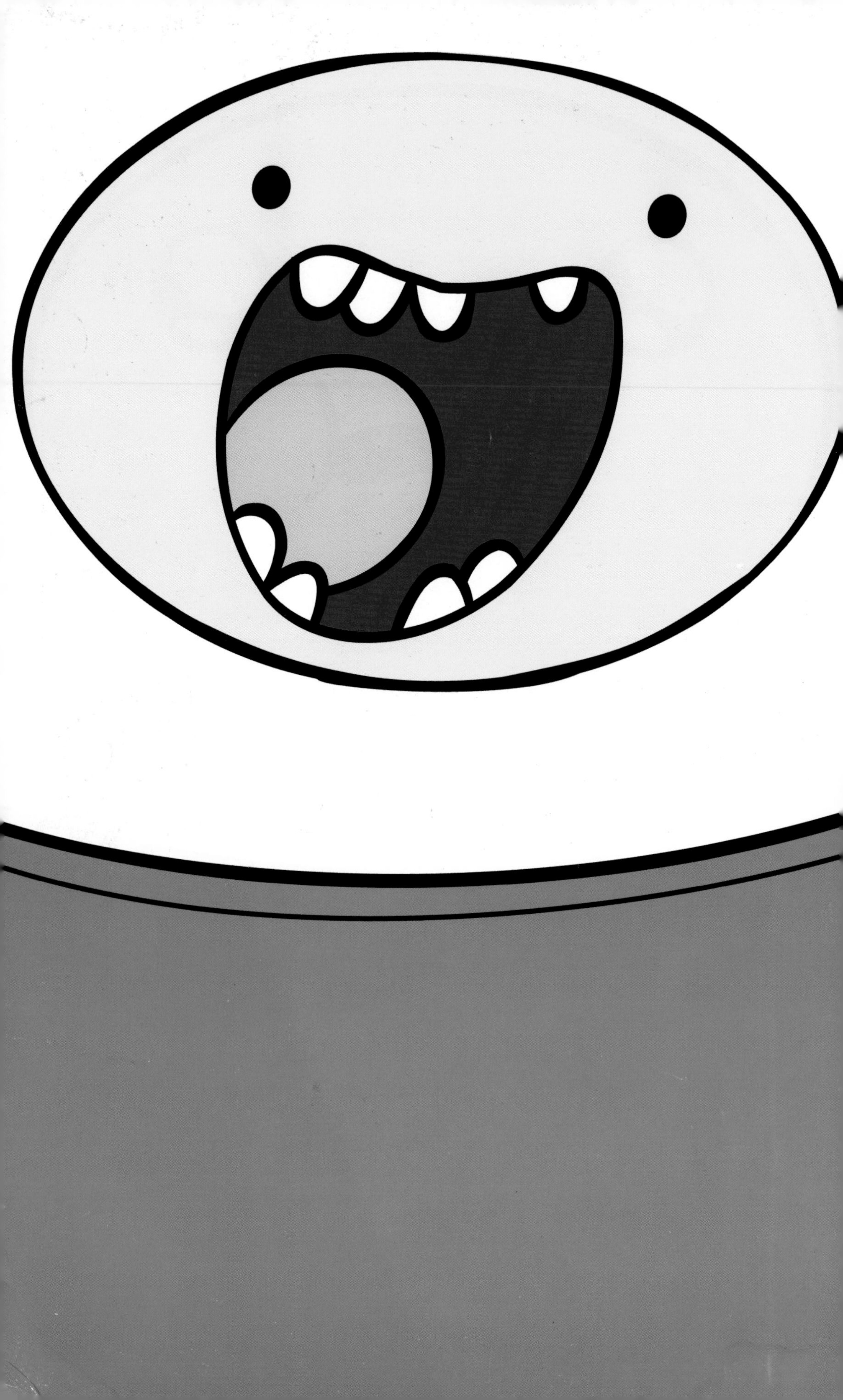

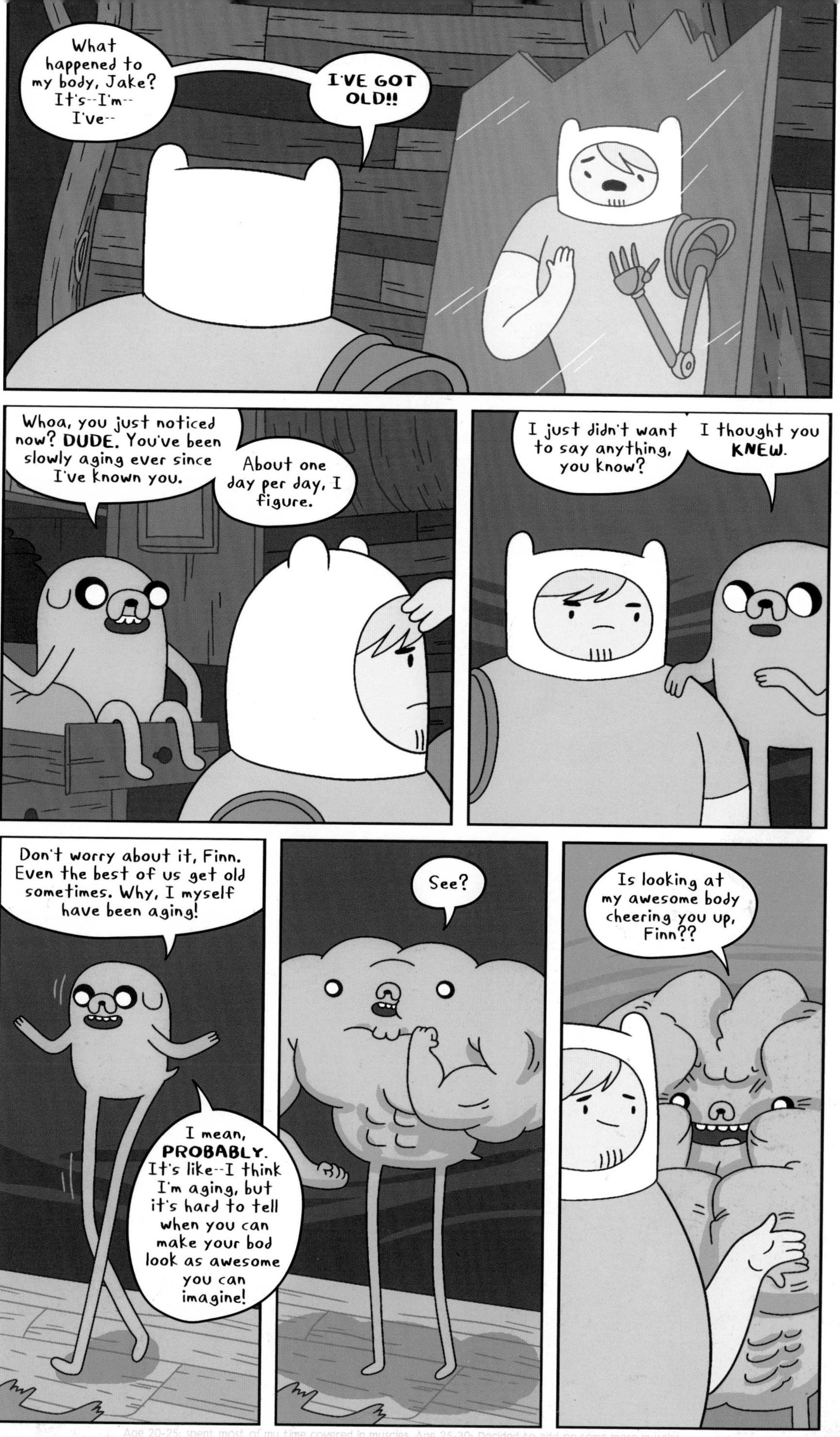
What happened to my body, Jake? It's--I'm-- I've--
I'VE GOT OLD!!
Whoa, you just noticed now? DUDE. You've been slowly aging ever since I've known you.
About one day per day, I figure.
I just didn't want to say anything, you know?
I thought you KNEW.
Don't worry about it, Finn. Even the best of us get old sometimes. Why, I myself have been aging!
I mean, PROBABLY. It's like--I think I'm aging, but it's hard to tell when you can make your bod look as awesome you can imagine!
See?
Is looking at my awesome body cheering you up, Finn??

Age 20-25: spent most of my time covered in muscles. Age 25-30: Decided to add on some more muscles.

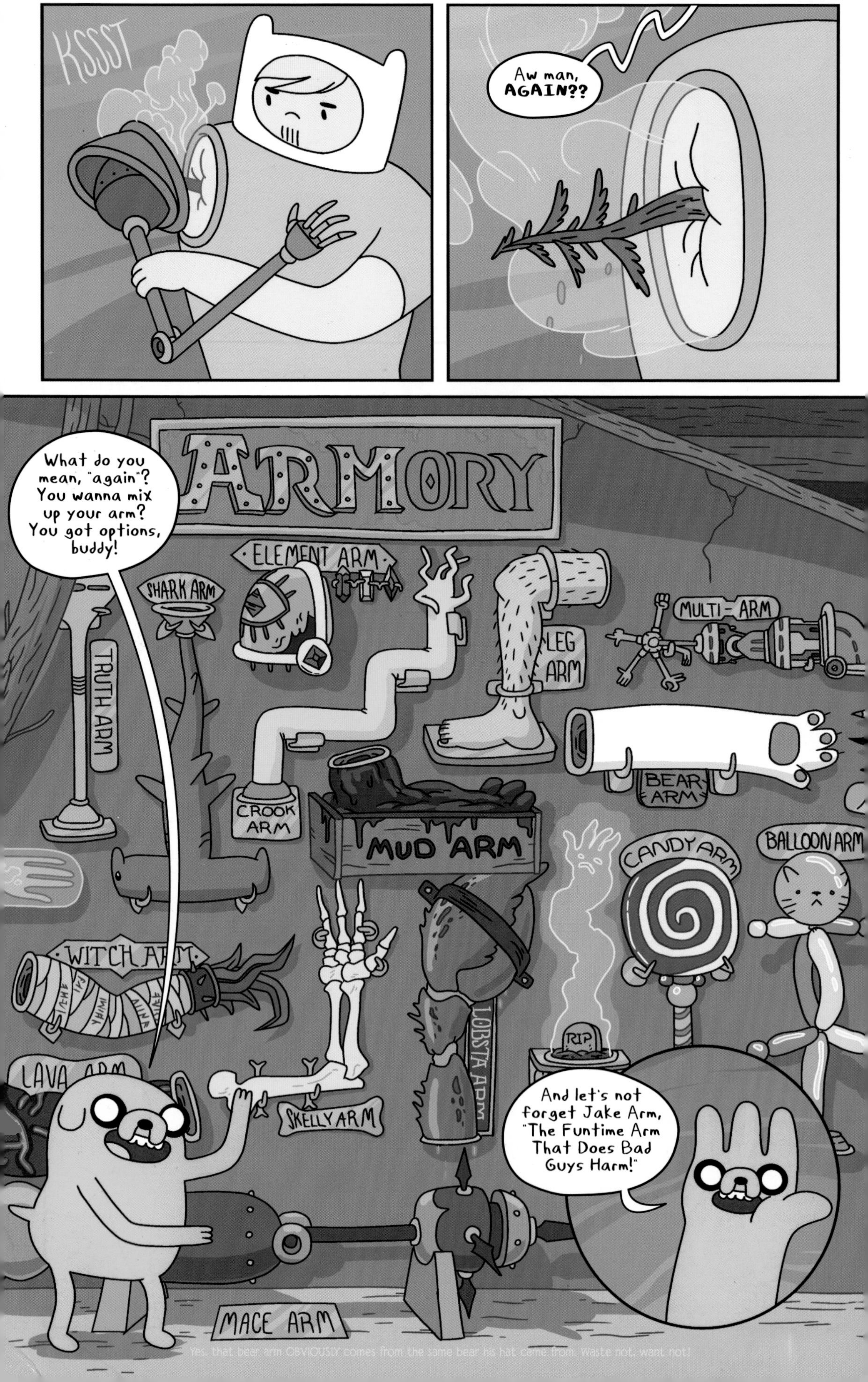
KSSST
Aw man, **AGAIN??**
ARMORY
What do you mean, "again"? You wanna mix up your arm? You got options, buddy!
ELEMENT ARM
SHARK ARM
TRUTH ARM
LEG ARM
MULTI-ARM
CROOK ARM
MUD ARM
BEAR ARM
CANDY ARM
BALLOON ARM
WITCH ARM
LAVA ARM
SKELLY ARM
LOBSTA ARM
RIP
And let's not forget Jake Arm, "The Funtime Arm That Does Bad Guys Harm!"
MACE ARM
Yes, that bear arm OBVIOUSLY comes from the same bear his hat came from. Waste not, want not!

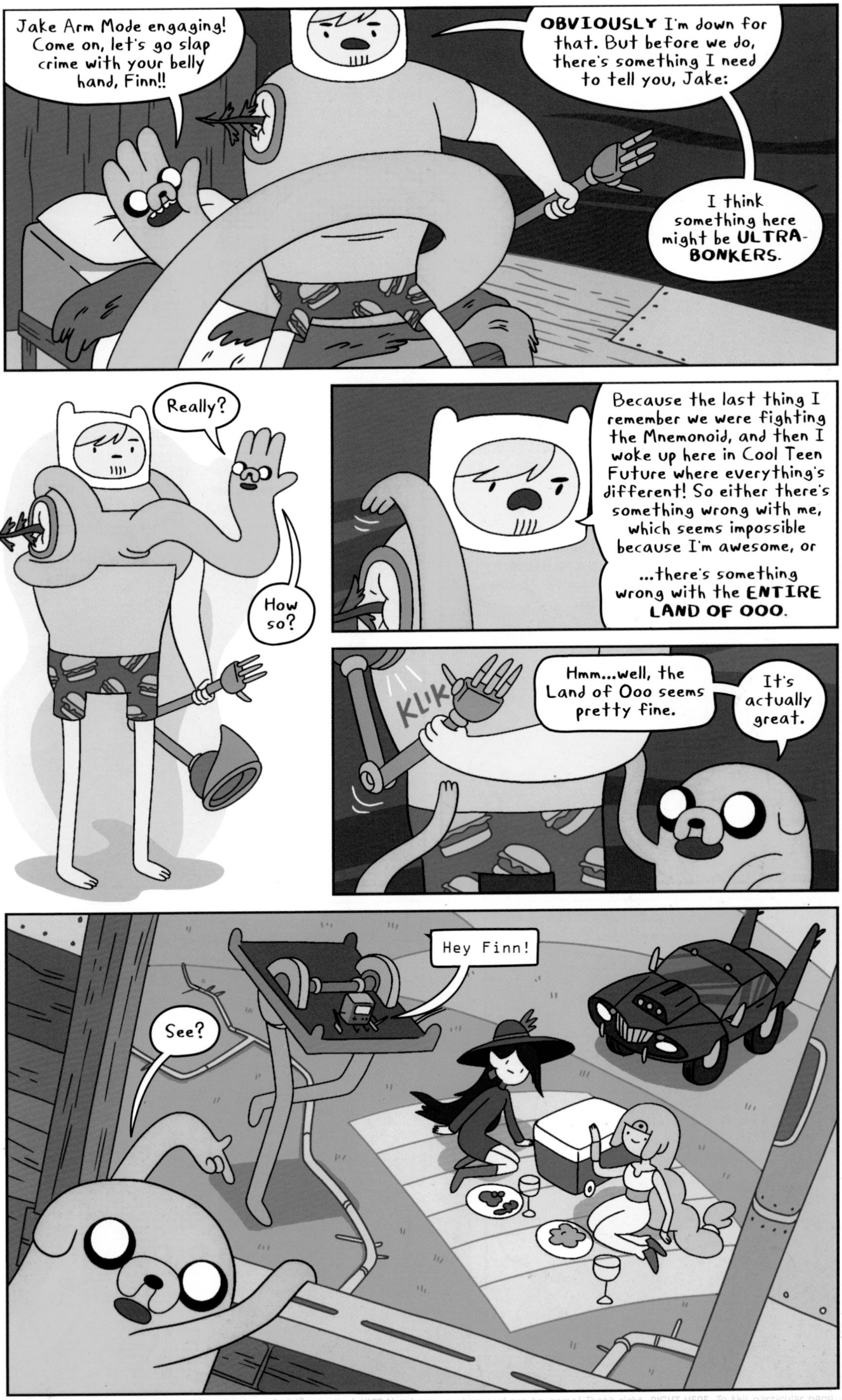
Jake Arm Mode engaging! Come on, let's go slap crime with your belly hand, Finn!!
OBVIOUSLY I'm down for that. But before we do, there's something I need to tell you, Jake:
I think something here might be ULTRA-BONKERS.
Really?
How so?
Because the last thing I remember we were fighting the Mnemonoid, and then I woke up here in Cool Teen Future where everything's different! So either there's something wrong with me, which seems impossible because I'm awesome, or
...there's something wrong with the ENTIRE LAND OF OOO.
KLIK
Hmm...well, the Land of Ooo seems pretty fine.
It's actually great.
Hey Finn!
See?

Other comics might show you something bonkers. But if you want **ULTRA**bonkers, you know where to come! That's right. **RIGHT HERE.** To this particular page.

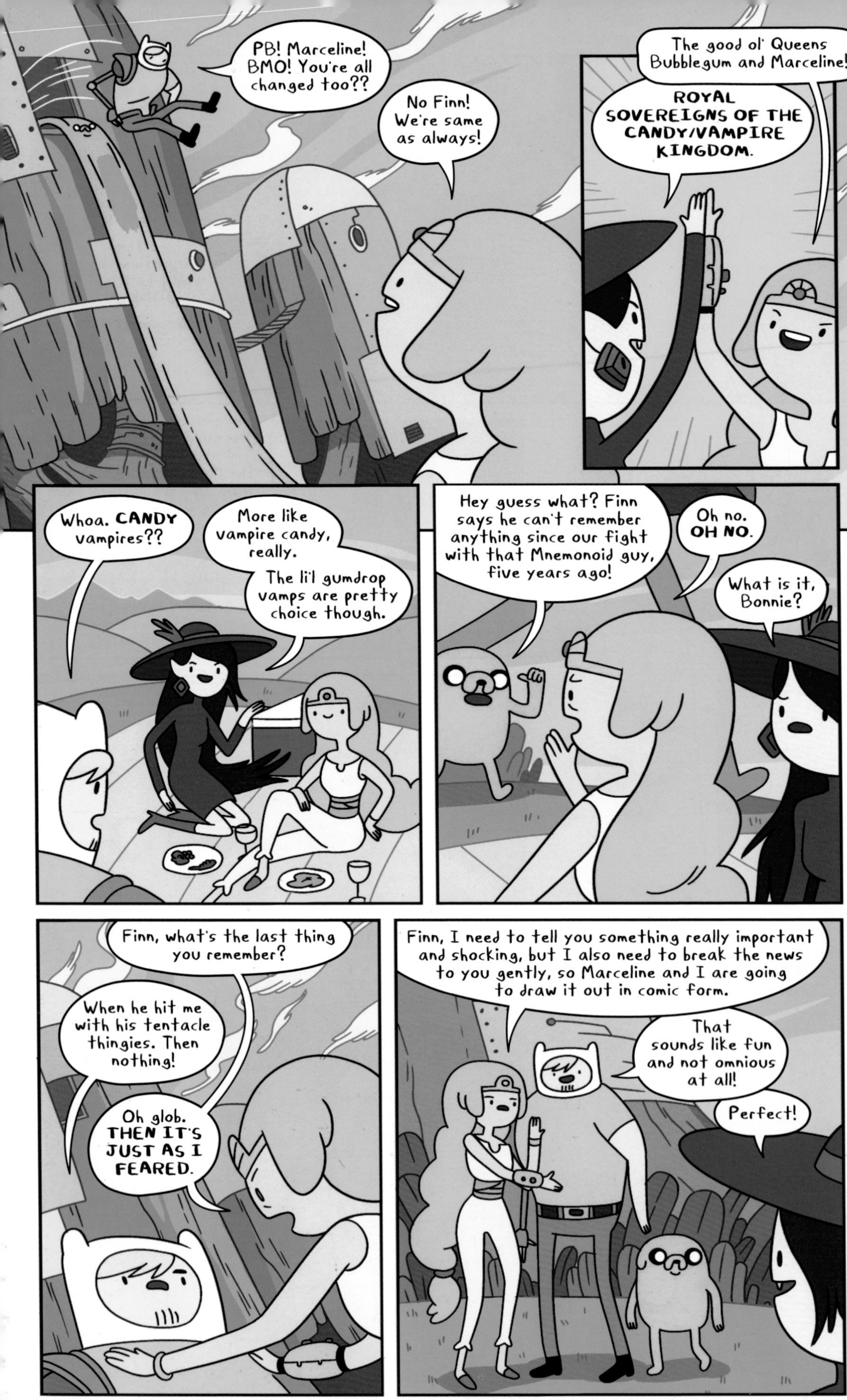
PB! Marceline! BMO! You're all changed too??
No Finn! We're same as always!
The good ol' Queens Bubblegum and Marceline!
ROYAL SOVEREIGNS OF THE CANDY/VAMPIRE KINGDOM.
Whoa. CANDY vampires??
More like vampire candy, really.
The li'l gumdrop vamps are pretty choice though.
Hey guess what? Finn says he can't remember anything since our fight with that Mnemonoid guy, five years ago!
Oh no. OH NO.
What is it, Bonnie?
Finn, what's the last thing you remember?
When he hit me with his tentacle thingies. Then nothing!
Oh glob. THEN IT'S JUST AS I FEARED.
Finn, I need to tell you something really important and shocking, but I also need to break the news to you gently, so Marceline and I are going to draw it out in comic form.
That sounds like fun and not omnious at all!
Perfect!

You may think delivering bad news is comic form is a silly idea, but this way at the end of the bad news you have a nice souvenir comic! Therefore it's Comics: 1, Quiet Conversation: 0.

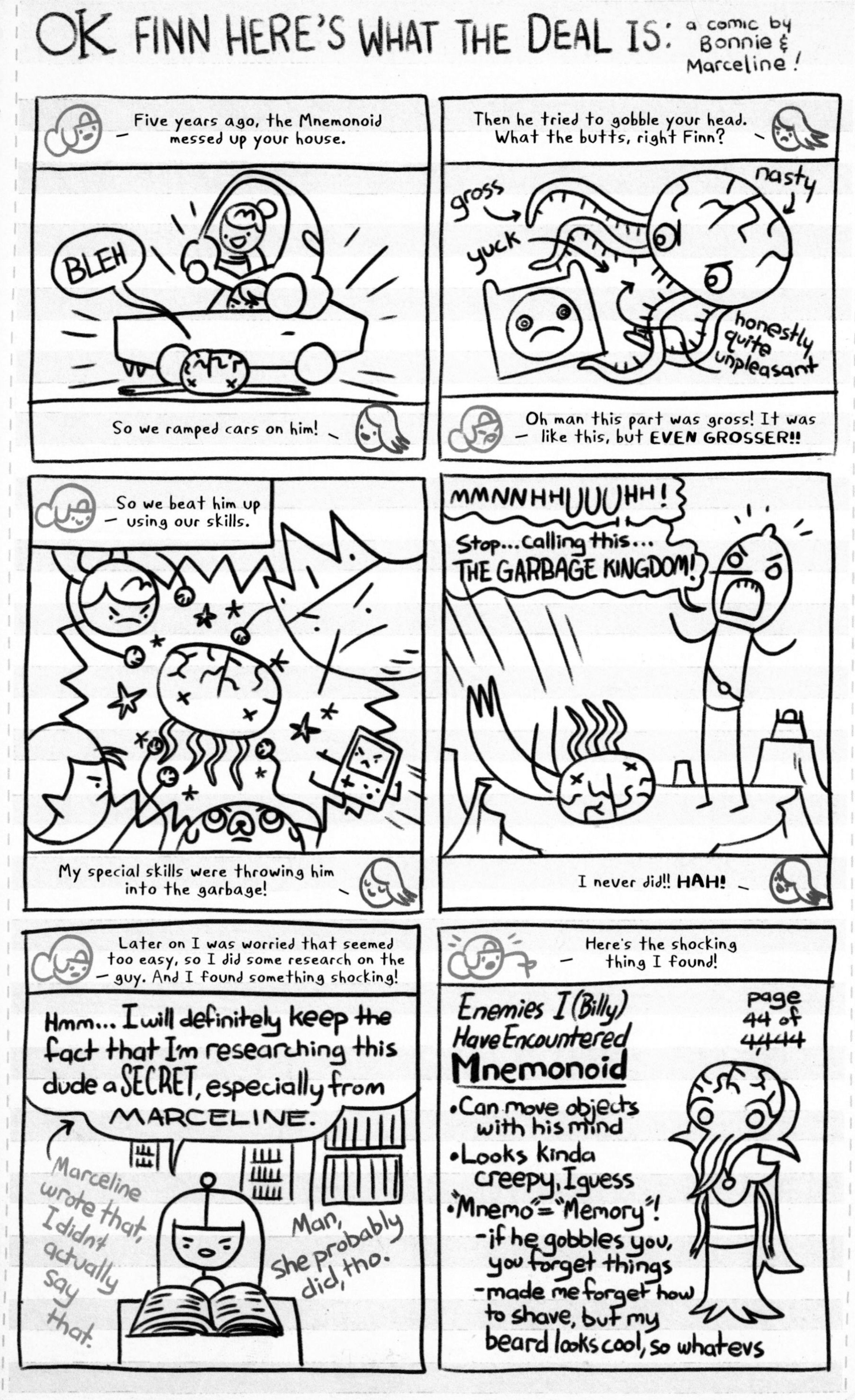

OK FINN HERE'S WHAT THE DEAL IS: a comic by Bonnie & Marceline!
Five years ago, the Mnemonoid messed up your house.
BLEH
So we ramped cars on him!
Then he tried to gobble your head. What the butts, right Finn?
gross
yuck
nasty
honestly quite unpleasant
Oh man this part was gross! It was like this, but EVEN GROSSER!!
So we beat him up using our skills.
My special skills were throwing him into the garbage!
MMNNHHUUUHH!
Stop... calling this... THE GARBAGE KINGDOM!
I never did!! HAH!
Later on I was worried that seemed too easy, so I did some research on the guy. And I found something shocking!
Hmm... I will definitely keep the fact that I'm researching this dude a SECRET, especially from MARCELINE.
Marceline wrote that, I didn't actually say that.
Man, she probably did, tho.
Here's the shocking thing I found!
Enemies I (Billy) Have Encountered
page 44 of 4444
Mnemonoid
•Can move objects with his mind
•Looks kinda creepy, I guess
•"Mnemo" = "Memory"!
-if he gobbles you, you forget things
-made me forget how to shave, but my beard looks cool, so whatevs

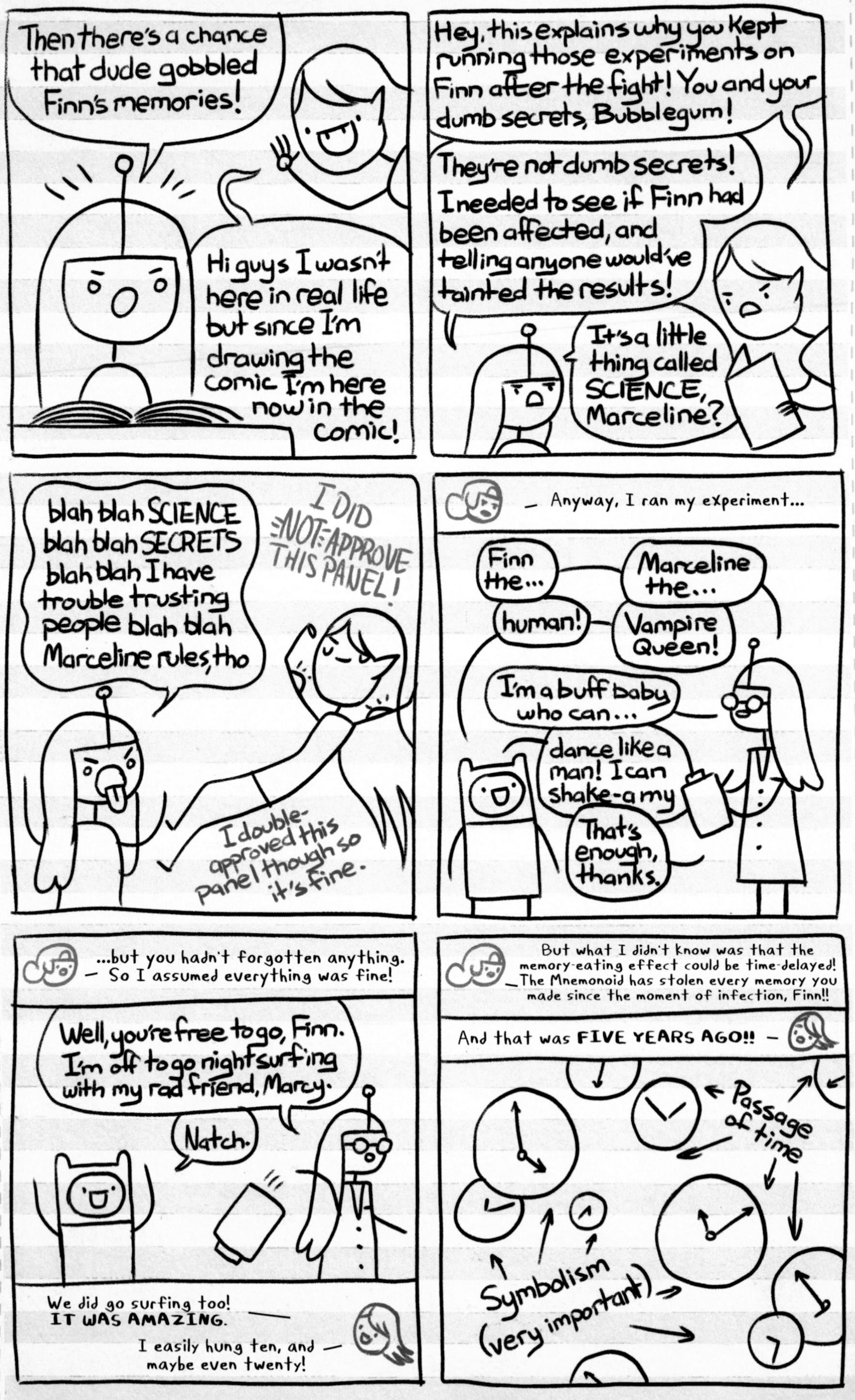
Then there's a chance that dude gobbled Finn's memories!
Hi guys I wasn't here in real life but since I'm drawing the comic I'm here now in the comic!
Hey, this explains why you kept running those experiments on Finn after the fight! You and your dumb secrets, Bubblegum!
They're not dumb secrets! I needed to see if Finn had been affected, and telling anyone would've tainted the results!
It's a little thing called SCIENCE, Marceline?
blah blah SCIENCE blah blah SECRETS blah blah I have trouble trusting people blah blah Marceline rules, tho
I DID NOT APPROVE THIS PANEL!
I double-approved this panel though so it's fine.
Anyway, I ran my experiment...
Finn the...
Marceline the...
human!
Vampire Queen!
I'm a buff baby who can...
dance like a man! I can shake-a my
That's enough, thanks.
...but you hadn't forgotten anything. So I assumed everything was fine!
Well, you're free to go, Finn. I'm off to go night surfing with my rad friend, Marcy.
Natch.
We did go surfing too! IT WAS AMAZING.
I easily hung ten, and maybe even twenty!
But what I didn't know was that the memory-eating effect could be time-delayed! The Mnemonoid has stolen every memory you made since the moment of infection, Finn!!
And that was FIVE YEARS AGO!!
Passage of time
Symbolism (very important)

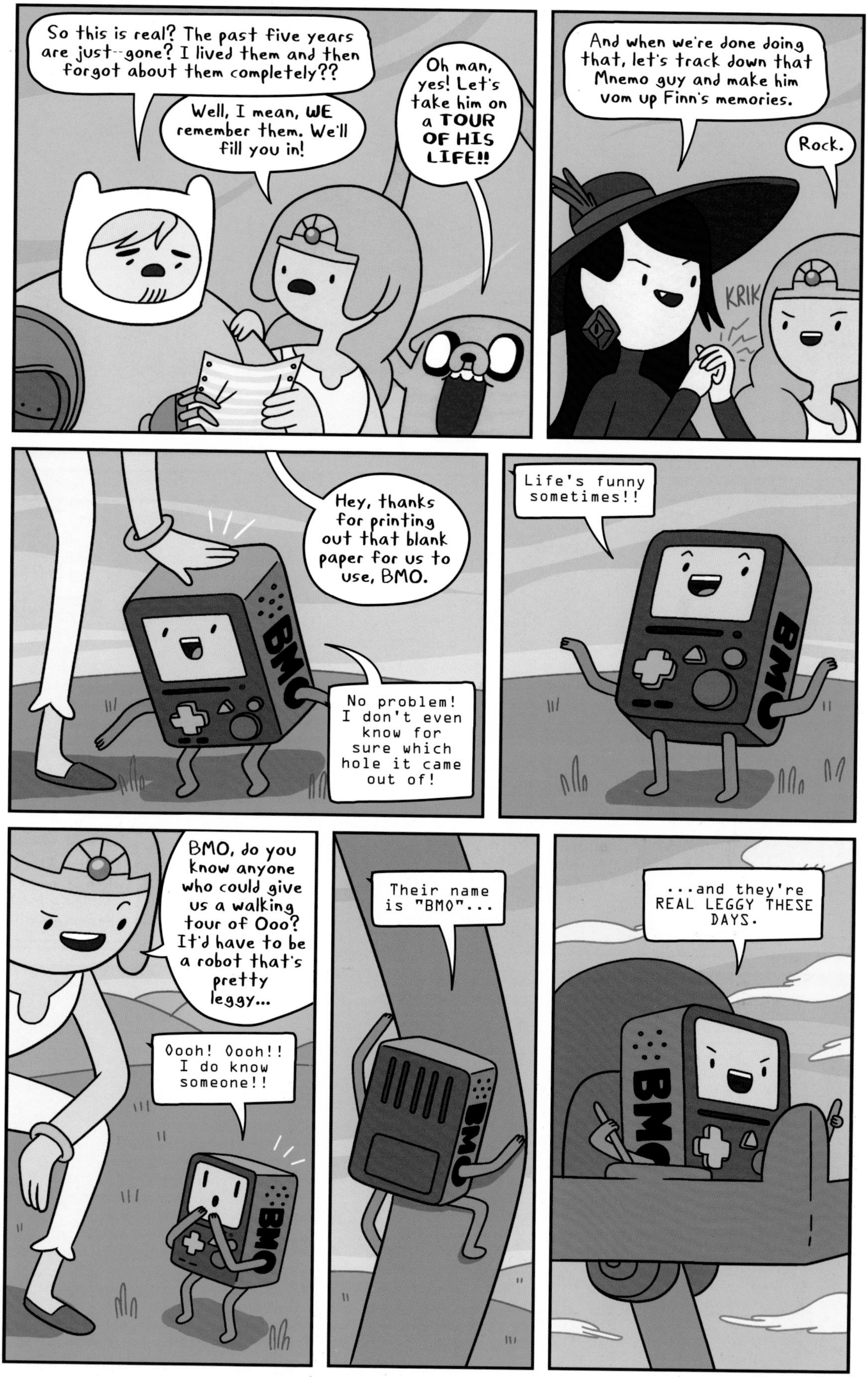
So this is real? The past five years are just--gone? I lived them and then forgot about them completely??
Well, I mean, WE remember them. We'll fill you in!
Oh man, yes! Let's take him on a TOUR OF HIS LIFE!!
And when we're done doing that, let's track down that Mnemo guy and make him vom up Finn's memories.
Rock.
KRIK
Hey, thanks for printing out that blank paper for us to use, BMO.
No problem! I don't even know for sure which hole it came out of!
Life's funny sometimes!!
BMO, do you know anyone who could give us a walking tour of Ooo? It'd have to be a robot that's pretty leggy...
Oooh! Oooh!! I do know someone!!
Their name is "BMO"...
...and they're REAL LEGGY THESE DAYS.

It's Adventure Time, with Finn and Jake! And BMO's supercharged legs!

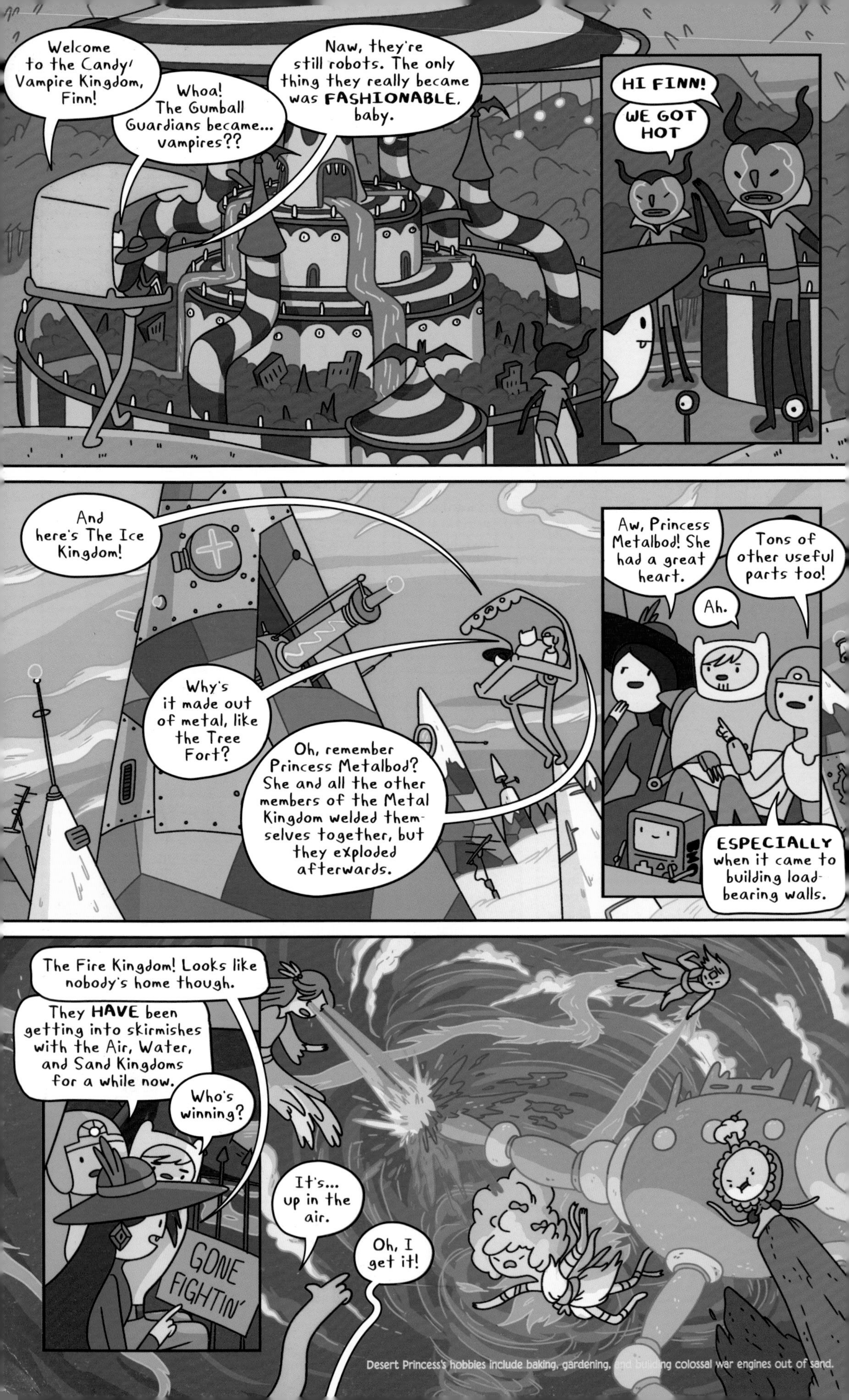
Welcome to the Candy/ Vampire Kingdom, Finn!
Whoa! The Gumball Guardians became... vampires??
Naw, they're still robots. The only thing they really became was FASHIONABLE, baby.
HI FINN!
WE GOT HOT
And here's The Ice Kingdom!
Why's it made out of metal, like the Tree Fort?
Oh, remember Princess Metalbod? She and all the other members of the Metal Kingdom welded themselves together, but they exploded afterwards.
Aw, Princess Metalbod! She had a great heart.
Ah.
Tons of other useful parts too!
ESPECIALLY when it came to building load-bearing walls.
The Fire Kingdom! Looks like nobody's home though.
They HAVE been getting into skirmishes with the Air, Water, and Sand Kingdoms for a while now.
Who's winning?
GONE FIGHTIN'
It's... up in the air.
Oh, I get it!
Desert Princess's hobbies include baking, gardening, and building colossal war engines out of sand.

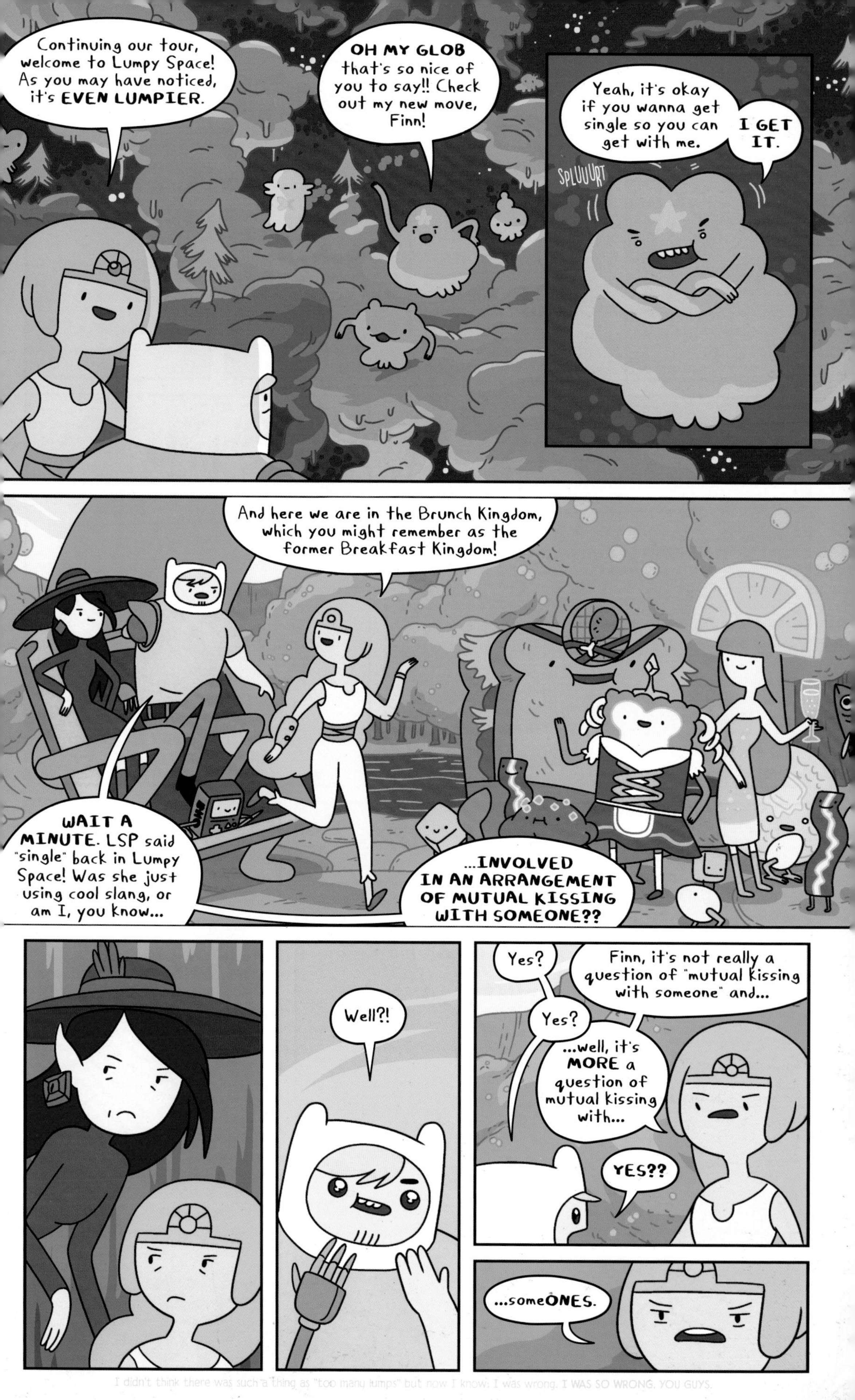
Continuing our tour, welcome to Lumpy Space! As you may have noticed, it's EVEN LUMPIER.
OH MY GLOB that's so nice of you to say!! Check out my new move, Finn!
SPLUUURT
Yeah, it's okay if you wanna get single so you can get with me.
I GET IT.
And here we are in the Brunch Kingdom, which you might remember as the former Breakfast Kingdom!
WAIT A MINUTE. LSP said "single" back in Lumpy Space! Was she just using cool slang, or am I, you know...
...INVOLVED IN AN ARRANGEMENT OF MUTUAL KISSING WITH SOMEONE??
Well?!
Yes?
Finn, it's not really a question of "mutual kissing with someone" and...
Yes?
...well, it's MORE a question of mutual kissing with...
YES??
...someONES.

I didn't think there was such a thing as "too many lumps" but now I know: I was wrong. I WAS SO WRONG. YOU GUYS.

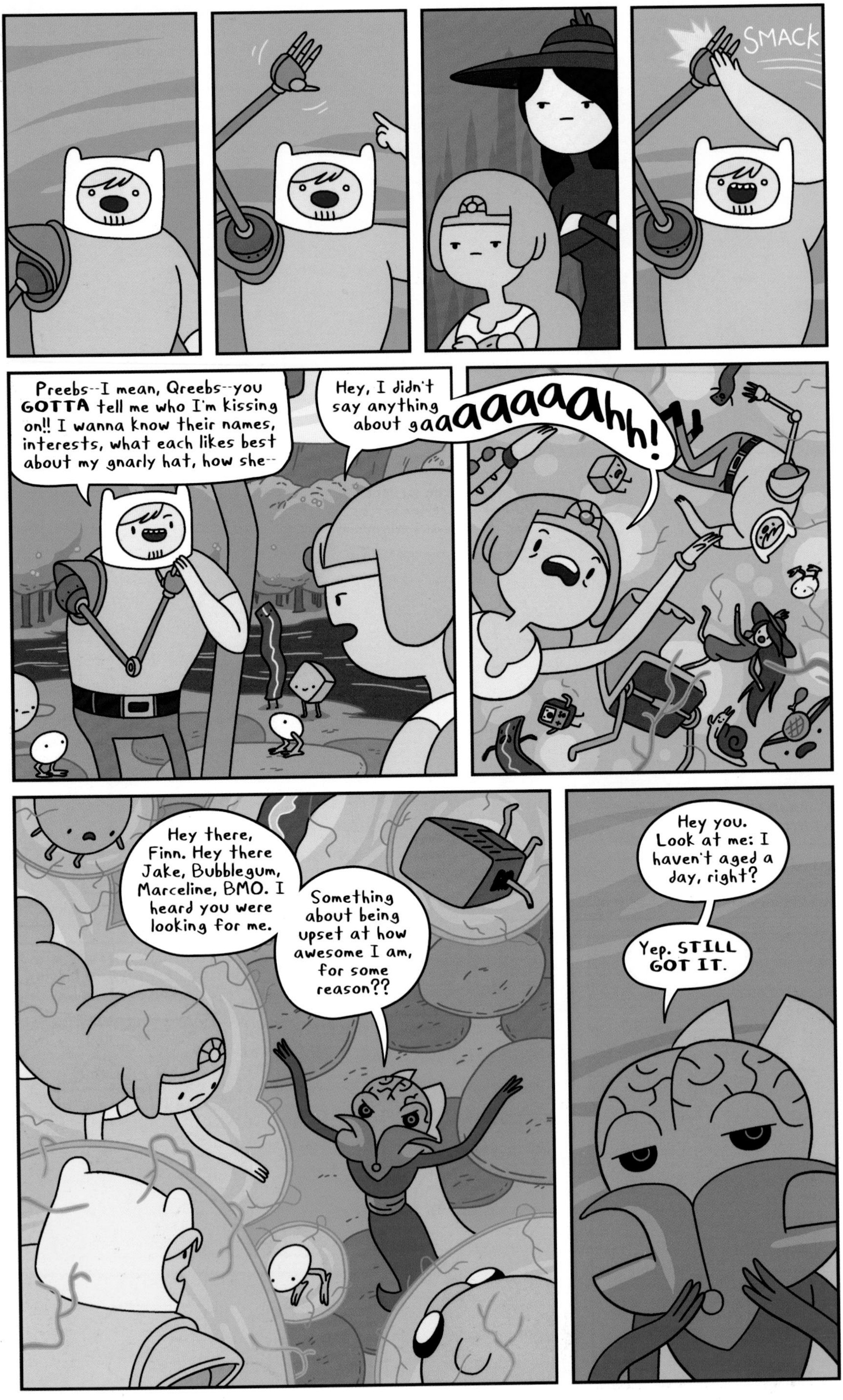
SMACK
Preebs--I mean, Qreebs--you GOTTA tell me who I'm kissing on!! I wanna know their names, interests, what each likes best about my gnarly hat, how she--
Hey, I didn't say anything about gaaaaaaahh!
Hey there, Finn. Hey there Jake, Bubblegum, Marceline, BMO. I heard you were looking for me.
Something about being upset at how awesome I am, for some reason??
Hey you. Look at me: I haven't aged a day, right?
Yep. STILL GOT IT.

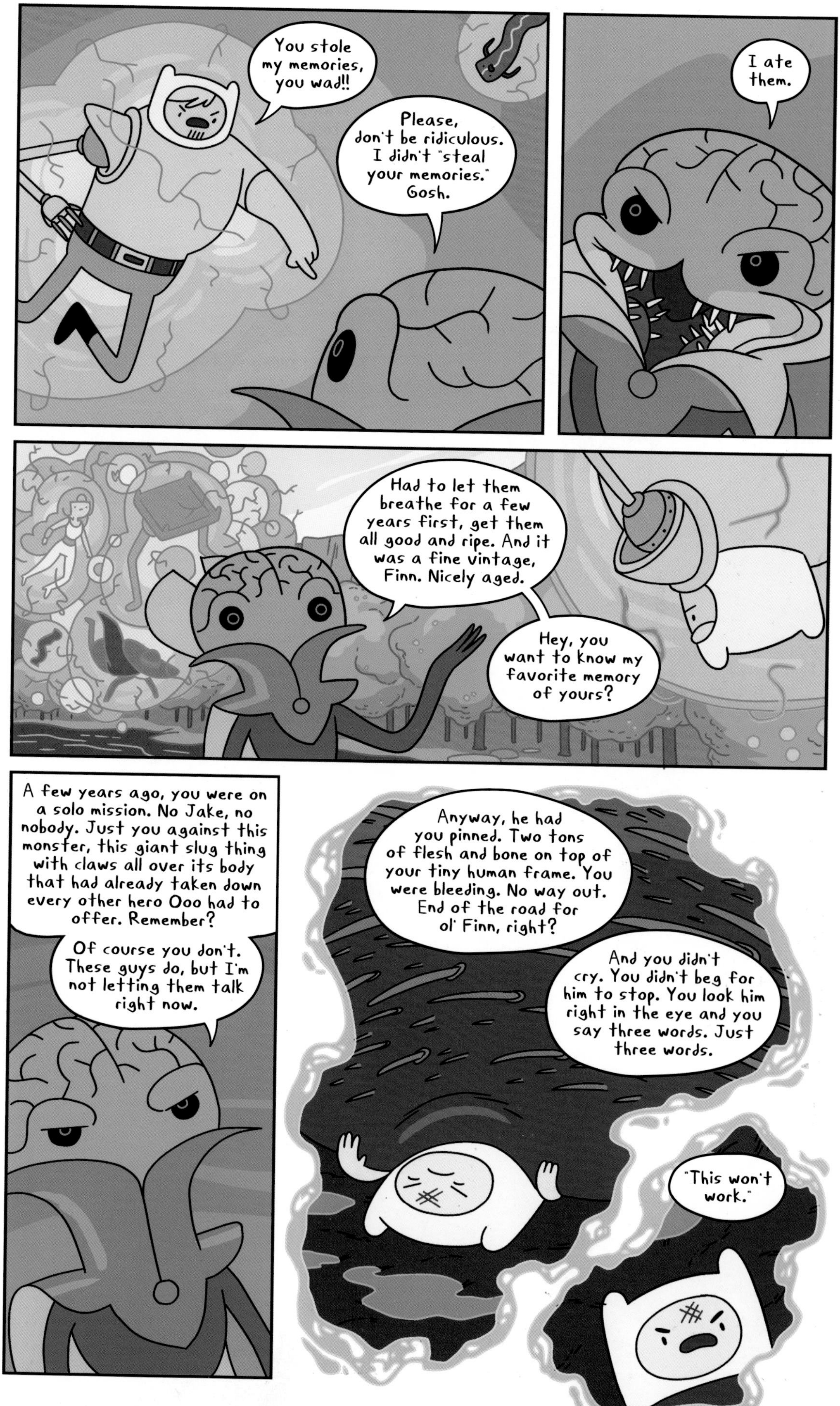
You stole my memories, you wad!!
Please, don't be ridiculous. I didn't "steal your memories." Gosh.
I ate them.
Had to let them breathe for a few years first, get them all good and ripe. And it was a fine vintage, Finn. Nicely aged.
Hey, you want to know my favorite memory of yours?
A few years ago, you were on a solo mission. No Jake, no nobody. Just you against this monster, this giant slug thing with claws all over its body that had already taken down every other hero Ooo had to offer. Remember?
Of course you don't. These guys do, but I'm not letting them talk right now.
Anyway, he had you pinned. Two tons of flesh and bone on top of your tiny human frame. You were bleeding. No way out. End of the road for ol' Finn, right?
And you didn't cry. You didn't beg for him to stop. You look him right in the eye and you say three words. Just three words.
"This won't work."

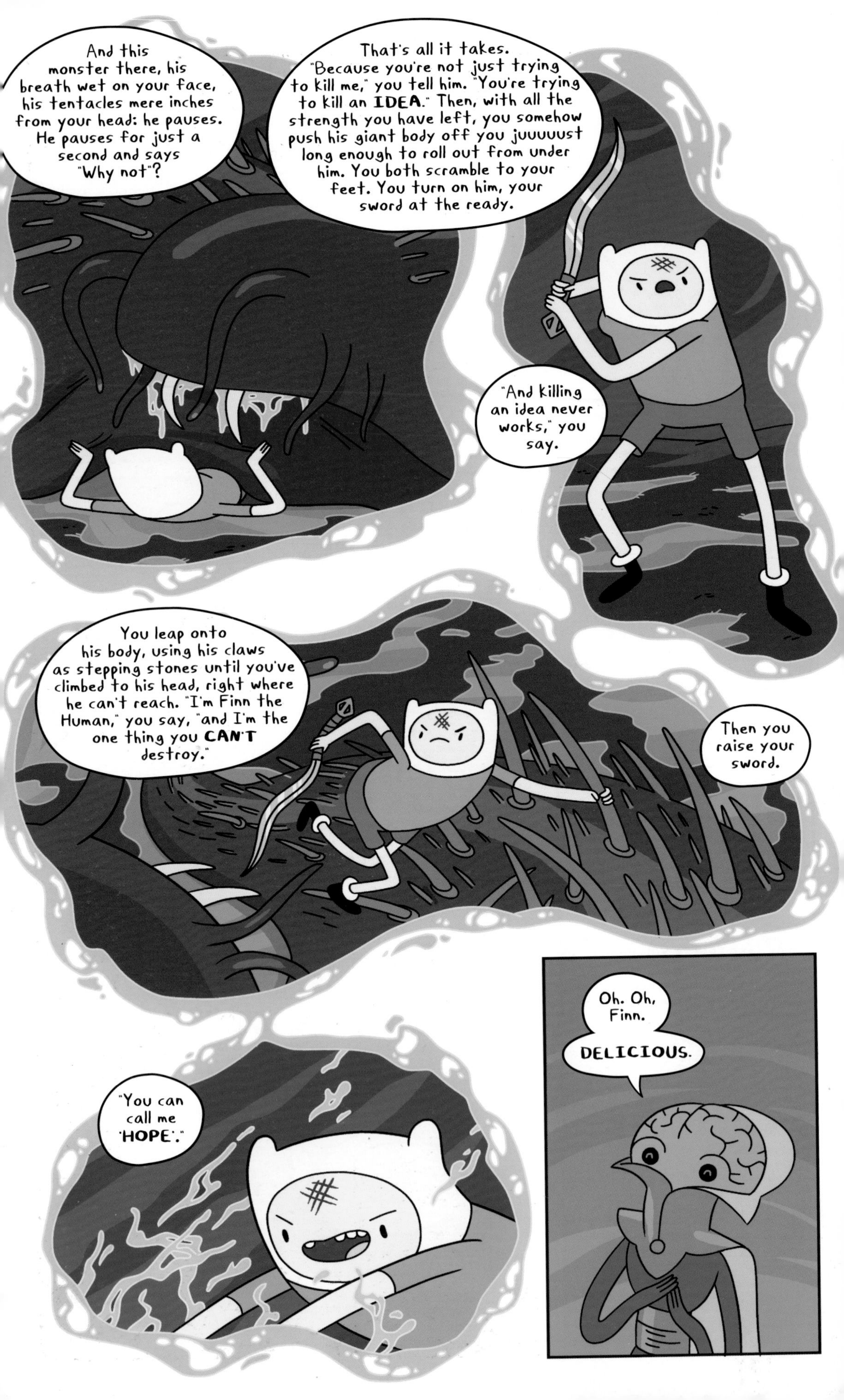
And this monster there, his breath wet on your face, his tentacles mere inches from your head: he pauses. He pauses for just a second and says "Why not"?
That's all it takes. "Because you're not just trying to kill me," you tell him. "You're trying to kill an IDEA." Then, with all the strength you have left, you somehow push his giant body off you juuuuust long enough to roll out from under him. You both scramble to your feet. You turn on him, your sword at the ready.
"And killing an idea never works," you say.
You leap onto his body, using his claws as stepping stones until you've climbed to his head, right where he can't reach. "I'm Finn the Human," you say, "and I'm the one thing you CAN'T destroy."
Then you raise your sword.
"You can call me 'HOPE'."
Oh. Oh, Finn.
DELICIOUS.

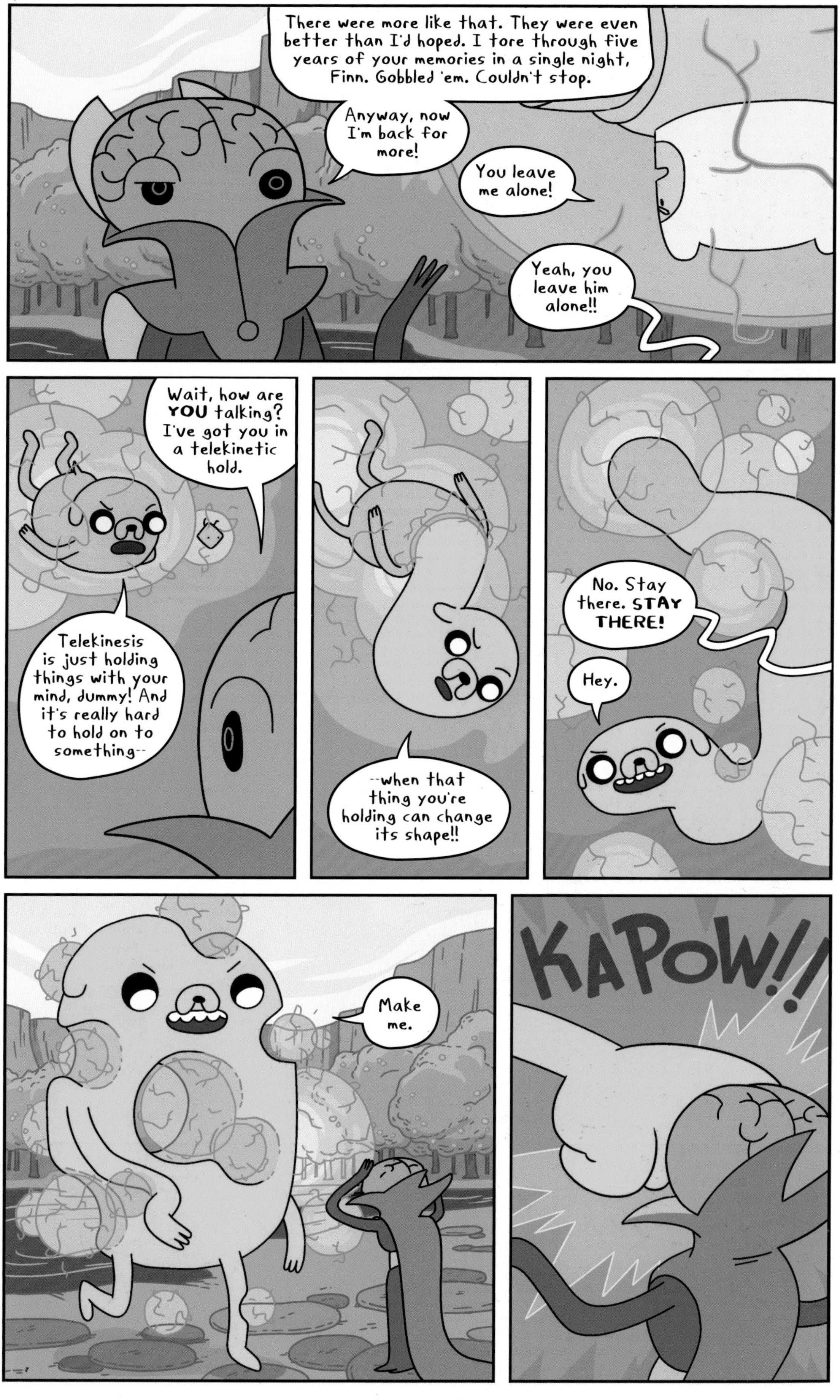
There were more like that. They were even better than I'd hoped. I tore through five years of your memories in a single night, Finn. Gobbled 'em. Couldn't stop.
Anyway, now I'm back for more!
You leave me alone!
Yeah, you leave him alone!!
Wait, how are **YOU** talking? I've got you in a telekinetic hold.
Telekinesis is just holding things with your mind, dummy! And it's really hard to hold on to something--
--when that thing you're holding can change its shape!!
No. Stay there. **STAY THERE!**
Hey.
Make me.
KAPOW!!

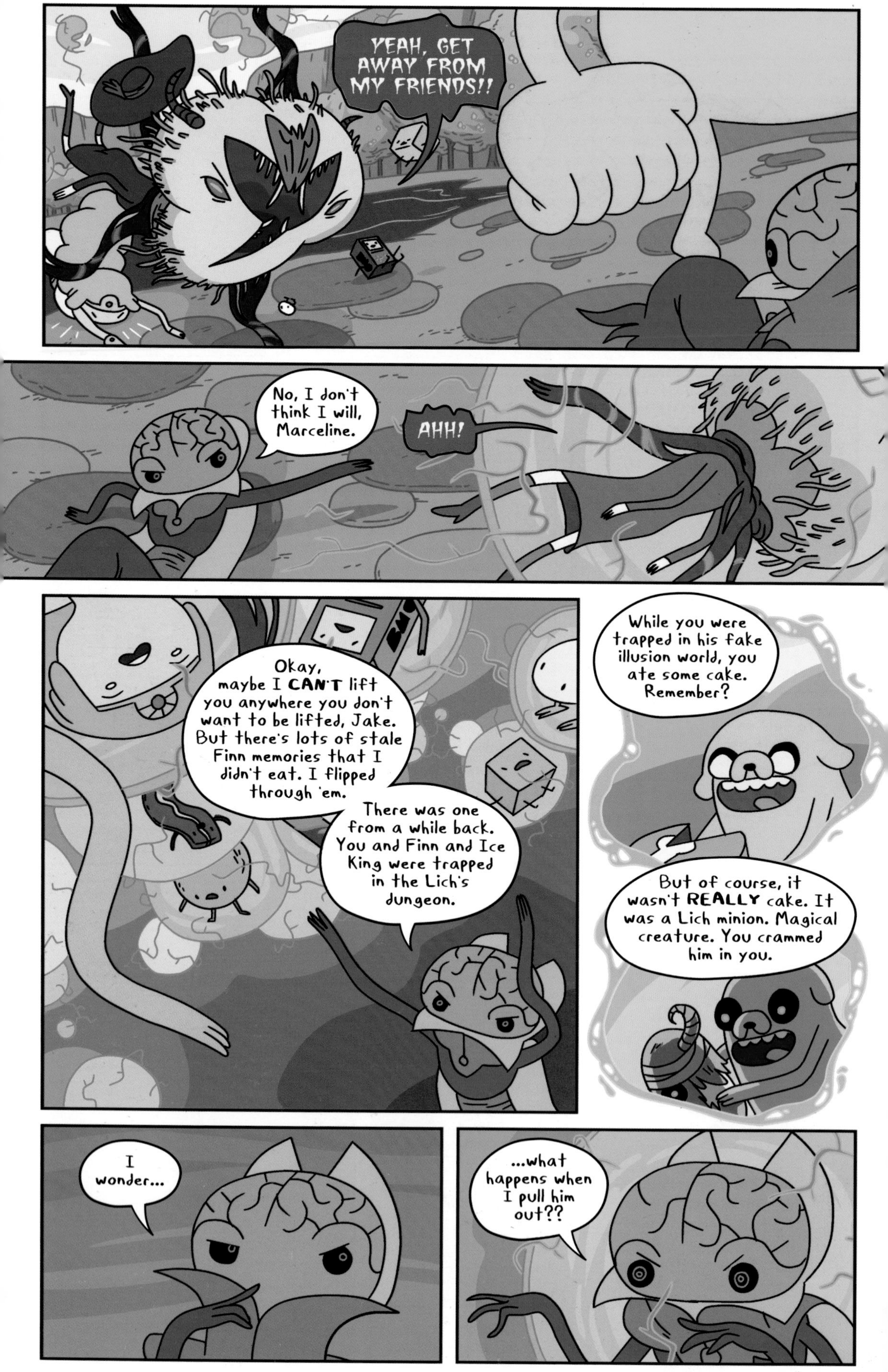
YEAH, GET AWAY FROM MY FRIENDS!!
No, I don't think I will, Marceline.
AHH!
Okay, maybe I **CAN'T** lift you anywhere you don't want to be lifted, Jake. But there's lots of stale Finn memories that I didn't eat. I flipped through 'em.
There was one from a while back. You and Finn and Ice King were trapped in the Lich's dungeon.
While you were trapped in his fake illusion world, you ate some cake. Remember?
But of course, it wasn't **REALLY** cake. It was a Lich minion. Magical creature. You crammed him in you.
I wonder...
...what happens when I pull him out??

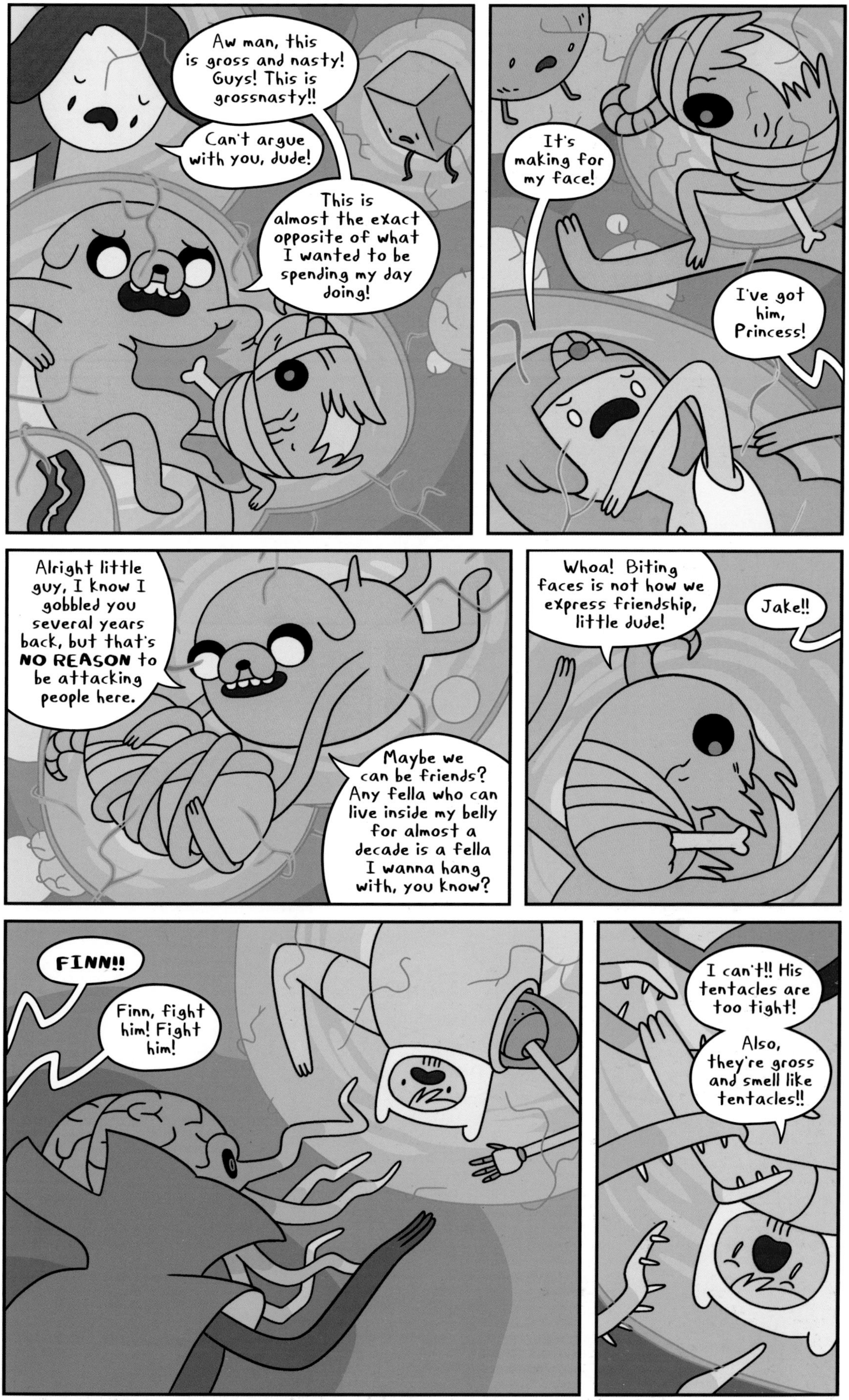
Aw man, this is gross and nasty! Guys! This is grossnasty!!
Can't argue with you, dude!
This is almost the exact opposite of what I wanted to be spending my day doing!
It's making for my face!
I've got him, Princess!
Alright little guy, I know I gobbled you several years back, but that's **NO REASON** to be attacking people here.
Maybe we can be friends? Any fella who can live inside my belly for almost a decade is a fella I wanna hang with, you know?
Whoa! Biting faces is not how we express friendship, little dude!
Jake!!
FINN!!
Finn, fight him! Fight him!
I can't!! His tentacles are too tight!
Also, they're gross and smell like tentacles!!

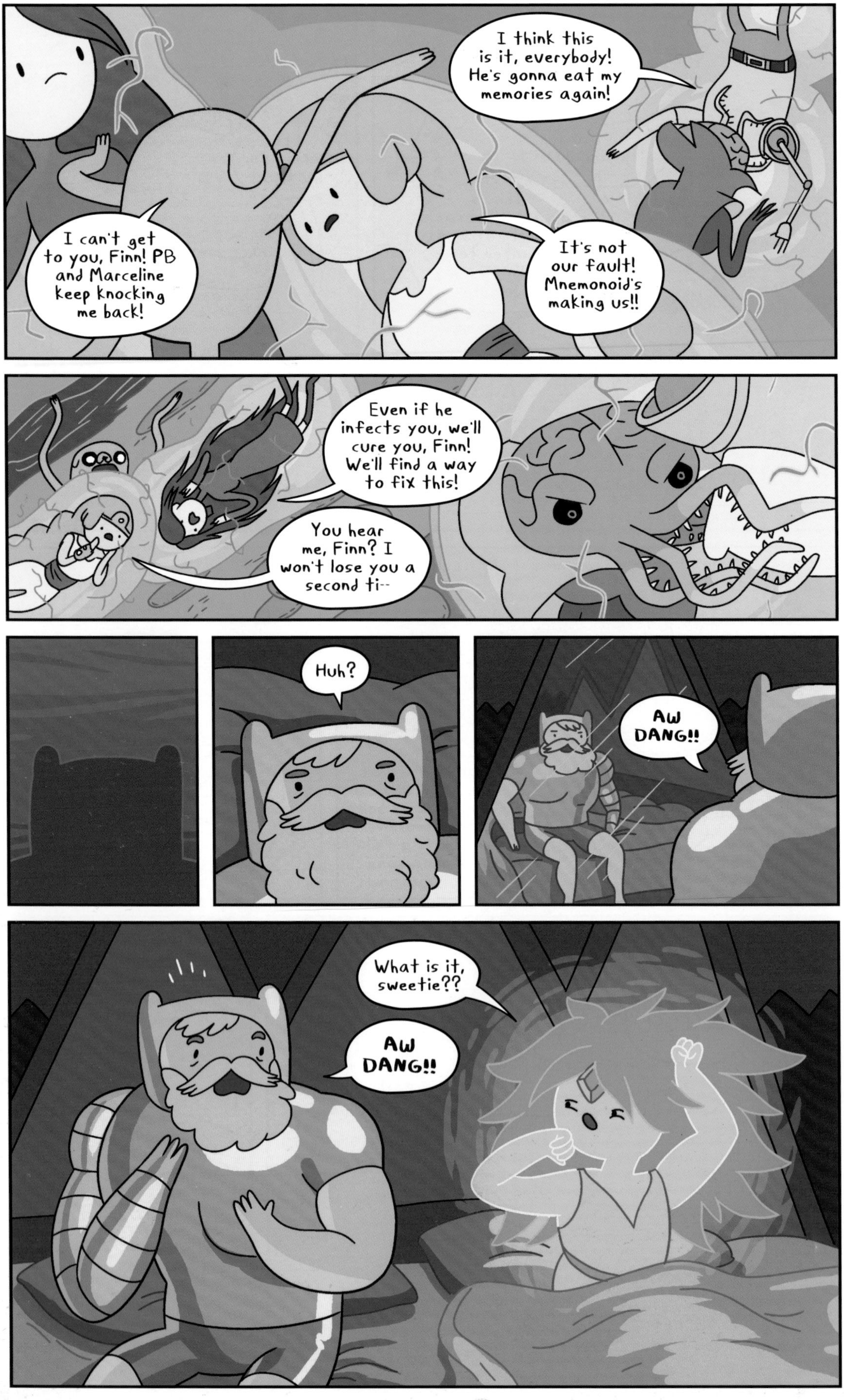
I think this is it, everybody! He's gonna eat my memories again!
I can't get to you, Finn! PB and Marceline keep knocking me back!
It's not our fault! Mnemonoid's making us!!
Even if he infects you, we'll cure you, Finn! We'll find a way to fix this!
You hear me, Finn? I won't lose you a second ti--
Huh?
AW DANG!!
What is it, sweetie??
AW DANG!!

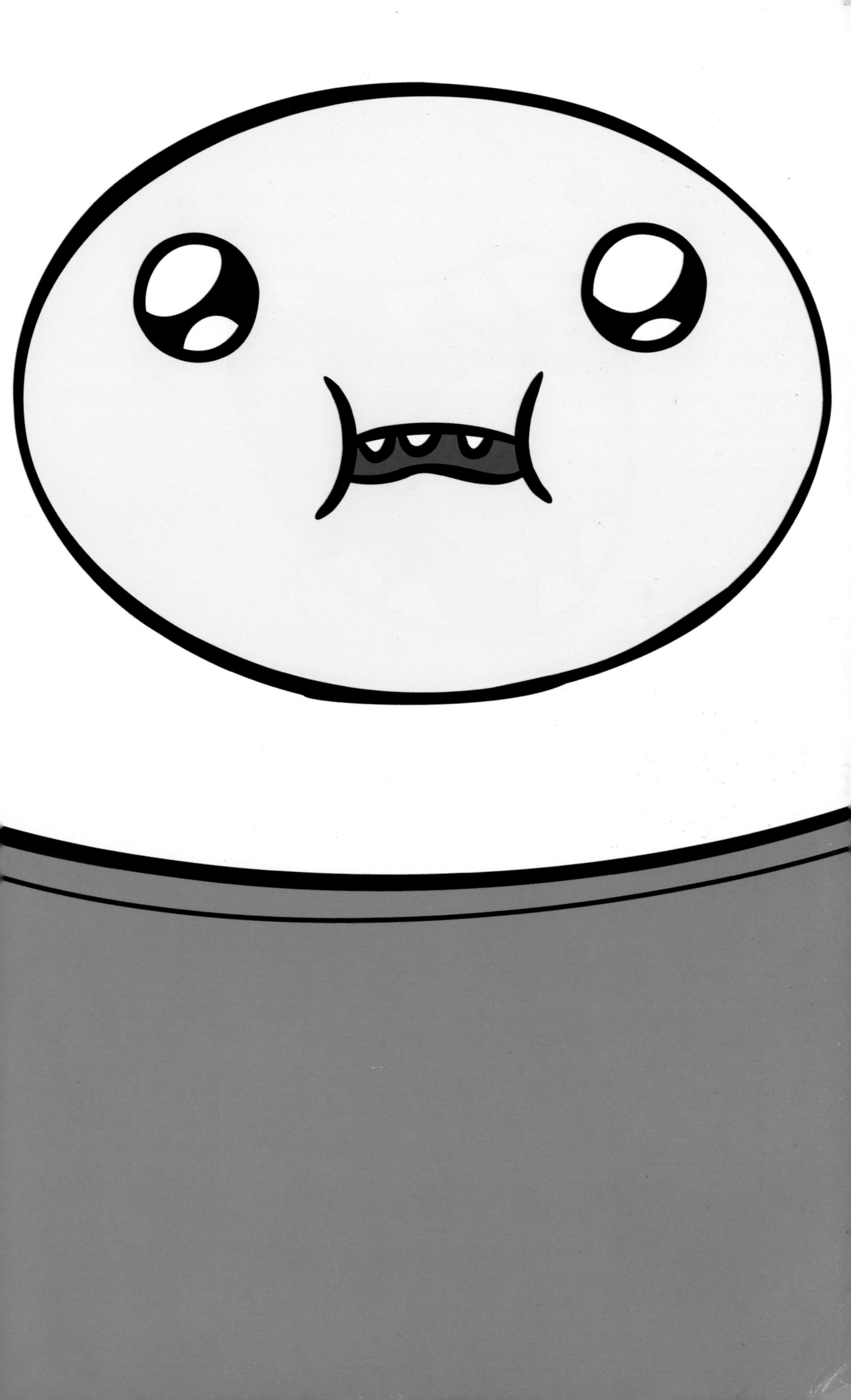

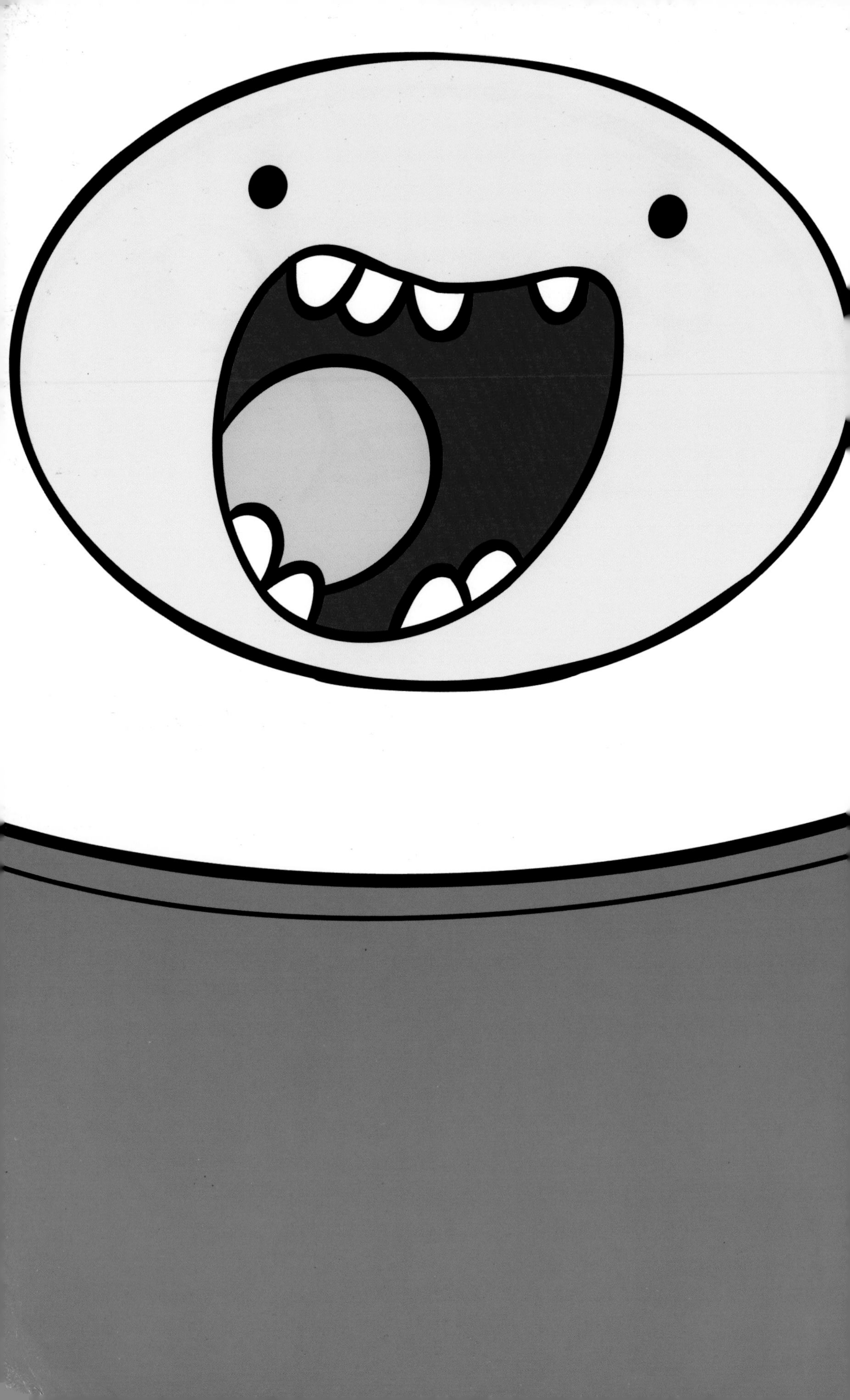

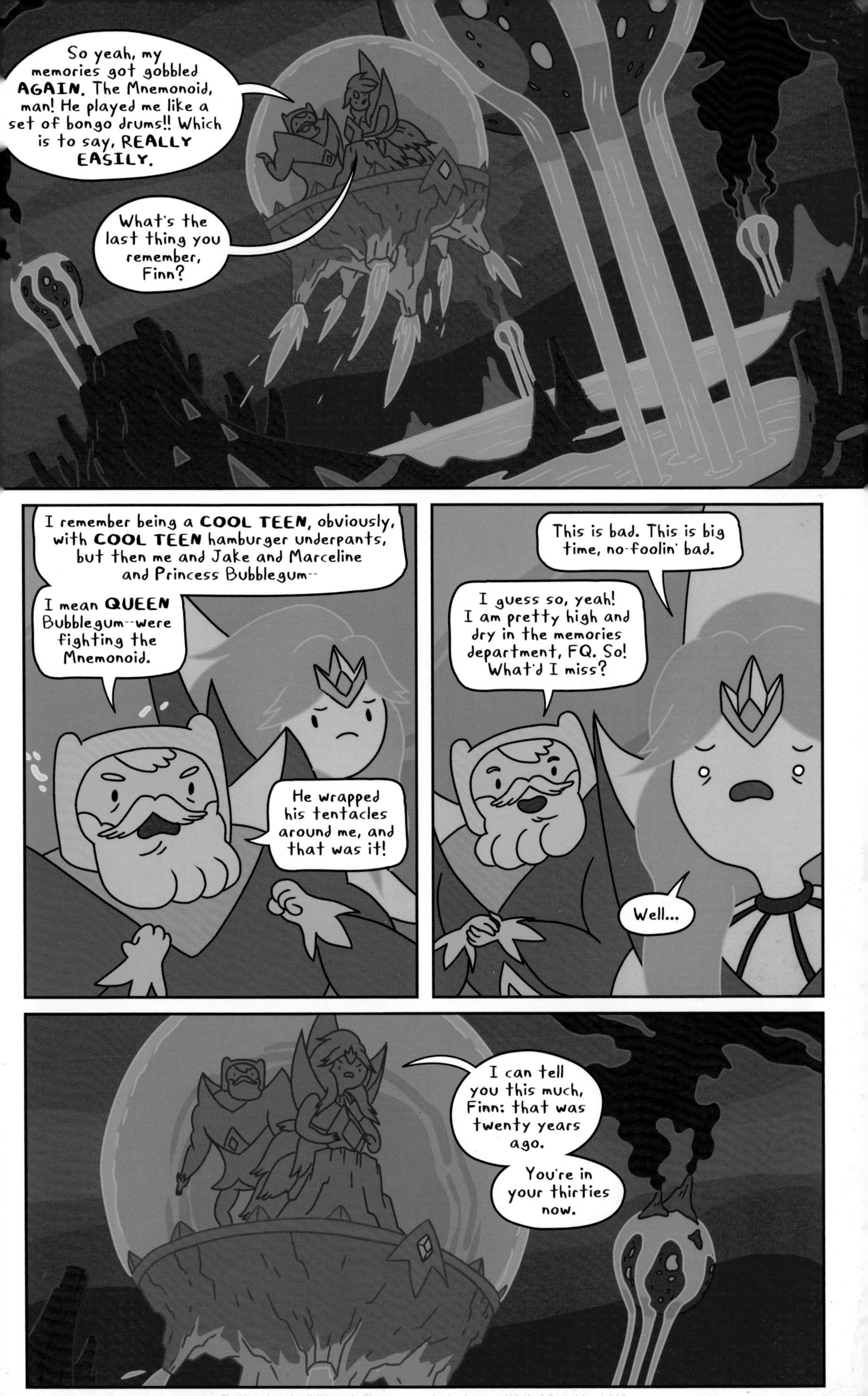

So yeah, my memories got gobbled AGAIN. The Mnemonoid, man! He played me like a set of bongo drums!! Which is to say, REALLY EASILY.
What's the last thing you remember, Finn?
I remember being a COOL TEEN, obviously, with COOL TEEN hamburger underpants, but then me and Jake and Marceline and Princess Bubblegum--
I mean QUEEN Bubblegum--were fighting the Mnemonoid.
He wrapped his tentacles around me, and that was it!
This is bad. This is big time, no-foolin' bad.
I guess so, yeah! I am pretty high and dry in the memories department, FQ. So! What'd I miss?
Well...
I can tell you this much, Finn: that was twenty years ago.
You're in your thirties now.

That's not so bad! It's probably awesome to be in your thirties! Probably, right?

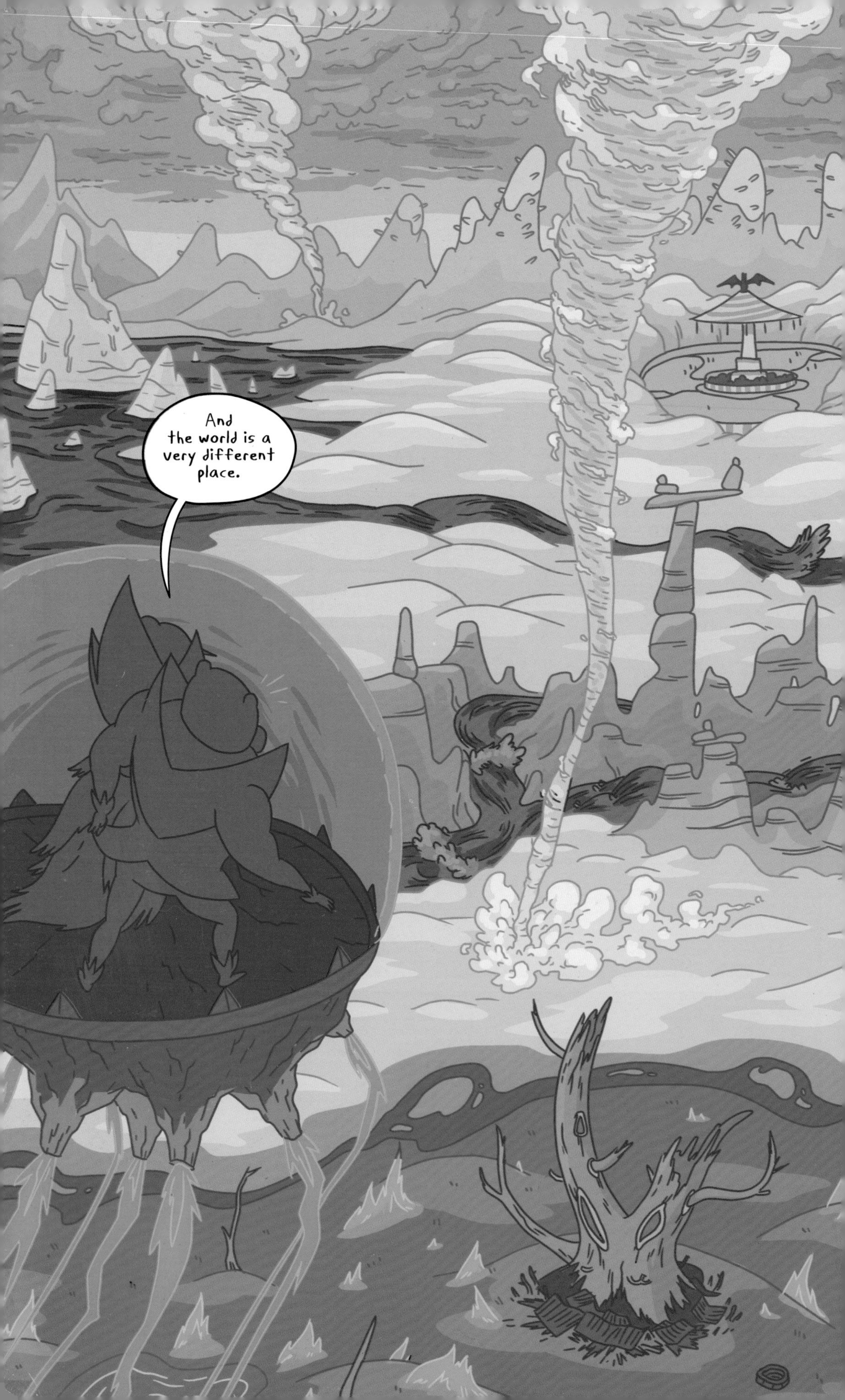
And the world is a very different place.

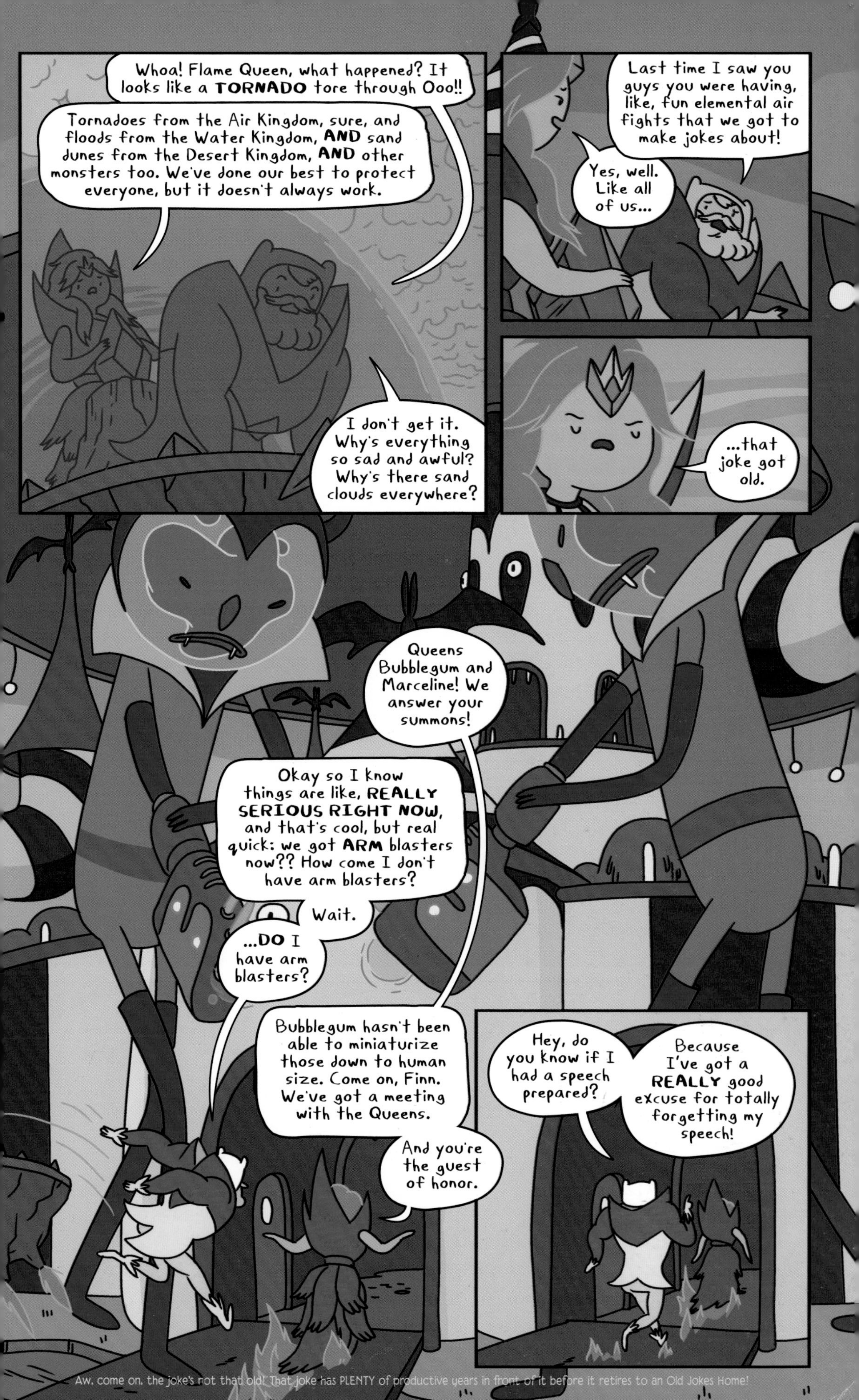
Whoa! Flame Queen, what happened? It looks like a TORNADO tore through Ooo!!
Tornadoes from the Air Kingdom, sure, and floods from the Water Kingdom, AND sand dunes from the Desert Kingdom, AND other monsters too. We've done our best to protect everyone, but it doesn't always work.
I don't get it. Why's everything so sad and awful? Why's there sand clouds everywhere?
Last time I saw you guys you were having, like, fun elemental air fights that we got to make jokes about!
Yes, well. Like all of us...
...that joke got old.
Queens Bubblegum and Marceline! We answer your summons!
Okay so I know things are like, REALLY SERIOUS RIGHT NOW, and that's cool, but real quick: we got ARM blasters now?? How come I don't have arm blasters?
Wait.
...DO I have arm blasters?
Bubblegum hasn't been able to miniaturize those down to human size. Come on, Finn. We've got a meeting with the Queens.
And you're the guest of honor.
Hey, do you know if I had a speech prepared?
Because I've got a REALLY good excuse for totally forgetting my speech!

Aw, come on, the joke's not that old! That joke has PLENTY of productive years in front of it before it retires to an Old Jokes Home!

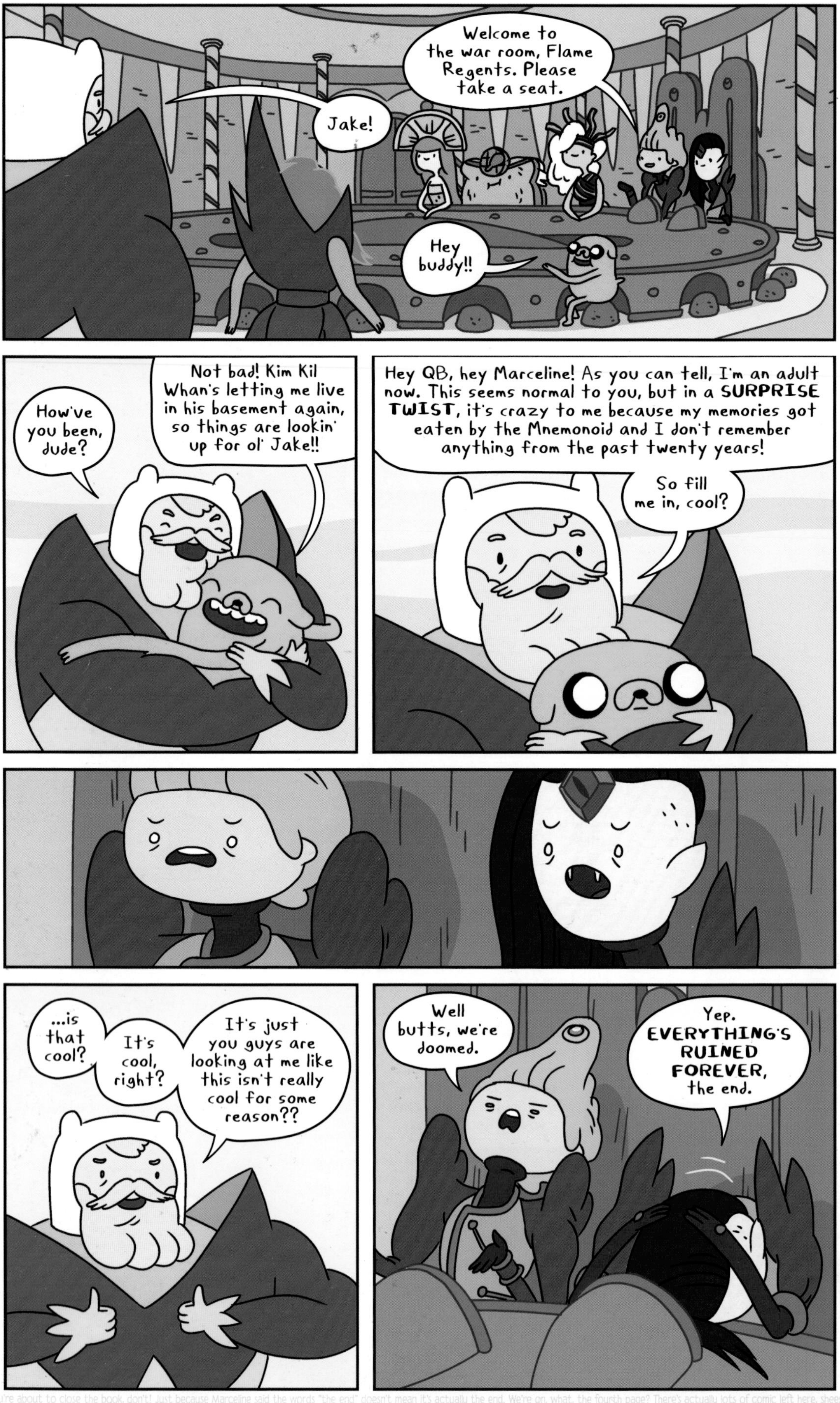
Welcome to the war room, Flame Regents. Please take a seat.
Jake!
Hey buddy!!
How've you been, dude?
Not bad! Kim Kil Whan's letting me live in his basement again, so things are lookin' up for ol' Jake!!
Hey QB, hey Marceline! As you can tell, I'm an adult now. This seems normal to you, but in a **SURPRISE TWIST**, it's crazy to me because my memories got eaten by the Mnemonoid and I don't remember anything from the past twenty years!
So fill me in, cool?
...is that cool?
It's cool, right?
It's just you guys are looking at me like this isn't really cool for some reason??
Well butts, we're doomed.
Yep. **EVERYTHING'S RUINED FOREVER,** the end.

If you're about to close the book, don't! Just because Marceline said the words "the end," doesn't mean it's actually the end. We're on, what, the fourth page? There's actually lots of comic left here, sheesh!!

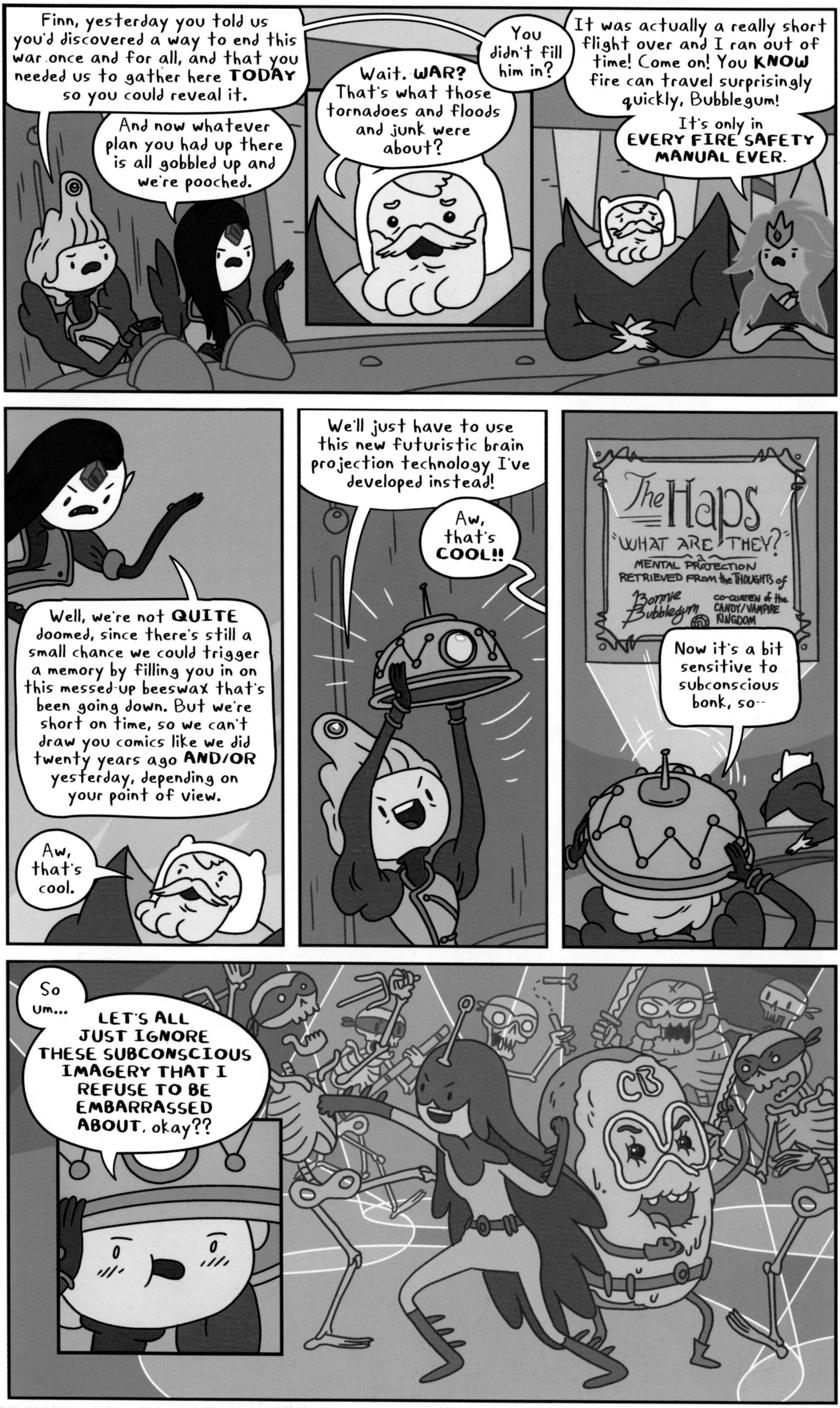

Finn, yesterday you told us you'd discovered a way to end this war once and for all, and that you needed us to gather here **TODAY** so you could reveal it.
And now whatever plan you had up there is all gobbled up and we're pooched.
Wait. **WAR?** That's what those tornadoes and floods and junk were about?
You didn't fill him in?
It was actually a really short flight over and I ran out of time! Come on! You **KNOW** fire can travel surprisingly quickly, Bubblegum!
It's only in **EVERY FIRE SAFETY MANUAL EVER**.
Well, we're not **QUITE** doomed, since there's still a small chance we could trigger a memory by filling you in on this messed-up beeswax that's been going down. But we're short on time, so we can't draw you comics like we did twenty years ago **AND/OR** yesterday, depending on your point of view.
Aw, that's cool.
We'll just have to use this new futuristic brain projection technology I've developed instead!
Aw, that's **COOL!!**
The Haps
"WHAT ARE THEY?"
a
MENTAL PROJECTION
RETRIEVED FROM the THOUGHTS of
Bonnie Bubblegum
CO-QUEEN of the CANDY/VAMPIRE KINGDOM
Now it's a bit sensitive to subconscious bonk, so--
So um...
LET'S ALL JUST IGNORE THESE SUBCONSCIOUS IMAGERY THAT I REFUSE TO BE EMBARRASSED ABOUT, okay??
CB

f you're about to ignore that second-last panel, don't! Just because QB said to doesn't mean you have to. In fact, let's all commit it to memory because it's actually pretty awesome and looks like a lot of fun!

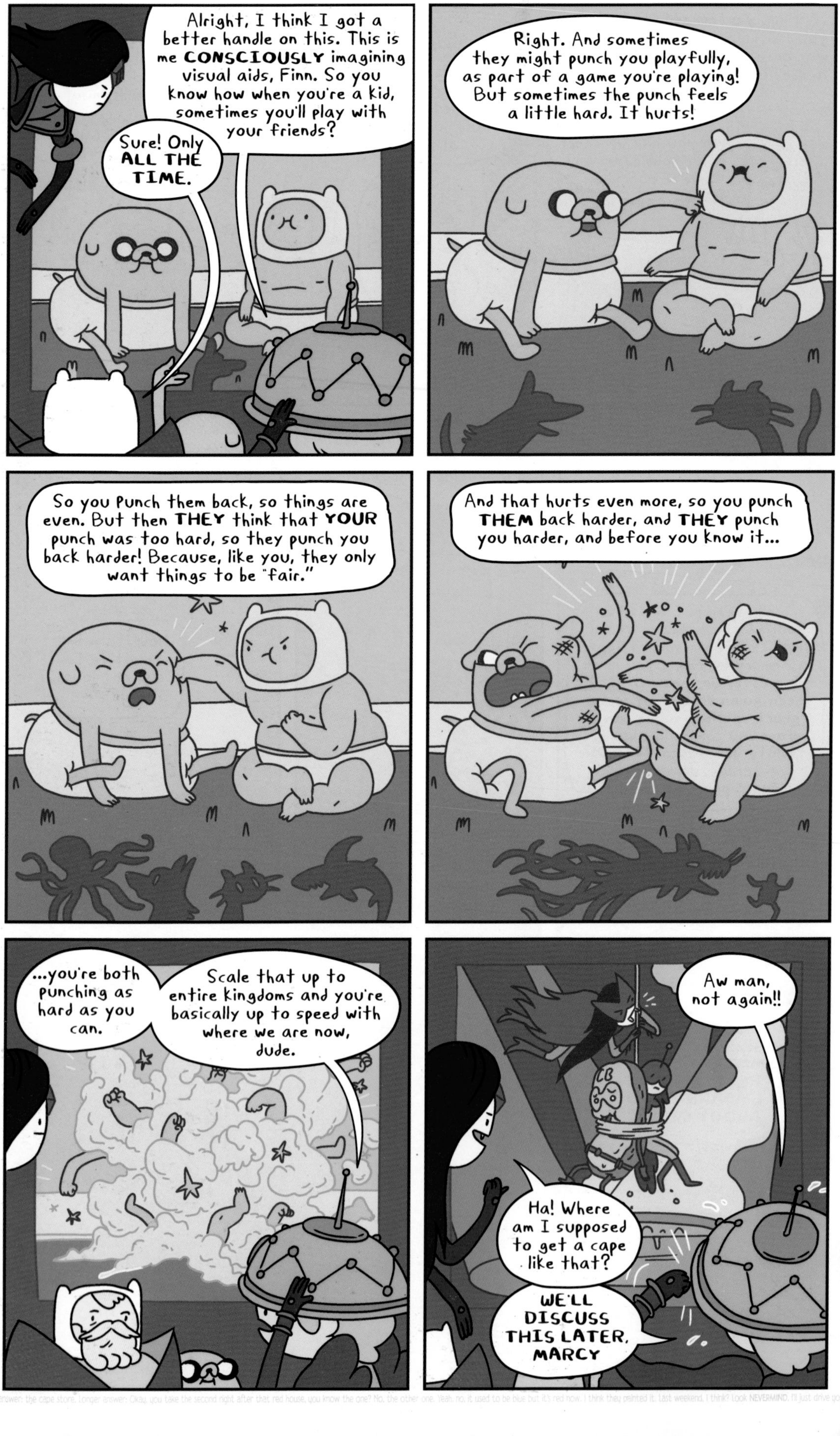

Alright, I think I got a better handle on this. This is me CONSCIOUSLY imagining visual aids, Finn. So you know how when you're a kid, sometimes you'll play with your friends?
Sure! Only ALL THE TIME.
Right. And sometimes they might punch you playfully, as part of a game you're playing! But sometimes the punch feels a little hard. It hurts!
So you punch them back, so things are even. But then THEY think that YOUR punch was too hard, so they punch you back harder! Because, like you, they only want things to be "fair."
And that hurts even more, so you punch THEM back harder, and THEY punch you harder, and before you know it...
...you're both punching as hard as you can.
Scale that up to entire kingdoms and you're basically up to speed with where we are now, dude.
Aw man, not again!!
Ha! Where am I supposed to get a cape like that?
WE'LL DISCUSS THIS LATER, MARCY

Short answer: the cape store. Longer answer: Okay, you take the second right after that red house, you know the one? No, the other one. Yeah, no, it used to be blue but it's red now. I think they painted it. Last weekend, I think? Look **NEVERMIND**. I'll just drive you.

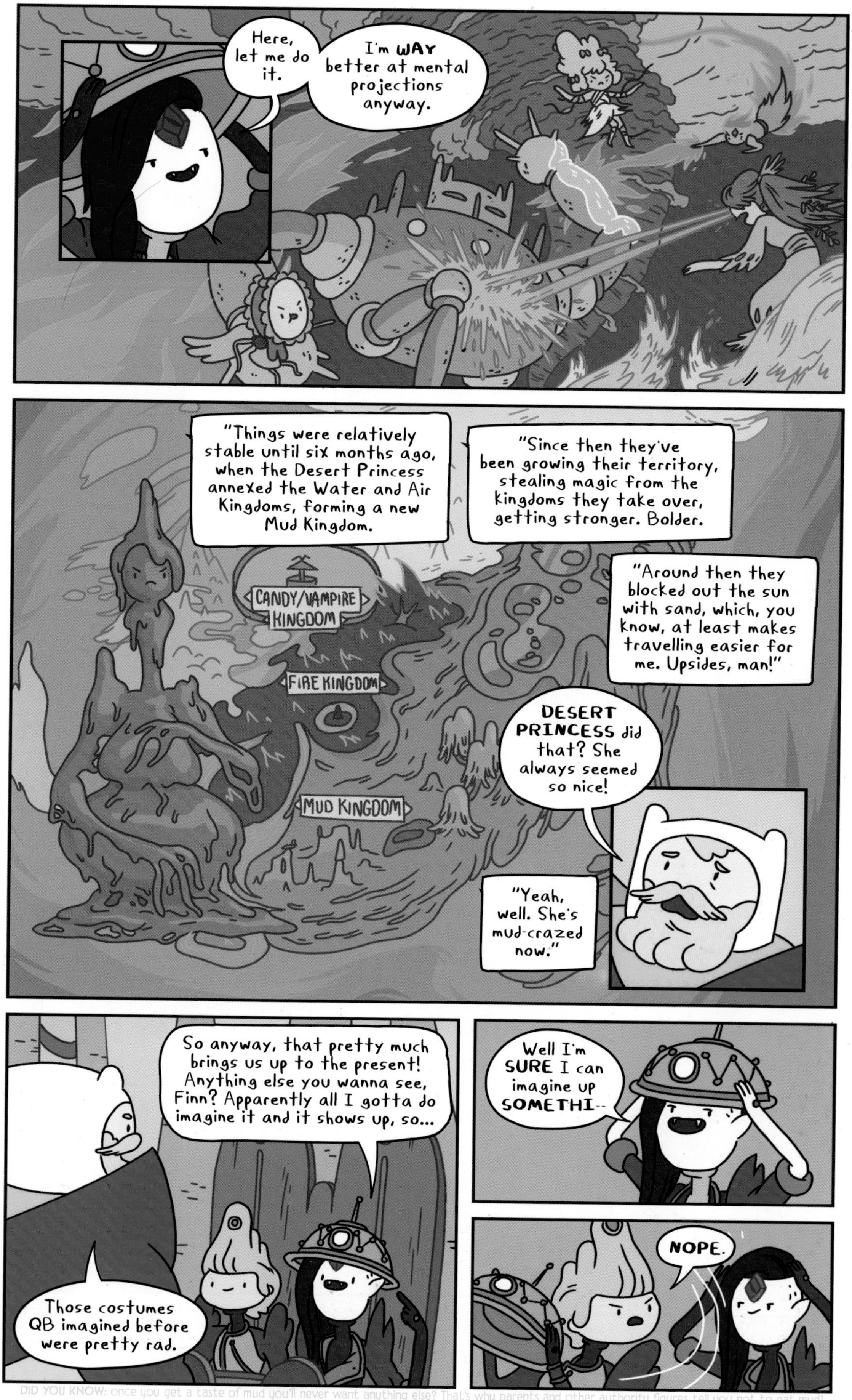
Here, let me do it.
I'm WAY better at mental projections anyway.
"Things were relatively stable until six months ago, when the Desert Princess annexed the Water and Air Kingdoms, forming a new Mud Kingdom.
"Since then they've been growing their territory, stealing magic from the kingdoms they take over, getting stronger. Bolder.
CANDY/VAMPIRE KINGDOM
FIRE KINGDOM
MUD KINGDOM
"Around then they blocked out the sun with sand, which, you know, at least makes travelling easier for me. Upsides, man!"
DESERT PRINCESS did that? She always seemed so nice!
"Yeah, well. She's mud-crazed now."
So anyway, that pretty much brings us up to the present! Anything else you wanna see, Finn? Apparently all I gotta do imagine it and it shows up, so...
Those costumes QB imagined before were pretty rad.
Well I'm SURE I can imagine up SOMETHI--
NOPE.

DID YOU KNOW: once you get a taste of mud you'll never want anything else? That's why parents and other authority figures tell you not to eat mud! **THEY WANT IT ALL FOR THEMSELVES.** This may or may not be an actual fact!

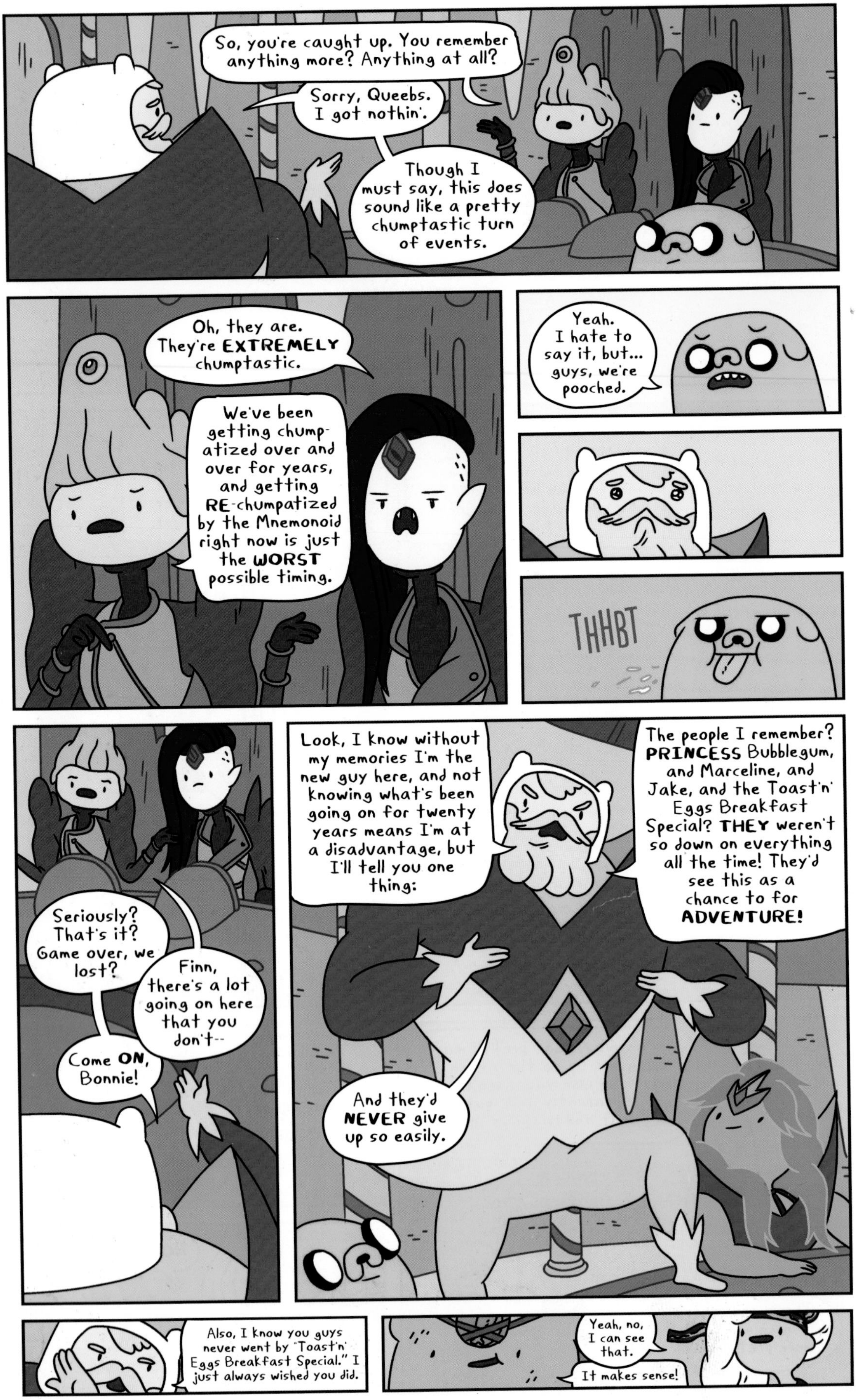

So, you're caught up. You remember anything more? Anything at all?
Sorry, Queebs. I got nothin'.
Though I must say, this does sound like a pretty chumptastic turn of events.
Oh, they are. They're EXTREMELY chumptastic.
We've been getting chump-atized over and over for years, and getting RE-chumpatized by the Mnemonoid right now is just the WORST possible timing.
Yeah. I hate to say it, but... guys, we're pooched.
THHBT
Seriously? That's it? Game over, we lost?
Finn, there's a lot going on here that you don't--
Come ON, Bonnie!
Look, I know without my memories I'm the new guy here, and not knowing what's been going on for twenty years means I'm at a disadvantage, but I'll tell you one thing:
The people I remember? PRINCESS Bubblegum, and Marceline, and Jake, and the Toast'n' Eggs Breakfast Special? THEY weren't so down on everything all the time! They'd see this as a chance to for ADVENTURE!
And they'd NEVER give up so easily.
Also, I know you guys never went by "Toast'n' Eggs Breakfast Special." I just always wished you did.
Yeah, no, I can see that.
It makes sense!

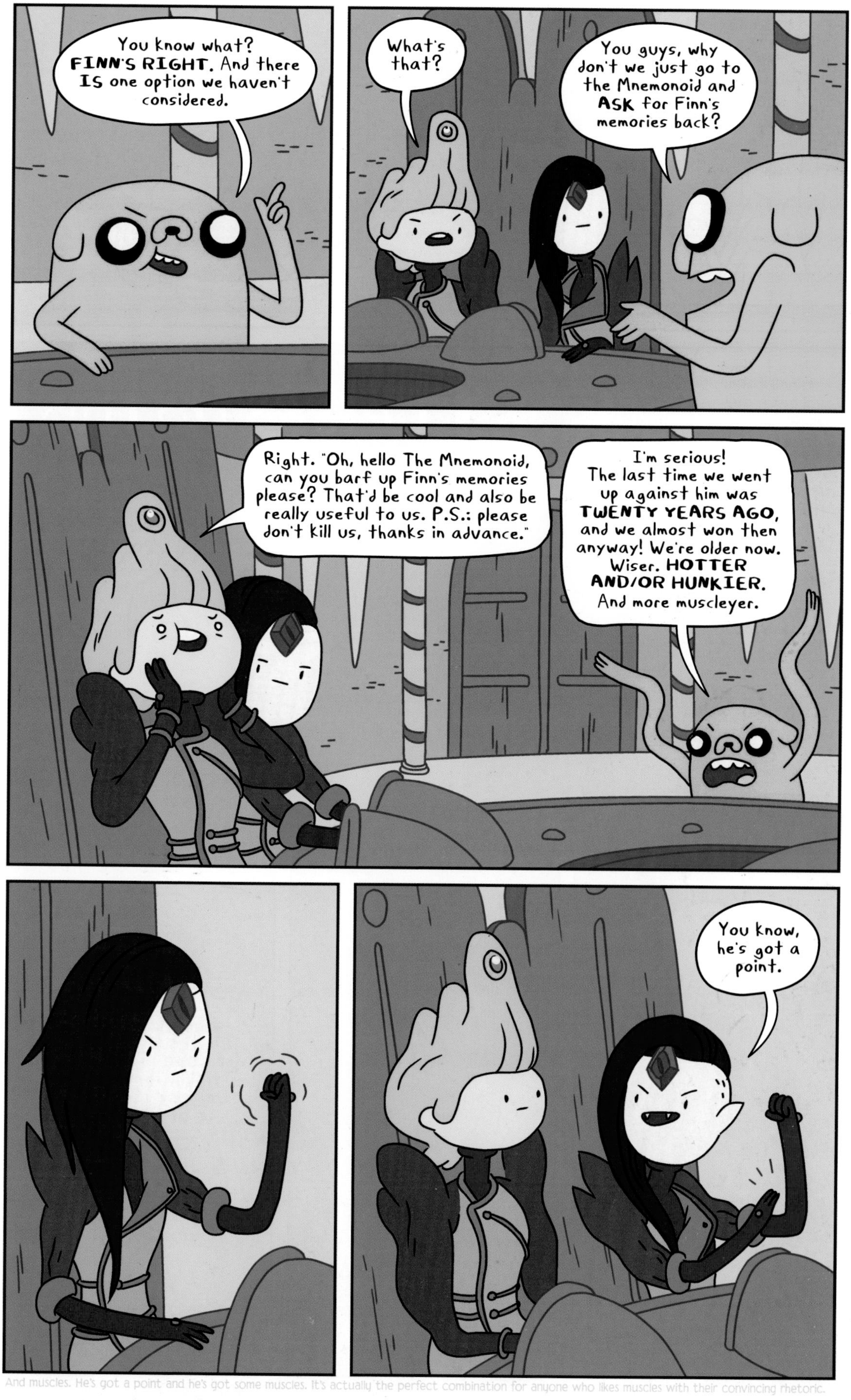
You know what? **FINN'S RIGHT.** And there **IS** one option we haven't considered.
What's that?
You guys, why don't we just go to the Mnemonoid and **ASK** for Finn's memories back?
Right. "Oh, hello The Mnemonoid, can you barf up Finn's memories please? That'd be cool and also be really useful to us. P.S.: please don't kill us, thanks in advance."
I'm serious! The last time we went up against him was **TWENTY YEARS AGO,** and we almost won then anyway! We're older now. Wiser. **HOTTER AND/OR HUNKIER.** And more muscleyer.
You know, he's got a point.

And muscles. He's got a point and he's got some muscles. It's actually the perfect combination for anyone who likes muscles with their convincing rhetoric.

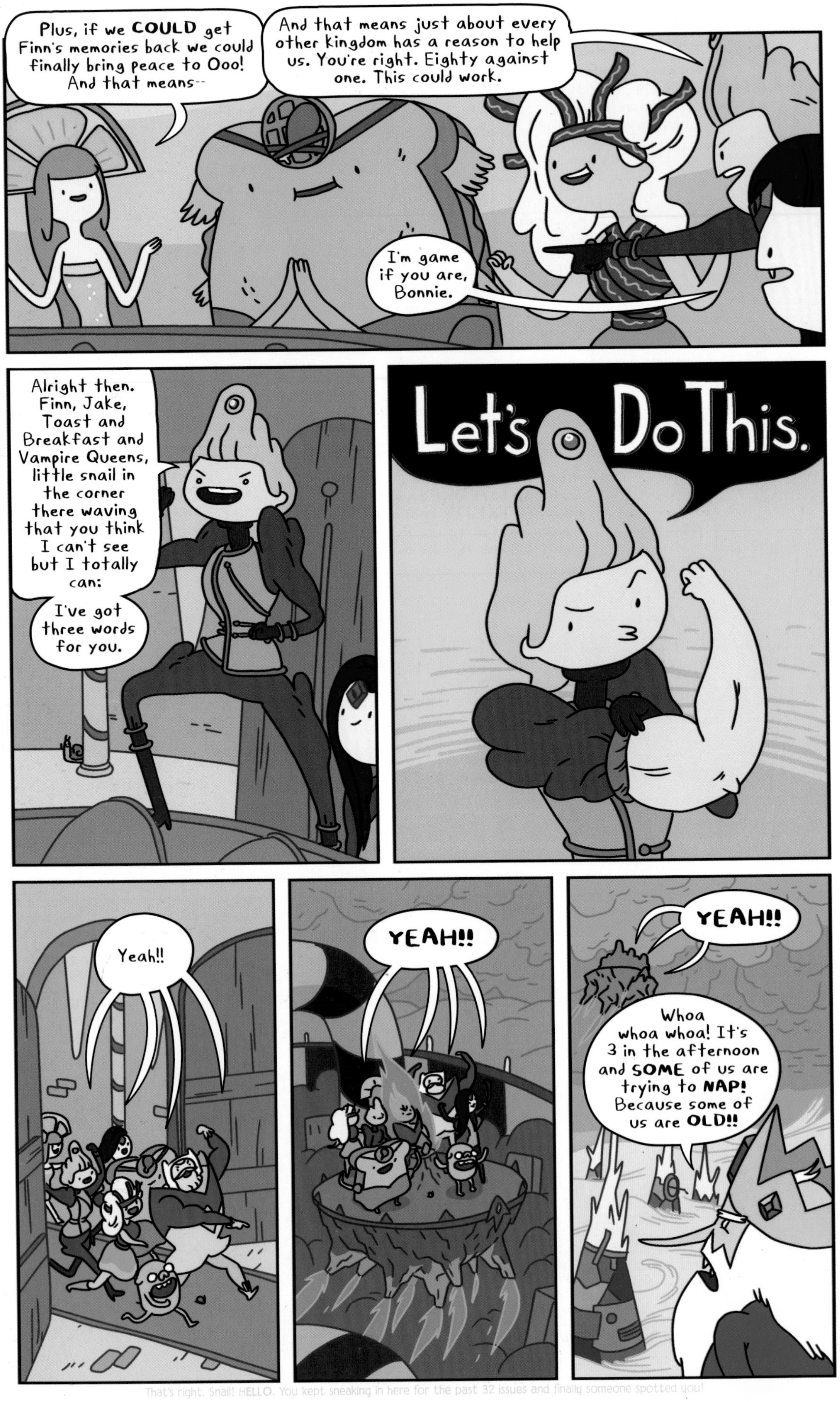
Plus, if we COULD get Finn's memories back we could finally bring peace to Ooo! And that means--
And that means just about every other kingdom has a reason to help us. You're right. Eighty against one. This could work.
I'm game if you are, Bonnie.
Alright then. Finn, Jake, Toast and Breakfast and Vampire Queens, little snail in the corner there waving that you think I can't see but I totally can:
I've got three words for you.
Let's Do This.
Yeah!!
YEAH!!
YEAH!!
Whoa whoa whoa! It's 3 in the afternoon and SOME of us are trying to NAP! Because some of us are OLD!!

That's right, Snail! HELLO. You kept sneaking in here for the past 32 issues and finally someone spotted you!

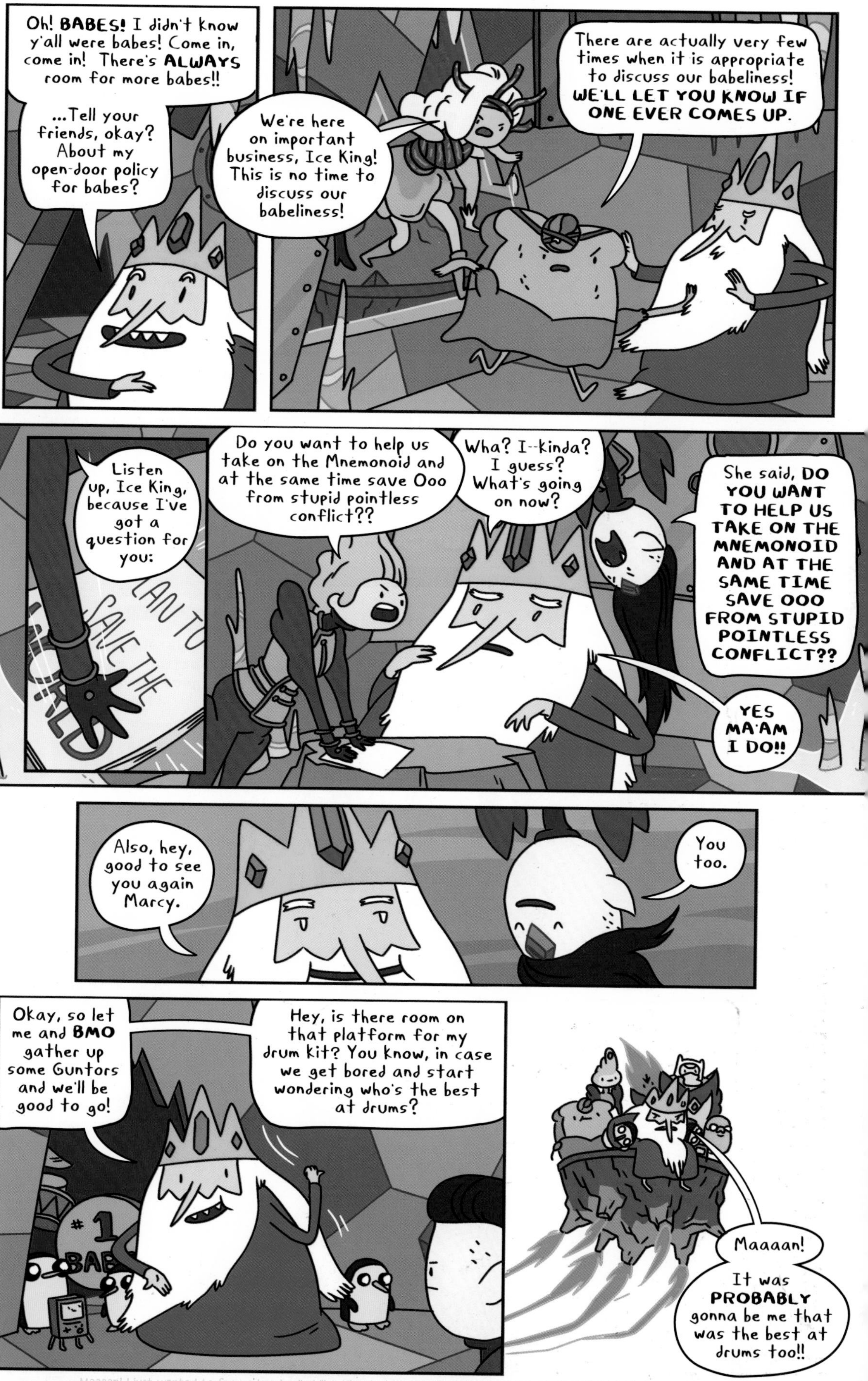
Oh! BABES! I didn't know y'all were babes! Come in, come in! There's ALWAYS room for more babes!!
...Tell your friends, okay? About my open-door policy for babes?
We're here on important business, Ice King! This is no time to discuss our babeliness!
There are actually very few times when it is appropriate to discuss our babeliness! WE'LL LET YOU KNOW IF ONE EVER COMES UP.
Listen up, Ice King, because I've got a question for you:
PLAN TO SAVE THE WORLD
Do you want to help us take on the Mnemonoid and at the same time save Ooo from stupid pointless conflict??
Wha? I--kinda? I guess? What's going on now?
She said, DO YOU WANT TO HELP US TAKE ON THE MNEMONOID AND AT THE SAME TIME SAVE OOO FROM STUPID POINTLESS CONFLICT??
YES MA'AM I DO!!
Also, hey, good to see you again Marcy.
You too.
Okay, so let me and BMO gather up some Guntors and we'll be good to go!
Hey, is there room on that platform for my drum kit? You know, in case we get bored and start wondering who's the best at drums?
#1 BAB
Maaaan!
It was PROBABLY gonna be me that was the best at drums too!!

Maaaan! I just wanted to form a band called "Ice King And His #1 Babes", and no, I actually DON'T think that's too much to ask.

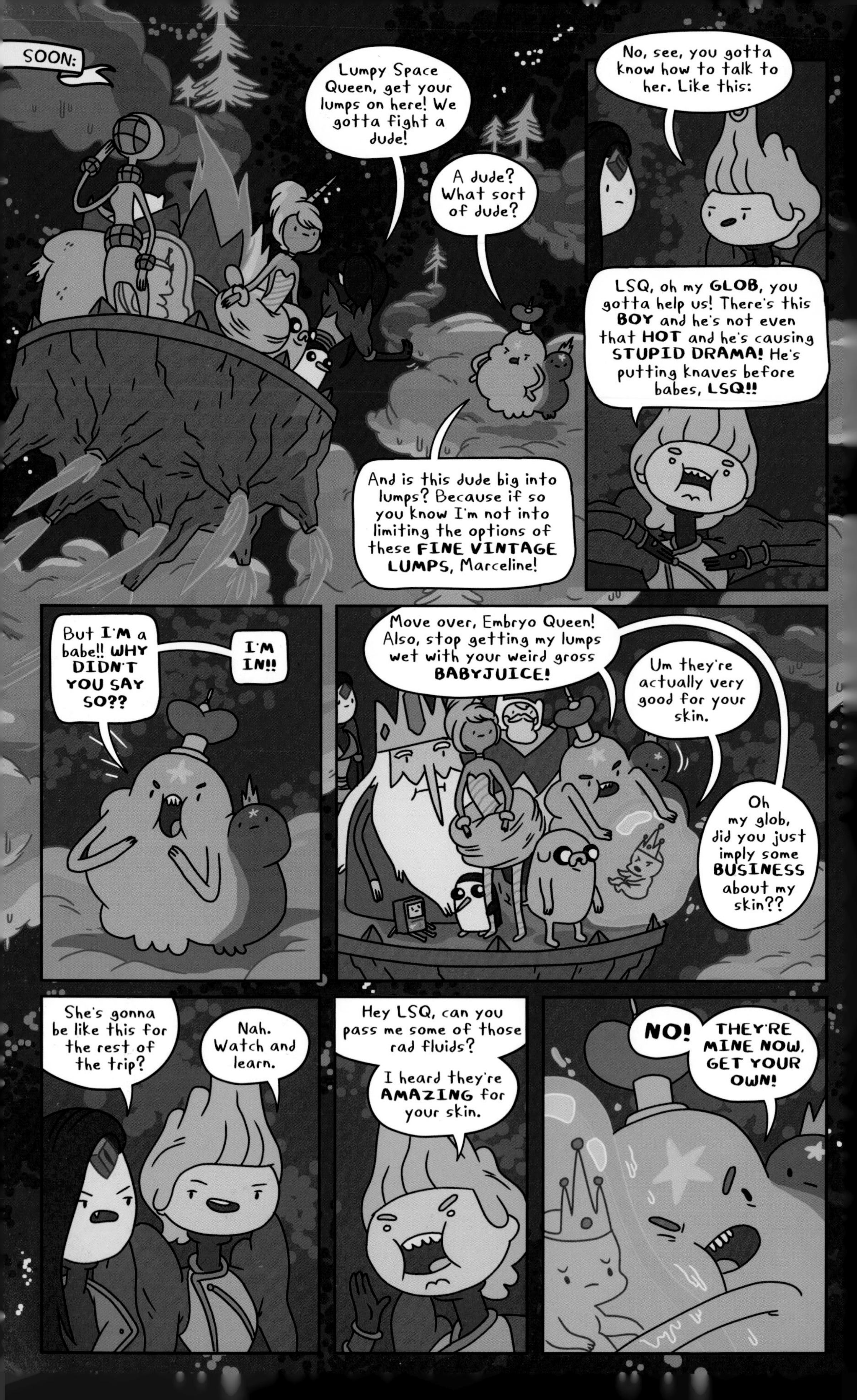

SOON:
Lumpy Space Queen, get your lumps on here! We gotta fight a dude!
A dude? What sort of dude?
And is this dude big into lumps? Because if so you know I'm not into limiting the options of these FINE VINTAGE LUMPS, Marceline!
No, see, you gotta know how to talk to her. Like this:
LSQ, oh my GLOB, you gotta help us! There's this BOY and he's not even that HOT and he's causing STUPID DRAMA! He's putting knaves before babes, LSQ!!
But I'M a babe!! WHY DIDN'T YOU SAY SO??
I'M IN!!
Move over, Embryo Queen! Also, stop getting my lumps wet with your weird gross BABYJUICE!
Um they're actually very good for your skin.
Oh my glob, did you just imply some BUSINESS about my skin??
She's gonna be like this for the rest of the trip?
Nah. Watch and learn.
Hey LSQ, can you pass me some of those rad fluids?
I heard they're AMAZING for your skin.
NO!
THEY'RE MINE NOW, GET YOUR OWN!

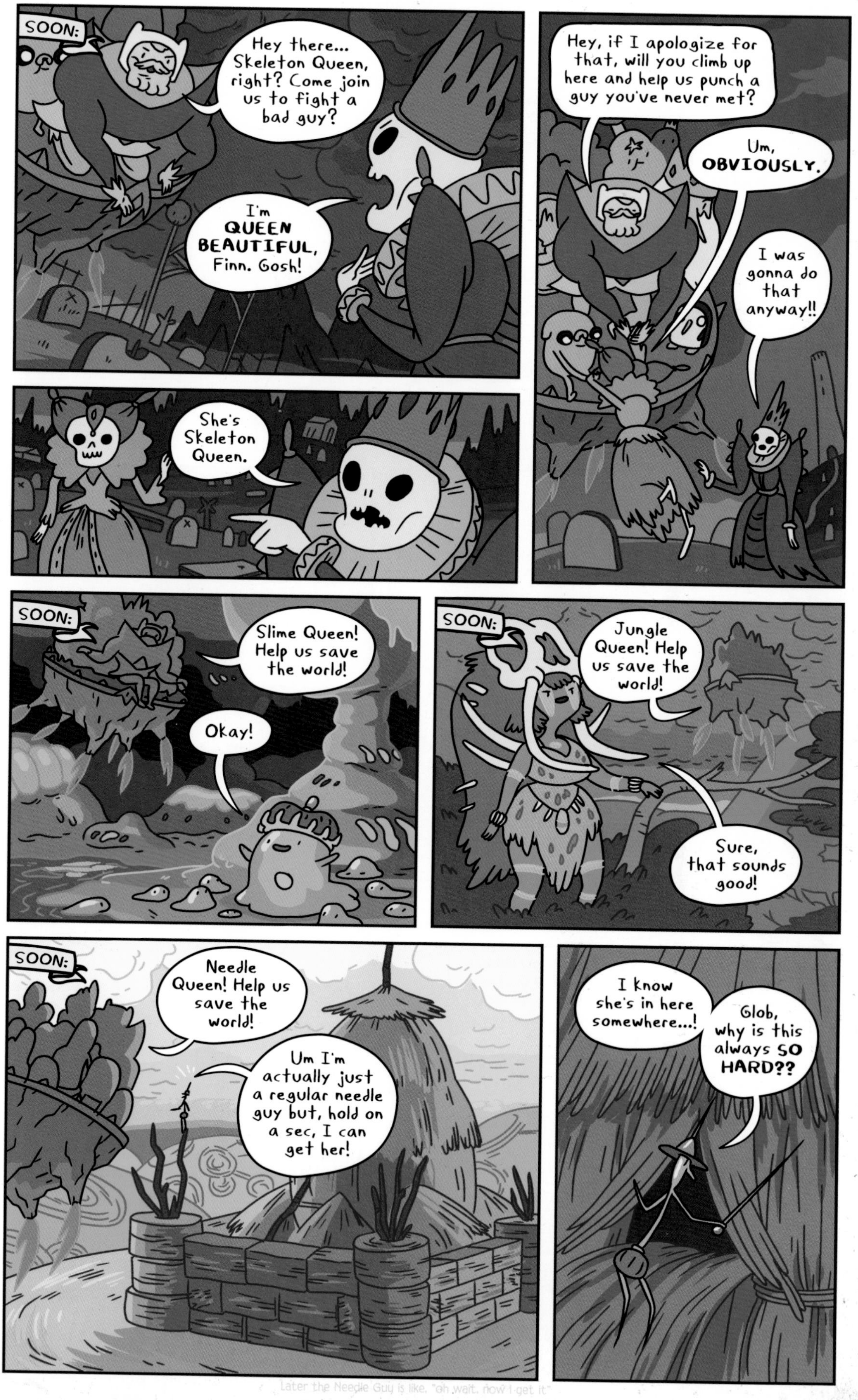
SOON:
Hey there... Skeleton Queen, right? Come join us to fight a bad guy?
I'm QUEEN BEAUTIFUL, Finn. Gosh!
She's Skeleton Queen.
Hey, if I apologize for that, will you climb up here and help us punch a guy you've never met?
Um, OBVIOUSLY.
I was gonna do that anyway!!
SOON:
Slime Queen! Help us save the world!
Okay!
SOON:
Jungle Queen! Help us save the world!
Sure, that sounds good!
SOON:
Needle Queen! Help us save the world!
Um I'm actually just a regular needle guy but, hold on a sec, I can get her!
I know she's in here somewhere...!
Glob, why is this always SO HARD??

Later the Needle Guy is like, "oh wait, now I get it"

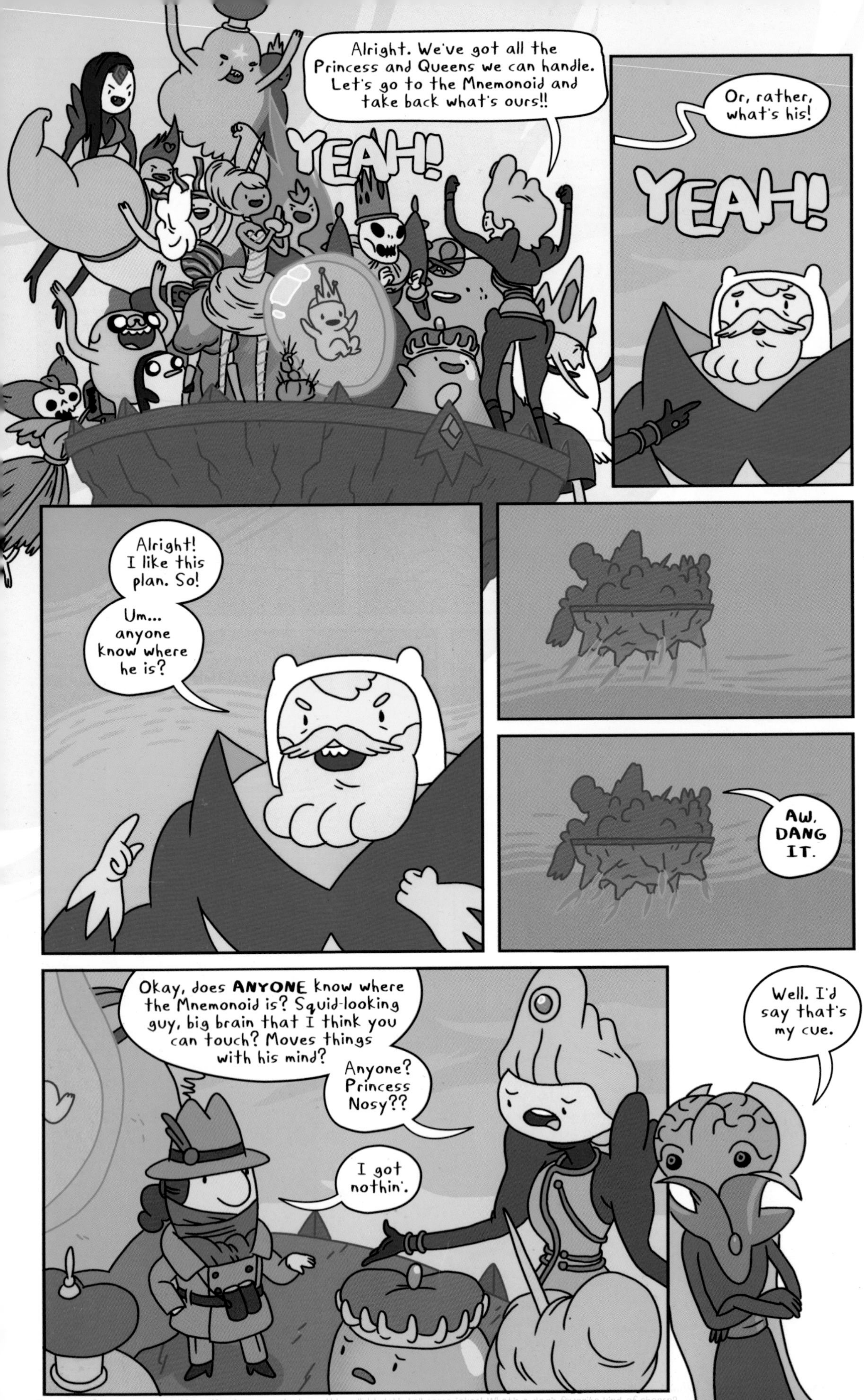
Alright. We've got all the Princess and Queens we can handle. Let's go to the Mnemonoid and take back what's ours!!
YEAH!
Or, rather, what's his!
YEAH!
Alright! I like this plan. So!
Um... anyone know where he is?
AW, DANG IT.
Okay, does ANYONE know where the Mnemonoid is? Squid-looking guy, big brain that I think you can touch? Moves things with his mind?
Anyone? Princess Nosy??
I got nothin'.
Well. I'd say that's my cue.

These next few pages are pretty action-heavy, so to keep things light, let's tell some jokes! What's a dog's favorite kind of cheese?

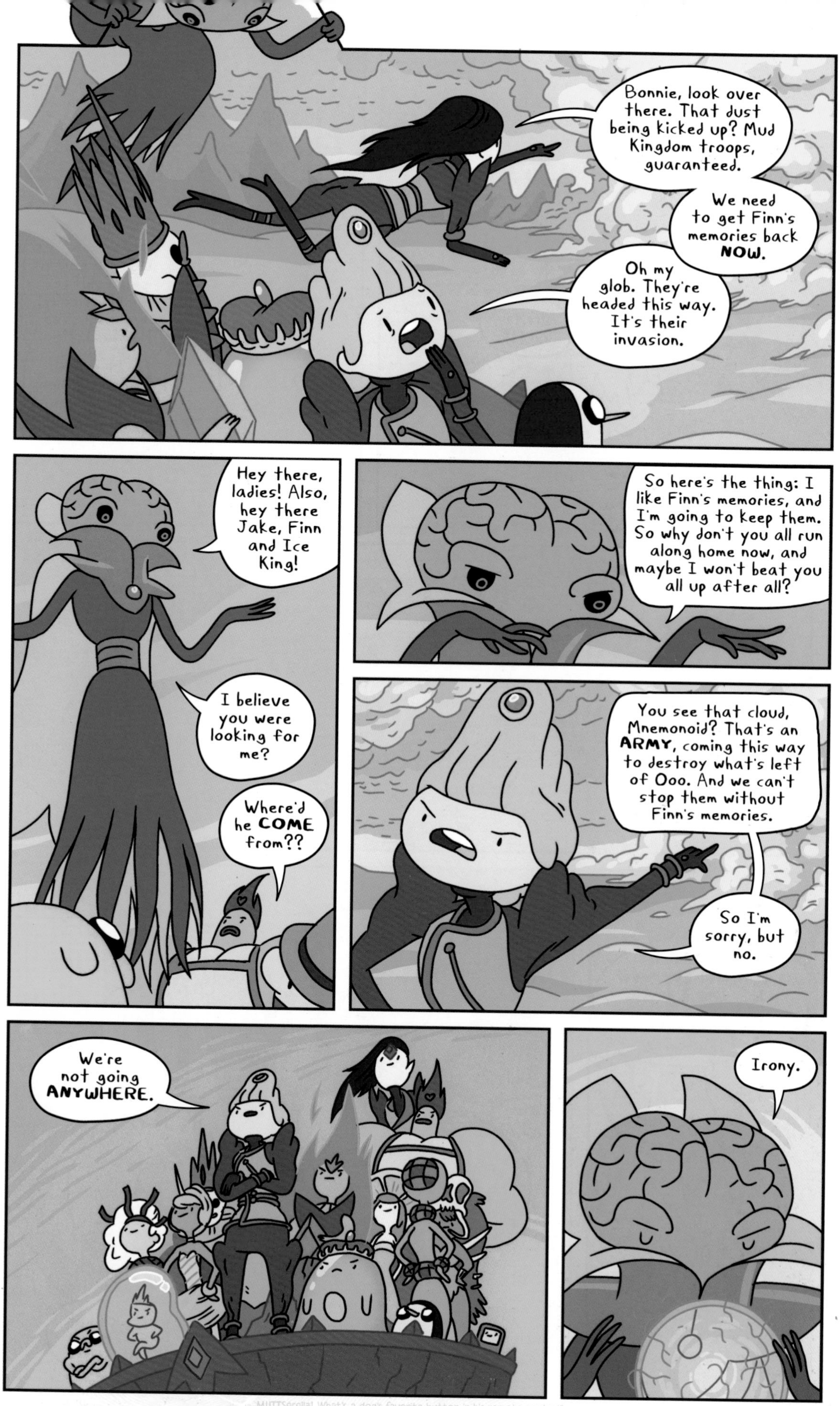
Bonnie, look over there. That dust being kicked up? Mud Kingdom troops, guaranteed.
We need to get Finn's memories back **NOW.**
Oh my glob. They're headed this way. It's their invasion.
Hey there, ladies! Also, hey there Jake, Finn and Ice King!
I believe you were looking for me?
Where'd he **COME** from??
So here's the thing: I like Finn's memories, and I'm going to keep them. So why don't you all run along home now, and maybe I won't beat you all up after all?
You see that cloud, Mnemonoid? That's an **ARMY**, coming this way to destroy what's left of Ooo. And we can't stop them without Finn's memories.
So I'm sorry, but no.
We're not going **ANYWHERE.**
Irony.

MUTTSerella! What's a dog's favorite button in his remote control?

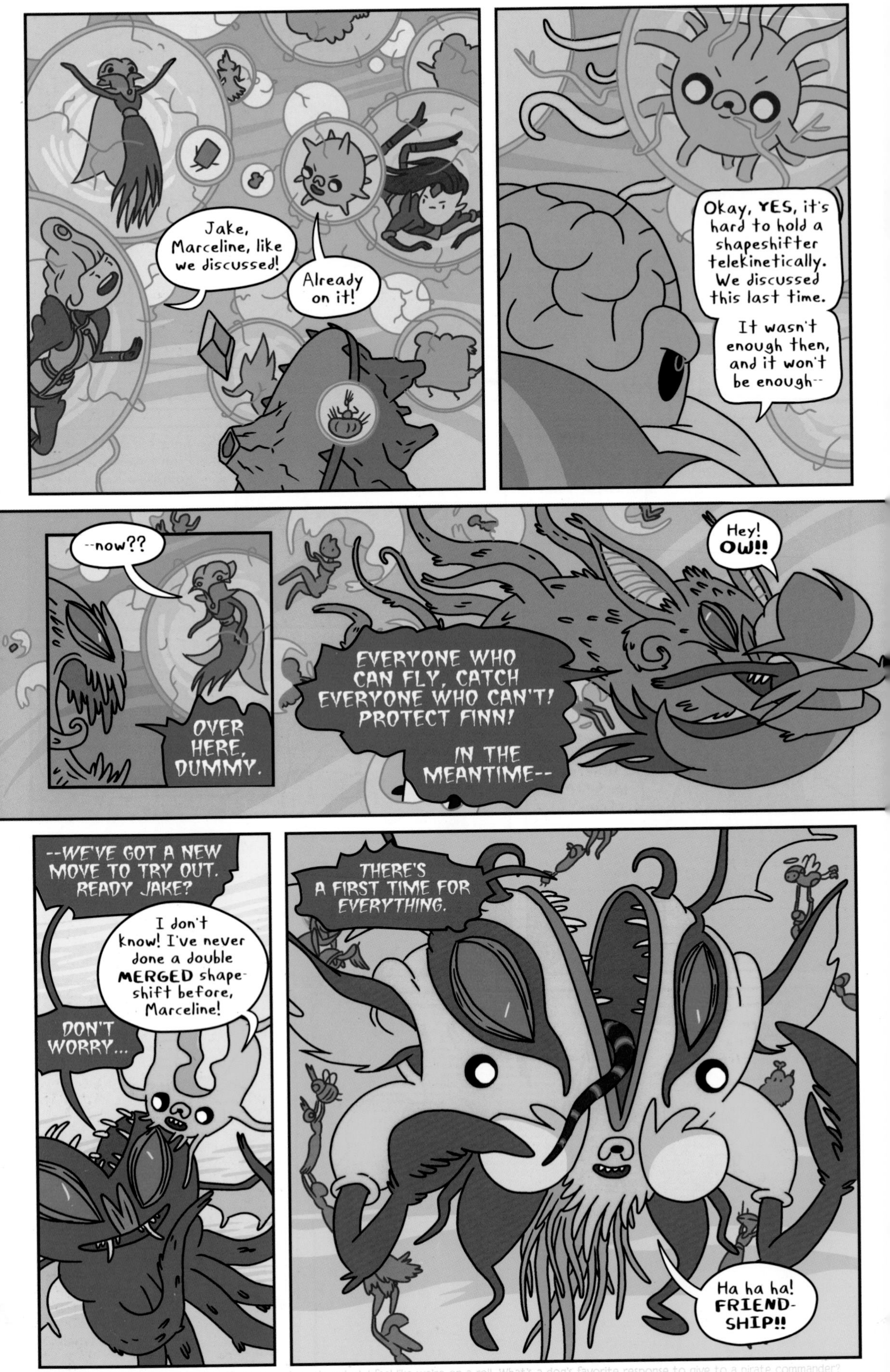
Jake, Marceline, like we discussed!
Already on it!
Okay, YES, it's hard to hold a shapeshifter telekinetically. We discussed this last time.
It wasn't enough then, and it won't be enough--
--now??
OVER HERE, DUMMY.
EVERYONE WHO CAN FLY, CATCH EVERYONE WHO CAN'T! PROTECT FINN!
IN THE MEANTIME--
Hey! OW!!
--WE'VE GOT A NEW MOVE TO TRY OUT. READY JAKE?
I don't know! I've never done a double MERGED shape-shift before, Marceline!
DON'T WORRY...
THERE'S A FIRST TIME FOR EVERYTHING.
Ha ha ha! FRIEND-SHIP!!

PAWS (like "pause"!). I'm making these up as I go along but I feel like we're on a roll. What's a dog's favorite response to give to a pirate commander?

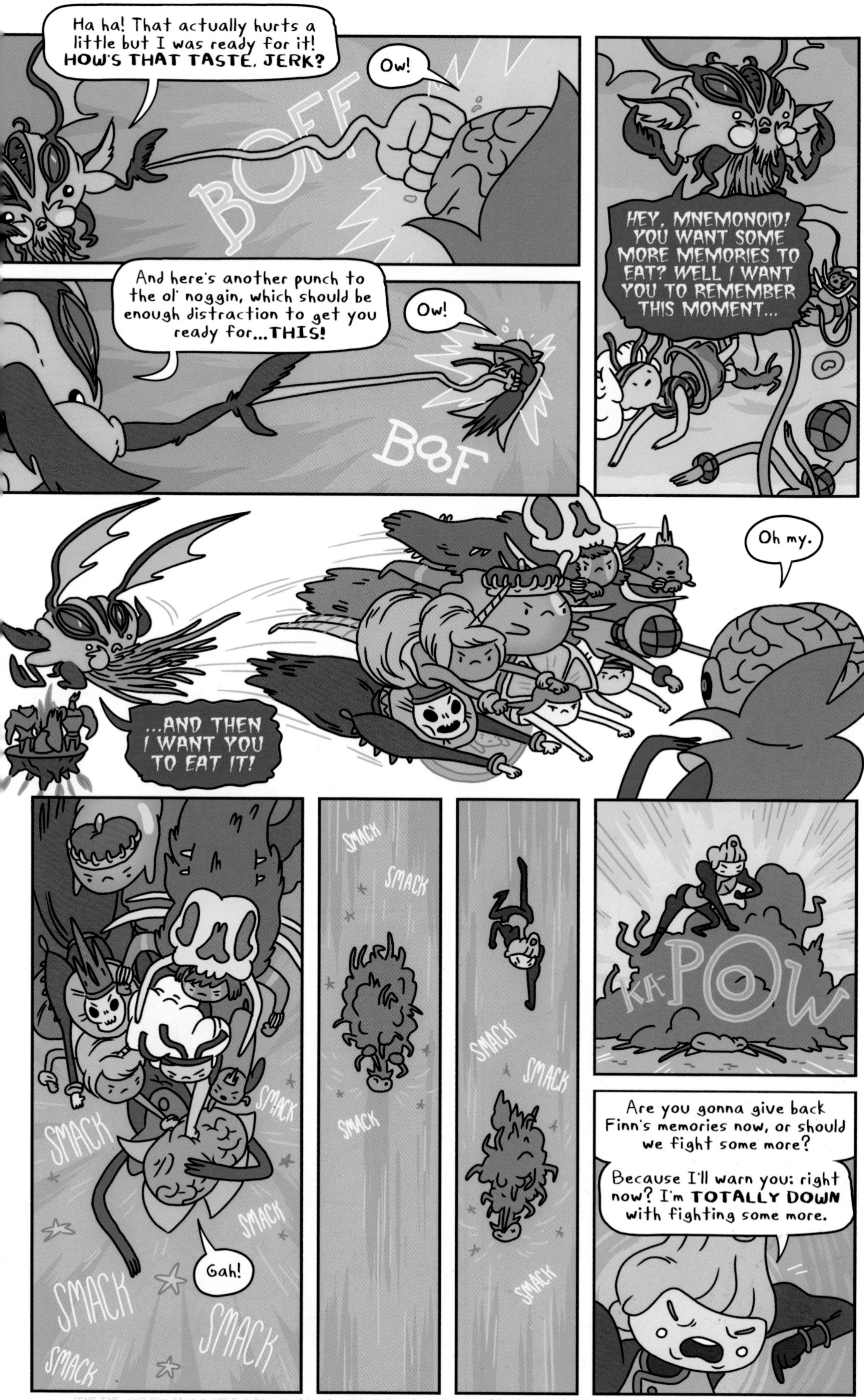
Ha ha! That actually hurts a little but I was ready for it! **HOW'S THAT TASTE, JERK?**
Ow!
BOFF
HEY, MNEMONOID! YOU WANT SOME MORE MEMORIES TO EAT? WELL I WANT YOU TO REMEMBER THIS MOMENT...
And here's another punch to the ol' noggin, which should be enough distraction to get you ready for...**THIS!**
Ow!
BOOF
Oh my.
...AND THEN I WANT YOU TO EAT IT!
SMACK
SMACK
SMACK
SMACK
SMACK
SMACK
SMACK
Gah!
SMACK
SMACK
SMACK
SMACK
SMACK
SMACK
SMACK
KA-POW
Are you gonna give back Finn's memories now, or should we fight some more?
Because I'll warn you: right now? I'm **TOTALLY DOWN** with fighting some more.

"EYE EYE, sir!" (like "Aye aye"? But "eye eye" because most dogs have two eyes? Look, comedy is hard, alright. We're all doing our best here.)

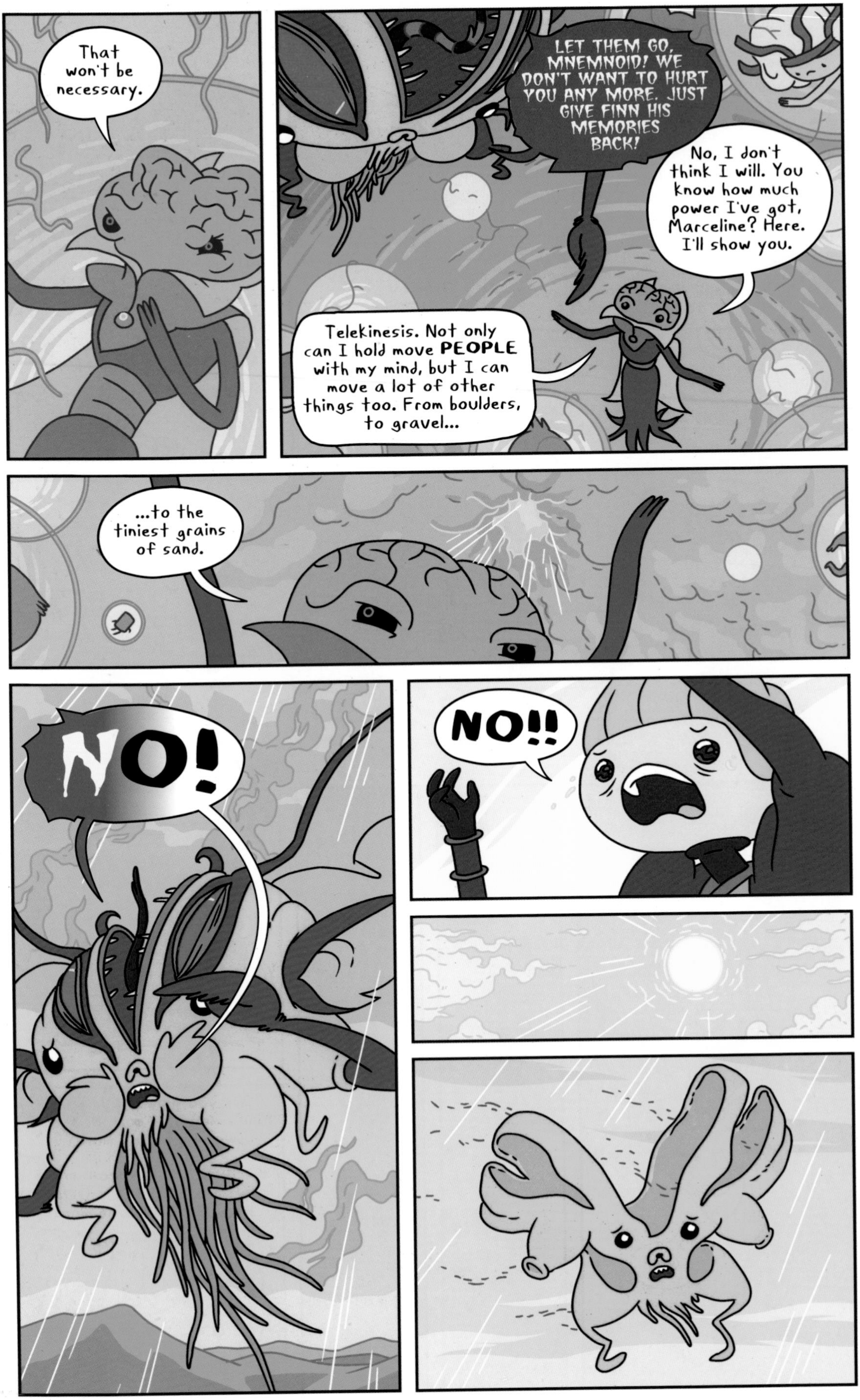

That won't be necessary.
LET THEM GO, MNEMNOID! WE DON'T WANT TO HURT YOU ANY MORE. JUST GIVE FINN HIS MEMORIES BACK!
No, I don't think I will. You know how much power I've got, Marceline? Here. I'll show you.
Telekinesis. Not only can I hold move PEOPLE with my mind, but I can move a lot of other things too. From boulders, to gravel...
...to the tiniest grains of sand.
NO!
NO!!

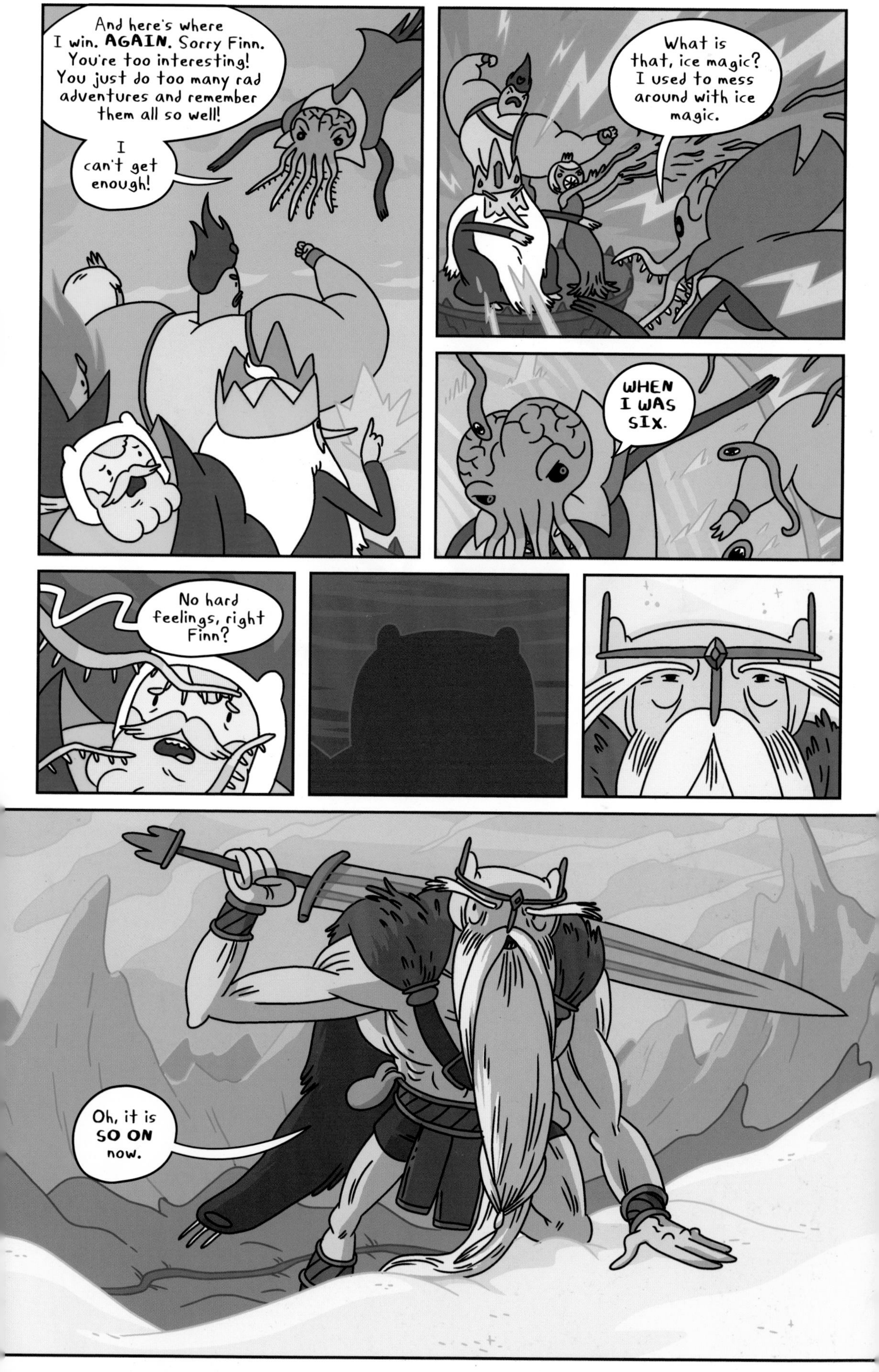
And here's where I win. **AGAIN.** Sorry Finn. You're too interesting! You just do too many rad adventures and remember them all so well!
I can't get enough!
What is that, ice magic? I used to mess around with ice magic.
WHEN I WAS SIX.
No hard feelings, right Finn?
Oh, it is **SO ON** now.

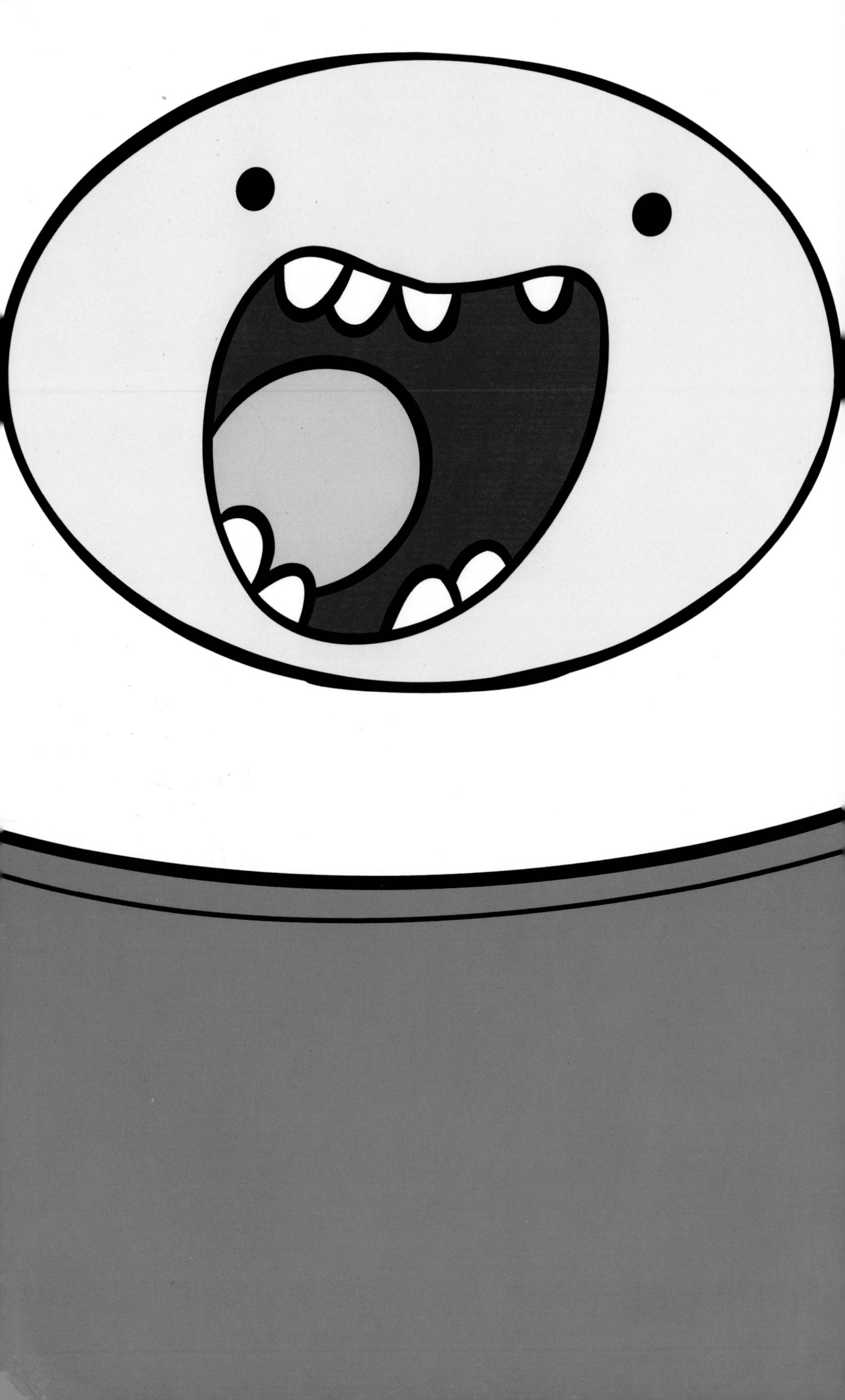

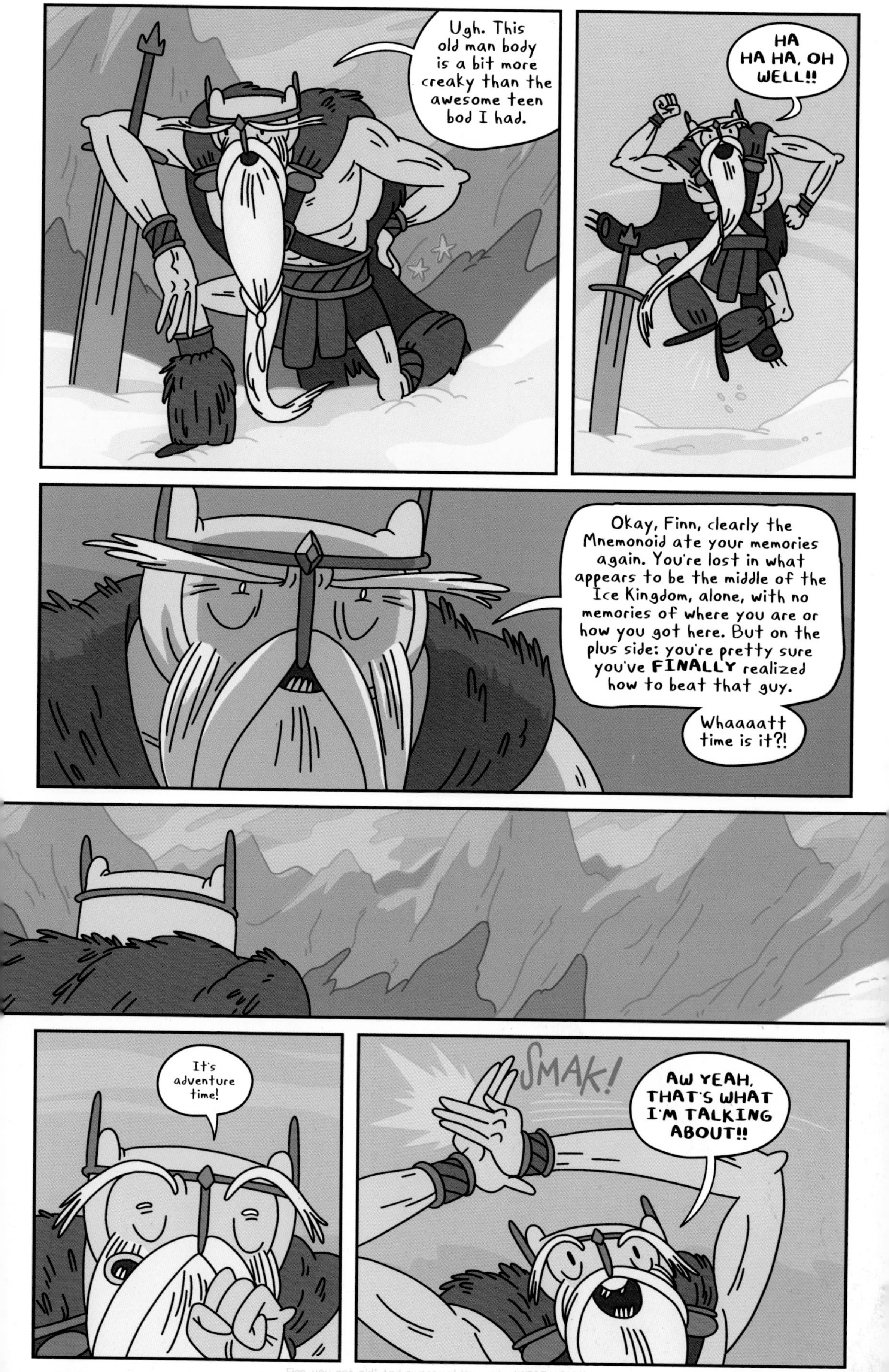
Ugh. This old man body is a bit more creaky than the awesome teen bod I had.
HA HA HA, OH WELL!!
Okay, Finn, clearly the Mnemonoid ate your memories again. You're lost in what appears to be the middle of the Ice Kingdom, alone, with no memories of where you are or how you got here. But on the plus side: you're pretty sure you've FINALLY realized how to beat that guy.
Whaaaatt time is it?!
It's adventure time!
SMAK!
AW YEAH, THAT'S WHAT I'M TALKING ABOUT!!

Finn, you got old! And awesome! You got...AWESOMOLD!!

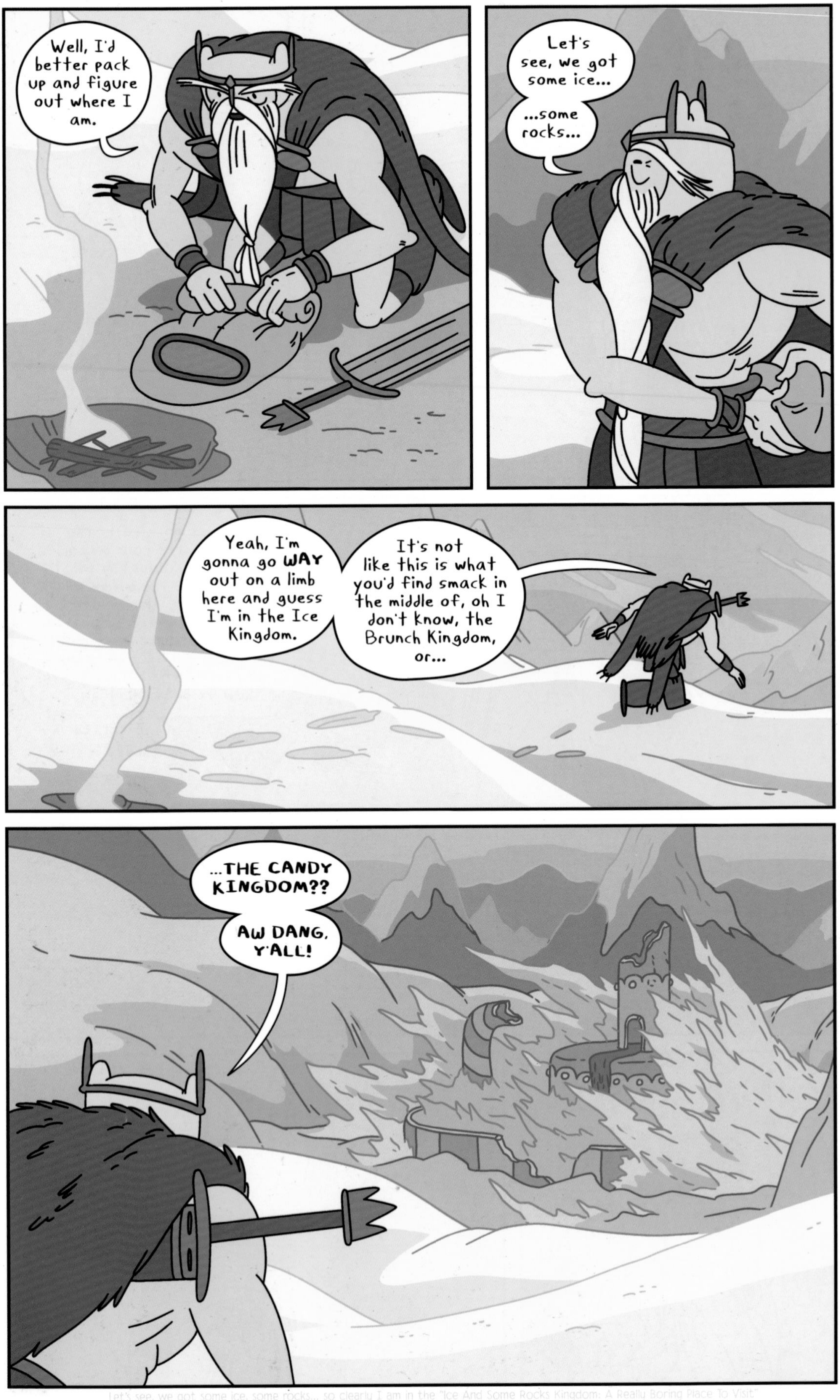
Well, I'd better pack up and figure out where I am.
Let's see, we got some ice...
...some rocks...
Yeah, I'm gonna go **WAY** out on a limb here and guess I'm in the Ice Kingdom.
It's not like this is what you'd find smack in the middle of, oh I don't know, the Brunch Kingdom, or...
...THE CANDY KINGDOM??
AW DANG, Y'ALL!

Let's see, we got some ice, some rocks... so clearly I am in the "Ice And Some Rocks Kingdom: A Really Boring Place To Visit"

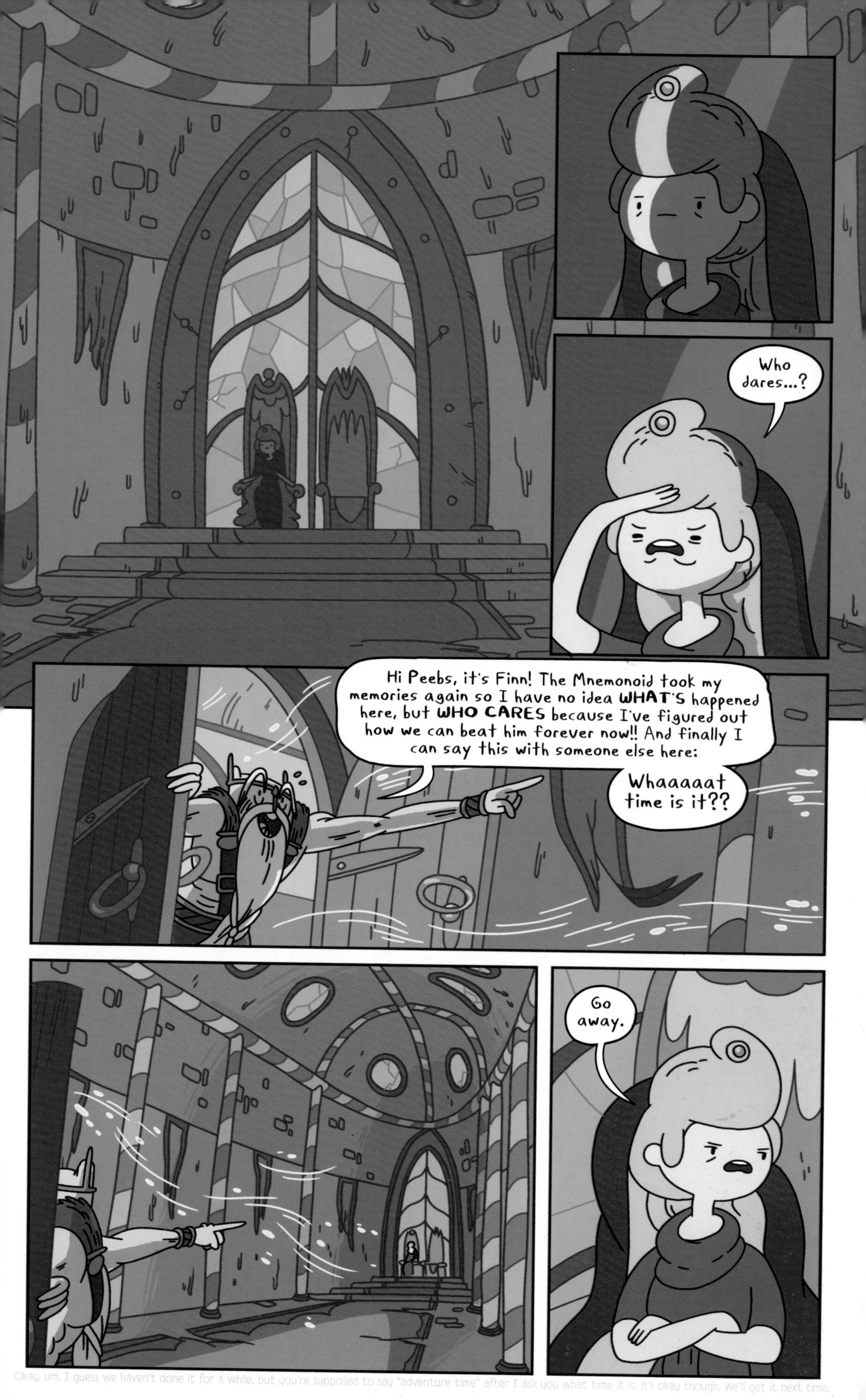
Who dares...?
Hi Peebs, it's Finn! The Mnemonoid took my memories again so I have no idea WHAT'S happened here, but WHO CARES because I've figured out how we can beat him forever now!! And finally I can say this with someone else here:
Whaaaaat time is it??
Go away.

Okay, um. I guess we haven't done it for a while, but you're supposed to say "adventure time" after I ask you what time it is. It's okay though. We'll get it next time.

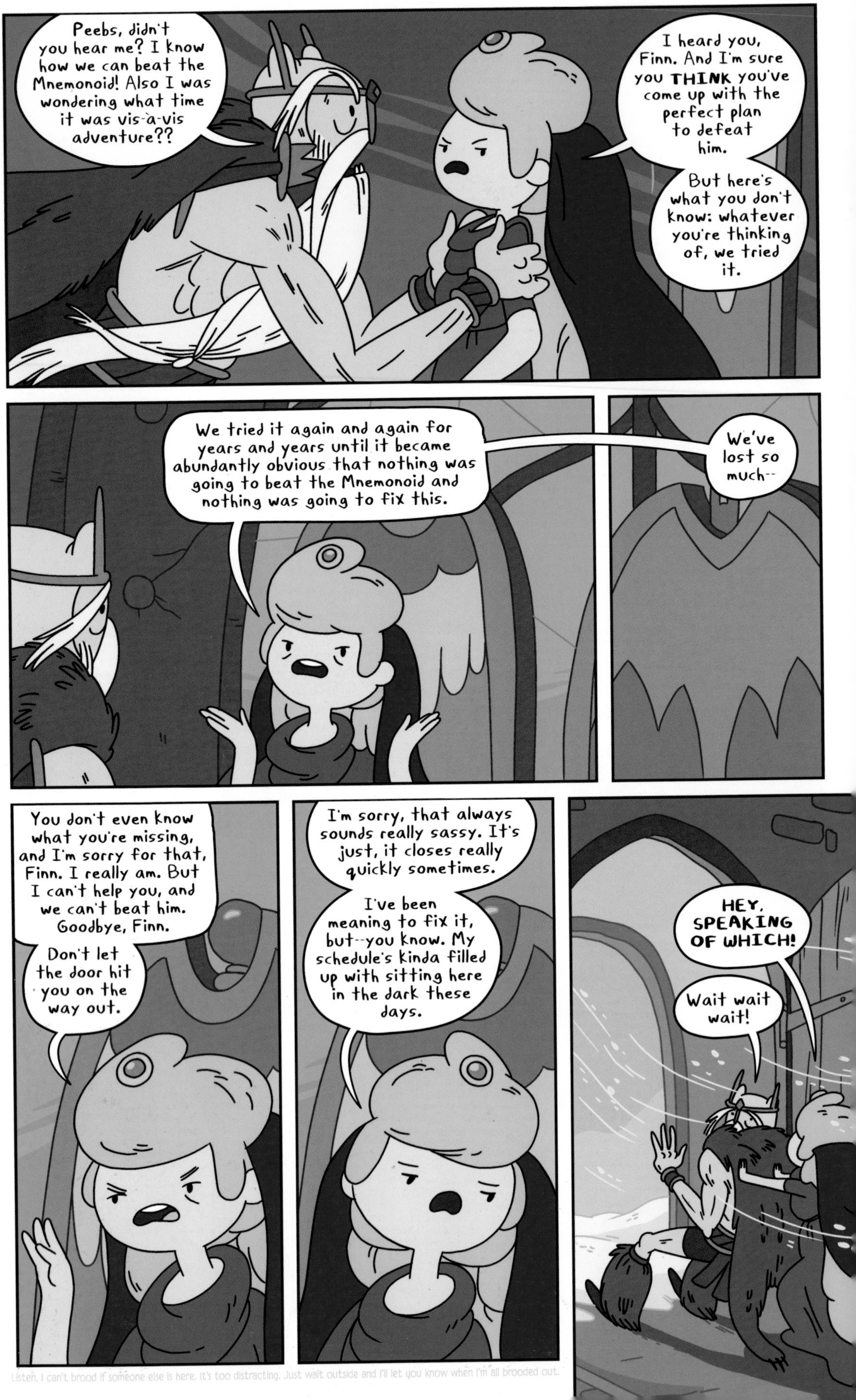

Peebs, didn't you hear me? I know how we can beat the Mnemonoid! Also I was wondering what time it was vis-à-vis adventure??
I heard you, Finn. And I'm sure you THINK you've come up with the perfect plan to defeat him.
But here's what you don't know: whatever you're thinking of, we tried it.
We tried it again and again for years and years until it became abundantly obvious that nothing was going to beat the Mnemonoid and nothing was going to fix this.
We've lost so much--
You don't even know what you're missing, and I'm sorry for that, Finn. I really am. But I can't help you, and we can't beat him. Goodbye, Finn.
Don't let the door hit you on the way out.
I'm sorry, that always sounds really sassy. It's just, it closes really quickly sometimes.
I've been meaning to fix it, but--you know. My schedule's kinda filled up with sitting here in the dark these days.
HEY, SPEAKING OF WHICH!
Wait wait wait!
Listen, I can't brood if someone else is here. It's too distracting. Just wait outside and I'll let you know when I'm all brooded out.

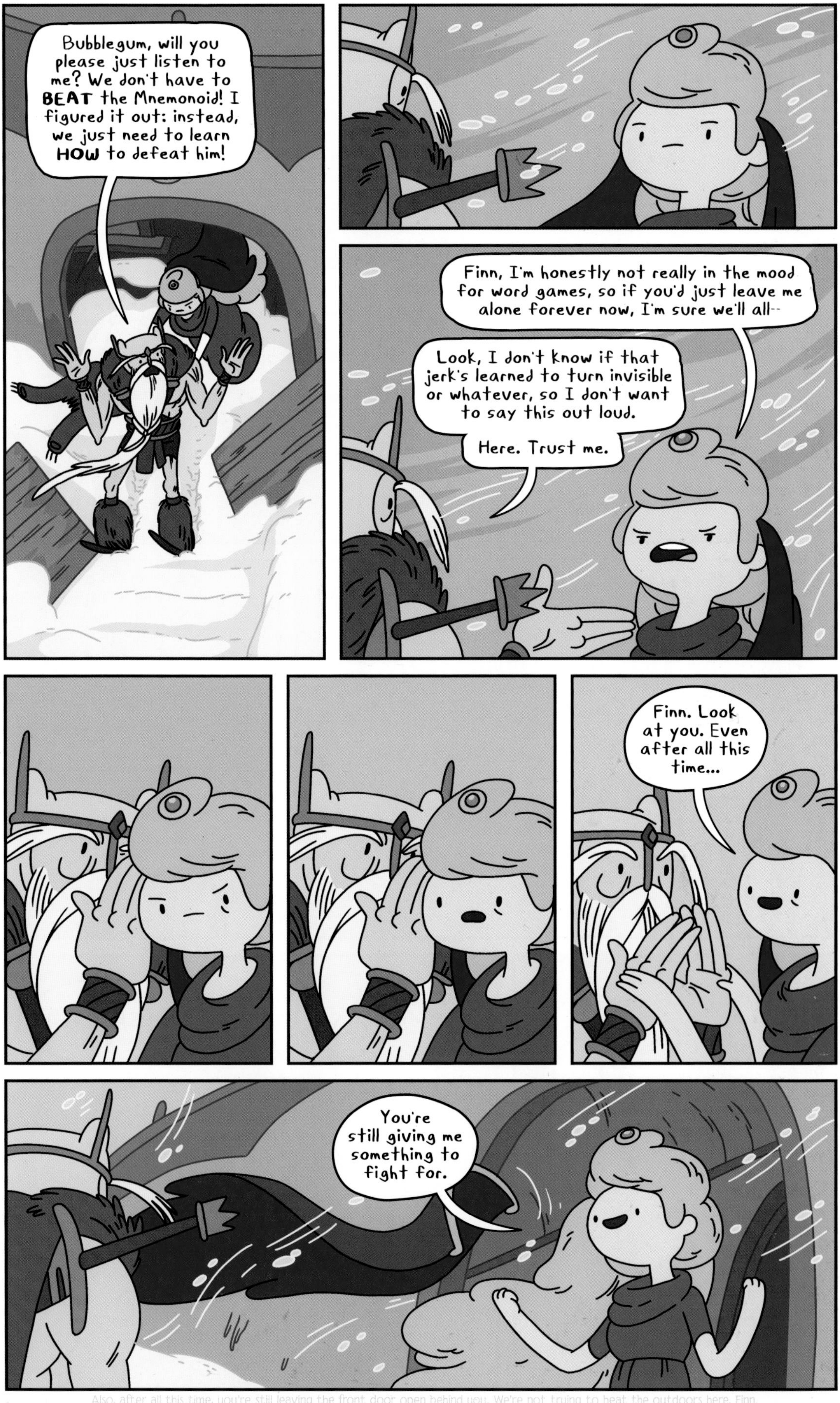
Bubblegum, will you please just listen to me? We don't have to **BEAT** the Mnemonoid! I figured it out: instead, we just need to learn **HOW** to defeat him!
Finn, I'm honestly not really in the mood for word games, so if you'd just leave me alone forever now, I'm sure we'll all--
Look, I don't know if that jerk's learned to turn invisible or whatever, so I don't want to say this out loud.
Here. Trust me.
Finn. Look at you. Even after all this time...
You're still giving me something to fight for.

Also, after all this time, you're still leaving the front door open behind you. We're not trying to heat the outdoors here, Finn.

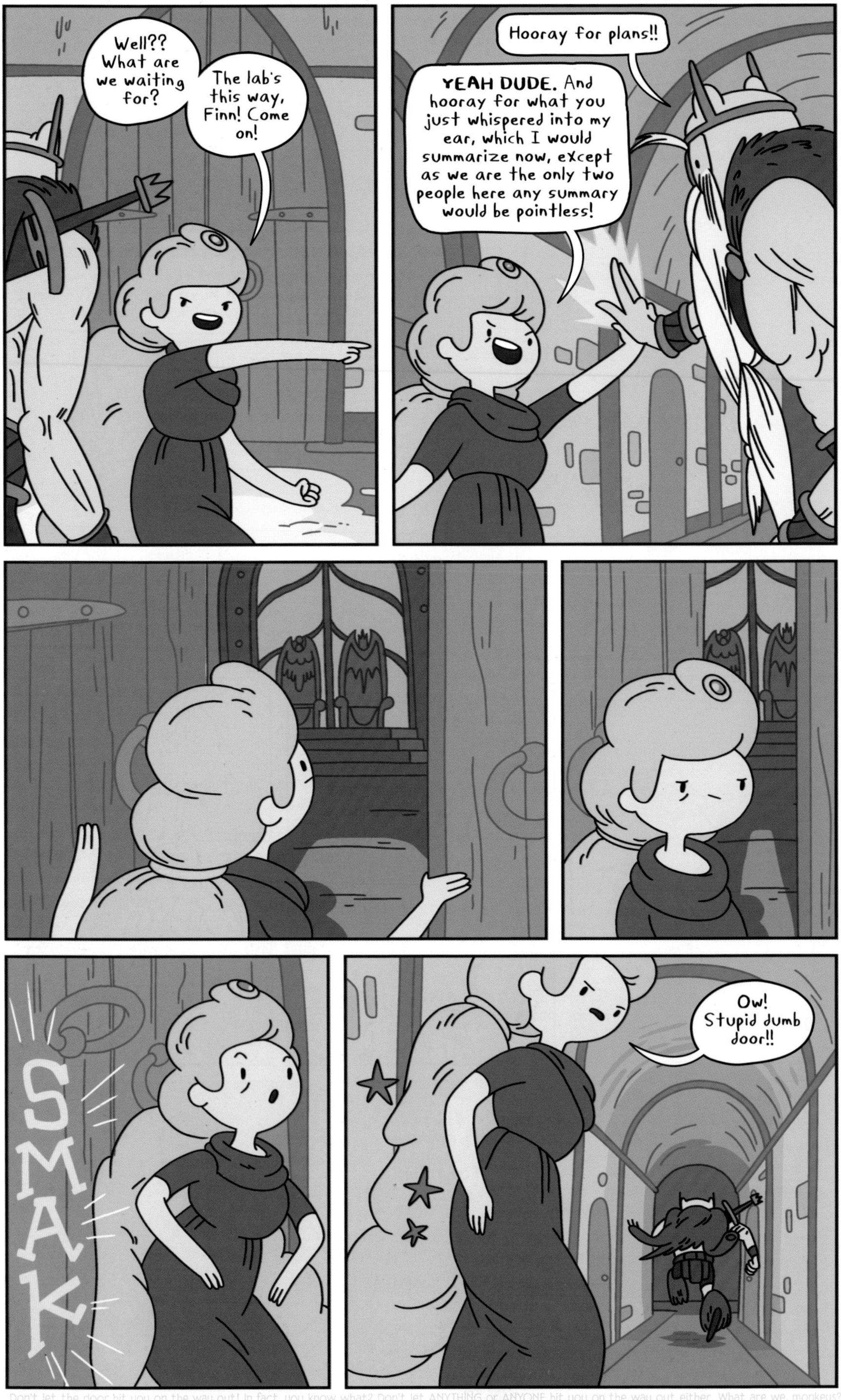
Well?? What are we waiting for?
The lab's this way, Finn! Come on!
Hooray for plans!!
YEAH DUDE. And hooray for what you just whispered into my ear, which I would summarize now, except as we are the only two people here any summary would be pointless!
SMAK
Ow! Stupid dumb door!!

Don't let the door hit you on the way out! In fact, you know what? Don't let ANYTHING or ANYONE hit you on the way out either. What are we, monkeys?

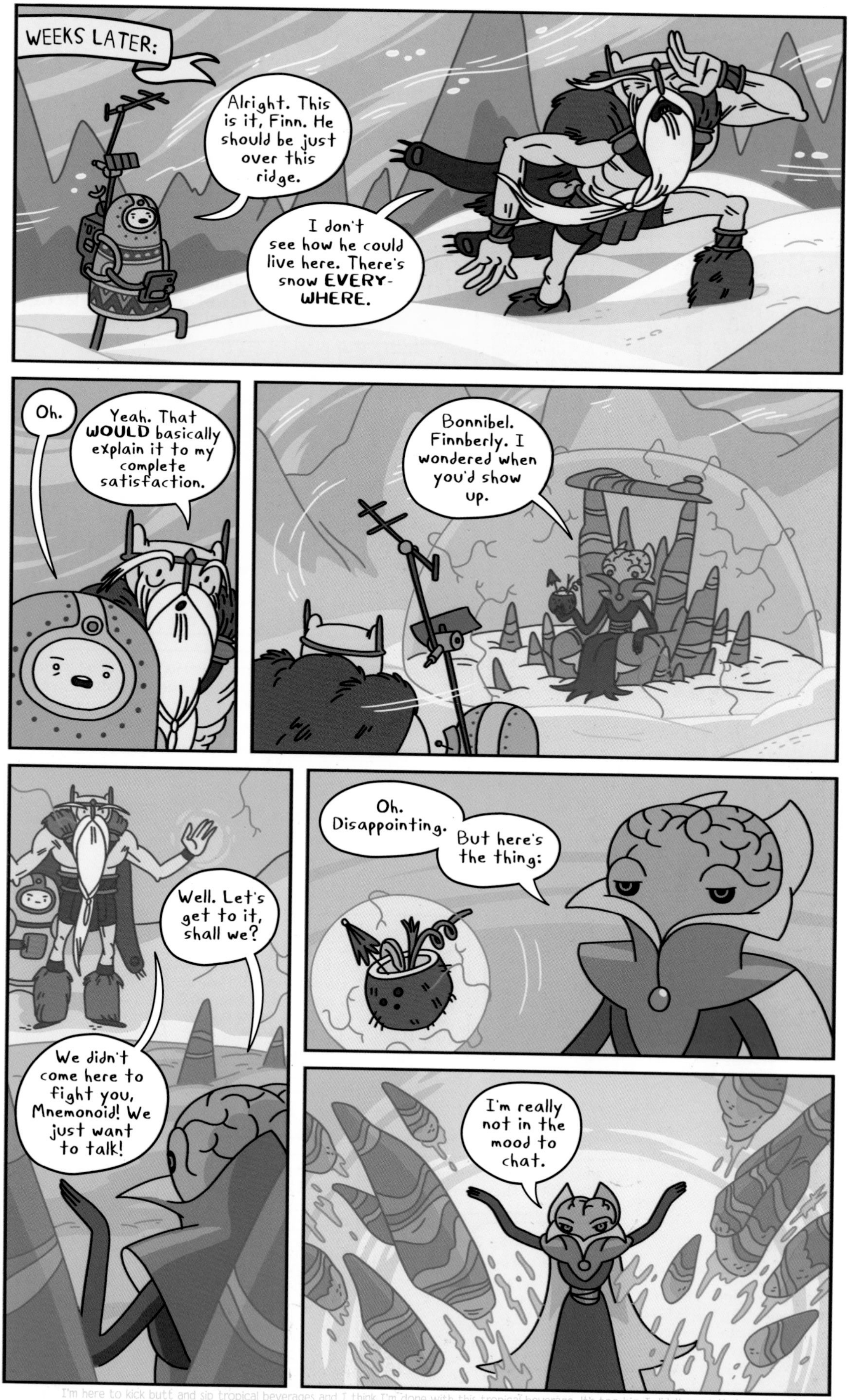
WEEKS LATER:
Alright. This is it, Finn. He should be just over this ridge.
I don't see how he could live here. There's snow **EVERY-WHERE.**
Oh.
Yeah. That **WOULD** basically explain it to my complete satisfaction.
Bonnibel. Finnberly. I wondered when you'd show up.
Well. Let's get to it, shall we?
We didn't come here to fight you, Mnemonoid! We just want to talk!
Oh. Disappointing.
But here's the thing:
I'm really not in the mood to chat.

I'm here to kick butt and sip tropical beverages and I think I'm done with this tropical beverage. It's too big. I didn't want that much.

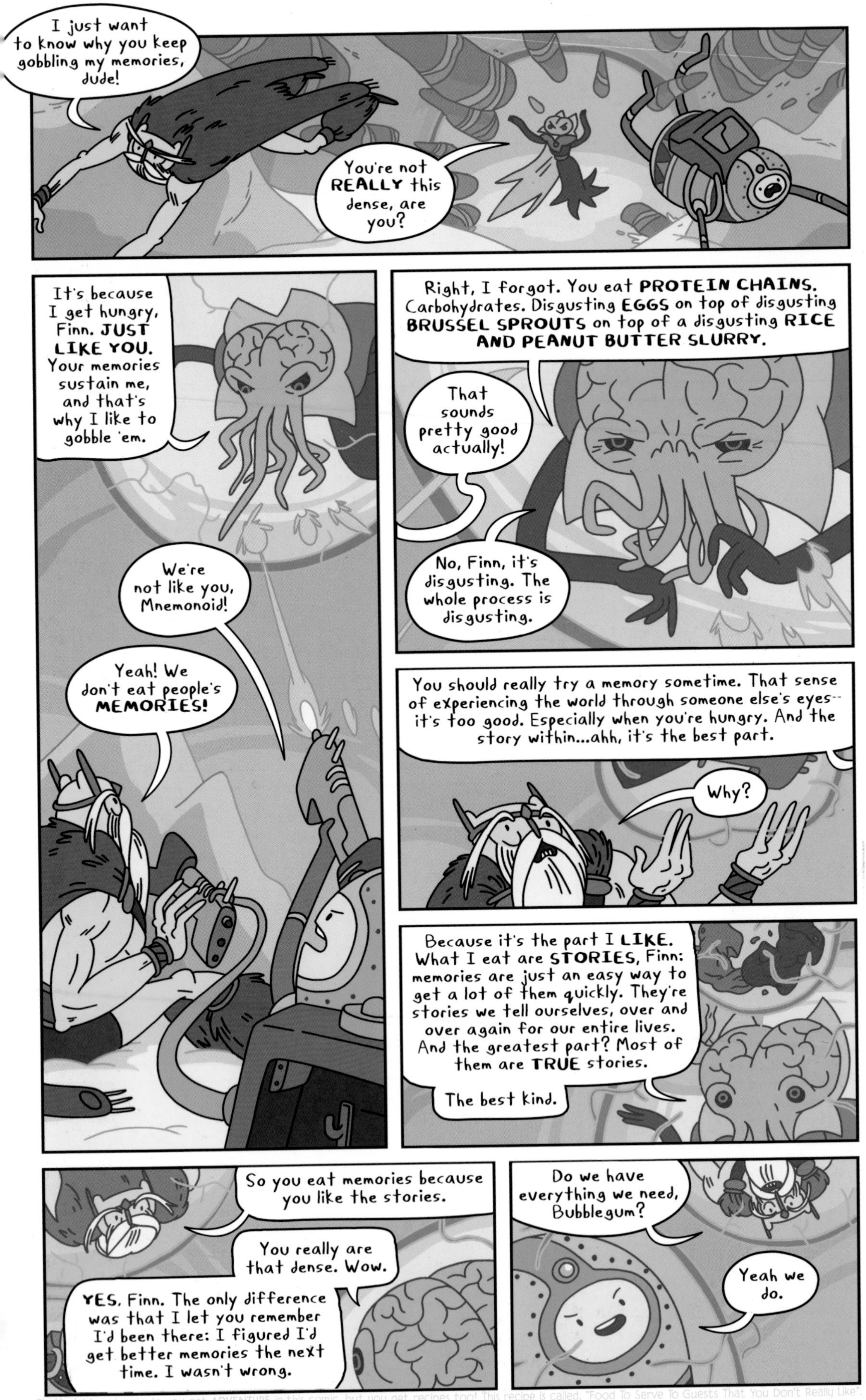
I just want to know why you keep gobbling my memories, dude!
You're not REALLY this dense, are you?
It's because I get hungry, Finn. JUST LIKE YOU. Your memories sustain me, and that's why I like to gobble 'em.
Right, I forgot. You eat PROTEIN CHAINS. Carbohydrates. Disgusting EGGS on top of disgusting BRUSSEL SPROUTS on top of a disgusting RICE AND PEANUT BUTTER SLURRY.
That sounds pretty good actually!
No, Finn, it's disgusting. The whole process is disgusting.
We're not like you, Mnemonoid!
Yeah! We don't eat people's MEMORIES!
You should really try a memory sometime. That sense of experiencing the world through someone else's eyes--it's too good. Especially when you're hungry. And the story within...ahh, it's the best part.
Why?
Because it's the part I LIKE. What I eat are STORIES, Finn: memories are just an easy way to get a lot of them quickly. They're stories we tell ourselves, over and over again for our entire lives. And the greatest part? Most of them are TRUE stories.
The best kind.
So you eat memories because you like the stories.
You really are that dense. Wow.
YES, Finn. The only difference was that I let you remember I'd been there: I figured I'd get better memories the next time. I wasn't wrong.
Do we have everything we need, Bubblegum?
Yeah we do.

That's right, not only do you get ADVENTURE in this comic, but you get recipes too! This recipe is called, "Food To Serve To Guests That You Don't Really Like".

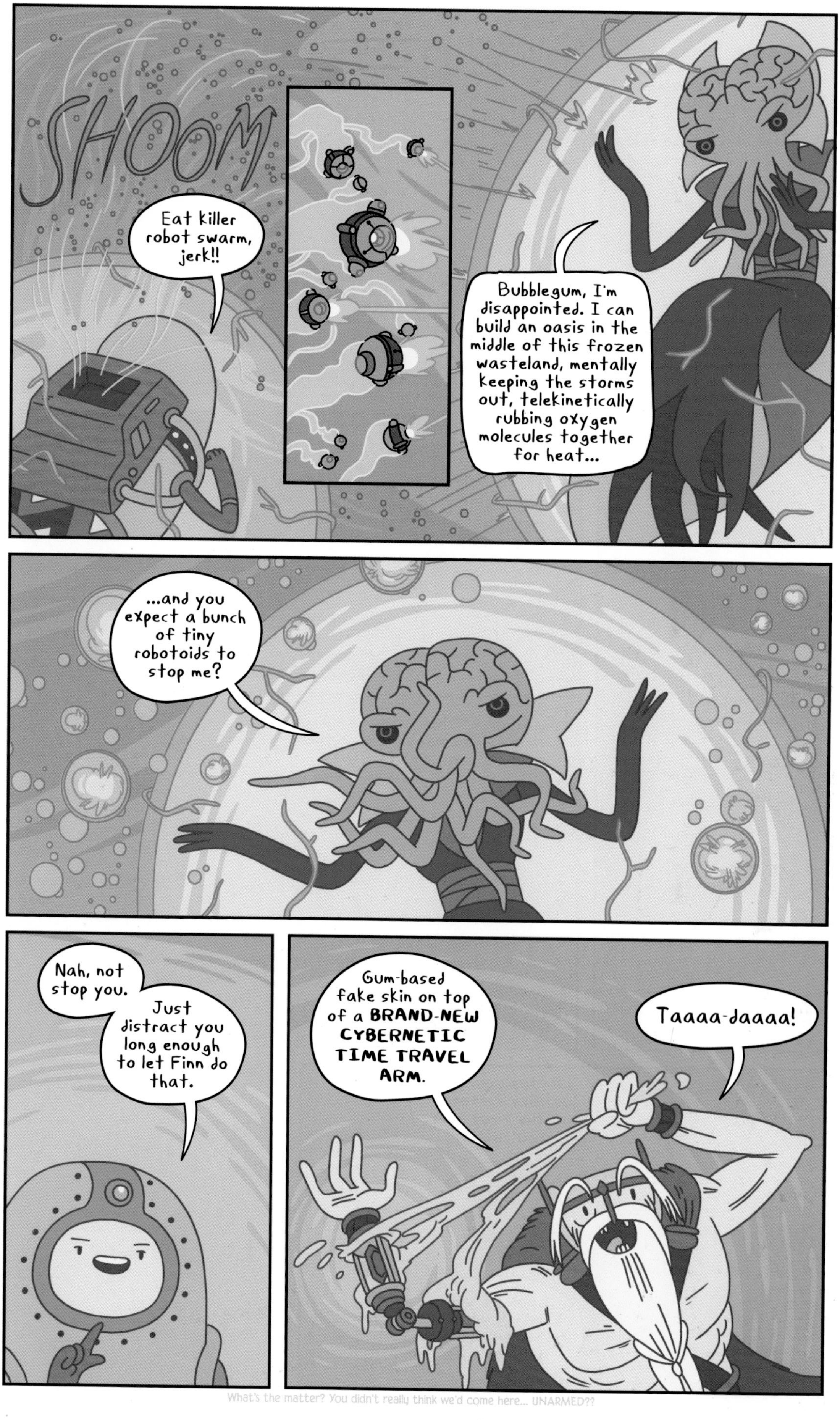
SHOOM
Eat killer robot swarm, jerk!!
Bubblegum, I'm disappointed. I can build an oasis in the middle of this frozen wasteland, mentally keeping the storms out, telekinetically rubbing oxygen molecules together for heat...
...and you expect a bunch of tiny robotoids to stop me?
Nah, not stop you.
Just distract you long enough to let Finn do that.
Gum-based fake skin on top of a **BRAND-NEW CYBERNETIC TIME TRAVEL ARM.**
Taaaa-daaaa!

What's the matter? You didn't really think we'd come here... UNARMED??

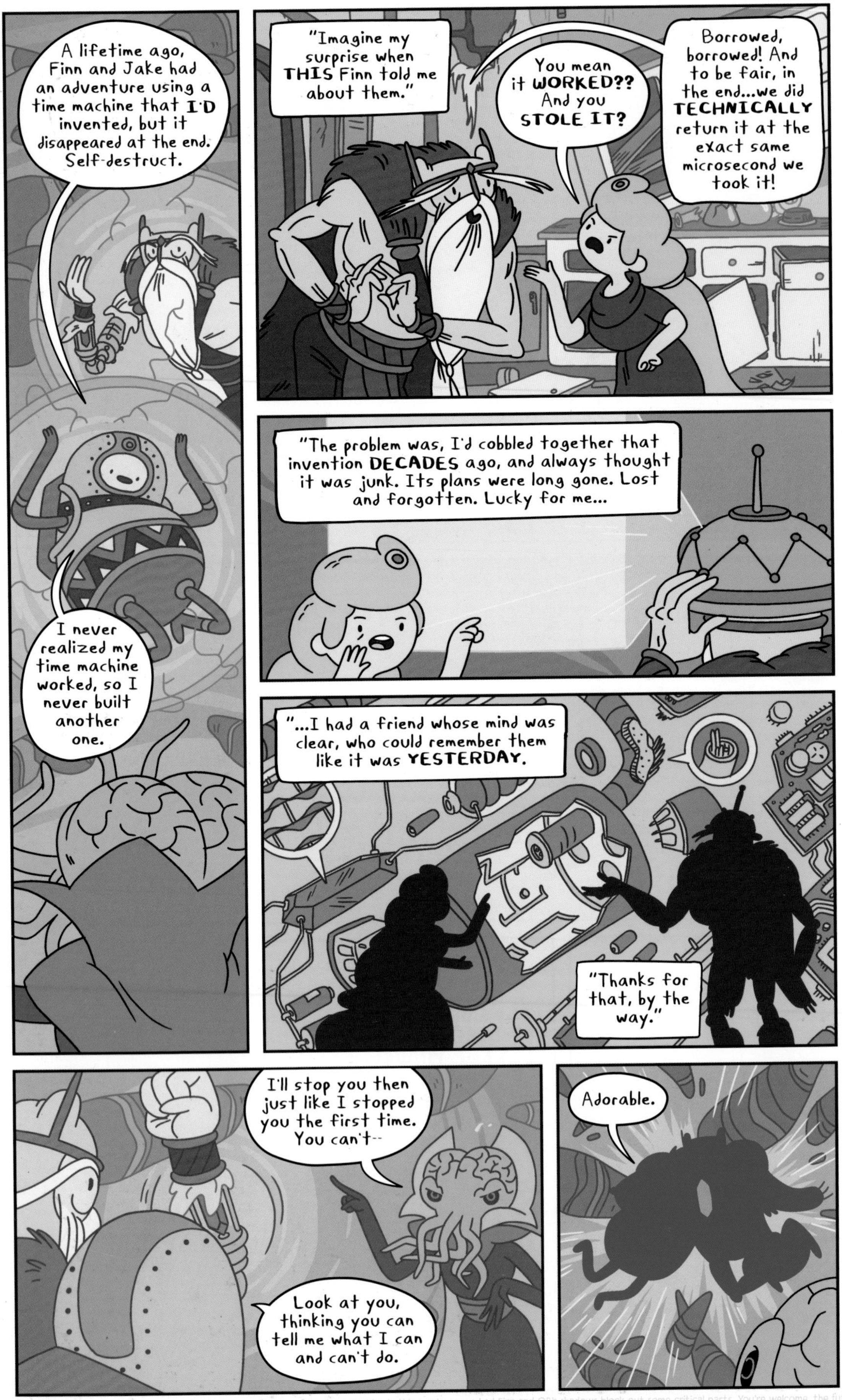

A lifetime ago, Finn and Jake had an adventure using a time machine that I'D invented, but it disappeared at the end. Self-destruct.
I never realized my time machine worked, so I never built another one.
"Imagine my surprise when THIS Finn told me about them."
You mean it WORKED?? And you STOLE IT?
Borrowed, borrowed! And to be fair, in the end...we did TECHNICALLY return it at the exact same microsecond we took it!
"The problem was, I'd cobbled together that invention DECADES ago, and always thought it was junk. Its plans were long gone. Lost and forgotten. Lucky for me...
"...I had a friend whose mind was clear, who could remember them like it was YESTERDAY.
"Thanks for that, by the way."
I'll stop you then just like I stopped you the first time. You can't--
Look at you, thinking you can tell me what I can and can't do.
Adorable.

We decided it was actually slightly irresponsible to present full plans for a time machine in this comic, so we had Finn and QB's shadows block out some critical parts. You're welcome, the future

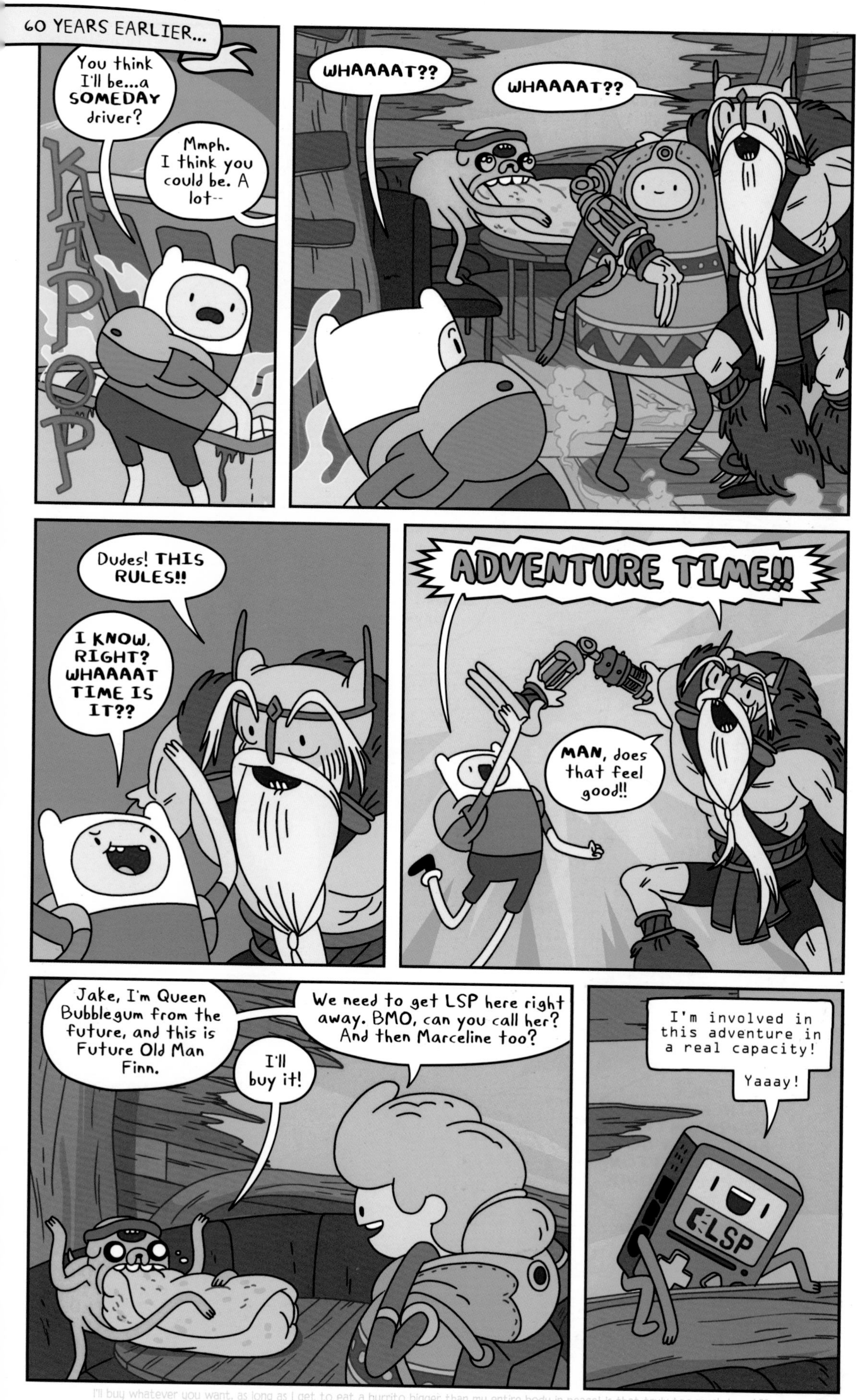
60 YEARS EARLIER...
You think I'll be...a SOMEDAY driver?
Mmph. I think you could be. A lot--
KAPOP
WHAAAAT??
WHAAAAT??
Dudes! THIS RULES!!
I KNOW, RIGHT? WHAAAAT TIME IS IT??
ADVENTURE TIME!!
MAN, does that feel good!!
Jake, I'm Queen Bubblegum from the future, and this is Future Old Man Finn.
I'll buy it!
We need to get LSP here right away. BMO, can you call her? And then Marceline too?
I'm involved in this adventure in a real capacity!
Yaaay!
LSP

I'll buy whatever you want, as long as I get to eat a burrito bigger than my entire body in peace! Is that truly too much to ask??

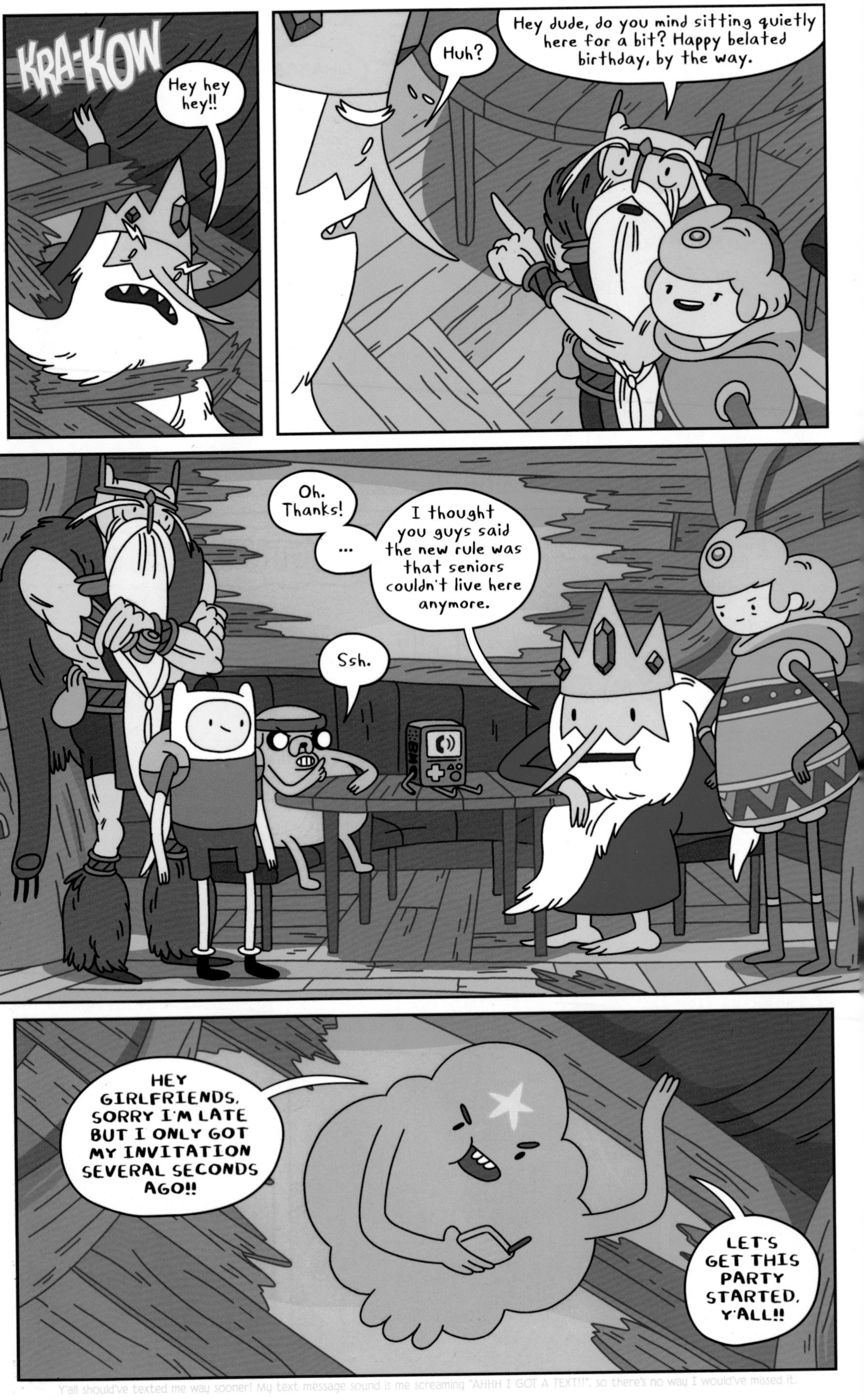
KRA-KOW
Hey hey hey!!
Huh?
Hey dude, do you mind sitting quietly here for a bit? Happy belated birthday, by the way.
Oh. Thanks!
...
I thought you guys said the new rule was that seniors couldn't live here anymore.
Ssh.
HEY GIRLFRIENDS, SORRY I'M LATE BUT I ONLY GOT MY INVITATION SEVERAL SECONDS AGO!!
LET'S GET THIS PARTY STARTED, Y'ALL!!

Y'all should've texted me way sooner! My text message sound is me screaming "AHHH I GOT A TEXT!!", so there's no way I would've missed it.

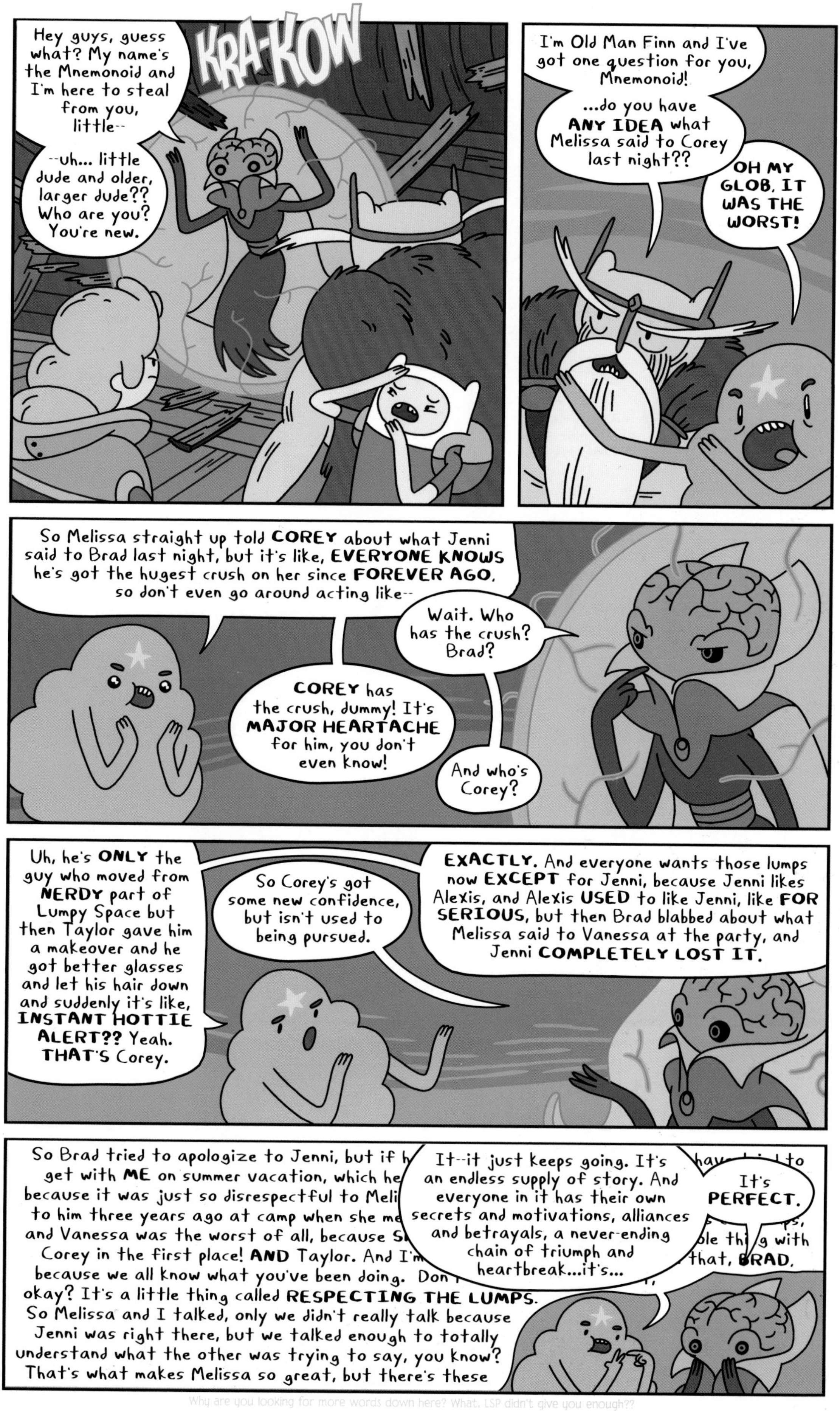

Hey guys, guess what? My name's the Mnemonoid and I'm here to steal from you, little--
KRA-KOW
--uh... little dude and older, larger dude?? Who are you? You're new.
I'm Old Man Finn and I've got one question for you, Mnemonoid!
...do you have **ANY IDEA** what Melissa said to Corey last night??
OH MY GLOB, IT WAS THE WORST!
So Melissa straight up told **COREY** about what Jenni said to Brad last night, but it's like, **EVERYONE KNOWS** he's got the hugest crush on her since **FOREVER AGO**, so don't even go around acting like--
Wait. Who has the crush? Brad?
COREY has the crush, dummy! It's **MAJOR HEARTACHE** for him, you don't even know!
And who's Corey?
Uh, he's **ONLY** the guy who moved from **NERDY** part of Lumpy Space but then Taylor gave him a makeover and he got better glasses and let his hair down and suddenly it's like, **INSTANT HOTTIE ALERT??** Yeah. **THAT'S** Corey.
So Corey's got some new confidence, but isn't used to being pursued.
EXACTLY. And everyone wants those lumps now **EXCEPT** for Jenni, because Jenni likes Alexis, and Alexis **USED** to like Jenni, like **FOR SERIOUS**, but then Brad blabbed about what Melissa said to Vanessa at the party, and Jenni **COMPLETELY LOST IT.**
So Brad tried to apologize to Jenni, but if
to
get with **ME** on summer vacation, which he
because it was just so disrespectful to
to him three years ago at camp when she
and Vanessa was the worst of all, because
with
Corey in the first place! **AND** Taylor. And
that, **BRAD**,
because we all know what you've been doing.
okay? It's a little thing called **RESPECTING THE LUMPS**.
So Melissa and I talked, only we didn't really talk because Jenni was right there, but we talked enough to totally understand what the other was trying to say, you know? That's what makes Melissa so great, but there's these
It--it just keeps going. It's an endless supply of story. And everyone in it has their own secrets and motivations, alliances and betrayals, a never-ending chain of triumph and heartbreak...it's...
It's **PERFECT.**

Why are you looking for more words down here? What. LSP didn't give you enough??

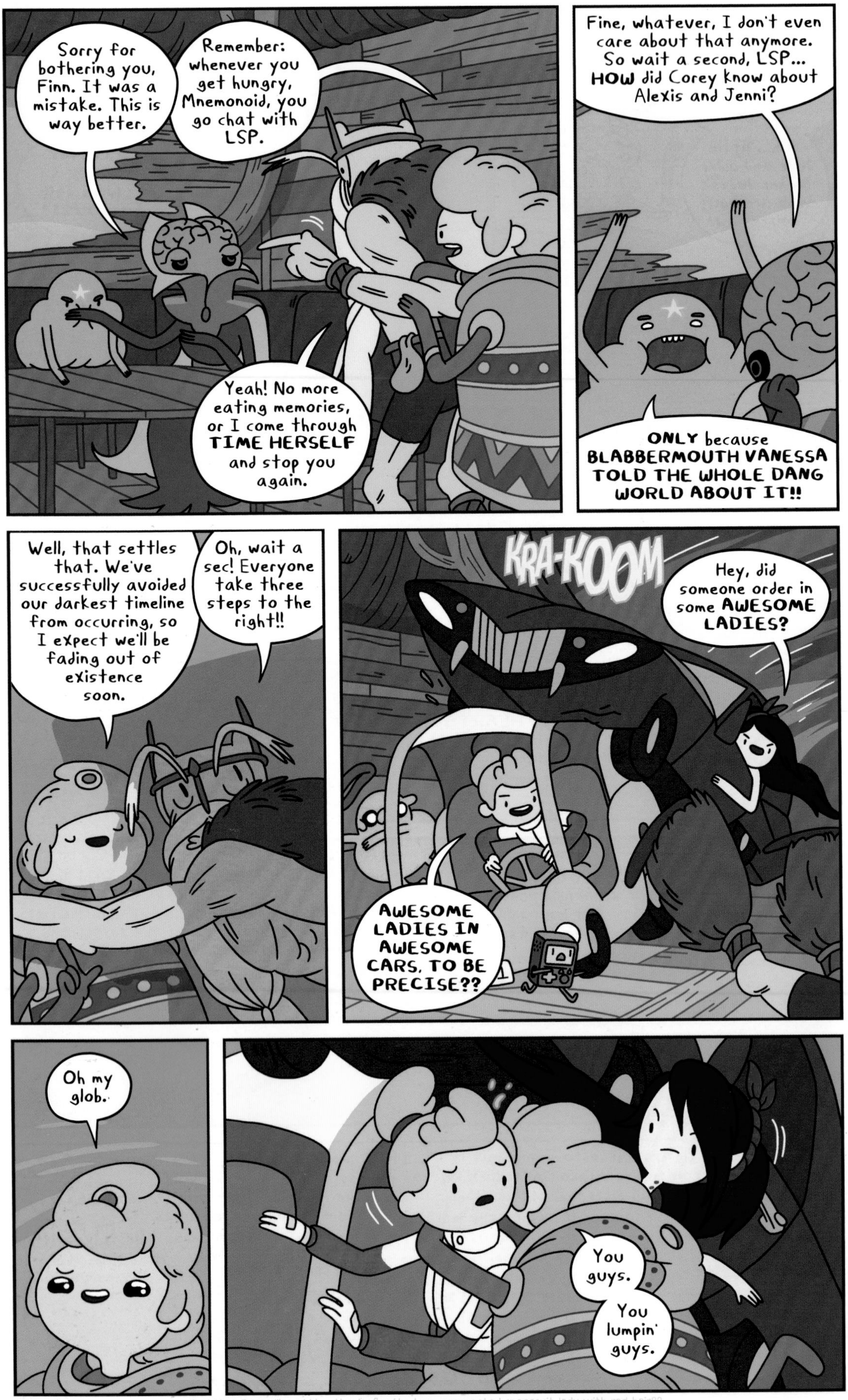
Sorry for bothering you, Finn. It was a mistake. This is way better.
Remember: whenever you get hungry, Mnemonoid, you go chat with LSP.
Yeah! No more eating memories, or I come through TIME HERSELF and stop you again.
Fine, whatever, I don't even care about that anymore. So wait a second, LSP... HOW did Corey know about Alexis and Jenni?
ONLY because BLABBERMOUTH VANESSA TOLD THE WHOLE DANG WORLD ABOUT IT!!
Well, that settles that. We've successfully avoided our darkest timeline from occurring, so I expect we'll be fading out of existence soon.
Oh, wait a sec! Everyone take three steps to the right!!
KRA-KOOM
Hey, did someone order in some AWESOME LADIES?
AWESOME LADIES IN AWESOME CARS, TO BE PRECISE??
Oh my glob.
You guys.
You lumpin' guys.

And then I was like, uhhh... thanks for the hug, unexpected spacesuit lady with rad hair??

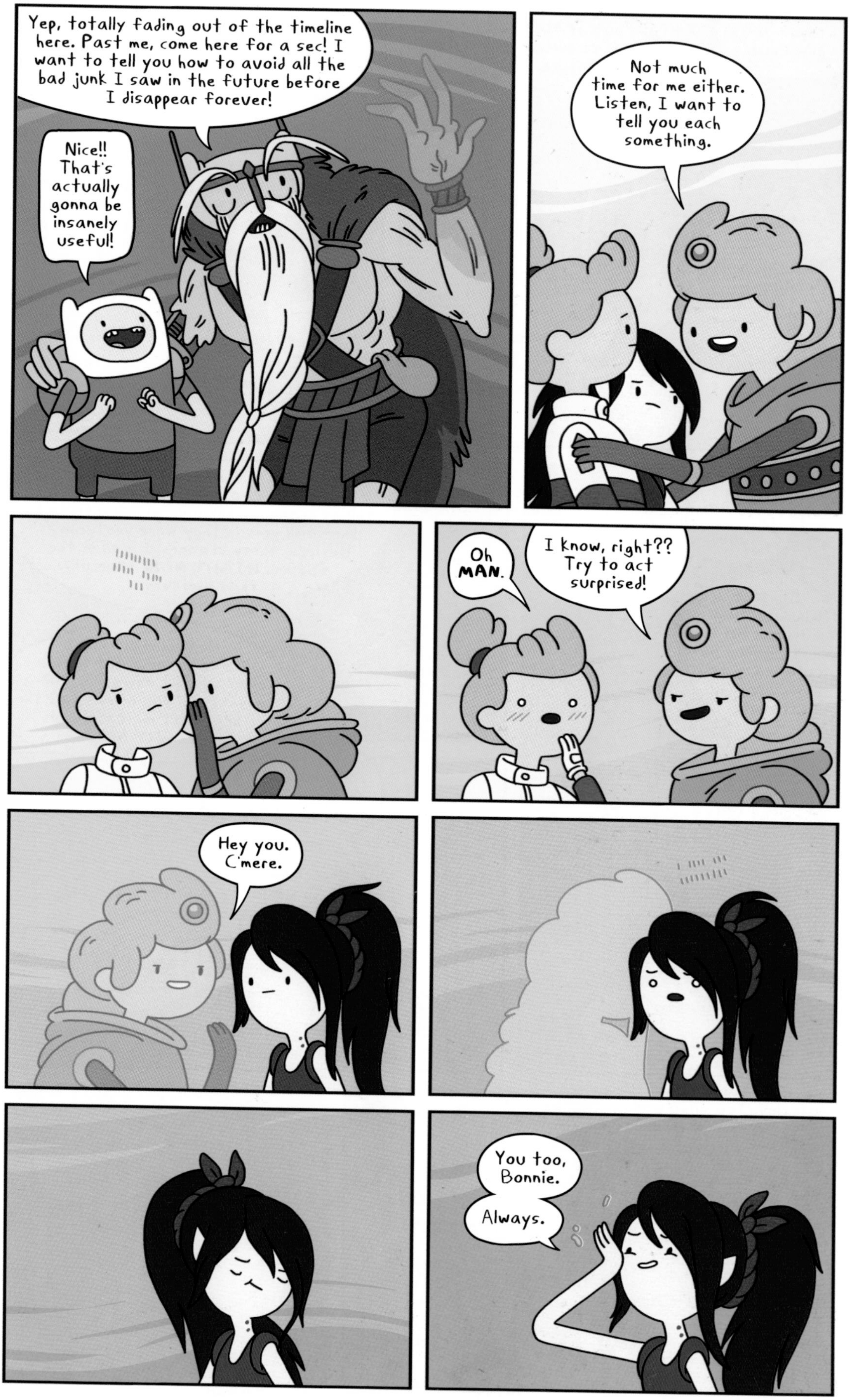
Yep, totally fading out of the timeline here. Past me, come here for a sec! I want to tell you how to avoid all the bad junk I saw in the future before I disappear forever!
Nice!! That's actually gonna be insanely useful!
Not much time for me either. Listen, I want to tell you each something.
Oh MAN.
I know, right?? Try to act surprised!
Hey you. C'mere.
You too, Bonnie.
Always.

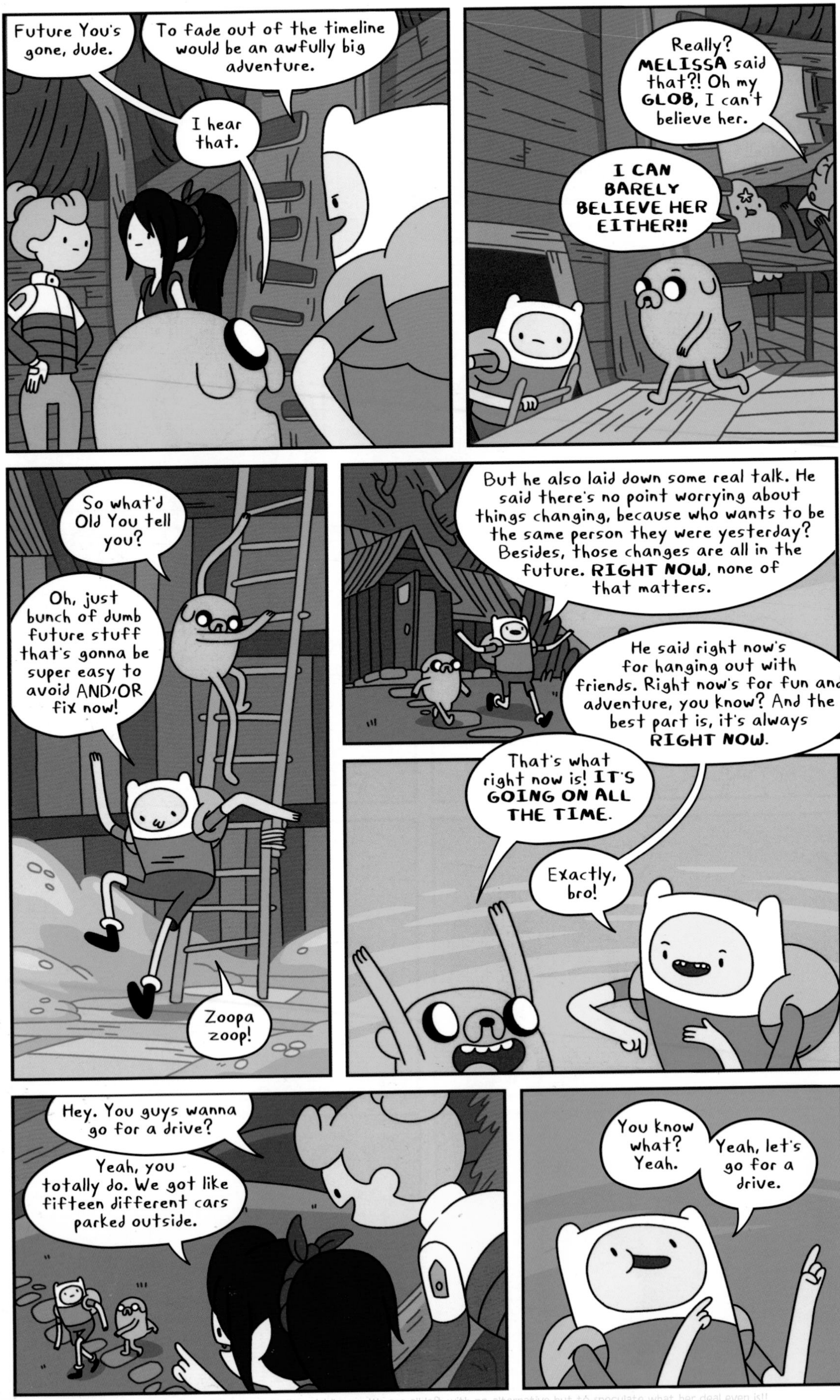
Future You's gone, dude.
To fade out of the timeline would be an awfully big adventure.
I hear that.
Really? **MELISSA** said that?! Oh my **GLOB**, I can't believe her.
I CAN BARELY BELIEVE HER EITHER!!
So what'd Old You tell you?
Oh, just bunch of dumb future stuff that's gonna be super easy to avoid AND/OR fix now!
Zoopa zoop!
But he also laid down some real talk. He said there's no point worrying about things changing, because who wants to be the same person they were yesterday? Besides, those changes are all in the future. **RIGHT NOW**, none of that matters.
He said right now's for hanging out with friends. Right now's for fun and adventure, you know? And the best part is, it's always **RIGHT NOW**.
That's what right now is! **IT'S GOING ON ALL THE TIME**.
Exactly, bro!
Hey. You guys wanna go for a drive?
Yeah, you totally do. We got like fifteen different cars parked outside.
You know what? Yeah.
Yeah, let's go for a drive.

To be fair, a lot of us can't believe Melissa right now. We are all left with no alternative but to speculate what her deal even is!!

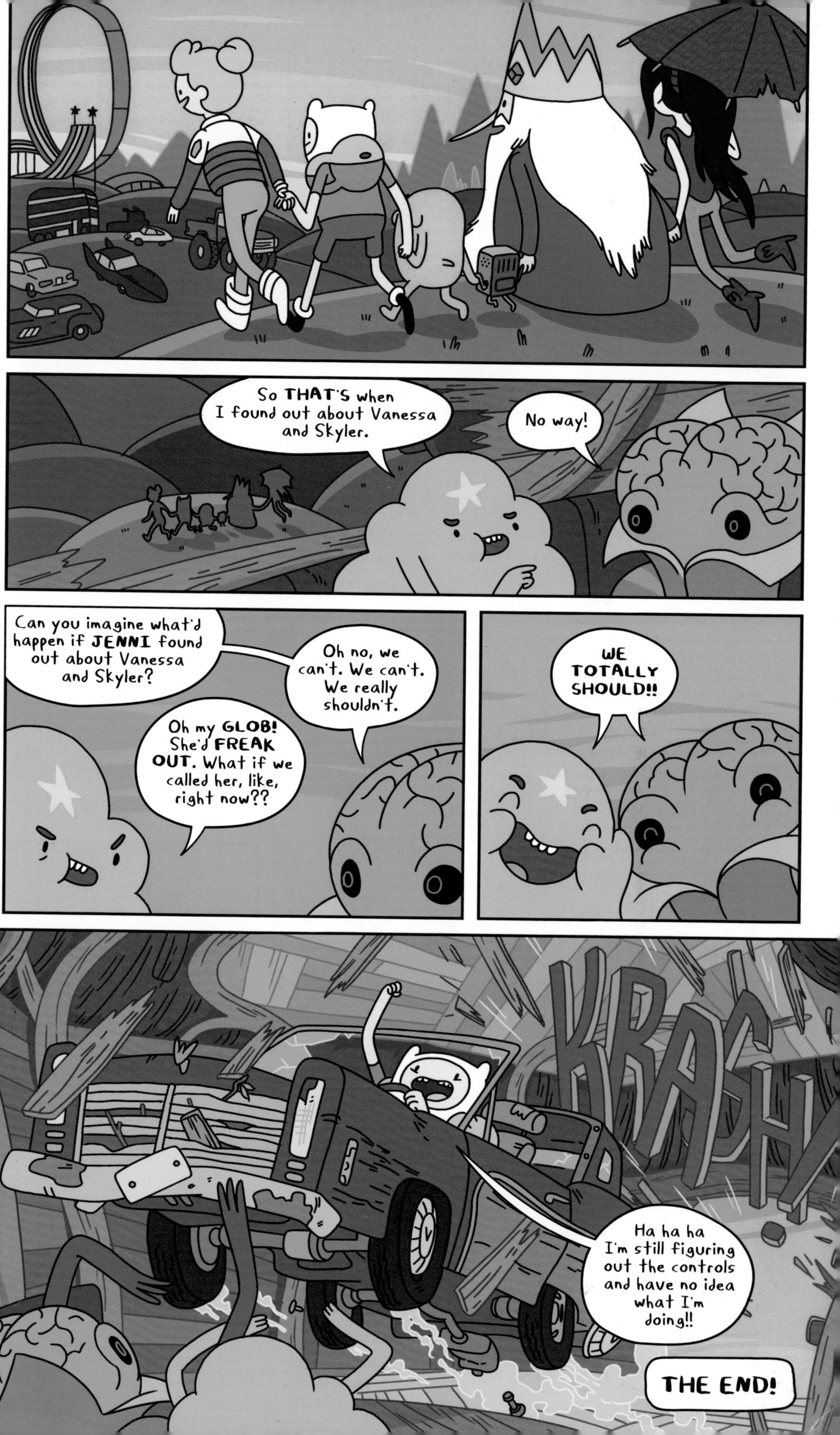
So THAT'S when I found out about Vanessa and Skyler.
No way!
Can you imagine what'd happen if JENNI found out about Vanessa and Skyler?
Oh no, we can't. We can't. We really shouldn't.
Oh my GLOB! She'd FREAK OUT. What if we called her, like, right now??
WE TOTALLY SHOULD!!
KRASH
Ha ha ha I'm still figuring out the controls and have no idea what I'm doing!!
THE END!

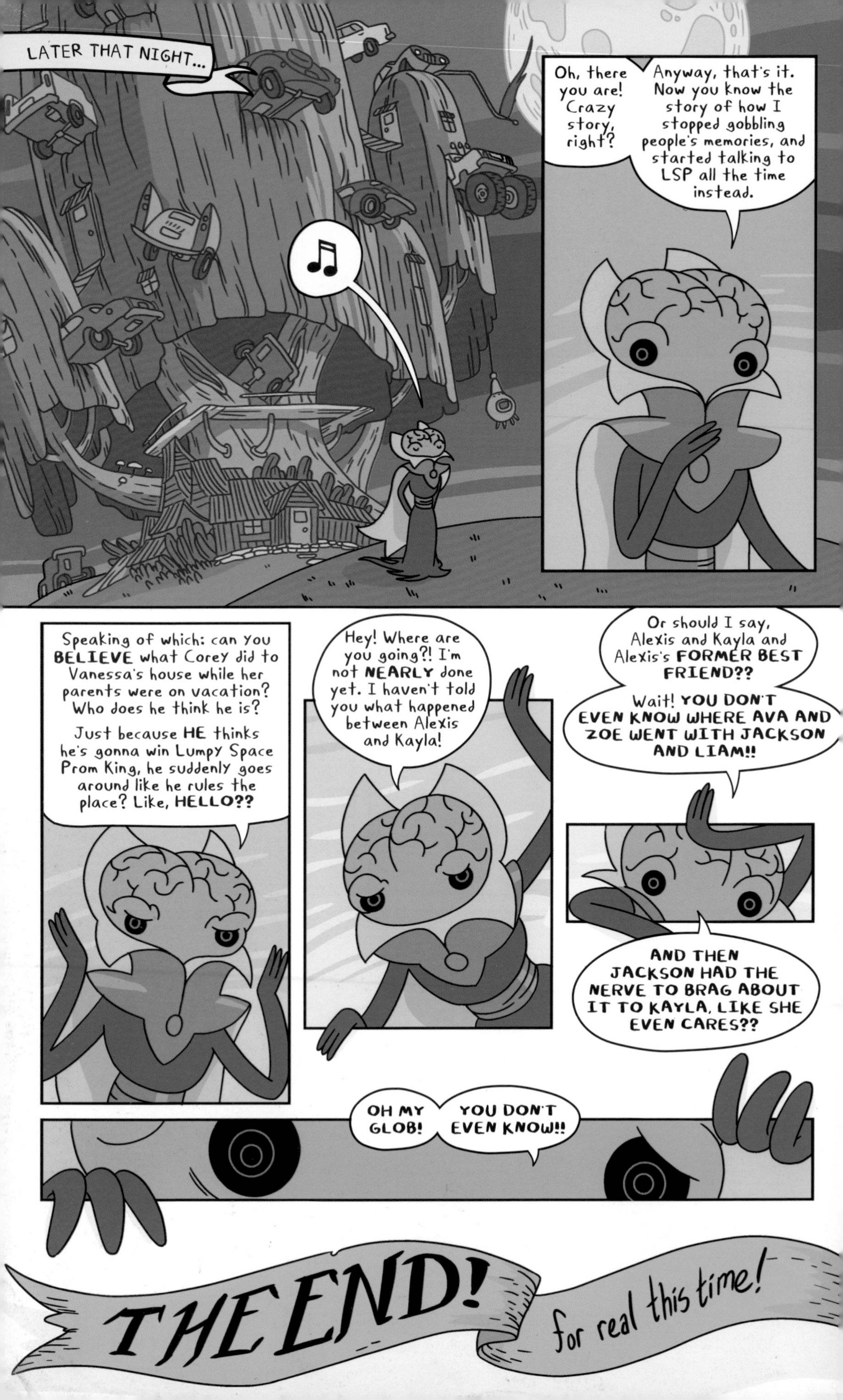

LATER THAT NIGHT...
♫
Oh, there you are! Crazy story, right?
Anyway, that's it. Now you know the story of how I stopped gobbling people's memories, and started talking to LSP all the time instead.
Speaking of which: can you BELIEVE what Corey did to Vanessa's house while her parents were on vacation? Who does he think he is?
Just because HE thinks he's gonna win Lumpy Space Prom King, he suddenly goes around like he rules the place? Like, HELLO??
Hey! Where are you going?! I'm not NEARLY done yet. I haven't told you what happened between Alexis and Kayla!
Or should I say, Alexis and Kayla and Alexis's FORMER BEST FRIEND??
Wait! YOU DON'T EVEN KNOW WHERE AVA AND ZOE WENT WITH JACKSON AND LIAM!!
AND THEN JACKSON HAD THE NERVE TO BRAG ABOUT IT TO KAYLA, LIKE SHE EVEN CARES??
OH MY GLOB!
YOU DON'T EVEN KNOW!!
THE END! for real this time!

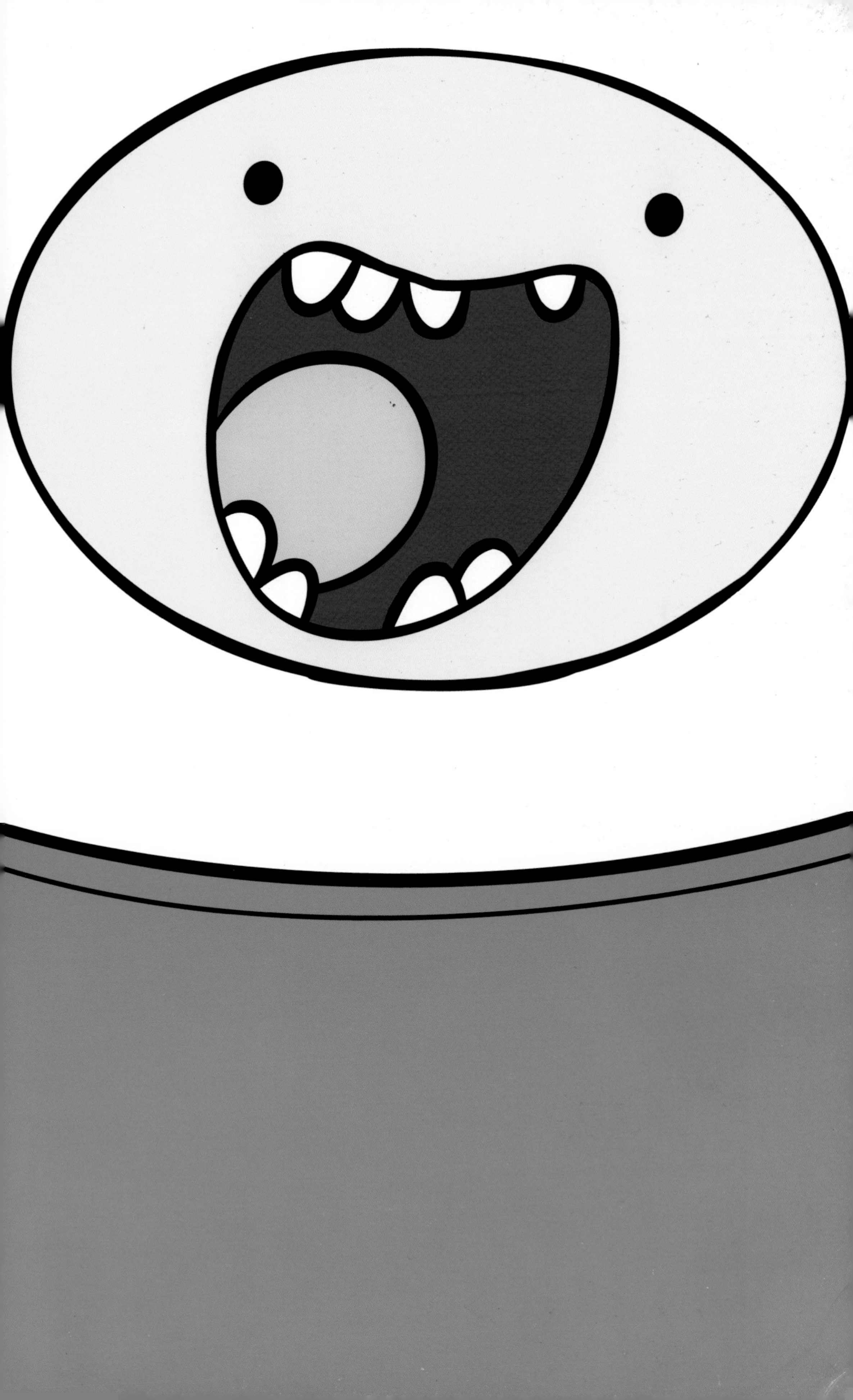

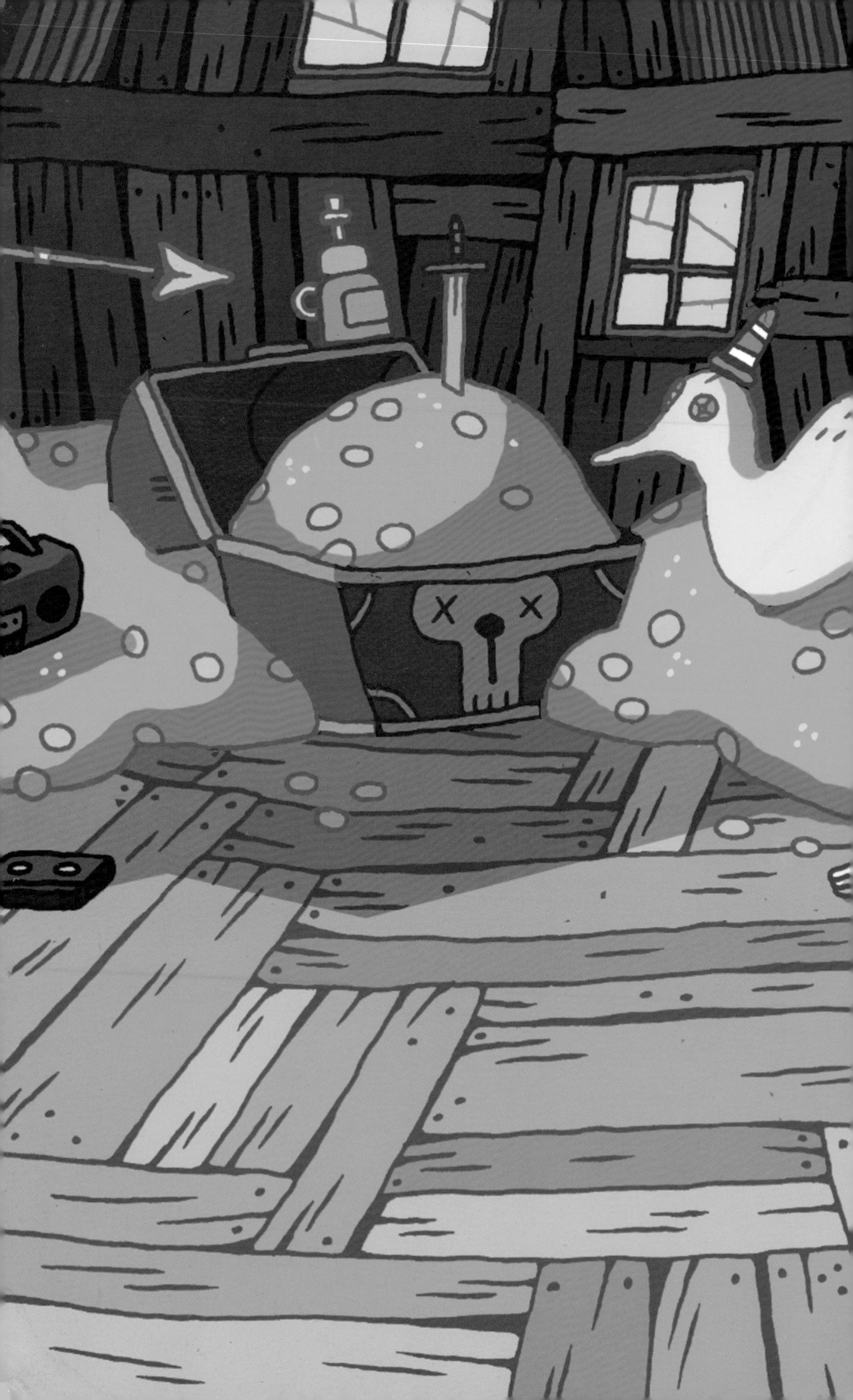

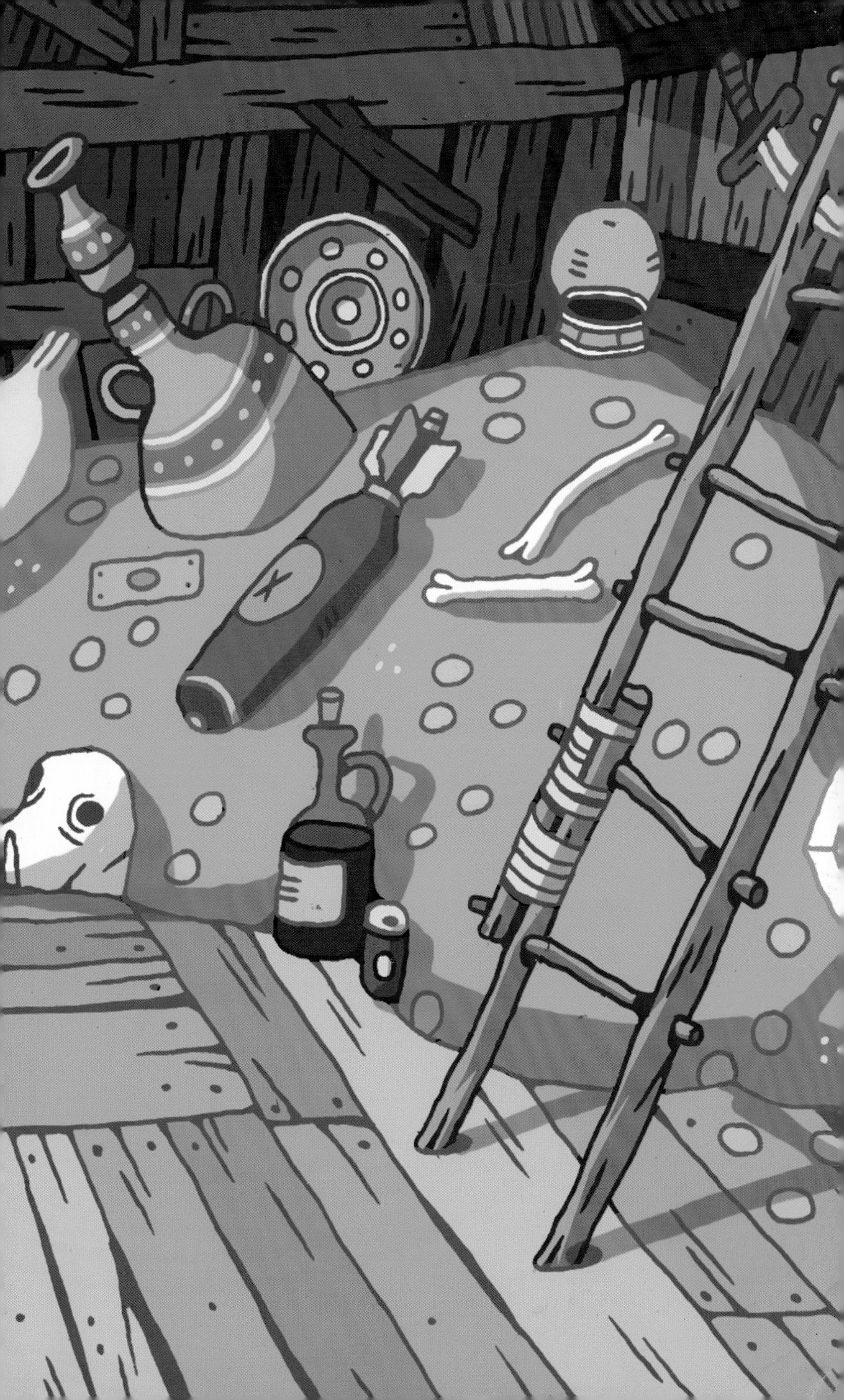

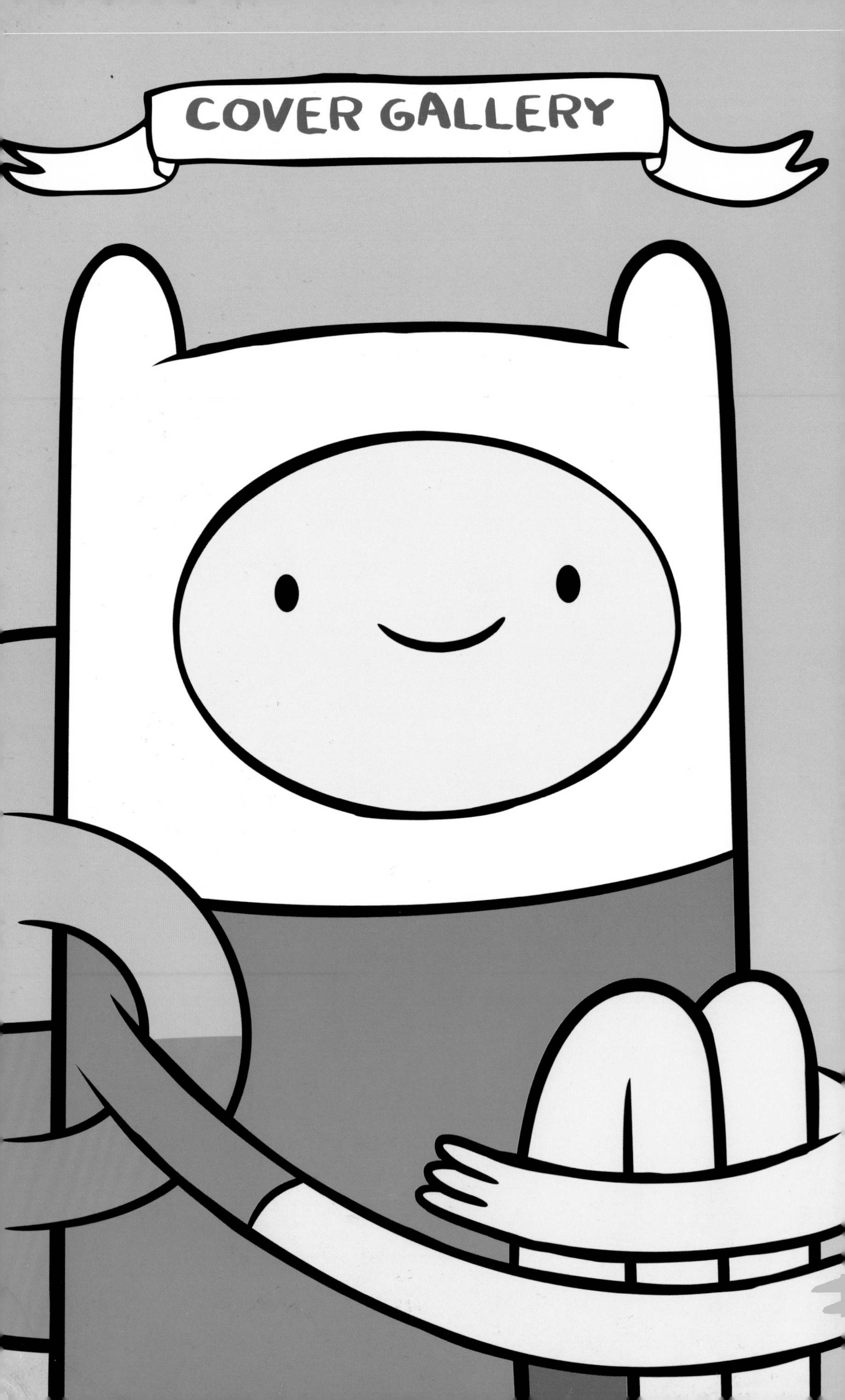
COVER GALLERY

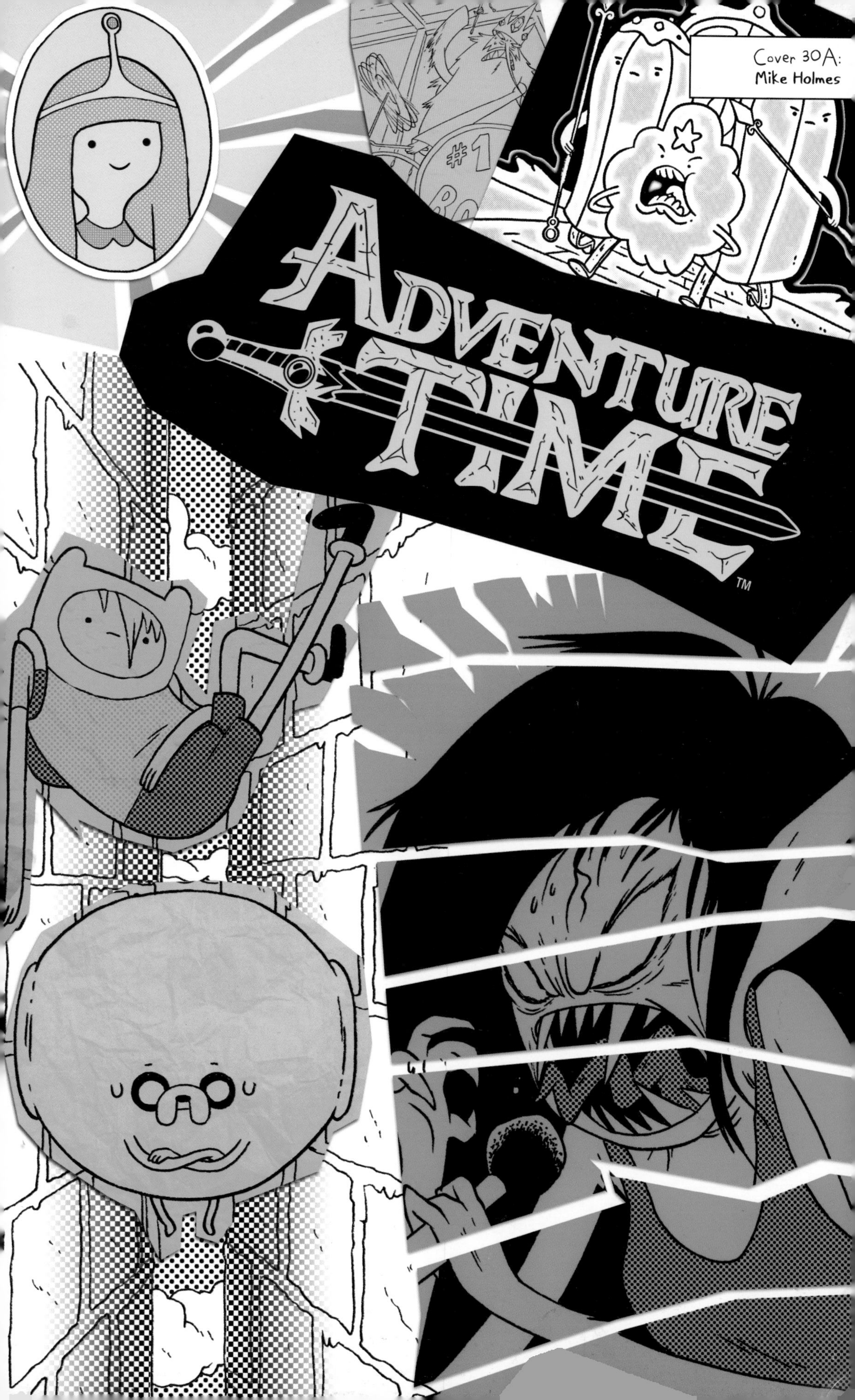
ADVENTURE TIME
Cover 30A:
Mike Holmes

Cover 30B:
Nick Iluzada

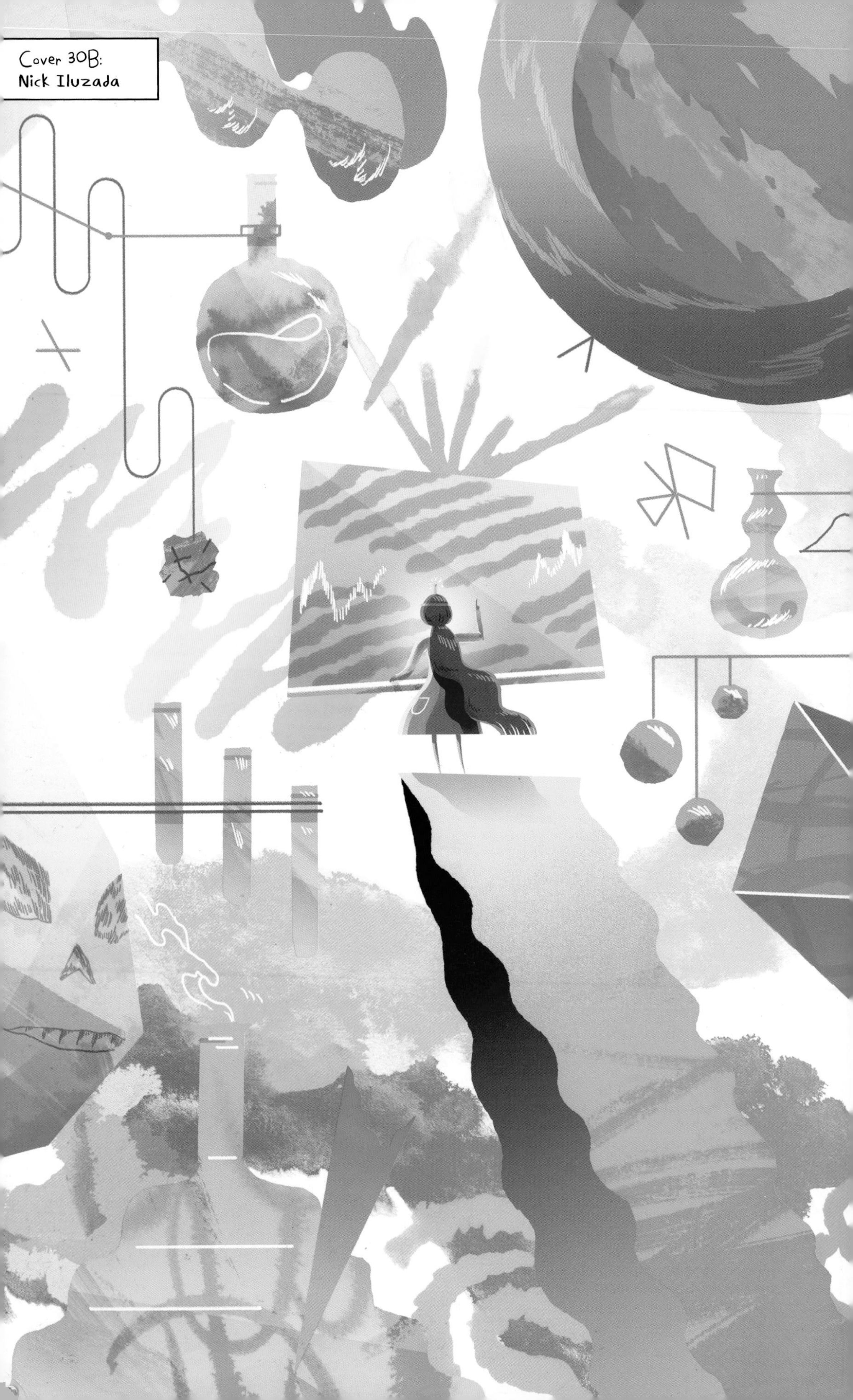

Cover 30C:
Luke Pearson

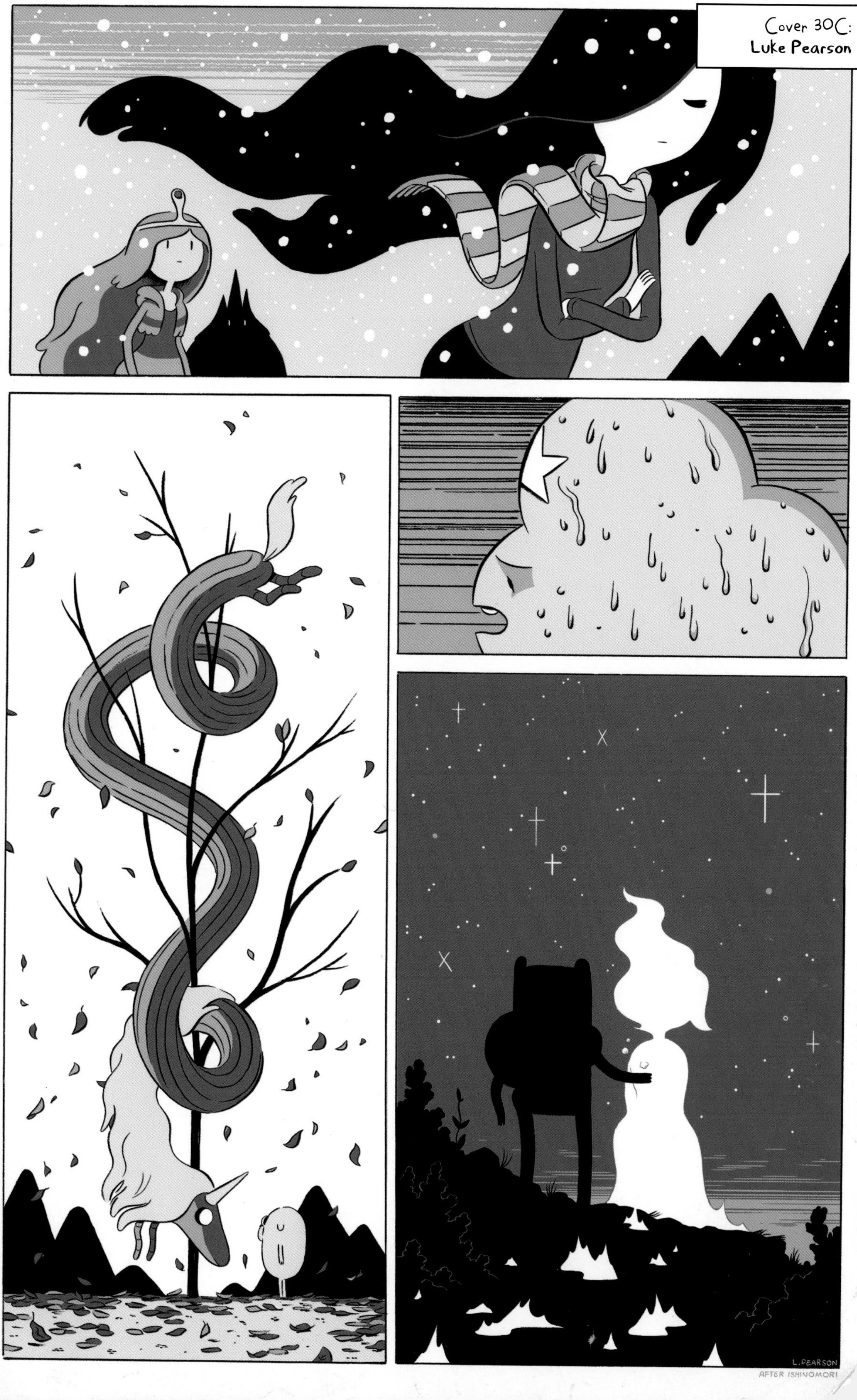
L. PEARSON
AFTER ISHINOMORI

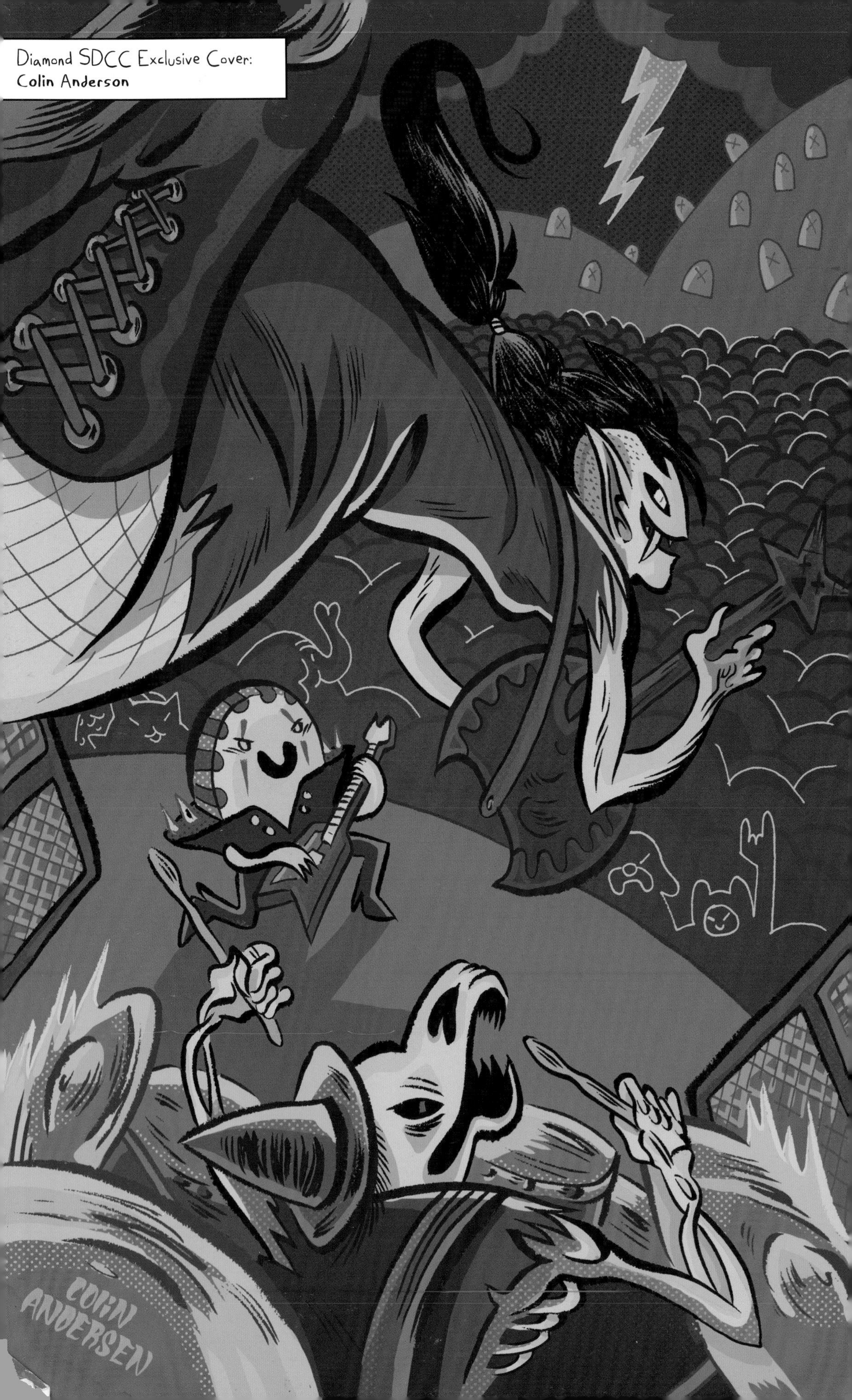
COLIN
ANDERSEN

Diamond SDCC Exclusive Cover:
Colin Anderson

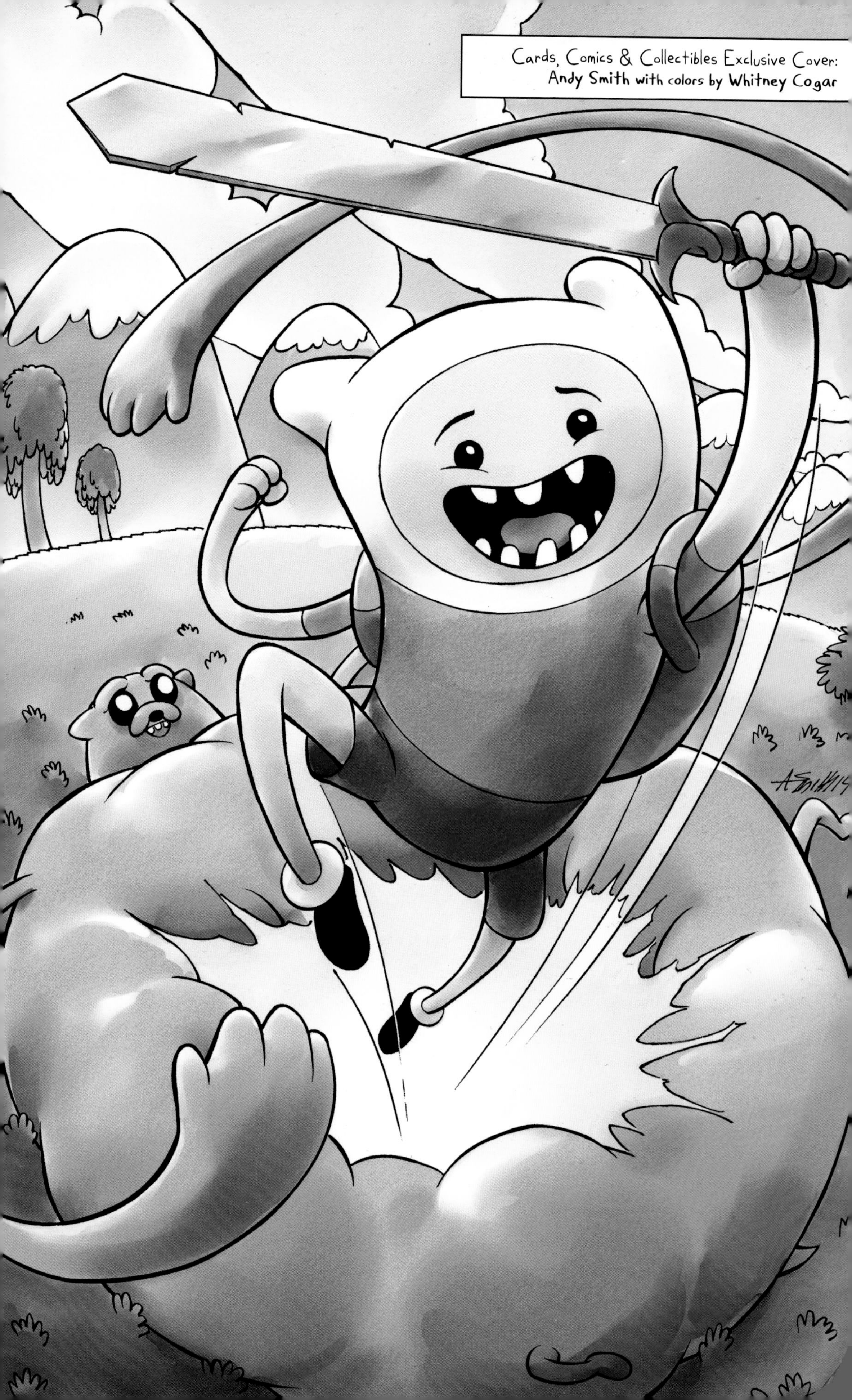

Cards, Comics & Collectibles Exclusive Cover:
Andy Smith with colors by Whitney Cogar

Cover 31A:
Kostas Kiriakakis

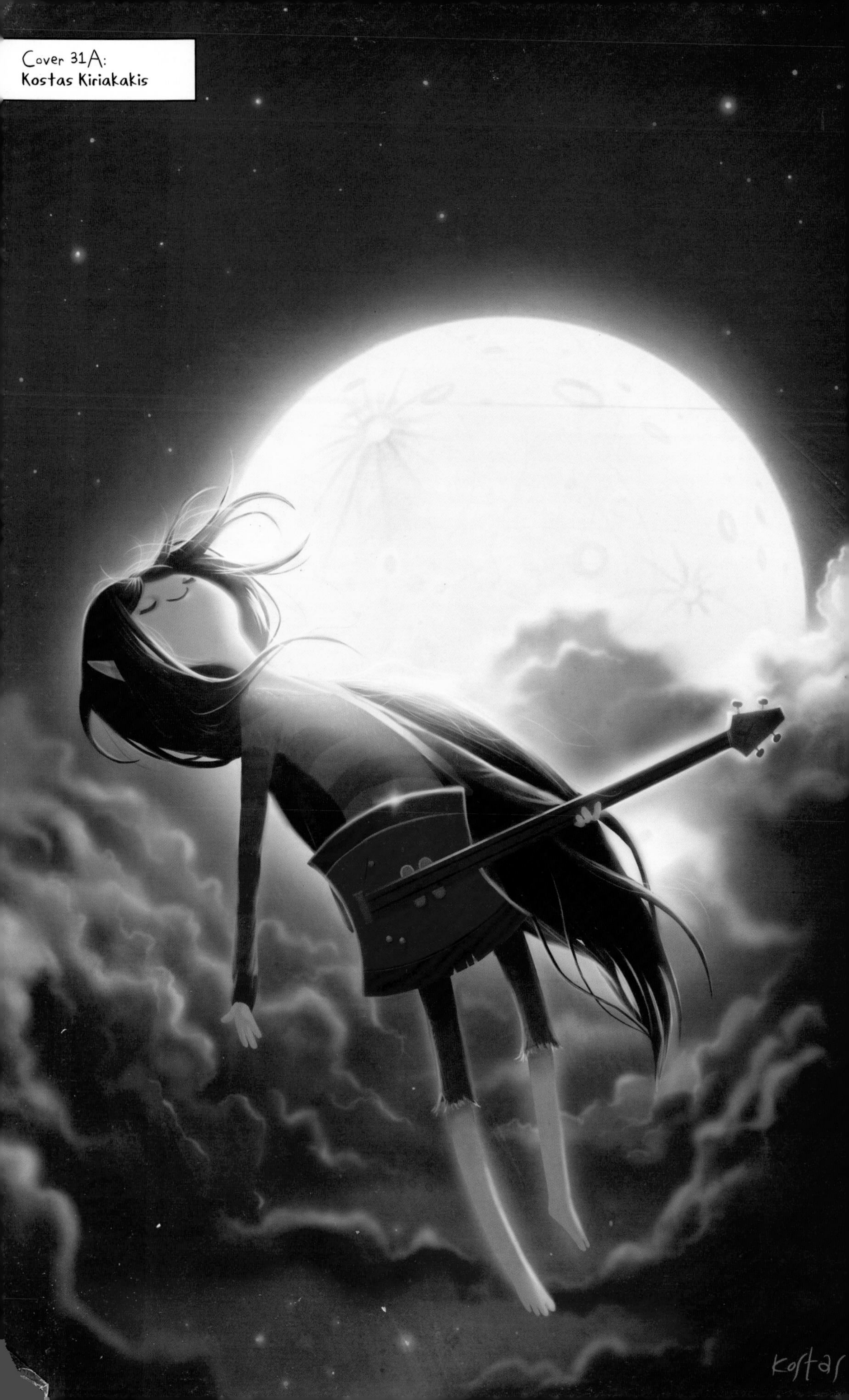
kostas

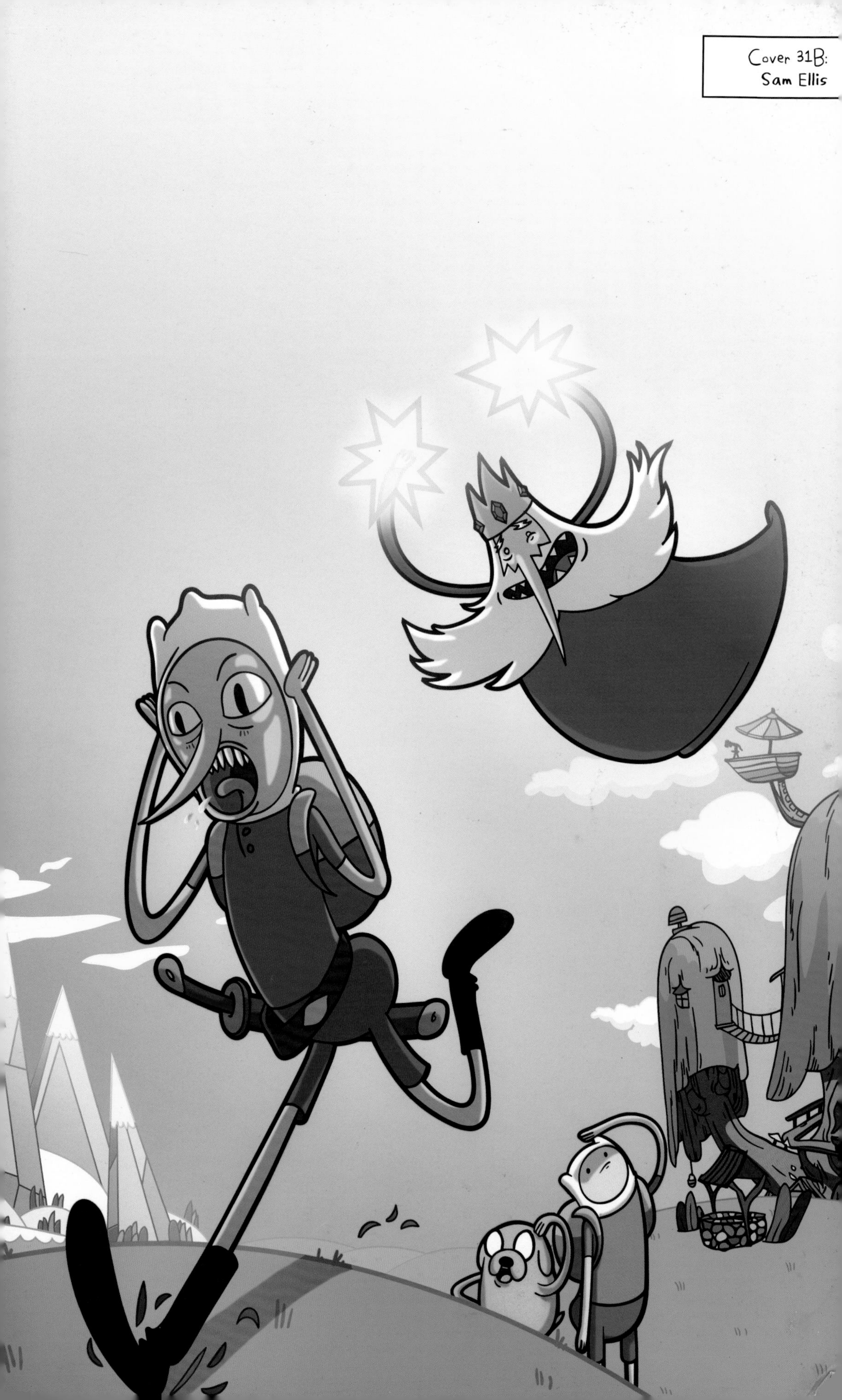

Cover 31B:
Sam Ellis

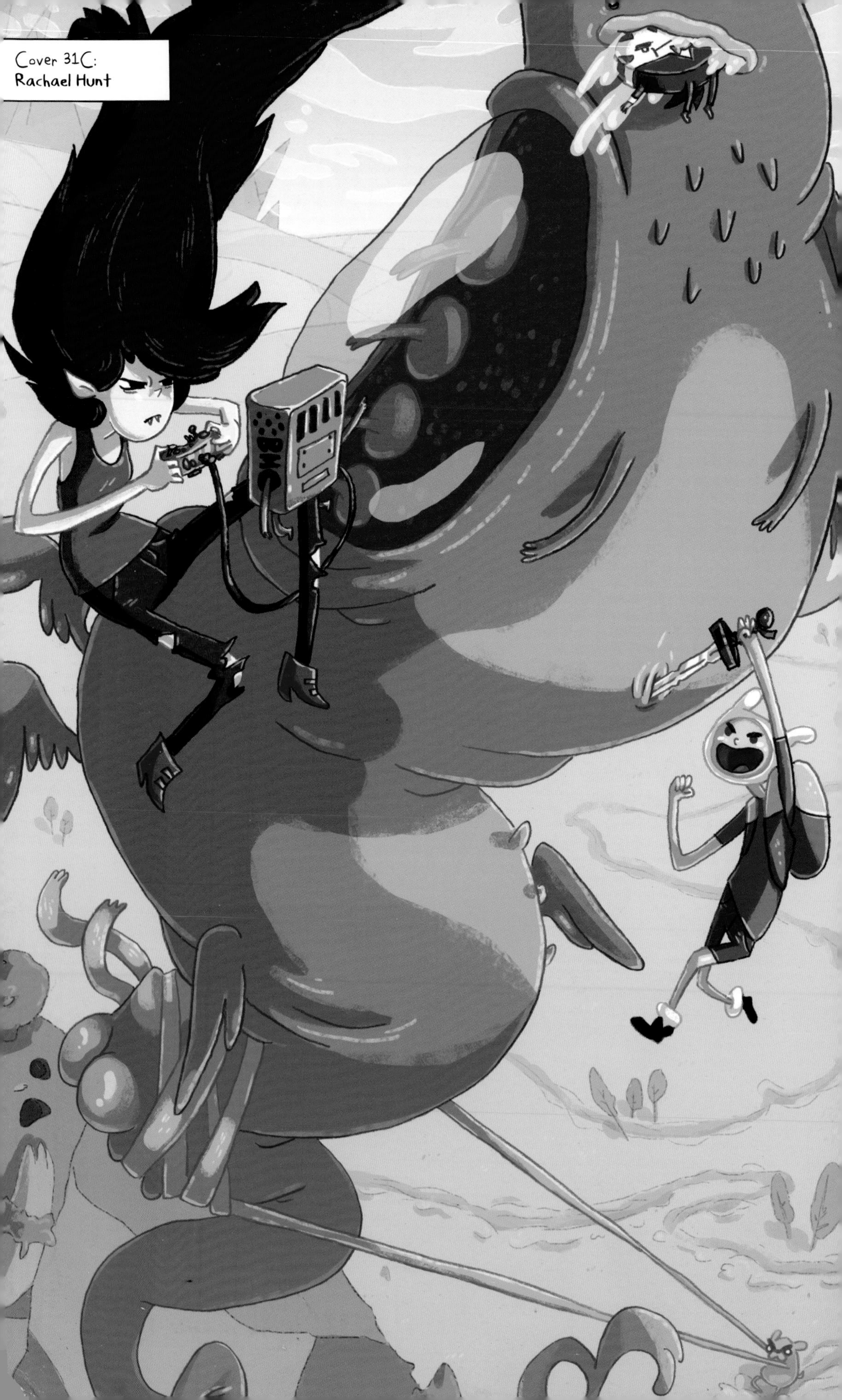
BMO

Cover 31C:
Rachael Hunt

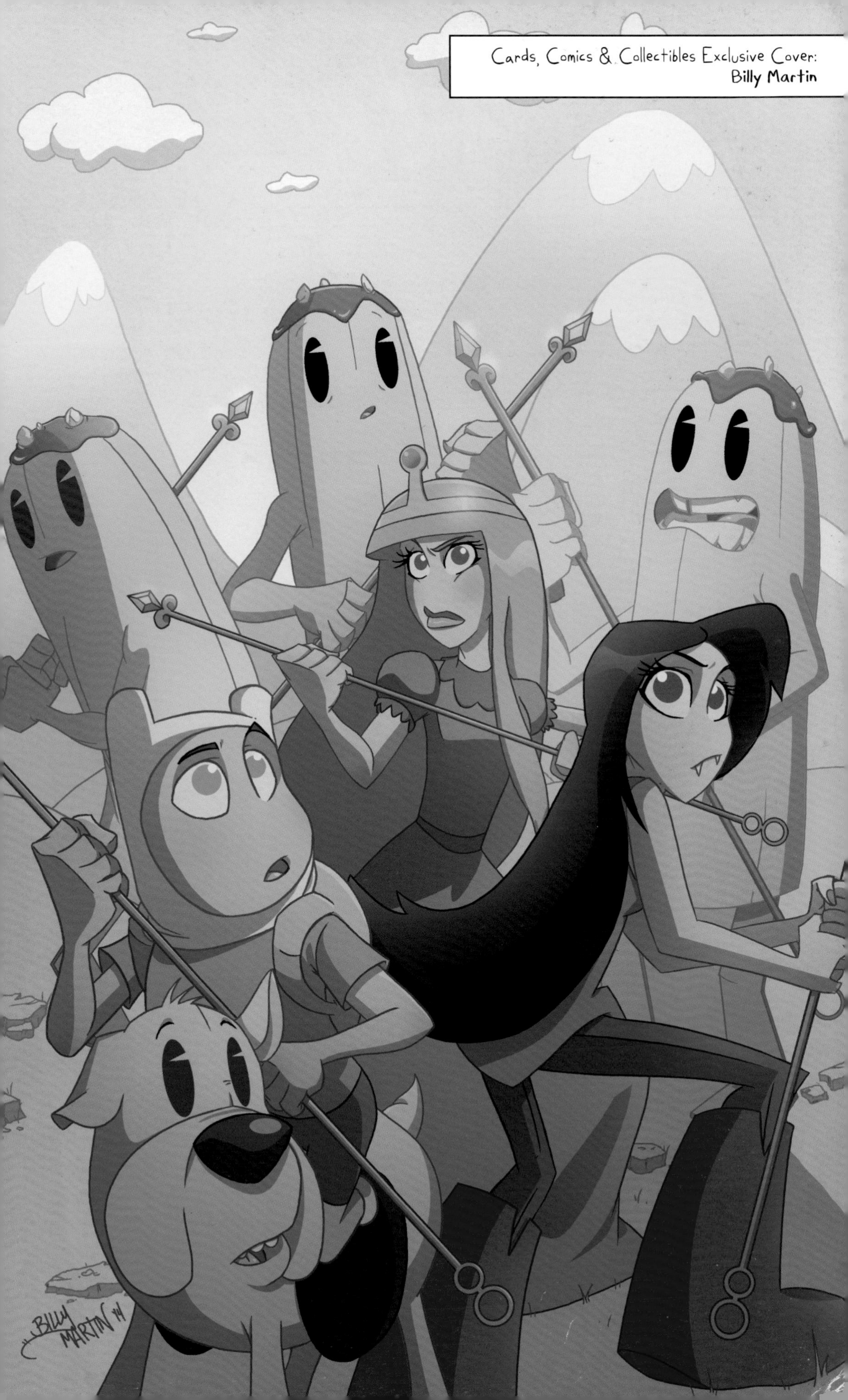
BILLY MARTIN '14

Cards, Comics & Collectibles Exclusive Cover:
Billy Martin

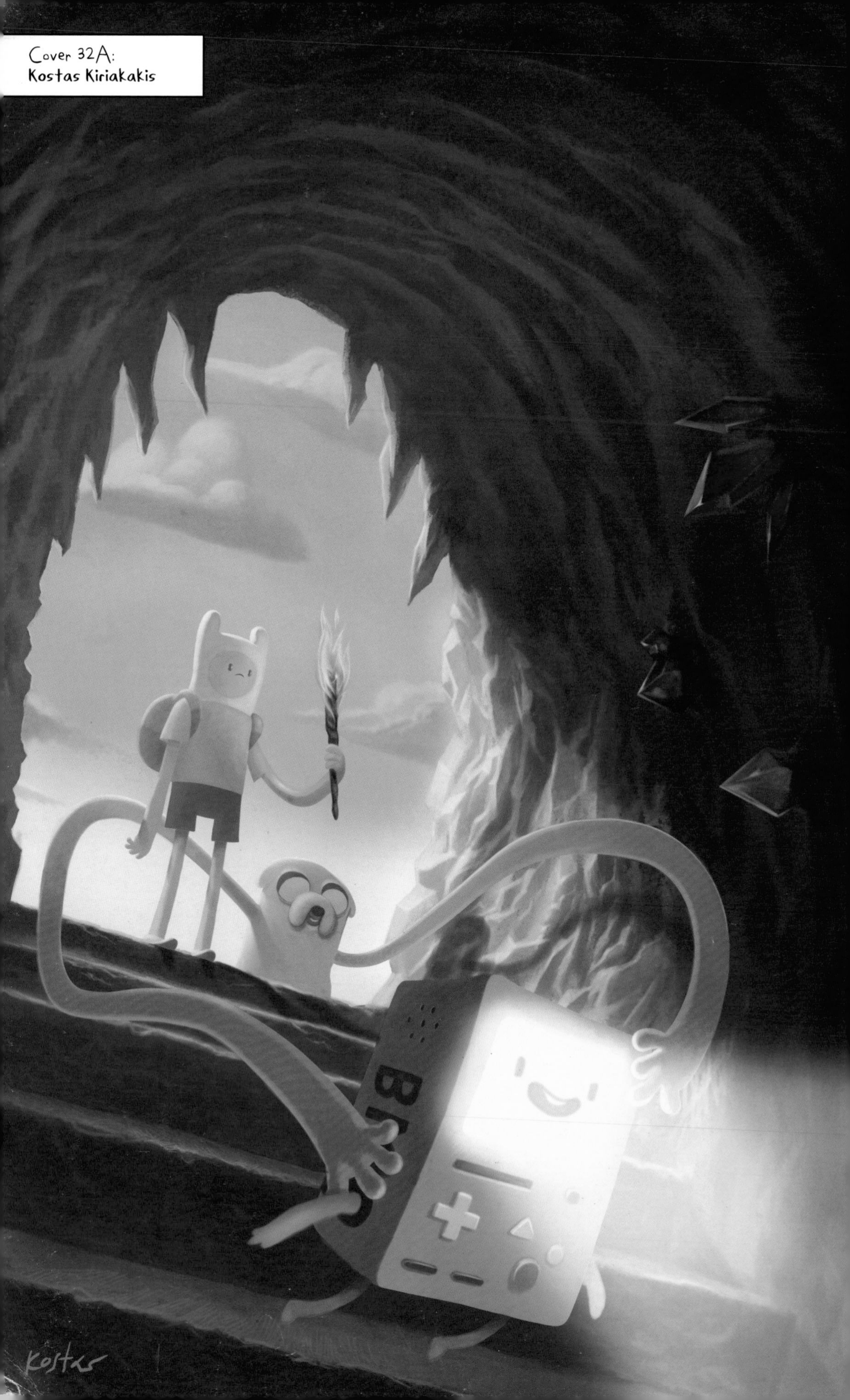

Cover 32A:
Kostas Kiriakakis

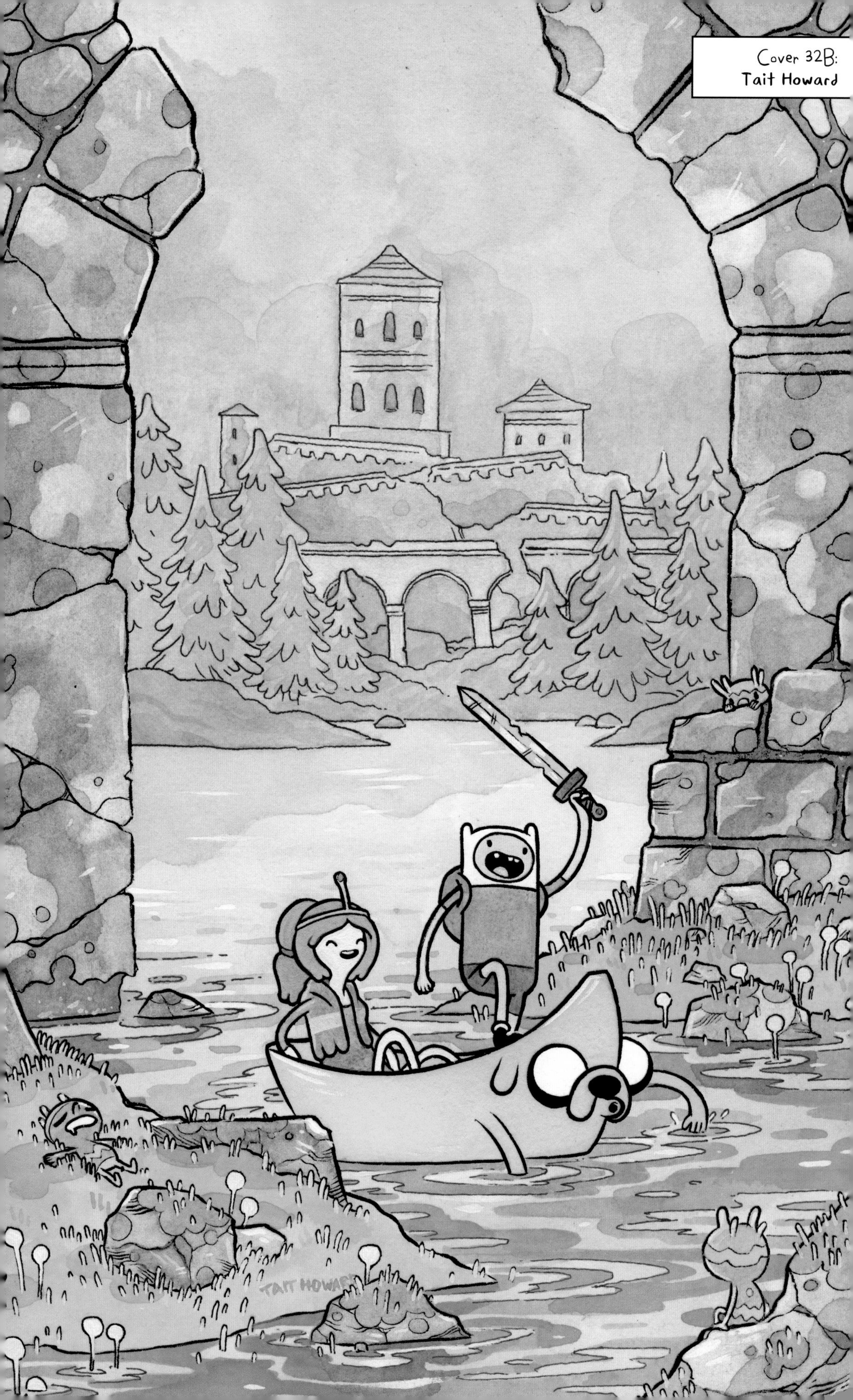
TAIT HOWARD

Cover 32B:
Tait Howard

Cover 32C:
Nikki Mannino

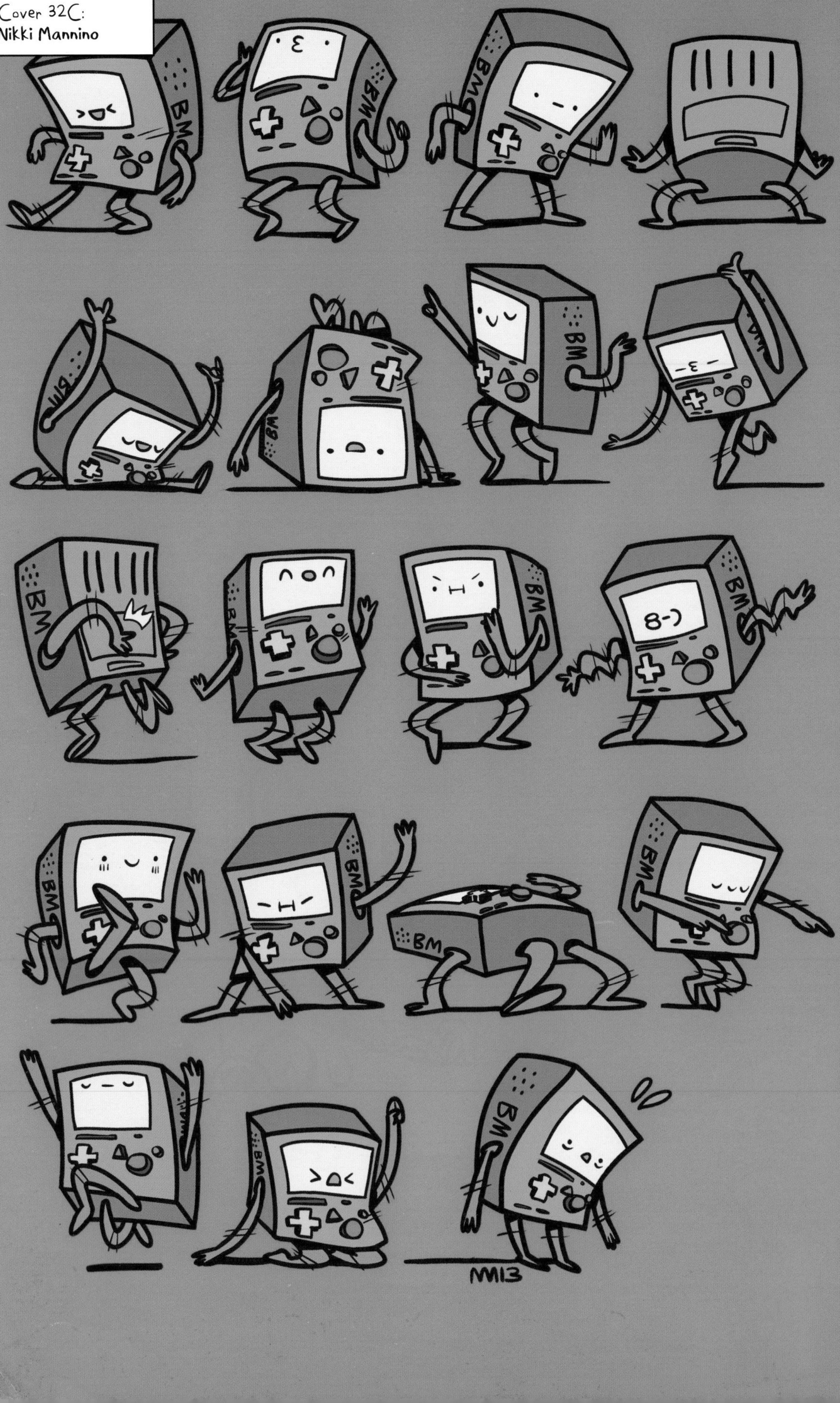
BM
NM13

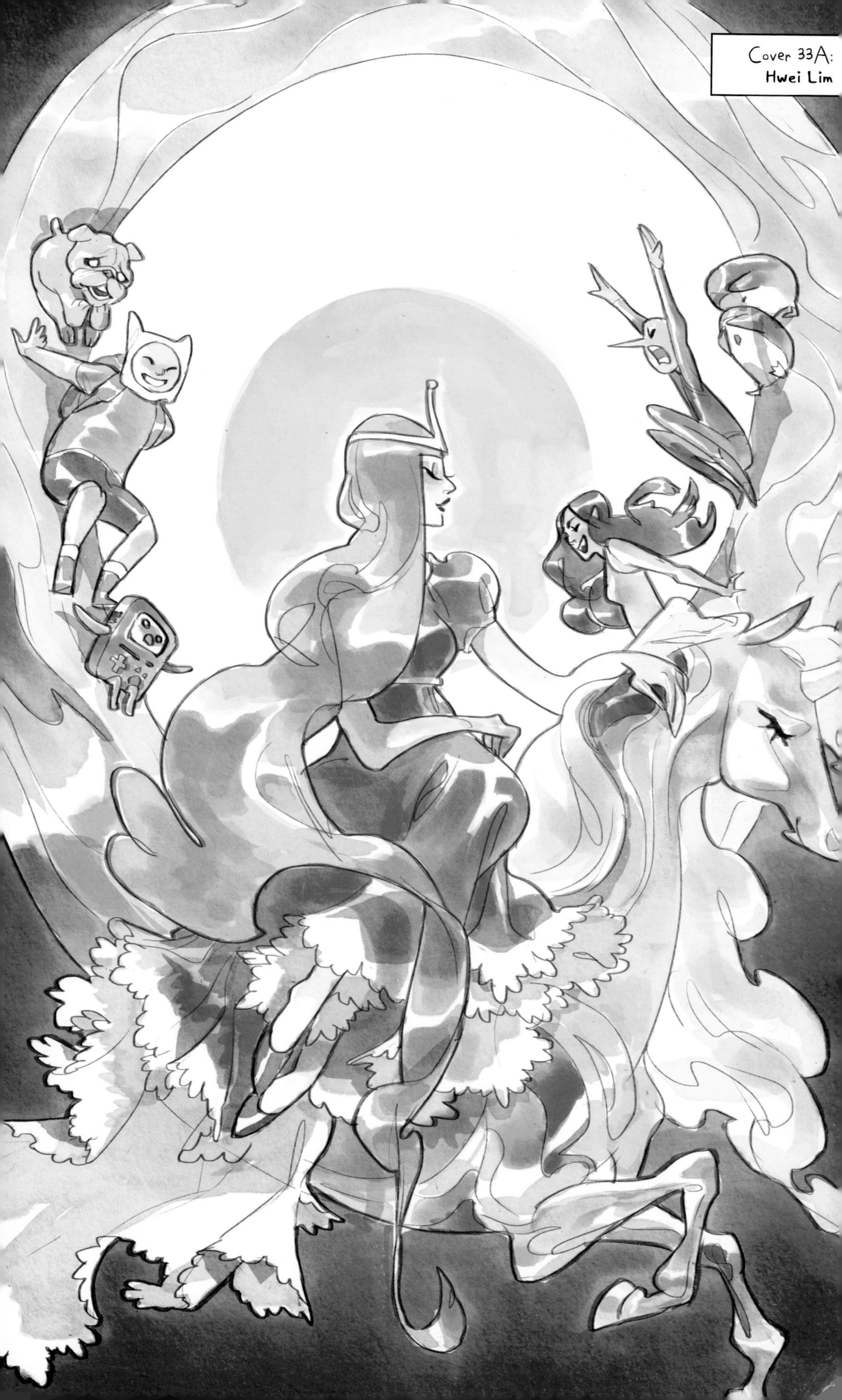

Cover 33A:
Hwei Lim

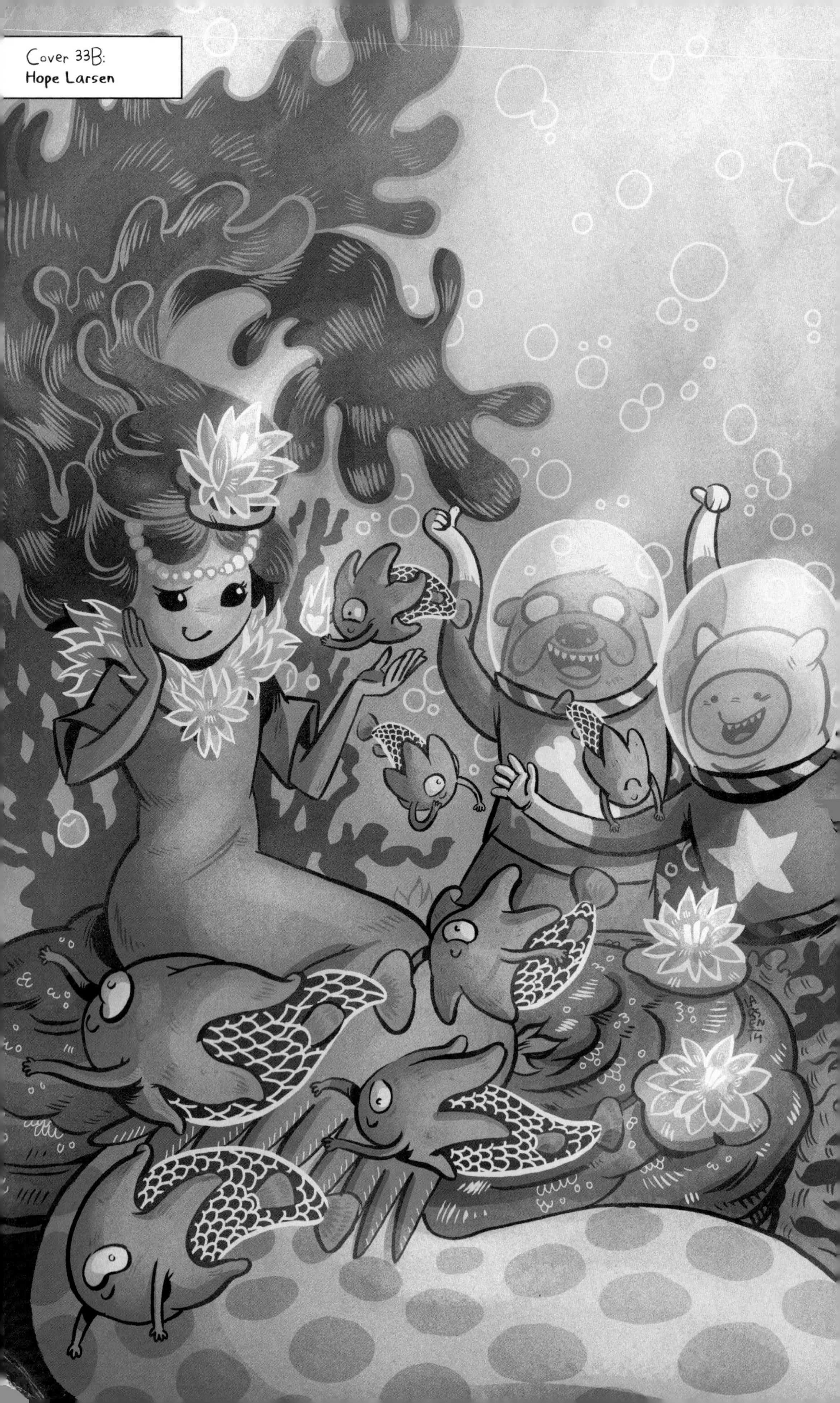

Cover 33B:
Hope Larsen

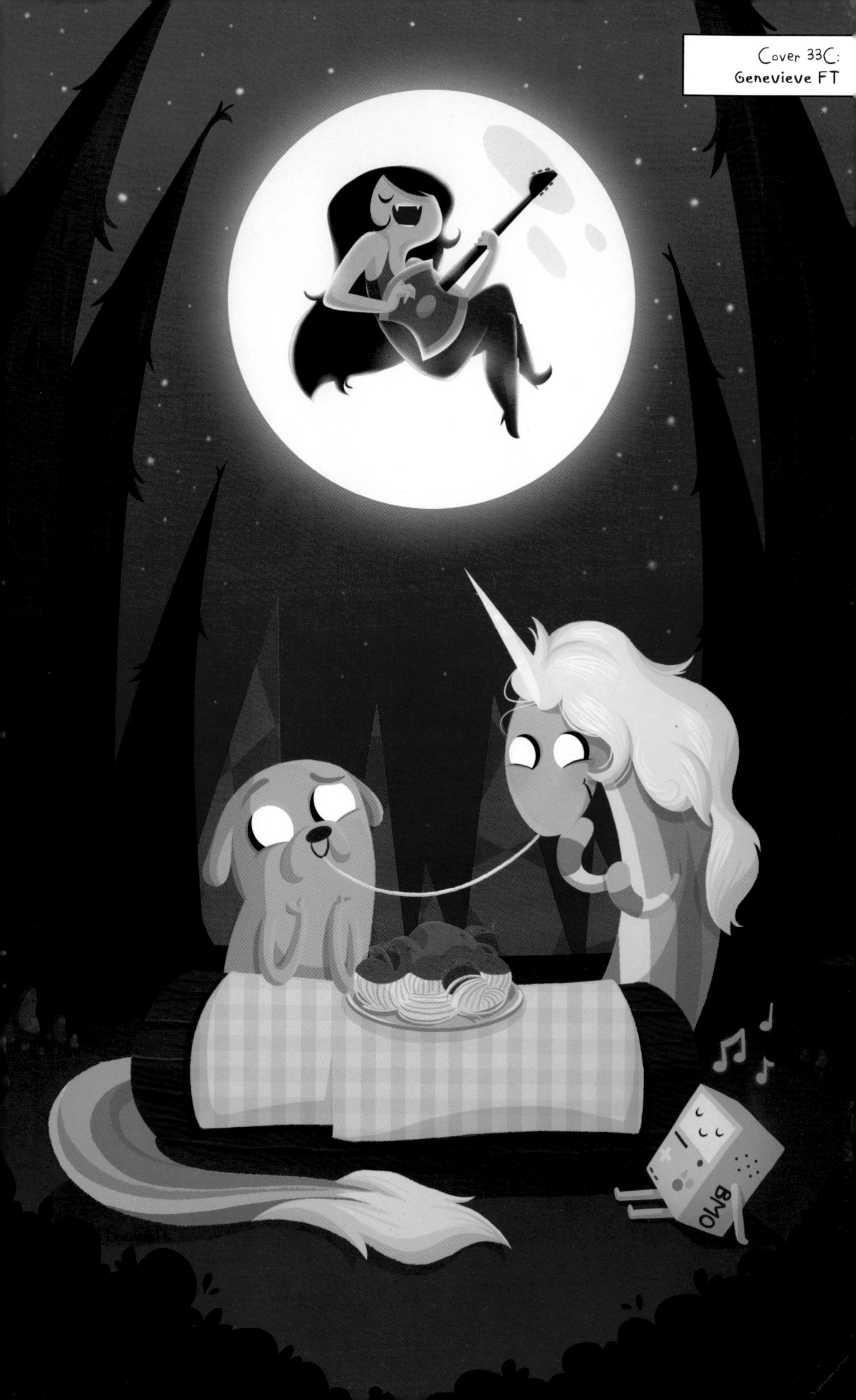
BMO

Cover 33C:
Genevieve FT

Cover 34A:
Stu Livingston

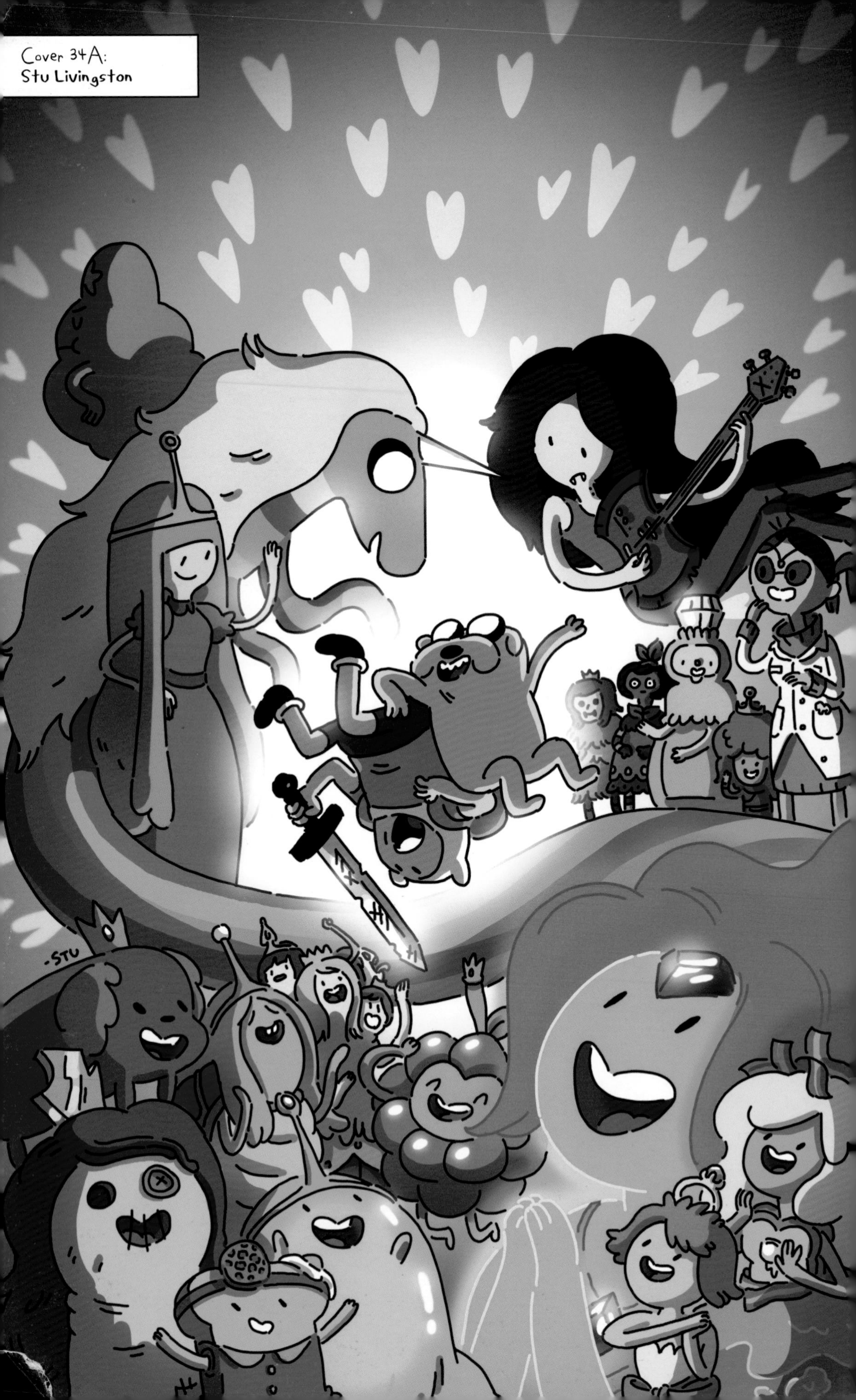
-STU

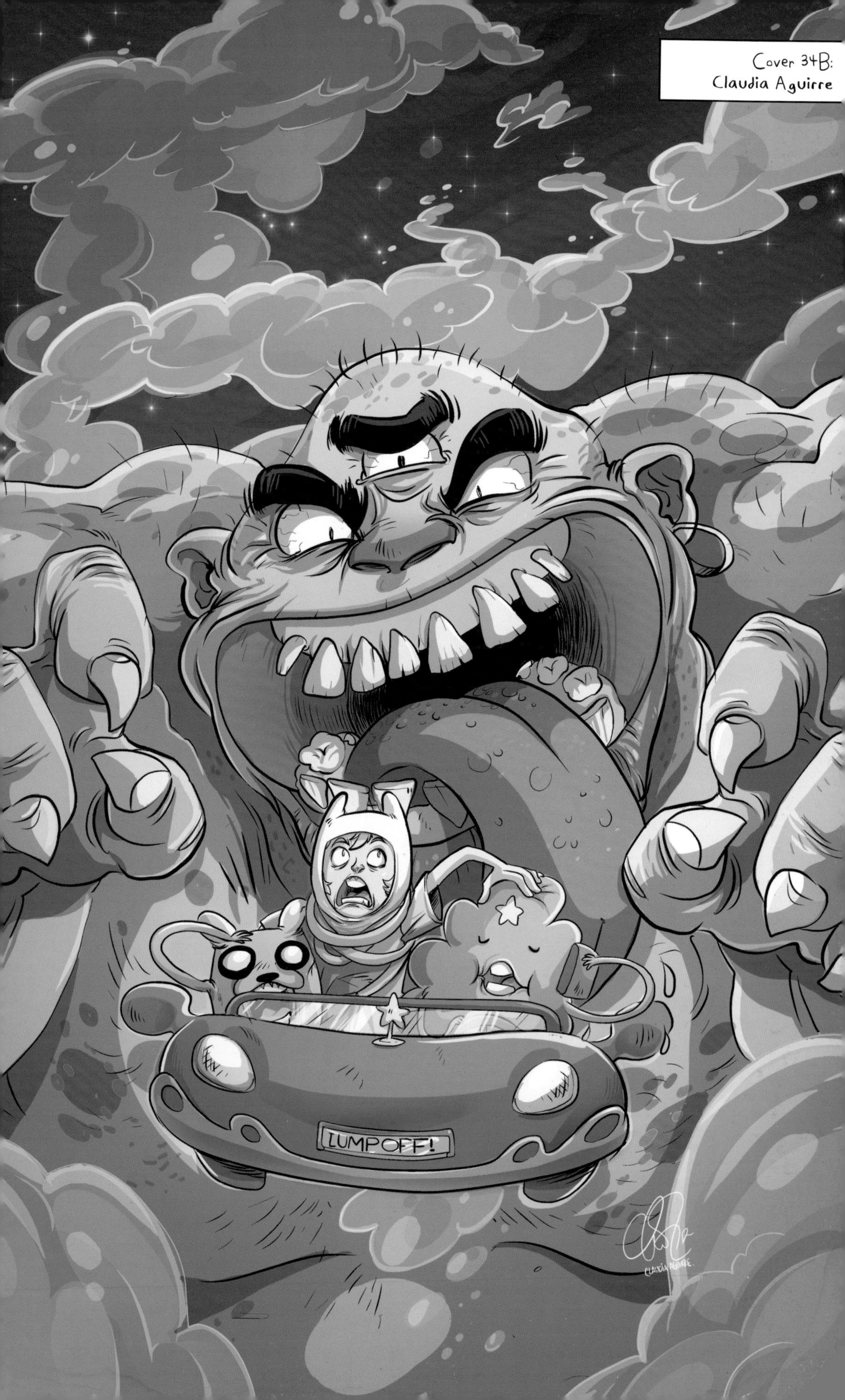
LUMPOFF!

Cover 34B:
Claudia Aguirre

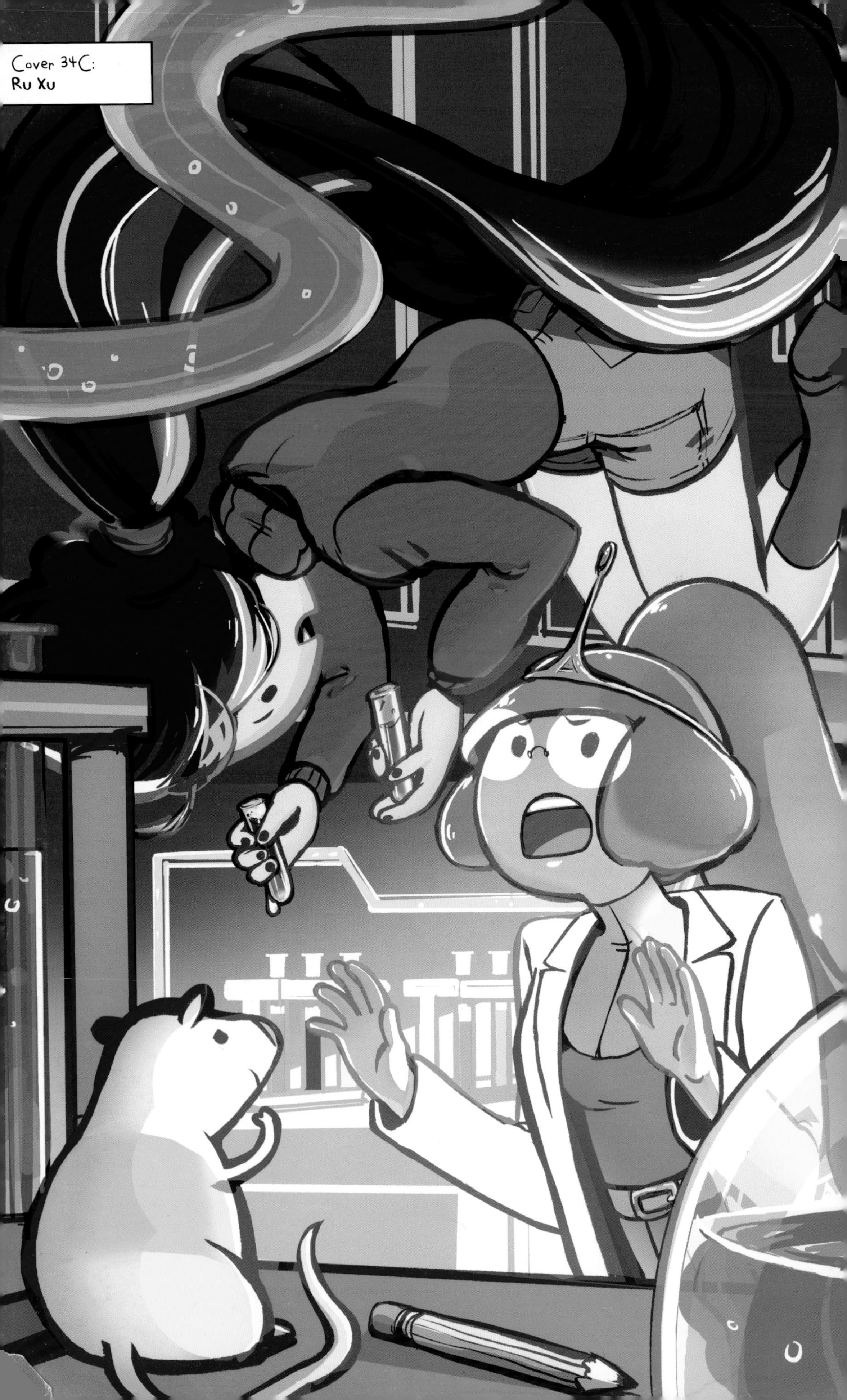

Cover 34C:
Ru Xu